Dave Barbarossa has earne(
drummer for over thirty ye,
Adam And The Ants, and Bo
He continues to be actively
projects, and is much in den   ... musician.
'Mud Sharks' is his first novel.

For more information, go to **www.barbarossabeat.com**

To Jenny

Mud Sharks

Best wishes

Dave Barbarossa

ISBN: 978-0-9567786-3-5

cover painting by Gene Barbe
cover design by Daniel Stewart
typeset by Steve at Ignite.
www.ignitebooks.co.uk

Printed and bound in the UK
by Biddles, part of the MPG Books Group,
Bodmin and King's Lynn.

For Esther, Lisa, Gerard, Louis, Simone, Gene, James, Joe, Anjelica, and Jasmine. Thanks to my friends Ian Fortnam, Trudi *chica-boo* Gartland, and Bridget Veal for their support and belief. And thanks also to Steve Pottinger at Ignite for the opportunity and David Allder for technical support.

In fond memory of Matthew James Ashman
3 November 1960 - 21 November 1995

for Alison with love

1

The Mauritian

I recall, through my fluttering eyelids, onion tips blackened in the pan. My stomach gurgled. I thought of the rivers proposed in geography this morning: Amazon, Limpopo, Mississippi; and held my breath. The smell squeezed my buds until the pips squeaked.

I'd not been allowed dinner at school. Usual stuff. Sent to the headmaster's door. Made to wait while everyone steamed through mash and stew and roly-poly and custard. All I'd done, right, was tip a book off a desk. *Nothing* in the great scheme of things.

He shook the frying pan with panache. "*Harry.*"

My name from his lips sounded like no other. The vowel was almost non-existent. The H a growl.

The Mauritian calling my name had arrived in monochrome. He surveyed this land of opportunity and vowed he'd take all or any of it. But he didn't quite understand. Poor friendless soul, black as coal standing there with his valise and elegant Coke bottle. He was the prince of the plantation delivered to Kings Cross in the dying age of steam.

The story goes, months later, now a swordsman at the Whiskey-a-Go-Go, he pulled an educated but needy girl. She was from Hackney, proud origins but bored by ambition, *obviously.* She wanted to make a statement and that she did because, in a few indecent months, there was me.

"*Harry?*" he beckoned.

"Yes, dad…" I said, from the kitchen door.

Grimacing theatrically, he shrugged his shoulders, twisted his neck left, right, left and exhaled. Onions hissed. He'd just

1

completed his daily workout; forty one-arm press ups (twenty on each arm of course), and the same amount of squats, twenty on each leg, and his breathing was slightly fast. "And, how was school?" he asked, pleasantly.

The kitchen was sensual, steamy and close. The smells overpowering because he never opened the garden door when he cooked.

Through the serving hatch to the front room, trumpets burst in and out. Foreign, nutty heads were playing on the stereo in there. A woman yelled disgracefully and the drums went chaotic; fours into threes, mad, risky pushes against the on beat, almost catastrophically late strikes on the off.

"Alright," I mumbled.

The grey nets that covered the lower half of the kitchen window shifted slightly. For a moment, I imagined making my way along a curtain, like the big one on the stage at school. My fingers searched for an opening. What was on the other side of the curtain was as vague as an early memory. As the fryer sizzled and the bass wafted through the hatch, I found a gap and entered a grassy space. Small, lost and scared, I was. I began to cry and call his name.

He appeared in an instant from behind the mottled trunk and scooped me up in his muscleman arms. Back in our living room, he rocked me and sung a patois lullaby in my ear. His voice was close as my own. I could detect his African antecedents in the strange gobbledygook, almost hear the family singing as they returned from the fields of sugar cane. Hypnotised, I flopped and snuggled deep.

The music through the hatch stopped. The vinyl crackled and I blinked into the kitchen. With the trees in the fields darkening through the window behind him, my one and only father stood at the cooker in black Y-fronts, his physique etched in ebony beneath the greasy, strip-light above. Without flinching from the spits of oil dotting the flattest stomach, he

2

prodded the meat around like a general with a toy army; slowly, deliberately, strategically. Fat popped and pinged in the pan. Onions hissed.

The next song started like a trick, with calming, mellow horns before the tempo ratcheted up dramatically. It was as if metal spoons were hitting all the pots and pans hanging over the sink. The vocalist yelled ravenously while ladle spanked copper bottom. I spoke through clenched teeth, "What's for dinner?" Trumpets shot through, obliterating my words. Teasing black tips peeked over the iron edge and my mouth leaked saliva.

"I said..." raising my voice above the track, "What's. For. Dinner?"

His reply fitted nicely into a restful, two bar break. "Steak. Porterhouse. With onions, and bread fresh." I wilted as the cacophony recommenced, this time with escalating brass jabs sizzling the meat to a climax.

A jet of flame flared, died, and the pan offset. Onions hissed. The vinyl scratched and ticked and his accent changed from the growl to shrill, posh incredulity. "Can't you smell it?"

I blinked and swayed. Was it to the beat, I wonder? "No, for us?" I asked.

"Ask your mother."

She wouldn't be in from work for a couple of hours. I felt drowsy with hunger. "Can I go up?"

He sliced bread, two thick slices and slathered them with butter. "No."

"Please, dad?"

"*Pa da di da...pa da di da.*" Smiling, he sang along to the new track seeping in.

As he slid the meat onto the plate, the muscles in his back squirmed like snakes in a sack. He gathered knife and fork and hid them on the plate. His long legs and tiny waist swept by the drawers in the little galley, *ever* in time to the beat.

First and foremost, my father was a performer, intensely aware of how he appeared even to me, surely the most insignificant spectator in his auditorium. He had a dangerous grace. 'A cuddly panther', one of the many, dottily besotted housewives whose shoulder he cried on had once said. He never tired of telling me what a champion, what a *stylist*, he was in his youth and once, when they'd left the hurdles up over the fields, he showed me his one-ten technique. His trailing leg was a flash to my eyes.

I teetered by the dining table while he smiled to himself (well, to himself so that I could see), before rejoining the simmering refrain oozing into the room. With a hip shake, so quick you wondered if he'd done it, he raised the plate to his nostrils and moaned, "Mmmm." His eyes were downcast. His cupid lips compressed like a meditating deity.

Meeting his moist beams with incredulity, I was freshly stunned at this week's injustice, this session's cruelty.

In the flecks of his iris, something soft and kind glowed from our pasts. My instinct was to go to him and curl up like a cub in his brown palms but my heart hardened and my 'not so cupid' lips curled with contempt at the whole scenario. In that second he sensed my derision and lowered his handsome head ready for the hors d'oeuvre, our predictable, one-way, violent ritual.

"Like you I was, like me you'll become," he growled, as if he'd just categorised me amongst the low, crawling things in a drained lake or an Old Testament lesson.

The thing was, my dad did love kids but only ickle bitty, baby ones. You should see the fuss he made as they slept, squashed against a mum's bosom in the sunshine. And those mums would look at me with such admiration, tell me how lucky I was to have a father so *natural*, so *in tune* with children. So yeah, he did love kids. It was when they began to walk and talk the shine rubbed off. He found

4

anything older than two years impertinent and strange, had no answers to their innocent queries, and despised their clumsy, gauche journey to adulthood. So at fifteen, rather than the apple of his eye, I had become the maggot in the core. An impediment that cramped his bachelor style, an unwanted result that had clipped his wings and, worse, tugged at his trailing leg just as he was trying to get it over.

"Sit!" he ordered.

With teenage reluctance, I slid into a chair at the table.

Offering his head to the succulent vapours rising from the plate, he proclaimed "How you have disappointed me Harry. I gave so much time... and care. There are boys of your age who do wonderful things... on the television. *They* make their fathers proud, they perform to a nation! They *win!*" His eyes shone with awe at these mythical students. "I fed you, my son, and look what you have become." He gazed mournfully from my holey boots, to my raggedy parka and finally, my startled hair. He hated my hair. He was bewildered that any male with an ounce of self-esteem would leave their house looking like I did.

He moved his arm. I flinched as if I were about to be burned by a cigarette. "Why do you *always* do that?" he asked, before shaking his head and attempting to regain his thread. But the beat had gone and all that remained were the damning lyrics. As he stood and moved from the table he spoke. "Your clothes, you look like a refugee, a gypsy. You ruin anything good. Don't you care about your appearance?"

Opening the fridge door, he reached inside and levered the cap off a frosted bottle of Mackeson. He sipped, and addressed the cold contents. "I can't believe I have produced such an ugly, graceless child," he told the eggs. He informed the butter, "The mother is flawed."

5

He pushed the door shut and, in the space between fridge and cooker, began stretching his quads. "You know, back home? I won *many* medals." His nose sniffed high as his whine ascended to addled-posh again. "*Extraordinary* achievements... best body..." He inhaled, flexed, exhaled then paused. Shaking his head as if unscrambling some excruciating mathematical theory, he announced, "You! I just don't *understand!*"

Sighing, I kicked at nothing. The urge to gob at the greasy calendar on the wall by the hatch distracted me for a moment. I wanted to see saliva drip in a glutinous snowball down the Alps and dangle magically in thin air over the lino.

His visage darkened. He growled, low and menacing. "You do *nothing*," he said, scanning the kitchen surfaces. "You walk about in your rags..." He patted and opened and closed cupboard doors. "...drag mud through the family name. What wrong did I do?"

Locating the salt, he lightened. "I showed you the right road, Harry, but you strayed and now you are a useless boy. Not pretty. I see other young boys on *Knocks Opportunity.* They are smart, their heads are held high. They will be *men!* But you..." And here he went super-posh, soaring, soar-ing, soaring. "For some *inexplicable* reason..." His voice plummeted. His eyes were that of a lizard's, cold and quick. "Have become, I find words hard at this point, some kind of... goblin?"

His lashes fluttered coquettishly and he put a hand (like a girl with a chipped tooth or braces would) over his giggling mouth, embarrassed by his eloquence.

He cut into the meat and tried to retrieve the tune that had ended. He wanted to illustrate his utter contempt for me, wanted to show me that his life, minus me, was all beauty, Porterhouse steak and *cha cha cha*. As his knife scraped the plate, the sinews in his forearms twisted and his shoulders rippled like bananas in black silk.

Closing my eyes, I entered the initial stages of sleep. His voice brought me around. "So, how was it?" His bicep popped as he forked a chunk into his mouth.

"What?"

"School." He chewed and sliced.

"Full of wallys."

"Everyone's a wally to you. *Big star.*"

I *had* to look at the plate. The meat was pink on the inside and charred on the outer. The onions glistened in oil and my stomach gurgled.

He studied my face and laughed.

Rage rocketed upwards and I was careless of the consequences. "I fucking hate you," I said, etching each word so there was no equivocation; I just wanted to get it over with.

I felt the whip of his hand and fell in slow motion, hitting the lino, frame by frame. Pulling me up by my hair, he lashed me left and right. Even though I'd experienced this degradation dozens of times, I still shook with terror and hopelessness.

I stared into the skirting's dirty, apricot gloss. All the doors and frames downstairs were painted in it. I could see the washed-out green matt it covered and then a pinky sort of hue, the cream gloss beneath that and finally, the wood itself, dark, flaked and battered. Geography again, the history of rocks and glaciers brilliantly revealed in layers. "*Ruin every meal I eat. My sight, get out of!*"

"*Great.*" I scrambled to my feet and sensed his leg bend for a kick. I bent over and hoisted my parka. "Go on, then!" I yelled.

Foot connected with arse.

Banging my head, I staggered to the foot of the stairs. I knew, even as the samba danced in, accompanied by knife, fork and china plate, that it was me that had the last laugh.

Later, as he mewed and purred to the wallys on the telly, I ghosted past the blue glow that framed the closed living-room door and, with my teeth, ripped the delicious fat from the rind of his cold remains.

2

Stay at yours?

I fell out of the cab into the sultry Hollywood night.

None of my lot were in the bar. A group of bright-eyed preppies were gathered around the jukebox. "*Don't you want me baby...*" they chanted.

I ordered a beer and knocked it back. As the dregs slid down the glass, I recalled Jeff's frenetic, five-finger shuffle across Miriam's hair and puked it back.

"*Gross!*" screeched the khaki party.

"Bollocks," I said and, to their horror, emptied it back down my throat and reeled away.

I wandered the hotel's staircases and corridors in the hope that someone - a stranger would do - would come out of their room and I'd be able to exchange a nod, maybe a word or two about the weather. But the doors remained closed.

Finally, desperately, I knocked on Christian's door. After a minute he opened up. "Room service?" I smiled.

Wordlessly, he turned away. By the time I'd exhaled, he was back in bed.

"Just had the weirdest scene, mate," I said.

One, wet eye stared at me over the duvet. He coughed. "Yeah, mental," I continued, gently bouncing against the wall behind me. "That drum rep, Jeff and his missus - "

He interrupted. "You see your dad at Christmas?"

"Yeah, we had a big do, friends over, cousins... I told ya..." His voice was muffled. "All the lying, Harry..."

Studying the weave in the carpet, I said "Nah, ain't seen him for years."

He pulled the covers around him. "One day you'll go back."

"I doubt it," I answered, sliding down the wall.

"Look at you, you're a success. He'll embrace you, get that old, fatted calf out, slit its throat…"

"Sometimes, I dream of going back and killing him," I said. "*'Like you I was, like me you'll become'*, he used to say..."

"The truth hurts, Harry."

"The truth... hurts."

As I repeated the words a memory, like a brick dropped in sand, quietly detonated in my mind. It was gone in a second.

Flinging back the covers, Christian shivered foetally. The bandage I'd put across his forearm a day or two ago had fallen off revealing the purulent, weeping hole. He rose and slowly walked towards the bathroom. His pants hung around the arseless top of his legs like threadbare nets. A beery glob of emotion rose in my gullet. "Don't, Christian. Let's have a drink, it's lovely out, warm."

"Warm?" he echoed, incredulously.

"We dreamed of this. We used to say what it'd be like, remember? On the Tube when it all started. LA and that…"

His hand wavered on the handle.

"*Come on*, Christian." I was practically crying now. "We can walk to Barney's from here, play pool. I'll let you win! We'll have a beer. It'll be a laugh."

"Nah," he whispered, flicking on the light switch.

"Sleep on your sofa?"

From beyond the bathroom door he said, "Do what you fuckin' like."

I couldn't bear being in the present with him, so I went back. Once, not that long ago, me and Christian stood in the lobby of the Edge Water Inn, Seattle. We were gig-addled, tour-knackered. Show after show had passed like the white lines beneath our bus's wheels. We'd lost all sense of reality and that mood was heightened by the sight of a fishing tackle shop in the middle of the lobby. Seriously, you could hire a rod and actually dangle it out of your hotel window until you got a bite. I remember asking the affable old boy that ran the shop what we were likely to catch.

"Mud shark," he said.

"What, real sharks?"

He held his hands about a foot apart. "Yay, 'bout so big."

So there we sat, late afternoon, pre sound-check, bags unpacked, gazing at the grey ocean, waiting for a bite from one of these mud sharks.

"*Fuck, fuck!*" Christian stood and his chair fell backwards.

"What, what?"

"I've got one, I've got one."

Dropping my rod, I danced around him. "Don't lose it."

"Fuck off, fuck off!" he yelled, straining and reeling in his line.

He looked away from the ocean and straight at me. I can see his face now: he was smiling, his eyes sparkling as his scrawny muscles worked away. "Got it!" he said, holding his line aloft while this tiddler thrashed about on the end of it.

"The bath, the bath!" he said.

"What?"

"The bath, you wally."

"Er... yeah."

Stifling my giggles, I watched his brow knit and knot as he gently removed the hook. A minute later, we had a shark in our bath. I phoned everyone. "Christian's caught a shark! We've gotta shark in the bath!"

I heard him yell behind me. "Oh no," I said laughing, "'e's got annuver one."

By the time the last of the crew had peeked into the bath-room, he'd hooked eight of them. They wriggled about in the tub while he leaned exhaustedly against the doorjamb.

11

"Don't worry," he said, panting. "I'm gonna throw them all back... then have a kip... get ready for tonight. Can't wait to play."

"Really?"

He nodded determinedly and said, "It's what we do, right H?"

Nodding encouragingly, I hesitated at the door. I wanted to stay in the moment. "It is," I said. "Why don't we, I mean, after we come off..."

Something flickered in an eye that no longer sparkled. It was as if he'd heard someone call his name from miles away. He saw my face and he knew, I know he knew. Bored by the charade, his lip curled in a snarl. "Oh, do what you fuckin' like," he said, closing that door on me too.

3

Beef Inc.

He nudged me awake. "What then?" he asked.

"What then..." I repeated, dazed.

He'd come from the shower and smelled of hotel potions and lotions but underneath, he stank. I tracked him from the sofa I'd spent the night on. He lit up and peeked through the shutters. Three jets of white light shot through the smokey room. He was wearing one of those oatmeal tracksuits. He'd bought about five of them in a truck stop in Wichita. It looked like he'd put his dad's clothes on by mistake.

Sitting up, I wondered if I should be somewhere else? Where were we off to today? A frisson of concern went through me - might we be late? I sank back knowing it wasn't worth worrying about. Bill would find us just in time and we'd be dragged on regardless.

I shuffled to the fridge and opened a Coke. It electrified me. Snot ran. Choking, I pulled the balcony doors across and let the California heat infuse the cold backs of my arms. Below, the preppies from the bar last night bombed the water in bikinis and shorts.

He joined me, full, furry tracksuit an' all. "Let's hear it then," he said, not taking his eyes from the frolicking students below. "This morning's episode from 'the philanderer's tale'."

Baking in half a minute, I peeled off my trousers and fell onto a lounger. He gazed at the hills and because of the light and angle of his face, I remembered when he and our singer vied for the title of 'most beautiful punk' in the dungeons and dressing rooms of London all those years ago.

In a laughing poolside splash, a ray from a sunspot made it to earth. It revealed a dented, grey man, incapable of joy. "Get on with it," he said, dogging his fag tetchily.

"What then?"

"You're the man with the great adventure. What happened yesterday... with the drum rep bloke? John. Wanker? Spanker…?"

It was my turn to look into the sunshine and it comforted me that, on the road, an adventure didn't occur until you told someone about it the day after.

Half an hour after yesterday's show I'd wandered back on stage. The residue of the set snaked between the aisles in the upper tiers before evaporating into the seats at the front. Andy, our roadie of long standing, was ordering the humpers about (he did little more than tighten a wing-nut these days). I handed him a beer. "Ta, H," he said. "What do you think of those new skins?"

"Were they new ones?"

"Yeah, the sponsor asked me to get your feedback."

"Why didn't he ask me?"

"You were supposed to meet him yesterday, at the after-show."

"Oh. Bollocks. Completely forgot." Which was true.

I didn't tell him why I had forgotten, nor about the somewhat unusual performance I'd given the all-girl duo that opened yesterday's show.

"You were indisposed," he said knowingly.

"I was, Andy," I admitted apologetically. I recalled the appointment the management had set up for me to meet the kit sponsor and other worthies after last night's gig. I was to go out with him, his Mrs and a muso journalist. I remember thinking, Thai? Maybe Malaysian? I was looking forward to an evening of normality when my metal detector was alerted by these suitably pierced Valley girls wandering back stage as we finished our sound check.

They were there to warm up the dribs and drabs, early doors. Peaches and Cream, they called themselves. Dripping with satire, they were. From the wings, I watched them stumble on stage like space cadets. Bronzed, tatty denim shorts, studs and bikini tops, they were the dreamy manifestation of the classic LA dolly, but it was all clever stuff.

From the first comic mis-strum on their acoustics, they had me. Their songs were short, folky essays on the frivolous, mall-addicted, super-rich species they grew up with. It was caustic, drain-clearing stuff, WASP piss-taking at its most delicate, and I loved it. To be honest, anything that tore holes in the fabric of celebrity and superficiality was alright with me. I'd been on the road eighteen months solid and hadn't a clue about what was real and what wasn't anymore.

After the gig, Peaches and Cream and me ambled along the strip to the Roxy, but it was packed and the nuances were hard to get. I couldn't nod sagely at their sly asides either, because I simply couldn't hear them. It was no quieter in The Rainbow, so I asked them back to my suite. Laughing, they responded in the negative, they said my reputation preceded me. I assured them my intention was simply to listen and learn. But that wasn't accurate because, once there, I offered to perform myself. My production, though heartfelt, wasn't quite what they had in mind.

"H?" Andy was staring bug-eyed down from his six foot four vantage.

"Wha?...sorry," I wiped the girls away and paid attention to my trusty drum tech. "Make sure I call him," I said. "Mind like a fuckin' sieve, nowadays."

"Well, what did you think?"

I nodded sagely, "Yeah, great gig, went down well..."

"*No,* the skins!"

"Oh, were they on?"

15

"*Yes.*"

"Sorry mate, sounded great... er... felt good, *response* wise."

"I'll call the rep."

"Definitely, do that. And, ta."

Back in the deserted dressing-room I gazed at our lavish american rider: a small pub's wine and spirits supply bowed a pasting-table. Flanking them were ice-bins brimming with bottles of beer. Cymbal-sized plates with innumerable and various salami and ham slices, selected cheeses and chopped veg, were arrayed like fans on an adjacent surface. All untouched. Accompanying them was a builder's bucket of guacamole and a flawless vat of salsa. The crisps and chips came in packets the size of pillows. All unopened.

Selecting a yellow sweetie from a bowl of a thousand, I longed for a fellow Englishman to share the irony of it all with me. "Andy," I called across the tennis court of a stage, "come out wiv' us?"

He shrugged from the base line. "Can't... got to sort out the routing with Bill. The get-in's awkward on the next one, and -"

"We'll have a beer at the hotel then?"

"Got something on later, H. Sorry."

"Don't matter..."

"Yeah, see you, H."

The previous night's performance for Peaches and Cream troubled me. I'd not exposed that side of myself to strangers before. I wondered if this public disclosure was a good or bad thing? Out here, they believed you should tell all without inhibition, it was unnatural to keep the darker stuff locked in. Every early morning show had some healthy, sorted-looking bod, committing emotional seppuku on telly.

It was resolution time again. In the cab back to the hotel I planned an early night and, in the morning, a proper go in the gym downstairs. Maybe a splash in the pool? I'd stroll up the hill in the sunshine and have something healthy to eat - Eggs Benedict I thought - and then, a really good book; educational, edifying, elucidating, on my own balcony. But, the songs, songs I had played a thousand times, still went round my head. The sounds and lights, the blurred happy faces staring up at me refused to leave and go home.

I paid the cabbie and entered the lobby feeling low and lonely. No book in the world would change that. The hours yawned ahead. Dreading the clunk of my door and the italicised fire/emergency procedure on the back of it, I went straight to the bar and marked time with margaritas and NFL on the telly.

At the end of the half, a grinning couple were at my table's edge. "Harry Ferdinand, right?" The man nodded assuredly. He was trim with a west coast jaw and fashionably barbered head.

Shaping the flat, civil smile that I kept by a molar in the back of my mouth, I answered, "Yeah, alright?"

"Jeff Kendall, Beef Drums?"

I stood and shook hands. "Oh Jeff, yeah, yeah, those heads, great sound... *response*-wise. Sorry about dinner last night, I - "

"Glad you liked the heads. Our people have been developing - "

"Sorry mate, sit down."

"Thanks, this is my wife, Miriam."

I gave her a peck. It was embarrassing. I was aiming for a chiselled, cherry cheek but somehow hit the mouth. And what a mouth... pursed, wet and warm.

"We're great fans, Harry."

"Well, ta for that. Let me get you a drink."

After the drinks arrived, I prepared myself for the inevitable, 'What cymbal stands do you use?' line of questioning but instead, there was an eggy silence with them beaming and me pushing my molar-grimace to its jaw-breaking limit. "Ja'come t'da show anight?" Incisive.

"You are asking if we were at the gig? Hell, yeah. We thought we'd see you at the party after."

"Nah, I... er... got this fatigue." True.

"Andy told us we'd find you here."

"Geezer's tireless." True also.

"Awesome performance, Harry."

Not really. "Ta. Erm… you play yourself, Jeff?"

"Never could. All that coordination, not my forte is it, babe?"

I'd not looked at his Mrs on purpose. I'd positioned myself so I could field him and keep an eye on the third quarter but now it'd be rude not to get a response, kit-sponsor-wife-wise.

She gazed into my eyes with a look of amused despair. "He's a *hopeless* coordinator, Harry."

"Well, I'm sure he's got his strong points, Miriam."

"I can't complain." She gave his thigh a squeeze but her eyes never left mine.

"Hey guy, you can really hammer those drums," said he.

"Ta."

"Where's the band? Christian, he's crazy!"

"Yeah, barking." I gonk-grinned. "They've left me on my own tonight, they fancied having a laugh."

"Have you been to the valley?"

"Er… not recently."

"We've got a new place over there…"

Jeff flicked the switch in yet another huge, white-walled room. "How much can you bench, Harry? Three-forty, sixty?"

"I dunno..." I said, looking at the stacks of weights and machines.

"The way you lash those skins, man, you must have power

18

to spare. Wouldn't you say, baby?"

I spun around. Miriam was framed in the doorway. "I'd say he's got plenty to spare, honey," she said, turning away.

We watched her sashay and lilt and giggle along the corridor and out of view.

"She's *such* a party girl, Harry."

"I'll take your word for that, Jeff."

In their expansive lounge overlooking the hills, Miriam put our album on. Smiling cheesily as the tracks went in and out, I thought of how loose and underproduced it sounded now and how rock-hard we'd make the next one when we got to Florida in a few days time. Sinking ever deeper into Jeff's black leather, L-shaped couch, I could almost hear, above the old ones, the new album's finished tracks with vocals and everything. I imagined the execs listening to the final mixes in their glass summits in Manhattan and nodding sagely, the smiles splitting their razored pores, their cheque-books flipping open.

"You're smiling Harry."

"I ain't heard this for yonks, Jeff, so raw..."

"We love it, play it all the time, in the car..."

"In the pool," she said.

"In the gym..."

She leaned forward and tapped my knee. "I love it in the gym, Harry..."

"Ha ha..."

They chopped a few lines, drank a little more, and then Jeff got down to brass tacks. "Miriam's a great admirer of yours, Harry. That right, hon?"

Across the room Miriam sprawled on the sofa. She giggled, stretching lasciviously, her eyes cloudy. My heart thudded.

"You think she's cute, Harry?" he said, coolly rattling the ice in his thick as a brick tumbler.

"Well a' course, yeah."

19

Placing perfect red nails on her skirt, Miriam slowly raised the hem. She wore sheer, hold-up stockings. She'd forgotten to put her knickers on. She smiled at both of us and, for a second, all the frogs and cicadas outside paused and time stood still.

"Top up there, fella?"

"Ta."

As he poured, his wife slowly disrobed and we appraised her as much as you would a wardrobe you had to get up some stairs.

"Here's what we should do," he said, putting his metaphorical pencil behind one ear. And while he made her parade, pout and pose it struck me as right and just that, from the great after-show harvester, I'd ended up a submissive, marital sex-aid in LA.

"Ok Harry, your turn...now *really* give me some rhythm, fella."

So with him sizing up the angles, I got behind his missus and enjoyed an insane business with his sporty, play-by-play commentary incapable of putting me off.

I blinked and exhaled at the recollection. "So, what d'ya reckon to that, then?" I said to Christian's track-suited back.

"Bout what?"

"Nuffin."

At the poolside the preppies marshalled in suntan order; boy, girl, boy, girl. "'Ere, Christian, remember them sharks in Seattle? How mad was that?"

He rolled over. His eyes were almost shut. "You know the trouble with you H, everything that comes out of your mouth starts with 'remember'." He rolled away. "You live in the past, mate."

"That's bollocks."

4

The 19th hole

Entering the kitchen via the fields at the back of our garden, I sensed a sweet, almost syrupy pall coating the house. Fear bubbled in my stomach. Stashing a few slices of Mothers Pride in my parka, I crept, breath held, towards the stairs. But I needn't have crept because maracas, cabassas and impassioned trumpets were going nutso in our front room.

A floorboard creaked underfoot.

His voice punctuated a half-bar break. "*Here!*"

I pushed the door open.

Through the Stuyvesant fug, my dad was at the garden end of the room performing a dance move so complicated (his arms were like a train's pistons in reverse while his feet shuffled quick/slow outlining an invisible hieroglyphic. Every now and then he'd throw his head back, but not randomly, the whole thing was a study in precise, mathematic repetition) that I, and the three women in there, looked on transfixed.

They wore miniskirts and boots with zips and their breasts pushed against the tight, multicoloured sweaters that restrained them. All were flushed pink, cooked by the radiator's dry heat and an afternoon's incessant rumbas, mambos and sambas. The empty bottles of Cinzano by the terracotta vase had been the perfect accelerant. I recognised the oldest of the three. She had a kid in the first year at school. I'd passed her as she waited at the gates a load of times.

When the music stopped, he held his pose. The women remained bewitched, motionless but dying to clap.

Breaking the spell, he picked up fag and lighter and triple-stepped to my side. A cervical vertebra or two compacted beneath the heavy hand fixing me to the gooey layer of dread beneath my feet. Crestfallen, he peered into the cornice. "*This* is Harry, my son. And he..." thick, mascara'd blue and green eyes followed his skyward gaze, "has broken into my heart."

All heads tilted in the direction of tramp-boy, chastised all day at school and in desperate need of a bit of *Hunky Dory* in the box-room upstairs. As the incantation went on, their pouting, crimson lips made me want to fold white slices into my mouth, one after another.

"He was a fine footballer, an athlete like me. He would score from any angle. He had control, finesse... a couple of years ago, dreams had I, but now... look at him, *how* could he do this to me?"

Even though *he* was a muscular bloke and *they* were three petite women, for a moment all four were identical, like abandoned kittens in the paper, looking pitifully up from their basket.

With all his masculine, uncompromising attitudes, his thing with women was one of effeminate camaraderie. He was never happier than when part of some sewing circle, bemoaning his bad back like they did their urinary tract infections or ill-fitting under-wiring. Nothing would excite my father more than bumping into a female acquaintance in a shopping aisle, and nothing afforded him more satisfaction than their agreement on his choice of lipstick or blusher.

Some men walked their dogs in the hope of attracting a dog-walker of the opposite sex; my dad walked me. I was a vehicle he used to inch his way up their woollen tights, the cur he called to heel to demonstrate command, the spanner he used to loosen a nut. He had many ways. He could elicit admiration by presenting me as cute (obviously challenging now) he could milk pity by announcing me damned (common), or worse, could spread the field by introducing me as his younger brother (excruciating - and the troubling new way).

Afterwards he'd strut and boast to me and mum. He'd like the barb to go right in, hook and pull. He wanted it known, in our house, that he was the great predator. Irresistible, *special*. We all knew who he'd fucked, wanted to fuck and who he was going to fuck, and not only did we know that, we knew why. Embittered revenge was the amorous motivator: revenge for his disappointing kid, his crappy, ambitious wife, this shitty country and the 'peasants' that took his dough on the eighteenth and at the bookies.

"Yes, yes," he plaintively brayed to the three there that day. "I myself have had to go to his school to be told of his misdemeanours. They thrash him there and I love my son..."

He discarded me gently and a pose of desolation was struck; right hand on heart, fingers of left hand pinching bridge of nose. "*Why?*" he whispered, head bowed. The compassion emitted raised the room's temperature further, stifling clear thinking. "Society's fault," one said.

"The schools lack discipline nowadays," said the woman in the know.

He put the needle on the record. "It breaks my heart," he whispered, rotating his shoulders and flicking his hips to the swishing guero.

I so wanted to tune out. I'd been doing it all day through Maths, Geography, and History, as well as during discussions behind the gym with my mates about new Martens and Shermans, stuff I'd only ever seen them wear. But his poxy beats. I hated the way they hooked me, made me sit up and pay attention more than any lesson.

"*Harry?*" His voice jolted me. "Is it not true that you are detained at school *every* night? Shirley, can you imagine the shame I endure?"

He put his hand on the knee of the woman in high

zippered boots, and dogged his fag in the onyx ashtray in her lap. His eyes never lost that twinkling hurt except for a split second, when they met mine to give me that baiting look of triumph, the secret one he gave me when he, alone, ate steak.

They mewed and simpered as he *cha cha'd* towards the Cinzano. "Poor man," someone sighed.

"Shirley, Viv, Rachel, when I was hurdling…in Mauritius, my trainer… a great man, said my potential superseded…"

Music drenched the room, muffling the giggles and gasps. But here's the thing: all the while I thought I was immune, inwardly railing against anything he loved, his rhythms were implanting themselves in my sinews and ligaments, attaching themselves to finger pad and wrist, causing my inner time-machine to memorise them forever.

"…according to one of the doctors, only athletes at their peak suffer…"

"Where is it?"

He lunged slightly, his slacks taut against outer thigh.

"Here," he said.

The one in the clinging woollen dress began massaging his lower back and then she moved her hand down. They all guffawed. Lashes flared coquettishly, though none batted more flirtatiously than my dad's.

I stood. "Gotta do me homework."

"You - "

"He's a great help with my maths, my *old man*. Don't be too long *daddy*, got algebra."

Anger bristled behind that bogus, bogus grin. "No, stay Harry… for me." He looked like a sick spaniel as he held out a pathetic hand.

I knew the game. He wanted to parade me for a little longer, demonstrate what he could produce with his genitals, given the right angle/temperature/cycle.

I left the room.

On the stairs, as timbales clattered joyously against a cow-bell, he took my hair. "Go. Into. The room front!"

"Why?" My eyes watered. The apricot background was a blur, the drum-rolls perfect, the triplets caning the two-tone skins.

His nails dug into my forehead. "It pleases me."

At that moment, ten years of odium poured by father onto son finally reached a tipping point. The cowbell marked the 'one' beat on its own. I imagined the rest of the ensemble readying themselves for a final, chaotic, drummy assault. I let him kick me for a laugh now. I even let him know (although it didn't stop him), that I wasn't keen on being slapped and cuffed for anything and everything. Seeds of righteous rebellion had sprouted and, like the four or five new hairs on my chest, they would not be denied. As the bass line wound its way around maracas and conga, I took another upward step.

He bent my head back further.

"What you gonna do, beat me up in front of yer slags…?" The words came out as the joyful vocal swept in. His grip loosened. The blood drained from his cheeks. I laughed with the singer. "Go on then!" I said, as exhilarated as the whole band that joined in.

"Where are you?" a lusty voice tinkled from the front room. The voice was not in tune or in time like mine was. Smirking, I turned my back and raced upstairs to the strings on the intro to *Changes*.

Finally, the piano chimed in and I traced a jumbled day backwards; a few drags with Bob and Pat on the alley bars before going in, a kip through register and sembly. Geography, English, and Susan's funny story (about her dog helping her with her homework) the only highlight of another crap day. A dinner-break fag behind the gym with the lads and their derision because I was always so unsuitably turned out. Mr. Driver's malign scrutiny as I skulked the waxy corridors, then a trip, nudge and nib in a doorway and inevitable banishment to the benches and coat-hooks outside the classroom. And there I stewed, scab-picking, clock ticking, inching towards home time and… home.

Scratching through my school shirt, I located the latest wiry, adult indicator. They were unstoppable. I counted nine of those little spider legs on my chest while *Eight Line Poem* played out. When I pulled my arm away, I felt a sharp twinge deep in the fibres of my shoulder. The pain wasn't as bad as it had been. The joint had almost repaired from the wrenching it had taken following another of his over-par rounds at the municipal golf course a few weeks earlier. Gently rotating my shoulder, I recalled how anxious I'd become. He'd missed his tee time and I'd waited with his bag while two sets of medium handicappers took his place on the first. It was rare that my dad would let anyone cut in front of him on any level. Compelled to break his 'wait by the washer ball' command, I went in search for him.

He wasn't in the pro shop or on the range, neither was he in the café talking to the cook about mutual, painful, lumbago. With my titanium burden rattling in my ears, I hobbled to the car park and it was there I saw him. Quad stretching, eyes a-flutter, he was engaging two young women between Transits. His double posh soared above the tree line that hemmed the out of bounds on the ninth.

Shifting the weight, I gave myself away. He waved amiably, said something to the women, and strode past me. I jogged to his side and on the first, pulled the driver from the bag. "Who are they, dad?"

He clicked his fingers. His gaze pierced the verdant distance. "Ball," he said.

We trudged up the eighteenth, the bag wet and heavy,

my trouser hems sodden courtesy of the high rough he found consistently.

Finishing his regulation three putts, he flung the putter away. As I bent to pick it up, his face was inches from mine. "Do *not* disappoint me."

I reared from his cologne. "What have I done now, dad?"

That was it.

He had this yellow Rover with a sunroof and that fucker went back if there was a rumour of sunlight.

I hated that car. If I saw it parked outside our house, I'd actually tremble with fear. Feel sick. It meant that he was home and I was going to get it. Sometimes, even if it was cold or raining, I'd turn around and go back to the alley bars simply to feel okay again.

But he loved that car. To assuage a season of violent, indignant rages, my mum took out a loan and bought it for him. He was like a child when he saw it; winding the sunroof back and forth, steering with one hand then the other, crunching the gears (he didn't have a clue about driving - never passed his test) and speaking double-posh really loud when pulling up to an obviously inferior vehicle.

The car was immaculate because I cleaned it. I kept his clubs spotless too. These were his golden chariot and burning spears. Whatever the truth behind our frosted front door, he was never diminished with this bourgeois weaponry.

When we drove from the course, the mood was all wrong. Instead of the usual blame game, (crap caddy - me, the shit weather, fairways too hard, muddy greens, the clubs - shafts too whippy - mum, same as me - the geezers he was playing with, all wankers to their dying day), he was preoccupied, expectant.

I feared the unknown streets that were not taking us home.

"Where are we, dad?"

"Do *not* disappoint me."

My stomach gurgled. Tell the truth, I was starving.

Outside a huge house in Hackney, my traps were given a fierce squeeze. In his golfing all-black he flexed, preened and rang one of the dozen bells on the door at the top of the stone steps. I sagged when the elder of the two women he was talking to in the car park opened it. "Your little brother is so cute…"

"We are very close…"

Genial, ethnic fiddles wafted us up the staircase.

On the coffee table were four glasses. The older lady (to be honest, I daren't even look at her face) gave me a glass of whatever they were all drinking. I sipped and winced (I now know it was aniseed). I was offered weird ovals in dishes (I know now they were olives and pistachios) but declined. My appetite had vanished. I felt sick with foreboding. Laughing, they conversed in French and scraps of something else. I tuned out and stared at a greasy print of some old sheep farmer until the older lady tried to engage me. "Tell me, Joe," she said. "Are you as good at golf as your big brother?"

I felt his gaze on my carotid, and shrugged.

He and the younger woman (who could have easily been in the sixth form at school) nattered unintelligibly outside an adjoining door. At the same time, the older lady took her place beside me on the sofa. She flattened the skirt on her lap with fingers adorned with chunky, yellow rings. Her tights were shiny. I could see her knees, they were bigger than mine!! Her perfume was as fierce as the unwavering eye she trained on me.

"Dad!" I blurted, as the door was about to close.

There was a moment of silence before it opened fractionally and the younger woman peeked concernedly through. My father appeared at her shoulder. He said something that only he found amusing, before pulling the now less frolicsome girl back into the room. The door clicked shut on them.

The older woman stood quickly. "Your father?" she asked, incredulously. Through the adjoining room's wafer plasterboard divide, a series of female protestations could be heard.

My stomach lurched as his roar shook the house. The door flew open and the younger woman fell into the room, sobbing. He was right behind her, his eyes flitting slits of anger. I was up but couldn't get around the older woman who had gone to her companion's side. All of them were ranting in French. Curling his lips into a familiar, evil pattern, he said something that had them gasping (I know now it was 'whores'). As they backed away, he tossed a few bottles around, kicked their crappy furniture and stormed out.

We three stood stock-still, our eyes, dry with shock. I came to, and legged it.

He snagged me by the arm as I exited the house, wrenching my shoulder so it burned and hung uselessly at my side.

"Dad," I whimpered in pain.

With dark mutterings, he flung me towards the yellow car. My head smacked the coachwork as I fell into the seat.

He drove and seethed. Posh he was. "You let me down. You disappointment me so, my only son. I will have my revenge."

As I was about to blab my usual, *'Sorry dad, don't hit me please, please, snivel, snivel'*, the agony I felt in my shoulder and the injustice of it all kept the entreaty behind my teeth. A new, clear perspective took residence in my mind; *big, married geezer tells prospective squeeze that his son is his brother then gets found out, and blown out, and becomes violently indignant!*

'No,' my insides said, 'this is not the way of the *real* world. This is wrong and strange and you, Harry, must not

29

let it go without complaint.'

We stopped at some lights and he took my ear. Normally, I'd have let him twist it until it stung, twist it so he knew he was winning, but because of my new perspective, I brushed his hand away with my good arm. "Don't," I said quietly, meeting his eye.

At another set he wound his window down. "Hey baby," he called to a passing female. "You look good enough to eat."

Horrified, she skipped away. He nudged me gently, "Sexy chick, eh?"

I cringed.

When he turned my face towards his, his smile was of the meat variety. Each of us knew that the final reckoning was approaching, the clash of cultures and ideals that would obliterate our biological connection. My stomach lurched again as he hummed his Latin refrain and shot away at green.

5

Acid Trip

For years it had been behind every door, the blackhand, forehand, serve and volley. I went to sleep with his addled, puppy-eyes studying me and awoke to his sneering scrutiny from the end of my bed.

My escape was perverse. I ingratiated myself with a gang of skinheads who, apart from the obvious problem with my complexion, appeared to enjoy my sanguine, rubber-lipped view of the world. Why I'd doubled my trouble is a mystery. Supplementary to them and him, I was determined to be the worst pupil my school had ever enrolled.

With the low autumn sun behind us, we shuffled through the plastic beads and took our seats in an incense-shrouded room in Holloway's claustrophobic bed-sit land.

They'd finally let me back in, the boys: Bob, Pat and Tone. I'd been hoping all week to be asked on another of their away-days but, after the show-up in English (silly Paki singing his head off again), I'd thought I'd lost my place. But here I was, part of the team, itching and twitching with anticipation.

Obviously, we didn't go in for register that day. We hung around the reservoir and waited for Bob's mum to leave for work then we sprawled on her flowery three-piece, opening beers and playing Roxy until our fags ran out. We were the sultans of skive, the Trojans of truancy.

Departing leafy Enfield and bussing it up Green Lanes, we alighted in the cosmopolitan mayhem of Highbury like the army in Belfast, all backward steps, secret signals, double-checks.

The plastic beads settled and laughter emanated from the floor above. Creaking footsteps then music (sitar and tablas) percolated through the ceiling. Tony sniffed and leaned into my ear. "'Ere, Gunga, Paki music," he whispered. I gratefully absorbed his contempt with a wonky grin of relief. He'd blanked me all week.

Footsteps thudded down and our host parted the beads.

"I'm Abdul," he said, plainly amused at our tough shrugs and smirks. "What about Saigon?"

"Ooh?" Tony returned aggressively, instantaneously, his verbal, Lonsdale left as unequivocal as ever.

Tony was by far the leeriest in our group. Sixteen last birthday while the three of us had just crested three fives. A head taller than anyone in our year, beefy and brooding, he scared the shit out of all the kids and most teachers too.

Like a jet's fleeting shadow or a slow, passing cloud, Abdul allowed a wistful smile to sail over us. His hair was black, shoulder-long and lank and a few strands were silver, like Christmas tree tinsel.

I took my place on a red futon between two sequin-studded cushions. My ugly DMs rucked up a greying throw and I thought, what must this bloke think of us in our school uniforms and bovver boots?

The back room was oblong. To the right of the fireplace was the beaded doorway we'd passed through. Through that was a dining room with a large bay that looked onto the street. Left of the hearth, was an alcove and then one big window overlooking the alley to the garden. The kitchen door was probably along that side of the house but because of the condensation on the glass, you couldn't see through it.

A low, sculpted wooden table was situated in front of me. Everything on it had a burn mark, the stain of fire.

Instead of papering the walls they'd painted them

different colours, mainly yellow, green and purple. The skirting was speckled and stripy, like a project in art the kids had taken far too seriously. Posters of eastern design adorned the walls; swirling, snake-headed deities looked to the east while whirlpool eyes screwed you out, their index fingers pointing to heaven, the Tube and the corner shop, simultaneously. I remember they'd hung carpets in the alcoves and left the floorboards bare. I thought that was particularly exotic.

The beers at Bob's had left my head as fuzzy as my hair but I couldn't deny I felt good. What alcohol I'd consumed had expunged the ominous clash on the stairs, the one where I told *him* to go back to his slags. Subtly, I rotated my shoulder, the ache had almost gone. With a mouth so dry I had to consciously prise the tongue off its roof or I'd gag, I gooned and made faces to amuse my betters.

Tony wasn't laughing though. He could handle drinking in the morning, but I'd never had so much before six o'clock. I wanted to spit. Outside, in the street or the park, I spat every, what, forty seconds? But that afternoon I had no saliva so I swallowed hard every twenty. Blinking and gulping, I began to read the italicised poetry on the poster above the fireplace. I'd like to think it informed my companions and me of the spiritual plane we would travel and the enlightenment attained at the journey's end. But, thinking back, it was simply pointing the way to the start.

Tony sniffed and bit the side of his little finger guardedly, as if everyone wanted a nibble. He was sprawled on a stool, his thighs stretching his bottle-green Sta-Prest to their satiny limit. Bob and Patrick sat on conjoined seats. The seats had armrests and they were pulling them up and down like they were plastic limbs.

"They're good," I said.

"Airplane seats," said Bob, pressing a button on the arm

and reclining. His amber ten-holes hove into view like dull, rising suns.

"Behave," Tony muttered.

Smiling sheepishly, Bob righted himself.

"Nah listen, we're all in dis to'gevah." Tony looked at me. My cheeks flushed with importance. "We're a team and we work as a team. So," here he glanced at our squatting host, preoccupied with the record collection that ran along the skirting, "everyone's got a job." His voice was quiet, the words said quickly. "We're in and we're out. Professional at all times. We're counting on you, Harry."

He leaned back and sniffed.

Although his face was large, pasty and bland, his nose protested. It could never cope with the oxygen entering it.

When I glanced up he'd returned to his nail.

Abdul stood, removed a record from its sleeve and placed it on the turntable. It took me a few tipsy seconds to realise that the lurid, pink cover wasn't my reflection.

As the first track crackled we nodded. Well, me and Bob nodded. Bob was the nearest thing to a proper friend in the respect he'd never cuffed me or been too harsh regarding pigment and antecedents. Pat was mute. Handsome, statuesque, like Bobby Moore. Well turned-out, model material, you'd say now, but I can't remember a single thing he ever said. Anyway, Bob and me nodded away. We searched for the musical pulse but found nothing to lock onto and ended up looking like a couple of blokes wordlessly agreeing.

Abdul didn't get into it either. The orange dart below the knees of his jeans remained static. He absorbed the music as if he were reading very small print on a label. His flimsy shirt hung over a substantial belt buckle, a twisted metal skull which seemed bigger than his waist. He actually wore sandals. You could count all ten tawny toes. He was the Afghan freedom fighter and we were four teenage civil servants (well, three and a sherpa) lost hiking.

Through brilliant white teeth he said, "That is *such* a happening track. Right, gonna make some moves. Wait here." As he turned into the afternoon sun, I noticed his chinny beard was silver-flecked too.

So we sat, fists and arses clenched, as his footsteps thudded up the stairs. The beads swung back and a waft of cooking infiltrated the room, spices, cumin and garlic, oil and chilli.

"Paki food," Tony noted eruditely, pulling a half-bottle of Johnny Walker from his Crombie and swigging. "Counting on you tomorrow, Gunga."

I nodded. He handed me the bottle and I opened my throat. Whisky ran out of my nose. Coughing, I blindly handed it back. Laughter spiralled as languidly as the synthesiser passage playing.

Arses and fists unclenched a little.

"Flash the ash, Bob!" barked Tony, from the dusty end of a mellotron.

I jerked awake as Bob patted his pockets. Tony stabbed the cigarette into the side of his mouth. "Soon as he comes back wiv it, we get the fuck out," he said.

Tony'd already been in borstal (that's why he'd had to drop down a year with us). He was sure the house was being watched. He'd been to football and was positive *they* were on to him because of a ruck he'd had at the station with 'that lot'. Tony could handle being inside but he didn't want to go back, he said.

Each of us had one of Bob's Embassys, the last of a packet of ten. We puffed uninhibitedly, blowing rings, trying out different grips on the filter. We were bold, for it seemed pointless censoring nicotine when we were about to embark on our psychedelic debut.

I wished Patrick and Bob's two-seater had been for three. Stuck down there on that futon, it was impossible to muck about. I felt like I did in class, cut away, the one person in thirty that just didn't get it. Through a diminishing tar circle, I scrutinised the words on that poster over the fireplace. I was amazed that people wrote and read things like that. We dealt in specifics, the lads and me. How many fags left? The time spent on the alley bars before going in. Tassels on loafers, yes or no? Pickled eggs, eat or eject at the back of a first year's duffle coat?

Footsteps tripped rapidly down the stairs so we puffed even more deliberately. Shiny, red nails bisected the rattling curtain. There were rings and bangles on the slender forearms that followed and, in a shimmering second, a real woman stood on the boards.

Her hair was an uncultivated mess of golden curls. "Hi people," she said, regarding us with a fair smile and the slow motion closing of her outsized, black lashes. She was tall for us, her movements unencumbered by high street clobber as she swayed from the hip. She was a clear, running ripple over us motionless stones.

I didn't need to look at Tony, Bob and Pat to know that they'd peeked then looked away. You didn't screw birds out where we were from, especially if you were going steady, and all three said they were.

As for me, I'd always been gargoyle designate so I gawped uninhibitedly. She appeared to be working an unseen hula-hoop but her gyrations would have been far to slow to keep one up. A hard-on stretched the grey trousers beneath my parka like a tent pole. "Alright," I said impulsively, instantaneously.

After scanning my face momentarily, she located my eyes. "Mmmm, *now* I am," she said, blinking rapidly.

My mouth hung open.

"I adore Crimson," she moaned.

Tony, with an angry snot clearance, snaffled atoms of disapproval. I looked at my boots, then sidelong at her.

Singing beautifully along, she had knelt and was flicking her way through the vinyl racked against the skirting. After a moment, she stood. With the sun at her back, her silhouette appeared diaphanous. "I'm Tania," she said, clutching an album of choice to her bosom.

Another weird stanza radiated from the speakers. Her anklets jingled and her locks bounced around her head like a merry-go-round. She was moving the fingers of one hand in a dreamy, weavy action when, at a change of key, she bent dramatically at the knees and tossed her head, left, right, left in time to that track's big finale. Her bejewelled navel was level with my eyes. Apart from my mum and a couple of furious lady teachers, I had never been this close to an adult female. Her cheesecloth shirt was knotted at the waist and her stomach was lean with fine, corn-gold hairs on it. I looked through her dress at her crotch, gulped and looked down quickly. She didn't even have sandals on! Her mouth was broad, it smiled encouragingly at nothing in particular. "*Ummagumma*," she said brightly, offering the record towards me. Was I supposed to reply with some equivalent nonsense? I felt small and momentarily sober beneath her, positive she was aware of the ecstatic discomfort she was causing.

Stopping in her tracks she said, "Hey, what about Saigon?"

To our mute shrugs she exited through the beads leaving a warm, mysterious space in her wake.

"State of her feet…" said Tony, sniffing. "Skate."

My tent collapsed.

Side one of King Crimson finally acceded so Tony stood, re-sniffed and flipped the vinyl over. On returning to his stool, he leaned forward and blew unerringly on his fag-end. Like us, it glowed obediently. "See, he don't muck about," he said. "And this geezer was asking for it and George done it. He don't care. George hates 'em." He glanced at me. Shamefully, I returned to my boots. "If he gets the hump, it comes out, dis long." He chopped halfway up his forearm. "Bayonet, SS, his granddad brought it back... I see it go in," he whispered, as the music jumped and juddered. "...*the geezer was crying for his mum... and he twisted it, called him a cunt!*"

Tony rocked out but we three remained staring at the crime scene on the floorboards.

Dragging victoriously on his snout, he laughed aloud and sniffed. Beneath his coat tails he appeared suspended, levitating on the helium of evil. "I'm up next," he said, casually examining a livid cuticle. He bit. "George said, the next nark that wants some? I can stick him. Right up to there..." He cut across his forearm again. "Wiv a twist."

We leaned out gradually.

Warm Watneys rose in my throat with its whisky chaser.

He rocked forward again so we did. Our heads came together. Mine was now on sickly springs. "Dis is the plan for tomorra night," he said. "We meet at the green. Not a word to no cunt. Teamwork and..." Heavier footsteps thudded above our heads. His lips came together like metal shutters.

We all rocked out.

Abdul breezed in. "Where are you going to do it?" he asked, as the pear drops settled behind him.

"Outside," said Tony, handing over the cash.

Counting, Abdul shook his head. "That's a bad scene. Four school boys walking around Stroud Green tripping out of their boxes. What if you're pulled?" He paused for thought. "You can do it here."

He knelt by the albums and after a few deft flicks of his

38

lean, brown fingers he pulled one out. "Gong. Good to trip to."

The stylus went on with a crackle and a pop and after a while, things got pretty swirly for me too.

There was a slinky, clever beat and mysterious guitar occupying a vacancy in my skull. I shook my head to clear it and, as I did, a solitary, speckled banana in a fruit bowl caught my eye. I watched the spots on it wobble awake then move up and down, as if searching for breakfast. "The spots are moving up and down," I said but, no one heard.

I can't remember exactly how Bob, Pat and Tony got on with LSD, but one thing's for sure, they all did a lot better than me.

Against the wall, by the beaded curtain, was a bass guitar. I'd never seen an instrument before, at least one that wasn't on telly. It was yellow and red, long and lewd. If I touched a knob or plucked a string, I was positive there'd be dire consequences for all of us. I arse-shuffled from it fearfully.

After ten minutes on this class A journey I decided to ring for my stop. Perhaps I'd visit that corner shop and buy a Mars, or go over Finsbury Park and have a kick-about? When I attempted to stand, the sequins on the cushions glistened while their shiny little mouths gaped angrily in the negative. I stayed put. Somehow, mixed in the fruit bowl, a voice had changed from a purr to a harsh, goading rattle. The music was growing far too loud and cacophonous to enjoy or understand. Smiling through gritted teeth at the gryphon in the poster on my right, I swooned when it smiled straight back.

A figure stalled in front of me. I watched with incredulity as it mutated, like the guitar, into an elongated, luminous oblong. I shook my head again and again but couldn't dislodge the mad marbles rolling about up there. The banana's spots gave no respite, proceeding to pulsate and swell to the size of tennis rackets before evaporating into tawny fragments across the ceiling. I bent my neck, tracing them as they vanished in the web-encrusted corners and received an instructional elbow to the ribs for my troubles.

A cymbal crashed and my whole being reverberated on its frequency. The sibilance was excruciating. I protested. My head slumped forwards and sideways, my mouth spewing nonsense. Hands that felt like electric shocks pawed and prodded. I screamed as a red water-wall rose over my eye-line like an unstaunchable nose bleed.

Someone was sitting on me; urgency in the room, anxious chatter. "Just in case..." I moaned, bewildered by the dancing yellow spots. Tania whispered near my ear. I reached for her lustrous tresses. Abdul swore, regretting opening his door, and Tony returned some ripe, anti-hippy abuse. On the low table in front of me, copper trinkets and cups throbbed before igniting. I pressed my hands to my face. The whole room was engrossed in flickering, orange flame. Screaming, I ran towards the swirling beads of freedom.

6

The Café

At ten thirty I absconded. Past the big bedroom, where my mum lay sleeping after her travails at office and sink, and downstairs, where I paused, heart racing, outside the closed front-room door. As I stepped into the kitchen, my father chuckled at some squealing triviality on TV. Rolling a slice of Mothers Pride from his plate and stuffing it into my mouth, I left the house.

Ghosting through the battered gate, I entered the copse at the edge of the fields that backed onto our garden. For a couple of seconds, banana spots floated across the crescent moon. I looked behind me. All the lights were off in the house on the right of ours. An old couple lived there and they never spoke to us. Ours would have been in darkness too but for the thin, blue beam outlining the ground-floor window.

Peering through the branches at the house on our left, I noticed Susan's curtains were drawn. A soft glow shone reassuringly through and, for a moment, my impending criminality was forgotten.

My father's low laugh smothered a burst of phoney applause. A fiery belt of apprehension had me gagging on the dough in my mouth. I spat it out, booted it into the air and ran through the murky fields, shivering.

We - me, Bob, Tony and Pat - passed some glorious houses on the way to the park. Most were in darkness but every now and then a spacious front-room was illuminated like a theatre's stage.

"Nosey cunt, ain't ya?" Tony barged me over a low, front garden wall. "*And* a bottler," he said, screwing his septum into his sockets with a righteous sniff.

"What?" I looked to the gnome by my head for support.

"Shittah."

I got to my feet. "I ain't."

His flat face was inches away. "We said we'd all go in and you bottled it."

I reared fearfully. "My mum's alarm didn't go off…"

"Your kind just can't get up in the morning. It's proven…"

With that he turned, flobbed a mile and walked towards the park gate.

The frustrating thing was that I *was* up earlier than him. I'm always up early. The sound of that lock sliding outside my bedroom window has me scrambling for my trousers every day of the working week.

Stepping into the fields that morning, the first rays etched branch and goal post in the mist around me. A flash of colour against the far, long wall accompanied by a cheery echo had me sprinting at top speed.

Her dog saw me as I stumbled in a muddy, rutted goal-mouth.

"*Ter-ry,*" she sang as the little grey scamperer hared straight at me. Immediately, I set off barking and yapping, racing around a centre-circle with the fluffy ball at my heels. Finally, I keeled over and let him nip my arm and lick my face with his stamp-sized tongue.

"You're all muddy," she said, hugging her dog to her. She offered the ragged tennis ball that initiated our morning ritual.

Her hair was shorter than any girl in our year. No way would she melt into the mousey, shoulder-length herd that migrated in and out at the sound of the bell. That didn't mean she wasn't the trendiest girl in the third year, by miles. This morning, she wore Levis, monkey-boots and a rhinestone-encrusted Budgie jacket. It was another of her gorgeous mysteries that she could get up, change into one set of clothes, then go home and change into another all before school.

Anticipating her smile shifting from her dog to me, I quickly looked away. I only looked at Susan when she couldn't see me. If she caught me at it, across the desks, say, or in the pungent chaos of the dining hall or even here, over the fields at the back of our houses, I'd avert to the blue/grey ends of my boots. Catching her eye was like staring into the sun, for me.

There was mud on her toecap. I removed it with my finger. She reddened. "You didn't have to do that... they're old..." She changed the subject. "Are you going to school today, Harry?"

My eyes didn't leave her boots. "Nah." That morning, I was far too fragile to walk through those rusty gates.

"And the reason is...?"

"Nuffin," I said witlessly, which was at odds with the gobby schoolboy, unafraid to answer the teachers back, I normally was. How could I tell my glossy-haired, teenage apparition that I'd been up all night watching brown tennis rackets turn into bananas then guitars, then into people and back again, with a grunt? How could I tell her that I knew I was going to get into the deepest trouble that night, but didn't give a fuck?

She stepped away. It was the signal.

I took a deep breath, bent my back and hurled the ball into the grey canopy until it disappeared.

What would usually happen is, she'd jump and clap while Terry whizzed in addled circles for a few seconds until the ball landed, *plop*, half a pitch away. But that morning, she didn't look at her dog but at me. It was as if she sensed my reckless intent. And what was weird is I didn't look away either, as if I knew she was concerned. We just stared at each other. I think that if she could communicate telepathically, she would have said, 'No, don't do it Harry', and, if I'd been

43

able to reply through a similar conduit, I'd have said (because you are permitted more syllables with ESP), 'I have to. It's gone too far, Susan'.

In the end we just smiled at each other. Soon, we were laughing, and for a few seconds it was as if nothing could tune in or break that particular connection.

"What you smiling at, *Wally*?" Bob brushed grass off my fluffy head.

I blinked into the present. "I *always* get up."

But he'd walked on. I jogged and caught up. "What happened today, Bob?"

"Nuffin," he replied. "Just Tone said last night on the bus on the way back from Abdul's, you know, 'the orders' and you said you'd be up for it. He thought you bottled it cos you bunked off school."

"But I'm here…"

He smiled, chopping at his forearm with one hand. "Lucky for you. He was well narked when you weren't at register."

Walking through the woods I was reminded of what a brilliant park it was. You could play twenty-a-side in three different games there was so much of it. And, if there wasn't enough to make teams, there was always 'centres and headers', 'Wembley' and 'three and in'. The woods were great to ride your bike through and, when Wimbledon was on, you could play tennis in the dusty, red courts until the parky came and shooed you off. There were swings and slides for little kids and a brilliant waltzer that me, Bob and Patrick finally knackered. And lastly, there was the café by the huge lake that Patrick's dad and brother fished in.

I strolled between rhododendron and holly bushes; a lit cigarette was wafted beneath my nose. I sucked on it greedily. Its chemicals emulsified the fearful, vile juices bubbling in my guts. Of course I didn't tell anyone I was petrified;

brickin', bottlin' and shitttin' it. Yesterday I'd taken LSD and it hadn't gone well. Tonight I was gonna 'do' somewhere. I just hoped I'd be better at burglary than I was at drugs.

From the woods, we emerged on the crest of the hill and gazed down at the substantial wooden cafe by the lake. In the moonlight, it looked like something from a film. A creepy old house at the still water's edge.

"You ready?" Tony asked.

With a wave of nausea, I flicked the last of my Number Six into a bush and the four of us jogged down like horseless cowboys.

In the summer this café was so busy, you couldn't see the flaxen grass for picnic blankets. The bins overflowed, attracting the manic, quacking ducks on the lake while bikes and bags were trustingly abandoned because everyone knew each other over there. On Sundays, it was as if the whole borough had turned out for some great event, a concert or an eclipse.

In winter the café was forlorn, open only during the day to serve cups of tea to pensioners after they'd finished their one, slow lap around the lake. Tony said there were fags, chocolates, crisps, tins of Coke and Fanta in there, enough to make a good few bob from at school and youth club. Even a tramp like me could buy something 'decent' to wear with his cut, Tony said.

We loitered outside the creosoted rear of the building. No cigarettes were allowed and we had to keep our voices down. This was business, Tony told us.

"Look Harry," he spat between his feet and put his arm around my shoulder. He stunk of fags and Brut, sweat and Party Seven. I was repulsed and attracted at the same time. "You said, you were the best climber."

"Er…"

The water lapped gently on the lake as he continued. "On

45

the bus, when you were puking and crying, I asked you and you said you were."

"Can't remember."

I felt his muscles contract before pushing me away. "Going back on it now, are ya?"

"Nah, nah..."

Wearily, he shook his head and sniffed. "Good climber, right?"

"I am, but - "

His eyes shone in the dark. "Can't you handle it, *chocolate drop*?"

I bristled. I lived to be useful, part of a team. I wanted the crook of his arm. "Course."

"Then over you go. Bring the stuff to the fence and pass it froo."

"Ain't you going with me?"

"It only needs one."

Suddenly, I was alone in the café yard and the lads were the other side of the fence. I still can't remember climbing over.

Tony passed a big screwdriver through the slats.

"Do the lock and get in there. Fucking hurry up."

I hesitated.

"Parky'll be here any minute. Don't bottle it, Gunga."

"I won't," I muttered.

Sweating in the chill, I levered the door with all my might.

Then I was calm. I knew where I was in the dark; I'd been here a hundred times buying a lolly or a Coke, bike left on the grass outside with many others. I stood behind the counter and for a couple of seconds, imagined serving some little kids ice-cream. Giving them a serviette to wipe their mouths because it melted in a second in this park in the summer.

Peering through the slats, I watched them leg it up the hill. "Well, help us over?" I called, but no-one did.

I hardly had the strength to heft a crate across and climb on it. Straddling the fence, I let my body weight tip me over. As I stood to pull away, I snagged myself on a nail. With my heart galloping, I threw myself forward and my trousers and Y-fronts ripped open.

They were near the path at the top of the hill when I limped up. My legs were jelly. "I'm knackered, Bob," I said, bent over and panting.

His face was beaming. "You did it, Harry."

Sweat poured into my eyes making me squint and blink.

Tony spoke. "We'll divi up." Squatting, they opened the holdalls they'd brought with them. My bollocks froze as I joined them.

Boxes were torn open and everybody had their share. There was nothing left for me. "What about me? I did it."

No one replied.

"What about a couple of packets of Rothmans?" I asked Tony. "And a ginger ale?"

"Tough," he said.

"That's not fair."

He turned on me, legs astride, chin raised, mouth snarling. "*Fair?*" he said, vacuuming oxygen from the woods. "Listen, nigger, you shouldn't even be here. This is our country."

"Wanker," I whispered.

A flash went off the second his nut recoiled.

Through the earth, voices were muffled, footfalls remote. "Leave him Tone, he don't understand…"

A slug in salt, I shrivelled in the dark, breathing.

Their Blakeys clipped the tarmac like hooves as they strode to the gates. I stood and limped after them.

Bob handed me a crushed-to-powder packet of Ready Salted as I reached his side. "Truth hurts, H," he said, and, with my conk throbbing, I surely knew it did.

7

The Police Visit

The following morning was Saturday and although I wanted to see Susan in the fields, I eschewed early morning tennis and stayed undercover. The trip to Holloway, the robbery and the shameful divi-up had drained me. I was still in my dusty pit at twelve. Sleep was far from restful though. The weekend rancour oozed through my pillow. Slamming and screams bled into my dreams turning flowers to monsters as I stooped to smell them.

"Your father said to get up!"

I peeked at the bespectacled, breathless woman with the black-bouffant framed in my doorway. Her sleeves were rolled up and a bleachy whiff pervaded.

"Why?"

Pulling a damp, jet tress from her brow with pink Marigolds, she said "He says you're a lazy bones."

" 'Ark at the great workaholic," I mumbled through the blankets.

"Don't shoot the messenger."

I raised myself and blinked, ready to trump her banality with another of my own. "He's…"

A cliché died on my lips because I was met by an unusual sight. For a moment, my mum's normally preoccupied façade had vanished and one of genuine concern, bordering on affection, had replaced it.

"What?" I said.

Her rubber finger trembled on her lip. "Who did that?"

I sat up, alarmed. Had I pissed the bed? *"What?"*

But the scaffolding went back up. The impenetrable lattice that shielded her emotions and kept her from suicide, or

flight, or murder, returned in a blink. "Look in the mirror."
She left the room.

"Panda," I whispered.

Even with my shade, the resemblance to Chi-Chi or
An-An, (they were the Chinese pandas all over the news)
fascinated me. My nose was bulbous and tender to the touch,
my eye sockets swollen yellow, blue and black. Inspecting
Tony's handiwork I thought, this is what I look like on the
inside, this is how I am, and I felt kind of good and proud.

Back in bed, I placed *Hunky Dory* on the turntable because
the booming racing commentary from the TV downstairs
filled every corner of the house. The piano tripped in and,
staring at the ceiling, I pressed my hooter until I couldn't
bear it. Inside a minute, Bowie was besting O'Sullivan and,
luxuriating in Mick Ronson's own black-eyed embellish-
ments, I hunted blissful sleep.

It happened during that line, '*Mamas and papas insane*'.
It was as if the track had been infiltrated by an outside
agency. As if it were being remixed inside the wires that
ran from deck to speakers. But it wasn't the record that
had changed, it was something in the house, something so
unusual that it felt as if the building had tilted a couple of
degrees on its axis. I sat up. It came to me. The TV was off.

"Off..." I whispered.

Once on, the TV never went off. It was vital. Our home's
artificial lung. Without its gales of laughter, hysterical
commentators and cheesy theme tunes, we'd have to look at
each other and speak.

Craning my neck, I sensed the atmosphere had altered in
my bedroom too. The air beneath my closed door eddied
coolly. I felt it against my battered face.

The front door was open.

"Open..." I whispered.

Thunder rumbled downstairs. "*Harry!*"

"What have I done now?" I wondered, shuffling from my room, defiant, fearful, resolute and entirely culpable.

Creeping onto the landing, I peeked through the banisters at the front door. Two of them: coppers, blue uniforms, shiny boots and peaked caps stood at our threshold.

My father looked comparatively small in his neat, all-black, slack and polo ensemble. "Harry?"

I poked my head around the top of the stairs. "Yeah?"

At the sight of these two, grim, hatchet-hard upholders of the law, all my ACAB and 'kill the bill' stuff went flying out of me. Then I really shit it because my dad was wearing his 'bad back' grimace. To the casual observer it meant that he had pain in his lumbar spine. To me and mum it indicated the wounded panther, a cornered beast ready to fight for its life.

I gulped.

With a sugar-sweet smile he beckoned me to his side. "*This* is my Harry."

"I'm not dressed."

He hissed. "Down. Now."

So down I padded, one hand pinning my ripped Y-fronts together so my oh so guilty ball-bag wouldn't give the game away.

Placing his hand on my shoulder, he toed the door shut. If he was trying not to alert the neighbours to this week's family shame, he'd forgotten about the other panda, the one outside with the flashing blue light and yakking radio.

One of the officers brushed the golf bag causing the shafts and heads to rattle. Everyone was looking at my face.

The club-brusher spoke. "Nasty ol' black eyes there, Harry. How'd you get them?

I daren't look up. "Accident."

Dad interjected in double posh. He'd put this stupid voice on whenever he was near any white man of authority, or in a suit, or uniform. As if sounding like John Gielgud would somehow make them colour-blind. "They *want* to ask... you... "

The thin-faced, blue-chinned constable held up his hand. "Please, Mr Ferdinand..." I sensed my father's perceived humiliation at being interrupted in his own hallway. "Harry, where were you last night, around eleven?"

" 'Ome."

"So you don't know anything about a break in at the café in Grovehills Park?"

"I been in, ain't I dad?"

He laughed nervously, his lashes fluttering like an embarrassed contestant. Take the money or open the box? "I heard his *awful* music upstairs," he bleated. "He stole corn-flakes..."

Wrong answer. The contemptuous look the blue-chinned one shot him was very similar to the sneer Tony offered me on a daily basis. He spoke with a sigh. "So, you weren't out with Patrick Carpenter, Tony Moor and Bob Wynch? We've heard you were seen with them."

"Yeah... er... we *were* out but not *that* late..."

Dad held up his hand. His eyes gleamed with good citizenship. "Yes. He told me. Those boys are criminals. They beat my son. Look." He offered my discoloured boat as evidence. "They endeavour to criminalise him," he continued with cod eloquence. "He told me they were to rob somewhere yesterday."

"I never said..." He pinched the rubbery tendon between neck and shoulder. I wilted while he looked to the game masters for approval.

The club-brusher cocked his head. "So, *you're* saying it was them that broke in, Harry?"

A nail-biting squeeze sent me knock-kneed and mute.

"He will not tell because he lives in fear," my paternal

barrister replied. "*I* am reporting to you what *he* has told me."

I felt like swooning. They were looking into my craven soul while at my side, my dad blinked and pouted like Miss Enfield.

"We'll proceed. Thank you for your time."

He waved the law away as if they were his aunt and uncle on their way back to the old country after a visit.

For a second, I thought of chasing after them and telling them everything; the nicking, the lying, playing with myself in English, the notes out of mum's purse, bogeys under the desk. As long as they didn't tell the boys it was me that told, I'd have admitted to anything.

My dad shut the door and leaned against it for good measure. He ran his tongue along his teeth. "So... you bring *policemen* to this house! On my mat door?"

Mum stuck her face around the kitchen corner. Again, I detected a weak link in that trellis but it wasn't there for long. She slunk back to the sink. The hot tap went on full blast.

He'll tire, I thought. He's been air-jockeying all morning. Surely the lawful humiliation on his doorstep would have sapped his strength? I thought about Bob. His mum will be in bits over this. I didn't even know if Pat had human parents and as for Tony... The golf bag rattled and I looked up. He'd removed his belt in a practised flash.

Left I guarded, but he struck right. Right I guarded, but he struck left. It was that natural timing and inimitable daily workout in effect. He feinted, I covered up, he connected with an exposed part. I rubbed at the sting. He lashed some fresh. I rubbed at that. Invigorated by his belt, nerve endings from past beatings sprouted like daffodils through a forest floor; their skyward-reaching tips new, enthusiastic pain receptors for the swishing leather.

I danced the hallway hop for a couple of minutes until he caught me across the top of the knee. As we drew breath, I managed to turn the door handle. If I could slither out and hobble around the corner, I could stay in the fields until it was dark and sneak into my room as he hunkered down for *Match Of The Day*. He hit me across my head. I felt the whip crease the bridge of my sorry conk. His voice faded in, in a boom of impassioned rage. "Criminal, criminal, *criminal!* My life you ruin…"

Wrenching the door open, I stumbled onto the front path. I looked for protection - privets, passing cars, citizens, bins - but he was at my side, his stride even as he examined his grovelling progeny. I had options: pride or pain? Three-piece hanging out in the cold midwinter or an unguarded flank? A full swing just below the ribs sent me skidding into the hedge by the bins. "Ruined my life, fucking child!"

Breathlessly, I crawled towards the gate and still, with tireless accuracy, he beat me. "No, no, no, *not* child now. *Big* man in trouble with the police."

As he grabbed a clump of coarse hair, my hands went to my head and my raggedy underwear dropped. Dedicatedly, unstintingly, he lashed my bare, brown arse on the flags outside our front gate.

With my pants around my ankles, I experienced a remote perspective. From helicopter height, I watched one ant chase the other round and around. A question was asked between rotor-blade wipes; "What is the point of pretending you are 'Mr Urbane Suburbia', 'Mr Private Good Citizen' when you beat the crap out of your half-naked son with a funky leather belt… in the middle of the street… at one o'clock… right after a visit from the local bill?"

And this *was* public. My nethers were exposed to numbers eighteen, twenty and twenty-two across the road, and as febrile curtains twitched I felt for my waistband, careless of the swipes across arm and back.

He struck again and again and then, mercifully, the

blows lightened. He stopped. The belt hung limp in his fingers and I had a surge of euphoria borne out of survival. With my body throbbing, I got to my feet and faced him. Our chests heaved in unison.

Something had affected my balance. I felt the urge to skid sideways but I sucked in my drool, kept still and looked unwaveringly into his bloodshot eyes. He recoiled, maybe only a millimetre or two, but he definitely backed up. Energised further, I took a forward step. I think I was about to say something like, '*Is that it? Happy now?*' But in that moment, my world shrunk to cringing shame. Across the road, outside number twenty's symmetrical, be-shingled driveway, Susan was hugging Terry to yet another new jean-jacket. This one had butterflies embroidered on the penny collars. Her face was ashen at the sight of me.

My dad pointed at my genitals and grinned.

I ran into the house.

8

Expulsion

Tatty parka flapping, breakfastless and groggy, I raced across the fields towards school. I had not the faintest idea that I was taking the first steps on a journey that would deliver me to the four points of the earth and back again.

I slid between the gates just as they shut.

Miss Clark hadn't been pasted all over her neighbourhood, nor had she recently been on the LSD. She'd had a restful weekend and was on the ball enough to see me mouth "Where's Tony?" to Bob at the end of register. Before he was able to reply, she'd banished me to the benches in the corridor outside. Disrupting the class.

Staring at the rows of coats, I tried to remember the all-exonerating, self-deprecating speech I'd put together for Tony but ended up day-dreaming about my ideal Christmas present and how I would get a hat-trick in games on Thursday. I never even had a shot.

I lost Bob and Patrick in the blazer exodus at the end of the lesson and couldn't go after them because Clark wanted to see me. Another detention was pencilled in. "I'm booked up for a month's worth, miss!" She shook her head and marked me down anyway. Consequently, I was late for the next lesson and told to sit at the front, diametrically opposite Pat and Bob who had booked in at the back.

Initially, Tony's absence appalled me. Then it filled me with hope. Perhaps they'd locked him up already and the inquisition at his buttoned-down Sherman would never take place. I willed Bob to give me a sign, just a nod or glance to say everything was OK, the police didn't come round and we were still mates. But, whenever contact was about to be made, some kid, some *pupil*, would come between us. Towards the end of the lesson, on a contrivance to the teacher's desk for a textbook, I managed to meet his eye. All I received was an indecipherable, shaking skinhead that reduced me to sweaty unease.

Satchels and holdalls went flying as I scampered towards the back of the gymnasium at morning break, but no one was there. I kicked at the halo of dog-ends, our own, term-length, noxious school project and felt like a soldier returning to his flattened house after the war. Looking away, I saw two shorn, bobbing heads beneath an Embassy cloud. They were progressing along the school wall at the far end of the football pitches.

"Oi!" I called, stumbling over the rubble, the sweet wrappers and exercise book pages. Cutting across the cricket square, I met them at the railings at the far end of the fields. They were heading towards Bob's. A morning giggling over pale ale and Roxy Music awaited but I was on the inside looking out.

They were sucking on fags and I wished I could inhale one hot drag to set me up. "Where's Tone?"

Patrick shook his handsome head. Bob wouldn't even look at me.

"I didn't say nuffin!" I pleaded.

Bob stopped. "Why'd they come round? My dad went mental."

"But - "

"Grass." The sibilance hissed like a rattler around my ankles. Their eyes stayed on me. It was as if they had me under a Bunsen burner in science and were waiting to see what happened when my skin came off.

Pat hardly ever spoke. He just looked great. What I remember him saying were things like, "*Nah, they don't wear turn-ups now, you wally*" or, "*You should have a stud, gold, cos it won't go all yella and weep...*" so when he actually put a sentence together that wasn't about Millets, I almost passed out. "Tony's gonna stab ya!" he said.

"Fucking grass, Ferdinand," said Bob, beckoning me to the fence. "He's on the run!"

"Is he?"

"He's really gonna kill you, Gunga."

"How can he if he's on the run?"

He gobbed straight into my face.

"You an' all, Bob?" I whispered.

By the time I unglued my eyes they'd gone.

Normally, after a show-up or some other misdemeanour, I'd put together a few nimble steps of the 'funky chicken'. That always made them grin, give me a fag, the end of their chips. On my own, staring into the traffic, I put my thumbs under my armpit, flapped my elbows, bent and slid. I bit my rubbery lip and summoned the battered shutters that protected me from hurt, but on this occasion, they refused to drop.

The bell rang across the fields, summoning the children back to their desks for the after-break lessons.

All around me kids were plonking bags down, unzipping pencil cases and opening exercise books for Maths with Driver. I hated this lesson and nine times out of ten just wouldn't be here. But where else was there? Rejection had sapped the rebel out of me. A kid nudged me and yesterday I would have lashed out, spat or swore. Today I cringed and shivered.

Then, through it all, I saw Susan shimmering at her desk. Welts on body and soul were irrelevant as I absorbed her clean lines and happy existence. Her eyes sparkled and her navy sweater met the white of her neck like the sea joins the sky. I etched a sad smile as she raised that clever brow and carefully arranged ruler, pencil case and text books in front of her.

He strode into the classroom like a gale that has doors slamming and papers flying. Spines stiffened as he surveyed the room from the blackboard.

"Good morning, 5R."

"Good morning, Mr Driver."

"Sit!"

Chairs scraped back. Amidst the coughs, wriggles and scribbles he droned away but nothing went in. My dishonourable discharge had dulled my wits because I loved those boys. A few days ago I had a country and flag but I'd blown it that morning with the police. Now I was stateless, a bottler, grass and traitor.

Driver was staring at me. "Sit down, boy!"

The command made no sense. My brain seemed stuck in sickly inertia. My knees wouldn't bend. *"Ferdinand!"* he roared.

Susan was looking at me. There was no sly smile.

"What?" I jerked awake, breathlessly.

"Stand on your chair."

"What?"

"If you can't sit down, stand. *Stand - on - your - chair!"*

Stepping on it, I wobbled upright. He wasn't entirely ruthless, Driver, he let the class have a good laugh at my expense for a few seconds.

"Right," he barked, "algebra homework…"

Mister Driver was the top, strutting heavy along the waxy corridors of my old school. He had speckled stubble that he never shaved or, if he did, he did it at night because it was always there in the morning like iron moss on his dimpled chin. He had a wide, sallow face, piercing eyes and played rugby at the weekends. Sometimes, in the summer, he'd wear his club colours - shorts too - and all the women teachers would give him the eye. He was obviously a physical sort of man. I couldn't stand him. The feeling was mutual.

I yawned and imagined whirlpool eyes peering from the dyslexic jumble on the blackboard. Soon, congealed banana spots were fragmenting across the ceiling as organ chords stabbed mercilessly to a slinky beat. I recalled the poem on Abdul's wall... "Go placidly amid the noise and haste and remember what peace there may be in silence…"

Kids near me glanced up from their books to snigger at my mutterings. I attempted to focus on the brown spots slowly passing overhead. The chair wobbled. Quickly, I grabbed the seat back for balance.

"Stand up, boy!"

My mouth was so dry. "I… I…" I mumbled.

Plastic pear drops swirled at lightning speed. They rattled like snakes in my head. *Grassss*. I wiped gob from my eyes, put my hands to my ears and fell. Tania's voice was imbedded in the sound of the surf. "Look at his back, Abdul."

Driver was standing over me. I began to count the little black shoots on his chin. "Play acting, boy, such a waste of space. Get back on that chair!"

I inhaled spices: garlic, cumin, Paki food. I whispered, "As far as possible, without surrender, be on good terms with all persons…"

"Are you laughing at me, *worm!*"

One after another, doors slammed shut in my head. At that moment it seemed that all sound - music, words, the wind in the trees - had ceased. There was nobody to turn to and nowhere to go. So I gave up. I just wanted to get it over with. "Why don't you fuck off, Driver."

Sequins floated as he grabbed both my ears and sort of lifted me backwards. Glancing left and right, to check the coast was clear, he smashed the back of my head into Miss Rand's geography project. She had mounted the best pictures and essays on *The Amazon Basin* on the cork wall-tiles. The back of my skull smashed through 3D forests and rainfall, felt-tip graphs into the breeze blocks behind them. He did it over and over, raging and pulling my ears, ripping out chunks of wiry black thatch. As my legs buckled and eyes watered, I could hear kids giggling - but not hilariously. It wasn't that funny. I mean, a great big rugger geezer smashing a fifteen-year-old's head into a brick wall just isn't.

When he tired of head banging, he took the back of my parka and lifted me so that my feet brushed the floor. "Ferdinand, you are the *worst* pupil in the history of this school." Pressing my face into his jacket (the stink of his adrenalised aftershave wasn't a million miles from Tony's a few nights ago), he sent me rocketing through the door. I stumbled into the musty blazers and coats on the hooks outside the classroom. As he dragged me along, his knuckles compressed the vertebrae at the back of my neck. I could hear the material ripping in my coat.

"Oi! You're tearing my coat."

"This rag!"

Outside the headmaster's office I choked on his breath, the staffroom standard: digestives, orangey tea and gastric reflux. "Do *not* move!" he said, rapping lightly on the door.

"Come," boomed the voice from inside.

He left me there. Shaking uncontrollably, I blinked back tears and snarled at the occasional, errand-running first year.

Behind the door the two great educators grumbled intelligibly and then, I heard…laughter.

Coincidentally, one of the earliest 'laughs' I had with my once best friend Bob, was outside this office. We were first years. I remember my teeth chattered as we giggled in fear of the unknown. I can't even recall the headmaster's name now. We called him Beaky. Grey suit, well over six feet but spare, the points of his elbows ever disfiguring the sleeves of his pinching, grey woollen suits. Bob and me had been exuberant but disruptive. Petty distractions, in late, laughing

60

and singing. It was an accumulation of events that had brought us to the end of The Beak.

As twelve-year-olds we stood in front of his huge desk. When at last he snapped shut his book and removed his half-specs, he embarked on a lengthy discourse. The subject, 'choosing the right road in life'. My eyes rested on the war medals in the display case behind him and adjacent photo: unsmiling, khaki soldier in the desert, the beret pulled low, rifle cradled in his huge hands.

He assured us that the school could be a great friend if the pupil was in reciprocal mood. 'Respect was a two way street' he said, pleased with his mastery of youth speak. He added that it was his duty to put young men like us on the right path. It was a duty he took very seriously.

I'd heard about these 'interviews', rumours and scary whispers from older boys that had inhabited the same, dog-end dotted carpet at the back of the gym. I thought, and Bob said he'd thought the same, that we were going to get off. I mean, he'd yakked away for a good twenty minutes and we'd nodded in all the right places. Then he stood, leaned across his desk and opened the door to an ancient cabinet. After what could only be described as a sigh of surrender, some-thing he'd never done in the war, he removed the cane.

He made Bob bend over the desk first and administered six whacks to the arse. I watched his wrist action. Unlike my dad, who went off like a dervish, Beaky was far more deliberate. He took his time, aimed and fired. Such was the crack and con-sequent grunt of pain from Bob, I muttered a swift, quivering prayer for forgiveness to the polystyrene tiles above.

I don't know if Bob was holding his breath, or if being bent over like that had squashed all the air out of his lungs, but when Beaky yanked him upright, his face was vermillion. He staggered and his green eyes, eyes that usually laughed at anything, glistened with sorrow.

61

Then Beaky took my budding Afro in his bucket-size hands and bent me over the desk. He had *looked* in control but his hand shook as his knuckles found the soft tissue in my neck. It was as if *he* was as terrified as I was and that really unnerved me. Old telly footage played in my panicky head: vanquished lines, grey columns of German prisoners, hundreds of them, guarded by a couple of our squaddies. Watching from the safety of the seventies, I wondered why such numbers didn't overpower their captors and escape. As Beaky ground my nose and mouth mercilessly into the desk, I finally knew. Inhaling in fearful expectation, I boaked on the stale smell of the green leather desk-covering. The first swipe was a shock. It sent electric waves of pain through my buttocks and into my thudding heart. The other five aren't even a memory now.

So, don't let other men tell you that it never hurt and it did you good. If you think they're telling the truth then they must have had a right limp-wristed sissy holding the cane. Because when Beaky, *Corporal* Beaky, set about your arse with the old bamboo, it stung into the night and the next day too.

The last caning I'd received was last term, for disrupting dinner I think. It may have been for missing detentions? Since then I'd been sent home numerous times. My parents had been called to the school and Beaky had informed all relevant parties that my next transgression would result in expulsion. It appeared to be that day's theme.

I touched the growing mouse on the back of head. It was wet. I looked at my hand. Blood glistened on my fingers and I began to mumble my tune. *"Now put your left hand up, across your face, your knees start a-trembling, all over the place."* Then I thought: fuck this.

I ended up in the toilets near the tuck shop. Looking into the mirror, I wondered why I never cut my hair. After all, everyone I admired shaved theirs to the bone. Why had I retained my clump? Not even the other coloured kids at school would dare to have such a nutty hairdo; black, curly antennae reaching into the universe for contact. As blood trickled down my nape, I took a huge inward gulp of air. My head ached, my nose and ears stung and the welts and slashes on my torso burned as they brushed against the man-made fibres encasing them. A wave of freezing melancholy doused me, locking my breath in tighter. Feeling faint, I imagined a black smudge in this white-tiled chamber. It was pulsating but the pulses were weak and erratic. The smudge was giving up, waxing hopelessly towards finality. If there had been a gun or a noose handy I would have done myself in.

Mongrel eyes returned the stare from the mirror and, gulping in the urine-scented air, I leaned heavily on the sink in front of me.

Fractionally, something gave. I leaned harder. The basin creaked and the grouting that ran along the tiled edge opened up like the ground does in a film when there's an earthquake. The pulse was strengthening, infusing. Tugging the sink half an inch from the wall, I heard a crunching sound as the mortar scraped rusty screws and ancient rawlplugs. I put my hips and shoulders into it and soon the whole thing was hanging by the waste pipe. I stood back and booted it. The sink fell and smashed into three.

I left the toilets with water jetting into midair.

In the first floor library, at a table in an alcove, I gazed at the playing fields and picked out the corner where I'd last seen Bob and Pat. From a shelf, I selected *The Catcher in the Rye* and opened it at the page where the bellhop whacks Holden Caulfield in the stomach. I felt myself buckle from a man-sized blow. I shut the book, sweating. For a moment I heard a hoarse whisper, saw bitten, livid fingertips. *'I see it go in… the geezer was crying for his mum… and he twisted it… sniff.'*

63

Fumbling through my pockets I found half a cigarette and lit up. The taste was tangy and the nicotine rush more gut-scouring than it had ever been. Blowing a few imperfect smoke rings at the ceiling, I let my fingers walk along the spines on the shelves in front of me. I stopped at *Fahrenheit Four Five One*. Opening it, I recalled a copy of this book had been strategically placed, along with a couple of others, in the kitchen hatch about a year ago. It was my mother's silent gift to me, an imperceptible nod between lifers.

Books were allowed. He accepted she needed them and had always had them. She had to read at work. It was there that she earned the money for green fees, tight black slacks, petrol, etcetera.

Arching his brow, he'd watch me secrete them beneath my holey school jumper. He was reticent to comment on things he didn't understand and what he didn't understand was of no importance. Most of what went on baffled him, I think he once said, '*Men do not read, they stand proud...like men!*' something like that.

In bursts between the hot tap, the mooing hoover and bitter oaths, she'd glance left and right and whisper, "Harry, books are your best friends."

As she scrubbed at a surface or sink or toilet, I'd accept her maxim with the surly, truculent shrug that befitted my stage in development.

That we had to suppress our mutual passion, made me despise her. We couldn't even talk freely about writers and writing without the great dictator sneering, shushing and looking with befuddled, bloodshot suspicion at our paper-thin union. I cringed with shame. How could she have chosen this person to be my dad? And she loathed me equally for putting a giant, foetal-shaped spanner in her university works. She could have read and read with impunity there.

But she'd been proved right. Bob, Tony and Pat, corporeal

64

friends, had turned their backs, but the authors my mum passed across remained loyal, eternal buddies.

I never managed to discuss a book with her. We never discussed anything at all. The jailor did all the talking. His voice boomed and roared at his outrageous treatment. I never found a minute to look at her and she at me and say, "So, mum, Steinbeck... that's America right? But not now..." I took a huge drag and coughed all over myself.

I would have torched that home of ours. Thinking in monochrome, I saw myself approaching it through smoke. It was a burned-down church. Relieved firemen, all smudged, drank cuppas brewed for them by our neighbours. Amongst the charred ruins, the prized terracotta vase lay in jigsaw pieces. Where the door had once been, his Slazenger bag was a gooey, smouldering mess of plasticised gold trim. My boots crunched glass and twisted vinyl as I entered. With its one fat eye smashed, the vanquished titan lay on its side. Its twin, telescopic hairs were so twisted, it'd be impossible for them to receive a signal again. Melted over the chrome table where it had sat, so smugly, were its entrails. Its silver/green brain was dashed beyond repair.

I touched a corner of the novel with the end of my cigarette and soon the pages were aflame. Practising my rings, I dropped the book and walked away.

The estimable Miss Rand was tidying the history display by the library door. She backed against the wall when she saw me. I raised my palm in apology. I remember her specs went all skew-whiff, like Eric Morecambe's.

Downstairs, outside Beaky's office, I waded into a lake, lace-hole deep. The fire alarm sounded. I dropped my fag in the water. *Grassss* it hissed.

I began to jog.

Coincidentally, it was Beaky's last year too. Since leaving the forces, he'd put in decades of sterling service and the school governors wanted to commemorate his efforts. It was decided that the children plant trees in his honour. Consequently, the fence that ran along the road side of the playing fields was lined with stick-like saplings. Heartfelt dedications on little metal plaques were set in front of them. These spindly limbs would grow into a row of leafy cedars one day. It was a wonderfully enduring gift. A natural barrier between this place of good learning and the roaring traffic on the A-road outside.

As I walked the field's perimeter, I snapped the first one in my path with a sensual contraction of my shoulder muscles. As it cracked, I felt one less lash across my buttocks, one iota of self-respect retrieved from Beaky's green, leather-bound desktop.

After a few minutes I stopped, caught my breath, and considered my handiwork. Four wrecked goalmouths and a dozen young trees snapped in half. I thought, they'll never grow straight and tall if they ever grow at all.

"Luck of the draw," I said, jogging towards the fence with the fire alarm fading behind me.

Back in the fields at the end of my garden, I lay, face-down on a tree levelled by the autumn storms. Distant sirens oscillated while squirrels scratched in the branches overhead. Through a gap in the clouds, the sun made a brief, valiant attempt to warm the copse. I raised my face from the moist bark to absorb its heat.

My palms looked like a detail from the pages of a DC comic, in part green, (stained by the saplings I'd so wantonly destroyed) and part red (from my bloodied skull, care of Driver). I gazed at our back garden's kicked-in gate knowing I'd never walk through it again. That certainty thrilled and frightened me. That gate would never be repaired. I'd walked through it a thousand times thinking, "All it needs is one

66

screw," then "All it needs is two screws..." then "Three..." Now it needed replacing. The top hinge swung free from the rotten post and all of its palings were missing, ground into the muddy patch either side of it. "Broken," I whispered, shutting my eyes.

My name from his lips sounded like no other. The vowel almost non-existent and the H, a growl. "Harry?" I blinked awake. My dad, his cheeks gaunt with stress, stared beseechingly at me from our garden boundary.

As sirens wailed, one muscular arm tested the gate but was unable to open it. You had to raise it an inch to free it but he didn't know that. "Harry," he repeated, pointing to his chest, impassioned. "*Me* the school have called." He was incredulously posh. "What have you now done to family *your?*" he pleaded, rocking the rotten old wood, gently.

I slithered off the trunk and prepared to sprint. It was then I heard their voices.

Through the trees they resembled crows in their Crombies. Tony and a couple of dangerous-looking older men were crossing the centre circle of the pitch, but one away from me. They walked in solemn uniformity, like coffinless ushers. Tony put his hands to his mouth. What he said would have been indecipherable to the untutored ear. Two syllables lost in a hectic lunch-break. "*Guuuungaaaaa!*"

I fancied I could hear his lungs fill for a second belt.

"Harry, how does one open this *appalling* thing? Unjust, criminal, careless world." Now in full Gielgud soliloquy, he rocked the gate violently, his Popeye bicep flexing, his eyes bloodshot. No longer puppy, more mad dog. "Cursed I am by your birth!"

"I ain't done nuffin..." I whimpered, my eyes flitting between Tony's mob and my furiously addled parent.

"For this crime you will be punished to the point that

67

never again!... will you transgress. Bones will break my son, bones will break."

"*Guuuuuungaaaa.*" They'd spread out. Hoots and football songs. "*Rule Britannia, a-g, a-g-r, a-g-r-o…*"

"I will have to beat you properly, this time, my only Harry..."

Stereo. Like that beat on *Five Years*.

"You hidin' in them woods? Monkey boy. Fuckin' Bill round my house…" They had encircled the copse. I ducked behind a tree.

"He's in there, behind that tree…"

"Good climber, monkey boy?"

I was looking straight at my dad and the unobtainable sanctuary behind him. Befuddled no more, he tilted his head and lifted the gate. "Ahhh," he sighed, stepping through with his nine iron.

"Where's the Paki grass?… *You're gonna get your fuckin' head kicked in…*"

I zigzagged in and out of view of my pursuers. The fact that I would inevitably become trapped between them and the wall at the end of the copse was firmly at the front of my desperate mind. I ran, gulping in the air, careless of the branches whipping my face.

9

Susan

"…You blown it monkey boy…"

I ran from trunk to hedge to trunk again. In front of me was the ten-foot high wall I had never been able to climb. Too short, too weak, no bottle.

My ankle twisted and I fell. Behind me, a twig snapped like a gunshot. I could smell their fags now and - my god - a whiff of Brut, Aqua de Silva, the Rover's leatherette pong. Watneys, malice… *murder?*

I staggered upright.

"*Harry.*"

Pulled to the ground, I rolled, shut my eyes and curled up tight. Metal scraped metal. I braced myself.

But I'd heard that metallic sound a hundred times. It was the movement of a cast-iron lock on the back of a sturdy wooden door. The door was seven-foot high and put there to repel the foreigner by a man that'd had just about enough of them. I heard it first thing most days.

"They've passed. Listen?"

Tony's war cries echoed away.

"And your dad's gone back inside."

Uncurling, I opened my eyes and took in the aroma of freshly mown grass. Above me, Susan blocked out the sky. "What's the time?" I asked, standing up and brushing myself down.

She had a watch. "Half two. All your coat's torn and your shirt's covered in blood."

"What you doin' here?" I asked.

"I walked out."

"*What?*"

69

"I walked out after Driver…"

"Why?"

"Because it isn't right to do that to a boy."

Beautifully irritated, she folded her arms when I laughed.

It was as if I had stepped into a watercolour. During spring and summer weekends you could hear her dad, Alan, and her mum, Maureen, at it from eight o'clock in the morning, the shears clipping, the mower rattling, chatter, chatter, the kettle whistling on the hour. Perched in the wasted apple tree at the back of our garden I'd watch the tops of their busy heads. My mum and dad never did the gardening; it would have been an admission of marital acquiescence for them to be on our muddy plot at the same time.

That afternoon, Susan's garden did indeed look like a painting. The clipped grass verge along the S-shaped path was as neat as any suedehead's fringe. Her dad had swept all the leaves into a neat pile at the side of the shed and, magically, not one had strayed onto the lawn. Rubbing the warm, golf ball-sized lump on the back of my head, I smiled. "You've never bunked off in your life."

She was framed by the trellis arch at the end of the path. It was woven with rose buds, pink and white. I read 'Head Girl' on the tiny, blue enamel shield on her starched shirt pocket. "First time for everything," she said, shrugging. Her pale lips were pursed with amusement at my amusement.

The dog barked inside the house.

"You'll get into trouble, Susan," I mocked.

"Then I'll contact the expert for advice." She arched her brow and the sun began to fade behind her like a giant, dying torch. "There was a fire and a flood, did you do it?"

Shrugging magnanimously at my biblical abilities, I watched her bite her bottom lip and blink with concern. "What are you going to do, Harry? There are police cars at the school. Fire engines as well."

"That's it. I'm never goin' back. They'll expel me anyway."

"What will your mum and dad say?"

"Ain't goin back dare, evah."

The dog yapped and clawed the kitchen door. "*Shhh*," she called over her shoulder. "Where will you go?

"Dunno, get a job."

"Doing what?"

"Dunno, go down the Job Centre."

Susan was perplexed, a rare sight. At school, she was top problem solver, never wrong. If, on a rare occasion, she didn't have the answer, she'd wear this blinking, addled smile as if she'd lost track. But, all the time her brain was whirring like a turbine. She wore that addled look now.

"Run out of answers, *Susan?*"

"Don't know what the question is, *Harry.*"

It occurred to me that not much more than a dozen words had ever passed between us, and now she was admitting she'd truanted so that she could see if I was alright. This unnerved me. Someone had mentioned she had a boyfriend, a kid at Grammar, sports star and academic. I imagined them going to galleries, and going on boats with him doing the rowing, with that pole... ducking under weeping willows.

"I've got to let him out," she nodded at the house.

"Go on then..."

She tapped her foot impatiently. "What about your clothes?"

"I'll buy some."

"With what?"

"Conkers."

"*Wally.*"

Her eyes were blue smudges of moisture and her hair was sticking out. Only I could have detected the tracks of a tear on her cheek. "Where've you been, Susan?"

71

"Do you want a clean shirt… for your job interview?"

I glanced at her house.

"Come on, Harry," she said.

I knew her mum and dad to nod at but I'd never dreamt of entering their domain. There was an unseen force-field around the Fernley's waist-high privet. They'd smile nervously at my dad and occasionally the mums would chat about school holidays and stuff but, in the main, they kept my iffy lot at a stiff, suburban arm's length.

She left my side, opened the kitchen door and Terry ran shuttles between our ankles. I bent to scratch him and felt my collar release from the scab on my neck. "Will it be alright, with your mum and dad?" I said from the trellis arch.

"They're at work. Do you like cream soda?"

"Er…"

"Or lemonade?" she said, walking up to me.

"Nah, I like cream soda more."

She took my hand and the utter exhilaration of her touch, her steering arm, and her breath anaesthetised everything. "Come on…" she repeated and I obeyed, powerless in her mighty softness.

In the kitchen, I inhaled cereal smells, her mum's Avon Lady perfume and a scintilla of sweaty dog. The sucky fridge door opened and the light from inside sliced a section of a spotless dining table in two. The screw cap hissed and bubbles popped as our eyes met. We finished at the same time.

The stairs were a blur, some prints of horses and a family photo on the landing (beaming Alan on a cliff, Maureen hugging up tight, windswept, sunglasses and a tartan blanket for the car).

While the other doors on the landing were glossed white, hers was navy and had 'Knock first - Susan's Room!' emblazoned on it. She pushed it open. On one wall was a poster of Bowie, Ziggy Stardust, the scowl and sequins, that blue

72

guitar. He gazed down on her at night. On the wall facing the bed was the poem from Holloway. I began to read, "*Go placidly...*"

"*Amid the noise and the haste,*" she wasn't reading the poster, she was looking at me. Her eyes were fierce as she spoke, "*and remember what peace there may be...*"

In silence we undressed and lay between her Daz-fresh sheets. We looked at each other for a long time until her cool, angel-light touch brushed the back of my neck and she kissed me with a mouth as perfect as any rose that grew in her father's garden.

Rib to rib, hip to hip, her freckled shoulder touched mine. When she dozed I watched her and when my eyes shut she studied me. We were guarding each other. Pressing close. Reassuring and reinforcing our flimsy afternoon against the fateful designs beyond the window.

With soft kisses and an unwavering gaze, she released thoughts and ideas that were buried so deep, I didn't know I had them. Holding onto each other we spoke of the future in muted voice.

"I want to do something... something different from everything," I said, breaking out of the whispers. Then I laughed at myself, unqualified, expelled, utterly useless.

"You can do anything you want, Harry, you're brilliant."

"What? Me?"

She stroked my neck as she spoke. "You say things, sometimes in class or to your friends, and no one understands. But I do, Harry." Her touch had managed to unlock every vertebra in my spine. I was like a puzzle returned to neutral after being jumbled up. "You must believe in yourself and not be frightened of... challenges."

"Challenges?"

"There will be many. You mustn't be afraid."

73

"Like what?"

She paused. A trace of befuddlement marred the clarity in her eyes. "Well," she continued seriously, "you're not very interested *academically* but you're not stupid, so you must be inspired. So, erm, your path..."

"What path?"

"Your path through life, wally."

"Oh."

"Your *path* won't be like a normal person's. Don't make that face. You'll have more choices. When you have them you'll have to be brave."

"Blimey," I whispered, confused but enthused. "Is that like what career officers say... like, on paths?"

"Yes. They advise. I'll probably go to the LSE and study economics. What did your advisor say about your options?"

"Didn't go in."

"Did you reschedule?"

Laughing out loud, I held and kissed her reassuringly. Once again her eyes became blue smudges of concern. "What happened when the police came round on Saturday?"

"About the café? My dad went mental."

"I saw."

"I know."

Recalling the whipping in the street, I expected a clammy rush of shame but felt nothing but relief at being able to talk to her about it. Up on one elbow she looked at me the way she did when reading the music during her morning piano recitals. "Why?"

"Why what?" I said, running my fingers through the fine clipped hairs on her neck.

"Why does he treat you like that?"

"Because of the way I am." Briefly, I imagined him; back pressed against the big rad laughing at some crap on telly then turning to me with a sneer before gravely announcing,

'Harry, what must it be like to be you? So despised and talentless?'

"He says I'll end up over the park with the drunks…"

Addled once more, she asked, "What drunks?"

"Over Grovehills."

Again, she shook her head.

"Ain't you seen them? By the lake? Tramps, men and women. They sit around and get pissed all day, singing and sleeping."

"He said you'll be like *them*. Why?"

"Because I'm not," and here I did become embarrassed, "a success?"

She giggled into my shoulder.

"Seriously, Susan," I said, gently lifting her face to mine. "He looks at the telly and points out all these wallys and says, 'look at his hair' and, on *Top Of The Pops,* he'll see some bloke and say, 'listen to him sing' and then he'll look at me and say, 'You're a failure. You're ugly and stupid. You'll never have a car or a wife'… stuff like that."

"But you *still* clean his car. You're always doing it."

"I don't…" I laughed.

She sort of patted my bonce. "I love the way it springs up, when you pat it."

"I do it once a week."

"At the barbers?"

"What?"

"I thought it went like that naturally."

I laughed with her. "Nah, clean his car, I mean."

"Oh. Does he threaten you to do it?"

"Funny enough, no. I clean his golf clubs too, and his shoes. I rub his back, he's got this bad back. Change the programmes over, I…" I realised how weird it all must have sounded to her. "I love my old man, think I always will. But he hates me."

"Since I can remember I've heard your family shouting through the walls. Dad turns the radio up."

"Sorry."

"It isn't your fault... but I think, what is so wrong with life *all the time* to make him so angry? At weekends there is *always* an argument. Screaming... your mum and dad... and then the Hoover goes on and the banging and then your mum cries, the front door slams and she runs past our house and then the telly goes on or that music, with all the drums - "

"It's Latin American - "

" - and then your mum comes back and it goes quiet and then the telly goes on *really* loud for the racing. It just stays on for hours. So *loud*... and your dad shouts over it and your mum screams back. It's *so* mad. What happens in there, Harry?"

"Just family life, I suppose."

She kissed me, and warmed by her sodary breath, I slept again.

There is no measure of the time we spent together, but day turned to night halfway through her smile.

"*What?*" I awoke with a start. This turning key wasn't in my dream. A door slammed downstairs.

Susan was already up, her school skirt on. The blue enamel badge glinted as she did her buttons up furiously. It was pitch black outside her window.

The *Jean Genie* sniggered as I put two feet into one leg and fell. My landing was disproportionately loud. In seconds, footsteps thudded past the grazing horses on the stairs.

"Susan!"

A beat. The door opened.

"You black bastard...!"

"Daddy..."

76

I was tossed onto the landing. The scab came away, stinging.

"Susan...!" I called out.

"Run, Harry!"

I took the stairs three at a time but couldn't open the front door. The man could fit a lock, that's for sure.

He roared and rumbled and Susan screamed for my rights. Turning from the door, my unlaced boot hovered over the first step.

"But he's got *nowhere* to sleep!" she implored from above.

"You certainly helped him solve *that* problem."

"Everyone hates him."

"Are you surprised?"

"He's a boy."

"He's a yob... useless drain on society... he'll go on the dole and I'll have to pay for him out of my taxes... mistake letting the bastards in."

At the door, I fumbled and tugged hopelessly.

Suddenly, Susan was at my back, her hot, tearful breath in my ear. She flicked the lock like she had my heart.

"Take this," she said, handing me a heavy, fur-lined pilot's jacket.

"I'll knock," I said.

"Run!"

I leaned towards one last brush of her lips but something pulled me from her. Looking back, I know it to be the fateful designs beyond the window: the dads - hers and mine - Tony, Old Bill, Beaky, Driver, everything that walked in that London borough. So I did as she said. I ran. I ran a long fucking way.

10

The Long Walk

Counting coppers nicked from mum's purse and the paper scrapings from the peg-pocket in his golf bag, I selected a bottle of sherry, Domecq, and a packet of ten Number Six. Stepping out of the offie and into the rapidly cooling evening, I glugged, then vomited the hot sticky syrup back into my mouth. But I didn't eject. I kept it in there, inhaled and slowly drew it down my throat. Shivering, I pressed my face into the brown, furry collar of Susan's jacket. It smelled like her pillow. I hesitated. I should run back and claim her. The lights changed to green. I swigged, boaked, swallowed and jogged on.

By the time I'd crossed the North Circ, I'd acquired a sherry tolerance. The taste reminded me of cough mixture; the bottle, Christmas adverts, top hats and canes.

Walking the cold, quiet streets, I became the detached auditor of my own fate. I calculated the only way was down. It was just as my father had so lyrically prophesied: 'Like you I was, like me you'll become.' Rubbing the welts on my hip, tender lumpy reminders, I swigged again. "Go placidly amid the noise and haste and, and remember… *remember… fuck!*" Even though I couldn't remember, I found myself repeating the opening lines over and over. If I didn't say them I'd hear Susan's impassioned pleading on the landing, feel the bottler's shame when she turned the latch and I fled.

Susan never pleaded; her chair scraped back, she stood and answered cleverly with that arched, sceptical brow. Swaying in the dark, I tried to recall one of her witty class-room retorts, clever digs to replay like bits of a song on the way back at home time. But the only tune my memory would allow was her animal beseeching for my rights. I should run back.

"Go placidly... *Bottler!*" I screamed, tearing blindly across the road.

I awoke on a bench near Wood Green bus station. A dark face peered down. I became alarmed. Had he dogged me in his four wheel banana? Was he about to rip the blankets away and thud and pummel? But there was a smile of concern on this tilting head. "Wha'appen, yout?"

Wiping and swigging I said, "Go placidly amid the noise and haste and remember - "

"Lemme tek dat."

"Nah." Hugging my seasonal tipple, I skittered away.

"*Boy?*" his voice faded.

I passed a shop I'd visited with the lads at half-term. Pausing, I gazed at two-tone suits and crisp Ben Sherman shirts in the window. I remembered that Pat said they were all 'so reasonable' and I didn't understand because I thought they were smart. 'The price, *coon*flake!' Tony informed me.

Taking a mighty wipe at my bottle, I became transfixed by a blue plastic bag. It was trapped on the tarmac, flattened and tattered by the wet, oily tyres that ran over it. I listened to its crackling cries for clemency as it attempted to dodge the roaring grilles aimed at it. Then, just when I thought it could take no more, a freezing gust lifted it as high as the lampposts. "We've escaped," I croaked, raising my bottle, enjoying its battered freedom dance until it shot leftwards, and impaled itself on the harpoon spikes of the metal railings.

Headlights passed, buffeting and spinning me. Tripping over the kerb, a car horn blared and tyres skidded at my back. I reeled across the road at Manor House and fell on the path that led into the park. Out of the corner of my eye I saw the sluggish clumps of street people grouped by the braziers at the Seven Sisters gates. I stood and veered away, suitably terrified.

The empty bottle went flying over a privet and on I reeled. I was many miles from home but somewhere not unfamiliar. Making my way up a path of cracked, ungeometric tiles, I rang the bell on the stained glass door at its end. The latch slid and a bushy, half-head peeked around the door.

"I go to school with Hassan - "

"He doesn't live here."

"Yeah, I know, but I know his brother, Abdul… and Tania."

"They're out."

The door slowly shut and, as it did, I inhaled spices, cumin and garlic.

A toe in my back had me scuttling away, taking a bin lid and some bottles with me.

"Hey, be cool…" The male face peering down was both surprised and amused. He sported red sideburns, they fizzed at his jowls while his eyes wrinkled with mirth. A second head joined him and their breath vaporised into the lamplight behind them. "Tania," I said.

"You know him, T?" said the man.

She shook her head. "Haven't a clue."

My bones were cold and stiff when I attempted to move. I winced at some ancient scar tissue resuscitated by the concrete's chilling effect.

The male head neared then reared. "He stinks. You been at the cooking sherry?"

He had a crop like a skin's but wore a duffle coat and beneath that, a multi-coloured, woollen jumper that a hard-nut wouldn't be caught booting in. With an unlit roll-up between his lips, he leaned in again. "It's a kid," he said, nodding assuredly.

"How do you know me, traveller boy?" She wore a cap, like a big mushroom. Like the ones in *Car Wash*.

"What's that smell?" I asked.

Her bangles jingled. "Patchouli."

The ginger man was talking to someone behind her. "Abdul... there's a kid here, he stinks of drink and he's lying in your dustbin. Modern fairy story man... I told you... fate and fable, it's coming..."

Abdul's head appeared between theirs. He baulked, fanning his nose. "He goes to school with my little brother in Enfield. He was here last week. Him and a few of his Nazi pals scored some acid. This dude had a very bad trip."

Patchouli overwhelmed me as Tania peered in. "My God, him! Gel, I told you, he went berserk! Had an *awesomely* bad trip. Remember his back?"

Gel loomed again. "You having a bad scene, little man?"

"I ain't little."

"No offence," he said, his brow furrowing. Creases appeared and vanished around his eyes as thoughts fluctuated.

When I righted myself, even I could smell it: sweet booze and sick. "I got three quid and I want to buy some LSD."

Abdul looked left and right. "Are you for real?"

"Here's my money."

"Keep it down, man."

Tania linked her boyfriend's arm. "He looks ill, Abdul."

Gel touched my forehead. I pulled away. "He is," he said, with some confidence. "Freezing out and he's running a temperature. Hot, hot, *hot*..."

"Look, are you gonna sell me some?"

"Yeah," said Abdul. "Definitely, but not out here. Not with the pigs hiding in the flower pots."

Again Gel nodded sagaciously. "The blight of surveillance, *Nineteen Eighty-Four*...it's coming, like a storm across the misty mountains," he said.

"Bottlers… fucking give me some… *hippies*… You're scared ain'tcha?"

They turned to each other in bewilderment.

Once again, my DMs rucked up their futon's grey throw. I shivered and hugged my knees.

Gel looked down. "And you can take *them* off."

He tapped his feet and patted his jeans manically as I began to unlace my Martens. Between thumb and forefinger, he picked them up and exited through the beaded curtain. I heard them land with a thud on the corridor's bare boards.

Abdul and Tania looked down from the airplane seats as I yawned. "You been jumped, dude?" Abdul said, smiling sympathetically.

"Nah," I said bristling, attempting to convey that no one would have the temerity to try it on with me. "Here's my money." I lay the crumpled notes on a sequinned cushion.

Gel was leaning against the wall. "Yeah, that's money for sure."

"Gel," said Abdul. "You got anything we could sell this traveller?"

He shook his head and smiled. "Not on me. Tomorrow though, got a lorry load coming in from the Netherlands."

Abdul met his smile. "Mine's coming from Pakistan, air freight, helicopter it into the garden." He rubbed his silvery chin apologetically. "You're out of luck; you'll have to go home."

"No… I can't."

Tania left her seat and knelt before me. She wore a purple poncho over faded blue flares. She looked like a little pyramid with the sun shining on the peak. "Something bad has happened to this boy," she said, peering into my eyes as if she were holding a lamp in the dark.

Gel looked down. "And you came from where, man? Enfield?"

"Yeah, walked…"

"You walked, that's like, ten miles?"

I shrugged and shivered. My eyes fluttered. I shook myself awake. "Drugs… bottlers…"

"Come back tomorrow afternoon."

"Nah, I want them now." I tried to stand. "Going down the station."

Tania put her hand on my shoulder. I fell back weightlessly.

"Please…" She shook her head, momentarily annoyed with herself. "What *is* your name?"

"Harry."

"*Please*, Harry, you can stay here tonight…"

"What?" Abdul glared at her.

"What's ours is yours." She turned to Abdul. "He's strayed from the path."

"I'll put him back on it *and* give him his bus fare."

"He's staying," she said resolutely before turning to me. "Harry, stay here one night and when you wake up, I promise you'll feel different."

I pulled the throw past my shoulders and stared into the whirlpool eyes of the deity in the poster over the hearth. "Go placidly, amid the noise and haste and remember…" As my lids fluttered shut I saw Susan's fingers trip the lock and felt the cold evening rush in. I leaned forward for one last brush of her lips but she had gone.

Tania woke me with a vast bowl of spicy broth.

"Time… please?" I mumbled, sitting up and tearing into the bread.

"Just gone midday."

I'd slept for twelve hours solid. "Blimey."

I ate while she put an album on. *Hot Rats* by Frank Zappa, a bloke in a funny hat and a big 'tache. My spoon scraped china to screeching violins.

"Hungry Harry," she smiled, swaying, anklets rustling.

"Er… sorry," I wiped my mouth. "Thank you."

"What's ours is yours," she said, pausing at the curtains with the plate. Her green eyes stayed on me. "What happened to you?"

"Nuffin."

"Bad scene?"

I shrugged.

"It passes," she said, tilting her head. "But, maybe not."

After she'd exited, I returned to the futon. Sated, foetal and warm, I gazed at the trinkets and vases, all bronze and gold, ruby cushions, sequins and beads. My eyelids fluttered and I experienced the strangest feeling of precipitation. It was as if a massive storm was about to break above me. I caught my breath. Had *he* followed me here? Had he given Tony a lift? Had black and white finally united?

Stupid. Sleep called. Shuffling down and deep I thought, he'll tire, he's got to tire. I faced the wall and searched for oblivion but something was in the way. Far away, thunder-clouds were collecting. Lightning bolts clashed unreasonably. Listening hard, I tuned into a wobbling thud so remote, its origin must be many miles away. Shutting my eyes, I pulled the covers over my ears but the muted, cacophonous blend tugged me from my dreams. The harder I tried to ignore it, the tighter its octopus grip on my senses.

Giving up, I blinked into day.

From my pillow back home, before radiators and ovens ignited, or when dad had an early tee-time and the TV wasn't on, I'd meditate in extended suburban silence. That silence was only interrupted by twittering birds outside my window or Susan's dog barking at their closed back door. Here, there

84

wasn't any quiet; cars and people passed by each second. Nor was there a moment void of sound inside the house; occupants padded across creaking floorboards, a toilet flushed, pipes clanged, records played, TV channels changed. There was always a raised voice, a laugh or a cough at a door.

The cartoon deity's ominously raised finger pointed the way and the words on the poster in the alcove spelled out the future. "*Go placidly, amidst the noise and haste...*" I uttered. But was that noise hasty?

It had to be the dustman, the bins banging and crashing carelessly against the cart or flung at the pavements, the lids slammed back on, hard.

Getting up, I parted the beaded curtain and peered through the bay front window. The bins lids were on. The one I took refuge by last night, brimming with rubbish. I pressed my face to the glass, looked both ways but saw no giant creeping truck.

Standing there, in the room by the road, the racket seemed closer but indecipherable. Turbulence percolated through the building, but it didn't undermine it, it warmed it. In a couple of minutes I became aware of a mathematic hint, a nod at repetition like a train on the tracks. I stepped out of the room and laced up my runaway boots. As I stood, last night's half-head, a full, shaggy-haired wizard of a man, nodded and retreated behind an over-glossed door. I wondered at his ominous move, was he silently warning me of the din overhead?

As his door clicked shut, I took a couple of paces forward and was instantly caught in an acoustic tractor beam. Step by upward step, the jumble and clanging gradually became clearer, purer, easier for the head to dilute, somehow. Was there some kind of factory or machine upstairs? I crept past varied-coloured doors, chipped skirting, torn nets, interesting light shades and peeling anaglypta. There was a motorbike carcass on the first landing and a showroom dummy dressed as a spaceman on the next. But I didn't put my arm around it because the heat emanating from above drew me, inexorably, towards it.

Outside a door at the top of the house everything made sense. Knocking before entering was futile. I opened the door and let the storm break.

Blasted by a wondrous contraption, with the ability to move air, rock house foundations and cause normal people to succumb to their basest urge, I stood gawping at the cold metal and turned wood. The glorious thing seemed to fill every inch of space with its jutting elbows. Its immobile hull squatted like something trained to kill. It was wild and alive, but at the same time, tame and obedient. Its pilot didn't even know I was there.

11

The Drums

He looked up, winked and finished neatly. Together we inhaled the thick primordial echo.

With the reediest roll-up hanging unlit from his lips, Gel said, "Greetings little man," then he nodded and resumed.

I felt like ape-jumping from surface to surface, baring my arse and giggling like a tickled toddler. The cacophonous racket bounced and ricocheted around the room infusing me with twitching delight. I held my breath as indecipherable textures bonded seamlessly, escalating in complexity only to be released by ear-splitting crashes that, in turn, initiated the next new, wondrous passage. But the beauty of it was, the massive gut-wrenching punch line was the precision. The mathematical dovetailing of beat over beat, layer upon layer was, for me, a glimpse at perfection. Order extracted from chaos, noise and mess. My bespoke lifeline. The drums.

I grinned like a gonk. Everything, I mean *everything* was forgotten, relegated to the far reaches of the fields, that crappy school and the black-capped judges in their semi-detached palaces. Gradually, an idea swirled and spread like black ink in milk: if this is how good it feels *listening*, how good must it feel *playing*?

On the evening of the first day I heard the drums, the pear-drops sparkled in a car's headlights and Abdul flicked open the ashtray on his armrest. "Well?" he asked.

Tania and him were sitting side by side on the airplane seats while I hugged my knees on the futon. She was moving her head in circular movements to some very strange wailing and wheezing from the stereo. "*Electric Storm in Hell*," she informed me before addressing her man. "I'm cool, Abdul."

"Gel?" Abdul asked.

"Ditto."

Abdul was concerned; their landlord wasn't keen on people crashing. If someone was sleeping in his house he wanted rent. He could get very heavy with dossers, Abdul said. I focused on a joss stick in an italicised bronze goblet. It was in the middle of the circular table between us. From it, a trail of incense tapered into the ceiling. To release his thoughts, Abdul parted his hair and fixed me with a sober gaze. "We agree, democratically," he said.

"We're a quasi autonomous collective, man…" Gel said from the alcove.

Abdul rubbed his goatee. "*If*," he continued, "by some miracle you get some dough; an inheritance, a job basically, and are able to contribute fiscally to our community... the futon's yours for as long as you want it."

The smoke turned into a hazy blue plateau as Tania gripped his hand and beamed at me.

"You can stay as long as you pay," Gel chipped in. "Way of the world, Harry."

"But you gotta hustle, man." Abdul nodded, and I nodded back in double time. "If the landlord catches you here, you tell him it was just the one night cos your arm fell off... and the hospital was shut…"

"Yeah," I said. "Gel said…"

"Abdul," Gel interjected. "I know a guy. Marios, Greek fella, runs a dress factory. I used to drive a van for him…"

The grown-ups left through the beaded curtain and I smiled at my guiding deity. I'd been there a day but it felt like the whole of half-term. There were no rules or abuse, just this slow, smiley environment, spicy soup and bread. No

Bowie or Roxy, but music of a sort. Couldn't they adopt me? I'd be happy to be head bead-polisher or master sandal-mender.

Tania popped her head through the curtain. "Hey, Harry, come to ours and watch TV."

The great pixilated god squatted in front of a poster of Che. It dominated the room. Shelves of books and records, more eastern trinkets and voodoo masks lined the walls but all eyes, as ever, were on the television. They were engrossed in an old film but I don't remember who was in it because *I* was engrossed in Abdul's *NME*. The articles and reviews were of no interest but the photos of the drummers on their gleaming, stage-lit kits were.

Just before nine o'clock the room began to fill. The shaggy half-head edged in and a couple of quiet, bulky girls from the room above took their place, cross-legged on the floor. Gel arrived last and propped himself against the doorframe with the ubiquitous roll-up teetering on his lip. The news item that had everyone excited was the riots in Soweto. Abdul swore at the screen as they showed the army shooting and whipping the scurrying crowds. Legs astride, he took the telly on, steaming into the politicians and commentators, countering their arguments with passionate ones of his own. I listened like I never had at school. I was brought up to believe the TV news was sacrosanct and had never heard anyone question the government's attitude to South Africa or any-where else. Why would you? Where I was from, you simply believed anyone in a suit with a microphone. To listen to some Camden carpet-seller getting the better of a talking-head on telly was revelatory. I wondered why I hadn't been taught that sort of reasoning. Why school had only been about repeating what was already written down.

The camera tracked the aftermath: armoured cars, dead

bodies, and women wailing over them. When Tania started crying I realised I was angry as well.

The mood lightened after the news. They smoked their rollies, opened bottles of wine and took the piss out of the shitty, light entertainment programmes that so absorbed my father back home. As they sniggered and mocked, I imagined his deep forest timbre. '*Look at that handsome boy*,' he'd announce, gesturing at some mini-suited child-star crooning into a microphone bigger than his head. '*Why isn't my son like that, proud. Look at his hair, cut like so…*' Then he'd put the backs of his hands just beneath his ears to demonstrate neatness and care in hairdressing before sneering at me, because you'd lose both hands and half an arm in my barnet. As with the newsreader, I was brought up to venerate the 'TV star' but around here they castigated the bow-tied 'comic' and derided the fawning audience for the mediocre stooges they were. Grinning, I listened to Gel and Abdul ridicule the tripping, docile dollies and slaughter the presenter making cracks about their tits. They tore into the useless insincerity of it all and I loved it, felt intoxicated by the abuse they doled out. They had squarely hit the head of a nail that had been sticking in my ribs for as long as I'd watched telly.

Abdul refilled his glass. "That guy's slacks, any tighter and you'd see what religion he is. Look into his eyes when he speaks. He genuinely hates these people… and they call it the 'nation's game'! The dude's got a bow tie on, for fuck's sake!"

Tania giggled into her wine as Abdul pulled the wings off some shitty, wheel-spinning, buzzer-ringing quiz show. The contestants were complete mugs, applauding the mouthy star while he ridiculed their whole family. I was reminded of the way the kids in my class would laugh at any crappy pun a teacher would make while I sagged at my desk, poker-faced and fuming.

90

From nowhere, fury raced up my windpipe. I stood and opened my mouth. "I've always hated that tosser; he takes the piss out of everyone, thinks he knows it all, *the cunt, I'd like to kick him up the arse... wanker...*"

Perversely, only the guffawing studio audience seemed to appreciate my analysis. The two girls from upstairs stood and left quietly. The shaggy half-head made his excuses and backed out too. I'd never seen the bloke take a forward step.

"What?" I said.

"A little heavy, brother," said Abdul. "It's only TV."

"Yeah, but everyone watches it... they just take the piss out of normal people... someone should stick up for them."

"Time and a place," said Abdul.

"Sorry."

"You don't have to apologise. They're rubes," Tania laughed, defending me to her boyfriend. "Who cares? I don't. Harry's right."

The sound of her laughter matched the way the curls danced on her shoulders, free and liquid. Abdul wasn't laughing though; he could go sober at the drop of a hippy hat. "Have you called your mother?"

"She's alright."

"You *must* call her, Harry. Tell her when you are going home."

"Really, she's happy for me not to be there at the moment."

With a few coppers Tania had given me I'd phoned my mum from the call box on the corner. She was livid. Well, as livid as she felt she needed to be in the circumstances. My mum only ever did or said enough to keep the peace, or start the war. Secretly, she was pleased I wasn't there with her and her husband. It was one less volatile ingredient to add to her dismal, domestic cake as well as one less unit to provide food, shelter and electricity for. She earned the money that paid for everything, including the new synchromesh gear box for the Rover - boy, could my old man crunch a gearbox. She never kept anything for herself. (There was nothing left after the rent, food, green fees and bookies tab, anyway.) I suppose if, on her wage, you could buy a new identity on another continent, she might have considered it. I think she'd admit, in the quest for a bit of p&q, she would have bought him a yellow speedboat.

Dad was - naturally - homicidal, she said. My clothes, records, books, any trace of my existence, had been incinerated in the garden. The spindly old apple tree had nearly gone up too, such was his conflagration. She said *of course* she longed to see me, but it'd be for the best if I made myself scarce for a few months, or at least until they'd stopped using temporary greens (he hadn't made a putt for a fortnight cos of me). They'd had the police round and the school had threatened *them* with the cost of *my* 'criminal damage'. Ironically, as she reeled off that last day's fateful litany, my money ran out.

On the way back to the house, boots undone, Susan's pilot's jacket hugging me, I reflected on the phone call. With me out of the way, my mother could concentrate solely on him. I was now somebody else's concern and we both knew that practically anyone else's concern would be healthier for my long-term prospects than his. So, in the pauses, secret signs and asides between the imprisoned and the free, I realised that I had conveyed my sympathy; she, her congratulations.

Although I'd confirmed that I'd called to my mum, Abdul remained in witch-finder mode. "Seriously, what the hell happened to you, Harry?"

"Nothing. Bit of bother at school."

They were all studying me as I tapped my right and left foot. "Thanks for the bath," I said.

"Cleanliness is next to godliness, so they say." Abdul stood up. "And you stank like a demon."

Laying on the futon, hands at my sides, the bead-light dotting the gryphon so it appeared that it too was nodding in concentration, I whispered, "Ready?" to my errant limbs. *One:* right foot on bass drum pedal and right hand on hi-hat - *and:* right hand on hi-hat only - *two:* snare drum with left hand and right hand on hi-hat - *and:* right hand on hi-hat only. *One and two and one and two...*

It was the simplest beat Gel could show me. I managed it a few times before falling off, the way you do when you learn to ride a bike. He said I was a natural. I disagreed. I felt like a berk as I flailed around, a drunk with an inner ear problem. Gel said, if you can dance, you can play. I told him I couldn't dance and he called me a pillock.

He was a good bloke, Gel. He took his time showing me how to hold the sticks, 'match' or 'orthodox', where and how to strike the skins, let 'em ring or kill 'em dead, rim shots and side sticks, twos, threes, fours... there was much to learn, decades of it. He'd let me batter his drums all afternoon while he sat, nodding, grinning, with a perpetual roll-up on.

I shut my eyes and tapped harder, faster. I became fractionally more accurate. "*One,* right foot - *and* right hand..."

12

First Rehearsals

There is electronic mooing in the fields downstairs. Bleach eddies beneath my door. I bury my head in the pillow.

Thudding, mooing, thudding up the stairs, the clack of the plastic hammerhead. Up a tone as it whines at a stubborn tread. An urgent, stabbing semi-tone on that until a phlegmy suck calms it. Mooing closer. A yelp of exasperation smothered by a rumble. Bang! The front-room door flung wide. Poor old hinges wrenched another millimetre. Slam! Sorry old, shocked, architrave cringing in its housing. *Grandstand* directs and my mother whispers madly, "*Fucking bastard man. I work all week and he does fuck all. He sleeps, golfs and fucks tarts and spends my wages. I cook and clean, cook and clean, bastard, bastard man.*"

I blink awake. It must be Saturday. My breath is a cloud.

Mooing moans and dies. Thudding footfalls. Wrestling Kent Walton chuckles cos it's funny. Wrestling, mum and dad strangle a hoover's boa neck.

Mum howls. Dad growls. "Fucking bitch, *my* money, the government gives, money… *my* back, the doctor says, keeps you in shoes, bitch. *My* life ruined by bastards, these…"

I pull the covers right up. Stomach gurgles. Layers of Mothers Pride, butter slathered on, sugar-sprinkled, tempt me downstairs. Lick the surface after. No crumbs, no evidence.

He says, "I fucking do it."

She says, "No, no, I will …"

The prize moos on. Then off. Then on. So precious, that Jules Rimet Electrolux. The royal purple trim hems the grey slotted mouth, unaccustomed to public speaking as it is.

"Every day do it, *I!*" says he.

Mum and dad balance on the landing and compete for a dust-free conscience. "A lie!" she accuses.

"Me you liar call?" he defends.

Under deep cover I chew my tongue.

"Why am I doing it now?" mum pleads to the judge on the landing. "The mud, the mud, fucking football mud - can't even do that *one. Bloodeee. Job. In five. Blood. E. Days...*"

"I will end it!" he roars.

As the covers are clawed back my tongue loosens. "No, no, no Dad, *don't...*"

My eyes open on a girl with green eyes and a man with red hair.

"Little man having a nightmare?" Gel looks down, comically sad. Tania attempts an embrace. I squirm away. "Sorry, sorry…"

She displays two, downward pacifying hands and exhales through her nose. "It's okay, be calm, calm."

Past her head I read 'Go placidly amidst…'

Gel brightens. "Saturday, little brother. Big day for you."

I gulp and remember. "What's the time?"

"Elevenish."

Along with Gel, Abdul, Tania and the girlfriends and wives of the band, I unloaded the equipment into a school hall a short drive from the house. I set the kit up in minutes. I'd become expert at it. The quicker I resurrected it in the room on the top of the house, the longer I could stay on.

While the musicians plugged in and tuned up, my boots squeaked and squelched on the freshly waxed parquet path that led from the hall to the classrooms.

Last term's projects and staff notices were still pinned on the corridor walls. I felt melancholy walking along. Devoid of children, the place felt eerie and mysterious; the rows of vacant coat hooks, saddening.

As if I'd caught my jumper on a classroom door handle, my school days inevitably tugged me back. Driver's wide, baleful face, two sizes too large, appeared to levitate at the end of the dim passageway. He was monitoring the busy dwarves that queued at the tuck shop I never had any money for. Through the reinforced mesh of a classroom door, I saw myself slouched at the back, flicking elastic bands. At an unheard command, I stood and walked slowly, yawning, tipping books off desks while the sniggering chorus played around me. The smell of lemon-scented shampoo drew me to a blonde head shimmering in the sunlight that poured through the window. On a desk were pens, books and rulers arranged in precise, geometrical fashion. I felt short, neat strands of hair between my fingers and was overwhelmed by the velvet vapours of cream soda.

I recalled an excerpt from that final afternoon. She insisted I dance the funky chicken on her carpet. She'd seen me do it for the lads. I detested that song. It had become my cringeworthy default when I'd shown myself up with Tone and the boys. It gave them a laugh and got me off the slaps and nibs and jacksy boots so I did it at least three times a day. The way she laughed as I bucked and slid across her room made me love it again. "Susan," I whispered.

"Pardon?"

I'd slid into Tania.

"Were you dancing, Harry?" She said out of one teasing eye.

I looked down and smiled. "A bit."

We were shoulder to shoulder while the guitars echoed along the corridor. "It's the smell," she said.

"What?"

"The polish. Coming back after holidays? I loved school, my friends, writing a diary about the summer. Did you like school?"

96

"Yeah… it was a laugh."

"I miss my friends so much. Is that why you're sad, do you miss yours?"

"Yeah, my mates…you met them. We did everything together."

"Do you still see them?"

"Nah, Tania. We move on, don't we?"

"But don't you wish we could just stop the world turning and stay at that point? Be at school forever."

I sat apart from the camp-followers. They watched from benches directly in front of the stage while I hung on the bars at the side. This wasn't Gel's bread and butter, the covers band he played for around London, this was something else he did. We were gathered to hear their new set; they'd been working on it for ages, Gel said.

It started with a poem, like a speech, ushering the listener into a tyme gone bye when Englande was merry and maidens were comely…

"Well, little man?" asked Gel, towelling himself dry after they'd finished to cheers from the twenty or so there. "What do you think?"

For around an hour the sounds had racketed around the bars and ropes, rebounding off the breeze-blocks to eventually die in the heavy red curtain behind the stage. It wasn't a question of liking what they played; it was simply the thrill of being so close to the instruments. Especially the drums. They sounded like guns in battle.

"Really good, Gel."

"Think John's pleased…" he said, glancing across at the singer/guitarist.

"Yeah," I replied.

But I wasn't convinced, because during the marathon set,

John kept stopping and reminding them all to, 'keep it down' and 'not speed up' and 'for pity's sake, get it *right* just once!'

Gel gave me a wink and walked over to the bass player. They stopped chatting when John joined them.

John, a bit like Driver, had a kind of aura about him. People shut it when he spoke. But there were differences. Unlike my old maths teacher, John had flowing, blonde locks (that, disconcertingly, reminded me a little of Tania's), he had a chest that went sort of inward, while Driver's stuck out like the prow of a ship. Their chins differed starkly too. Driver had one.

John did have some equipment though. Tons of it compared to everyone else: a huge amplifier, a couple of acoustic guitars and three electrics arrayed on stands. During the songs, he'd take one off and put another on to nods of admiration from watchers and band alike.

What lyrics I remember were to do with drinking cyder in the sun and being proud peasants. There was one that went on for ages about knights and damsels and I was annoyed with myself for wishing they'd hurry up and get to the end. They *were* accomplished players. I could appreciate the technique and care in what they did as much as I could a footballer that could trap a ball, square, and find his man. They started at the same time, stopped at the same time and they all wore the same smug grins when, I imagine, they played some diligently rehearsed pause, push or breakdown. During the extended solos, unfathomable stops and starts, tempo changes and olde worlde message, I felt a variety of emotions but the overriding one was envy. I didn't covet their ability, their pro gear and the ease with which they played, what got to me more than anything was the team work. I was envious of the unit, the *band*.

Recalling school days; the rope in my hands, skipping over benches and the view from the top of the bars, I heard

Gel call my name. "John, Si," he said, "We're nearly done. Look, let the little man have a go. He's got talent but he's not jammed before."

My heart thudded. It was as if my Dad and Tony had arrived at the back of the hall for country dancing. "Nah, it's alright…"

John shrugged and his curls danced just like Tania's as he unplugged his guitar. "It is late."

"*Man?*" Gel smiled his good, red smile.

Reluctantly, John nominated a guitar from the display. "Of course, it's a wonderful thing," he muttered, tepidly, "…to hear new talent."

Like tugging bedclothes in for protection, I pulled as much of the kit towards me as I could, while the other blokes plugged in and re-tuned. I went round the drums. I was so nervous, it was a miracle I hit any of them.

"Okay," said John, with a smile which was the spit of the weary teacher tolerating the slow kid in class, "a little 'twelve bar blues' for Gel's homeless acolyte."

"I'm not home…"

He counted in four and I was off, sprinting to get to the end before the rest. I won by miles.

John shook his head. His hands were held up in surrender. "You have to keep time, *man*. You were playing another song!"

"Yeah, sorry. Can we do it again?"

"I'm all out." He was sulking. He wanted to go to the pub. I could see his crystal-fondling girlfriend wincing in my direction.

"Come on, mate," I pleaded.

He forced another smile. "Okay. *One, two, a one, two, three, four.*"

And once again, we're off.

I could feel the groove and knew where I should sit but

there was something inside me that made me want to spoil it, change it and take it somewhere else. Their sound, what *they* played, was like a freshly rendered wall that needed a big old knob and bollocks drawn on it and I was happy to oblige. It was an odd response after the endless daydreams of playing with other musicians but, all I could think, was, *'faster, louder, harder'* and I couldn't deny it. It was like wrecking the fields or answering back. It was a dash for identity, I think. Sensing the bass player synching with me, I accelerated through the gears to *my* top speed. For a few bars we were flying. I felt ecstatic as we soared away then, with a twang, John stopped and when he did, so did everyone else. Not me though. I proudly hammered another thirty seconds on my own.

"Can we just, *just... stoooppp!*" He was flapping his arms, stammering over the fading cymbals. "It just *isn't* happening!"

Sucking in air, I looked up. They were all shaking their hairy heads, embarrassed at the slow kid. But I didn't see them. I was blinded by the residue of that minute when I led. Drummer's adrenalin coursed through me, making me bristle and spark, but - more than anything - making me want to do it again and again. I met John's eye. "Come on, mate?"

But he blanked my entreaty and gazed, Hamlet-style, at the audience for sympathy. Suddenly Gel was beside me, unscrewing the hi-hat clutch. His look said, 'button it and break it down'.

Negative vibes were emitted while I helped load the gear into the van. John was head honcho, some kind of musical genius and as far as they were concerned, I'd pissed in his couscous.

Shoulder to shoulder, Abdul and I hefted his unfeasibly heavy amplifier into the back of the transit. "Weighs a ton, dunnit?" I said, but Abdul wouldn't reply.

100

From the school gates I watched the van motor away. Those who couldn't get in that, travelled with John in his Merc. I was the last person out and there wasn't a place for me. Tania met my eye from the rear window. She wore a sad, clownish frown while everyone else laughed.

Hunching my shoulders against humiliation's icy chill, I followed through the cloud of diesel.

In the beer garden, the talk was of the band and John and how far they'd undoubtedly go. Through the laughter, reminiscences of wild times at uni and sojourns in Marrakech and the Camargue were overheard. I wasn't included in any of the pally, intimate circles so I sat at a table on my own, feet going, hands at it. Beat, beats, beats.

Gel bought me a pint but he didn't hang around. He was preoccupied by a girl in a duffle coat, pale blue to his navy. I could see him across the garden, tapping something out on the table, his rollie hanging on his lip while she nodded in time.

I Shot The Sheriff came on and I attempted to jam along with my fingers. I'd do that with everything I heard, now. After my first go on his kit, Gel had told me that I'd never listen to music the same way again. He was right. The minute I heard a song with drums on, I'd pick the beat apart and attempt to master it (if only in my head). In a few days, I'd doubled my musical pleasure and been set on a path of endless discovery. Screwing up my eyes, I tuned into the track. How did that bloke play those fills? He was doing it backwards, hitting things in the wrong places and then I remembered Gel saying that right and wrong didn't exist on the drums. There wasn't a formula, you did what *you* thought was right. *You* had to take responsibility, there's no-one that'll do it for you. But, even as I peered into the sound, concentrating forensically on what this drummer was playing, my attention faltered because of what had just happened. "Always at sodding school," I muttered. "What a show-up."

Doubt crept over the rim of my glass. Even though I'd only had half a dozen goes on Gel's kit (and it was the first time I'd ever played with anyone), I'd been dented by John's words and actions. With all that gear and the deference paid to him, he *obviously* knew what was what. Would I ever be good enough to play with anyone? I loved the drums more than anything. The thought of not playing with a bass player, a guitarist or singer, making actual music, was unimaginable. *Always* at sodding school.

The beer was strong. I couldn't knock it back like the stuff I used to drink over the fields with Bob and the others. It was spicy too, but not like curry, like… mince pies. Swallowing thick, dark mouthfuls, I felt as if I had a point to make but I didn't know what it was or to whom to make it. Nursing my chunky glass, feeling the smooth, cold bumps and hollows, I gradually realised how pissed off I was with that 'John'. He'd stopped me playing and made everyone hate me and worse, had me doubting myself. He'd done the same 'kill it before it grows' number on me that my dad or Tony would.

He was talking to the bass player and a couple of other blokes. They were sucking up to him as if he was Driver on sports day.

"Hey little man, you look like thunder." Gel was at my side.

"Blimey..."

"Here, drink up."

"Ta, Gel."

He handed me another foaming pint. "Listen, I gotta see a man about - "

"Who is he?"

"Who?"

"John."

"Just one of the guys."

"Why does everyone crawl to him?"

He laughed. "They don't, do they?"

"Yeah, look…"

Across the garden, John was addressing his fan club. Smiling and nodding magnanimously, his curls bounced in slow motion on his lincoln green lapels.

"Just naturally popular, I suppose," he said, practically levitating with excitement. The girl in pale blue fluttered her fingers at him. "*Man,*" he said. "I really gotta split…"

As he walked away, I swigged my beer and reflected on that five minutes on the drums. The way *my* sound had rebounded around a school hall of all places! It felt as if I was running fast, but not on my own… with a ball… down the wing, leaving them face down in the mud, weaving in and out, blades of grass flashing past my boots. "Gonna score," I slurred and then I looked at my glass, cold, smooth, but empty. I stood and the alcohol rocketed through me. I held the table, shut my eyes and breathed in hard.

Gradually, my focus fell on a popular, green silhouette a few yards away. It had siphoned off a couple of women in sort of Indian shirts and long flowery skirts. For a moment, I watched them fawn and pout and then, like everyone else, I too was drawn towards the greenness.

"Alright, John?"

He reared theatrically. It was getting dark and I thought, maybe he doesn't recognise me. "It's me, Harry, just done the drums… over school."

Behind their glasses, the girls grinned mischievously.

"Yes, young Harold, Gel's acolyte. Er… hi?"

"It's Harry and - "

But he had turned away to revisit his conversation. "And that's the problem with sanctions," he said, wistfully shaking his head. The curls bounced lightly. The women listened obediently. "We could all do *something*... but this government, and they call themselves *socialists*... the shame. Soweto is a watershed moment in our history as well as theirs..."

"Yeah, I saw that, what cunts..."

The women weren't smiling now. They weren't nodding either.

"Is that word necessary?" he said.

"What word?"

"The 'c' word."

"What, *Soweto*? Dats'n 's', innit?"

He pursed, puckered, then shook his bouncing curls. He was addled, posh addled.

"Yeah, mate," I said. "I fucking saw it, those fat coppers whacking 'em with their whips n' dat - "

"Shamboks."

"Wha?"

"The whips..."

"Yeah, cunts, makes you wanna go over there. Know what I mean? Fuckin' fight back."

The pucker softened, mutating into an apologetic, thin-lipped smirk. "Listen up, my fuzzy little friend, they'd eat you for breakfast." Then, he looked at the sky, crestfallen. He was tragic but instructional. "You've no idea of the iniquities, the injustice, the brutality! Have you ever been whipped, beaten?" He turned to the simpering hippy chicks. "There's the 'c' word and there's the 'n' word, negro and other - "

"What? Nig-nog? What about gollywog? Is that as bad?"

Together they inhaled the thick, dusky air with their mouths open.

As the rush of trouble thrilled me, I wished more than anything I was playing the drums. I could cause as much mayhem as I liked behind a kit. Nobody'd mind. But I wasn't, so I carried on. "They used to call me that at school, *nigger, paki* as well… it was close, never totted it up though…"

John's regret dripped theatrically. "Gel's acolyte - "

"*That's* not what you said. *You* said - "

"That is not a pejorative term, *acolyte*…"

They women laughed nervously as I butted in. "I know that, what I wanted to say *is*… that you make me sound like a dosser. I ain't. I'm paying to stay at Abdul's. I got a job in this dress factory… I ain't homeless…"

I wasn't being entirely truthful about being at work. I was going to the factory in Hackney in the morning, but I *had* been paying Abdul to sleep beyond the beaded curtain. I'd met my mum in a pub car park in Palmers Green a couple of weeks ago. It was strange to see her as others do. She presented her public face, a face I rarely saw. Anyone watching would have described a focussed woman, handbag clutched defensively, lap of skirt creased from sitting at a desk. They'd think she was waiting for a colleague and a working lunch.

I moved out of the shadows. The second she saw me, the scaffolding came up hard and fast. Her smile remained that of the office variety, but the eyes did not rest on me. Perhaps she was embarrassed out here? I knew the truth. I knew where she got dressed and drank her coffee, I knew of the eyes that balefully examined her as she rinsed her cup.

She asked about me how I was getting on. I said I was warm and dry of a night and usefully occupied of a day. My reply induced a flicker of attention. I could tell she wanted to ask what I was doing, but she bottled it. What inmate wants to be tormented by the interesting life of a released ex-con? Telling her about the drums would be cruel. It would shine a light on her limitations and conditions.

When I asked why she wanted to see me, she took a book from her handbag. "I thought you'd like to read this," she said.

What was it? The 'how to survive in London when you're fifteen, potless and clueless' manual? I read the title.

The author was French, his name unpronounceable.

She nodded at my furry collared jacket. "It's about a pilot, Argentinian, in the war."

I touched the collar. "It's Susan's," I said, opening up a vast plain of conversation. But, with a blithe inhalation, the topic narrowed and tapered to nothing. We returned to nods and winks. "Anyway," she said, looking into the traffic, "I just wanted to check that you were ok."

"Yeah," I said, examining my boots.

"I've got to go to work."

I watched her click away, the big old bouffant like a black, bothersome swarm above her head.

For a moment, I considered running after her. Maybe they'd give her a room? There was a vacancy behind the spaceman on the first floor.

That night, I placed Gel's nicotine-thumbed book about chariots and churches as alien space ships on the bare boards, and opened hers. I liked the books my mum liked. Laying back, I realised that I'd never told her that. I promised myself, now I was free, that one day I would. I turned first one page and then the next and four fivers fell onto my chest.

"What's your rent?" John's curious tone brought me back to the beer garden.

"Fiver. Get fifteen a week at this factory *workin'*, yeah? Tania thinks it's too much but I'm alright with a five. Only fing is, you're not supposed to tell the landlord. He's a bit of a tight-arse."

They didn't inhale at that. They froze.

"But," I carried on, pleased to have a toe-hold in things at last, "we have some good nights there, real laugh - "

Thawing quickly, John smiled at the women in turn. "Ah, yes, what nights, cultural, intellectual… *probably.* Sadly, not rhythmic, but we can't be gifted in all things can we, *young Harold.*"

The women were smirking and he was loving it.

"You ain't a teacher are ya?"

"We are all teachers, Harold."

"My name is Harry."

"*Harry.*"

Even my name seemed to amuse him, and I noticed when he was amused, like when he was pissed off, everyone around him was too. He was Tony in flares, Driver with curls.

I looked up and away from their sandalled feet at the setting sun behind the flats a mile away in Tottenham. "Anyway," I said. "I thought you were."

"Were what?"

"A teacher."

"How so?"

But I left them to it because the past, like the night, was inexorably creeping in. It was time to buy Gel a beer.

Like the smallest bloke in the scrum, I searched for him in the press of bell-bottoms and bum-freezers but never found him. Immune to the sideways sneers and frosty shoulders, I returned to the beer garden (with my lager in a straight glass). I surprised myself. I could remember every strike I'd played back at the school. Tottering around the grassy little plot, I sipped my pint and dreamed of another go on the drums. I was going through each virgin bar with relish when, through a blur of purple and orange fabric, I spotted a furious, green blob. John was jabbing his finger at Abdul and Tania. Hers and his locks were remarkably similar but her cheeks were pink and smooth while his were crimson and bursting. When he'd stopped ranting they all turned and looked at me.

I raised a friendly palm as Abdul strode towards me.

"Alright, Ab - "

"Did you insult John?" He interrupted angrily.

"Nah Abdul, he said I was homeless. Just told 'im - "

"You *can't* insult my friends."

"Ain't I your friend?"

"Don't be competitive, *dude.* You'd have been on the street if it wasn't for me."

"I give you a fiver!"

"We fed you and took you in, but - "

All of a sudden, Tania was at his side. "Abdul, it was our gift to give."

"Stay out of it, woman," he said, turning on me. "This is reality, *Harry.*"

"I know," I said.

"No wonder you are where you are."

"That's a terrible thing to say, Abdul," she said.

"What do you mean?" I asked.

"You know what I mean; you're one step from the gutter."

Tania put her hand to her mouth, "My god..."

And it was strange because I agreed with Abdul. I didn't want Tania to hear any of this either. "I'm gettin' a job."

"Moronic work. What about your prospects?"

"You said I shouldn't compete...you told me not to let the, erm, straights make me - "

"Get real, you have to eat."

"I am..."

"He's trying..." she pleaded.

He rounded on her. "You and your waifs and strays. I should never have listened to you. He was bound to cause trouble. He's a Jonah. One look at the scars all over him..."

"Sorry Abdul, I'll move out. I never wanted any - "

"*Shut up!*"

People were looking at us. Tania had put her hands to her mouth. She looked on the brink of tears. If I could have co-ordinated it, I'd have tried a few moves from the old funky chicken to cheer her up but I'd only have slid into the wall.

Abdul glared at me. "What are you going to do for the rest of your life, *maan?*"

"Dunno…" I felt very drunk and angry, but more than that, sad for Tania. I looked at her and tried to elicit a smile. "Be in a band… like the Spiders… in America… have loads of drums and let everyone stay at my place and never charge them a fucking penny…"

Her frown vanished. She threw her head back and laughed. With the sun setting behind her, she was like a golden bird defying the end of the day. I beamed, pleased that I was responsible for such a brilliant sight.

Abdul's curtains whipped his face in confusion. "Get real, Harry..."

But the fight had gone out of me as I gazed into Tania's laughing eyes. "Sorry Abdul, beer's strong…"

"You can be in what you like but you don't insult another man's friends."

"Sorry," I repeated. "Really am."

"Don't say sorry to me, go over there and apologise to John."

"Alright."

As I made my way across the lawn, they all stopped talking about Cambridge and the Bello and I thought, this might not be outside Beaky's office, or the alley with the boys shaking their shaven heads, but it's the old shaming ceremony - I'd know it anywhere.

"John?"

"Yes?" he said sulkily, tossing his locks. He was defiant, hurt but stoical as he awaited my grovelling apology.

Looking at his suede boots and sprayed on jeans, his embossed green jacket and finally, his bloodless, rectal pout, I thought, 'How old is he? Thirty? Older? And he's got all these mates and birds and amps and guitars and what have I got?'

The garden was spinning. My brain was fast but my mouth was slow. I was thinking about the last few weeks and wondering how the hell I'd ended up outside the shut classroom door *again.* I tasted honeysuckle, beer, fags and patchouli. Everyone was waiting to see what would happen when my skin came off.

To my astonishment, I shuffled, slid, and said, "…Buy us a drink you tight cunt."

The air left the grassy square in a mortified vacuum. I couldn't believe I'd said it but I knew I had. It was way out of proportion, but at that moment John embodied everyone I'd been saying sorry to all my life.

"Alright, don't then…"

I left the beer garden and staggered across the traffic lights on very disobedient legs.

It was as I swerved to avoid a lamppost that appeared determined to impede my progress that I heard my name called. Turning slowly and with no little care, I saw Tania skipping towards me in her Afghan coat. I flopped onto a garden wall. I sensed her standing over me. "I'm *so* sorry," she said.

Nets twitched. A finger tapped the windowpane. Her hand brushed the top of my hair. "Shall we have a cup of tea?" she said.

I looked up. "Where?"

Batting her black lashes with surprise, she said, "Home, of course."

"What about?" I nodded towards the pub.

Her smile vanished for a moment. "They'll be hours mopping John's brow."

I stood slowly. "Really sorry about that, Tania."

As we walked through the empty back streets, she giggled and gently barged me. "Did you enjoy the rehearsal, I mean the music?"

"Yeah, really good."

She walked backwards in front of me, mischievously searching my face.

"It was great hearing Gel play... specially," I said, as guilelessly as I could manage.

We stopped at the house with the cracked ungeometric tiles. She had her key out. "Come on."

I followed her jingling steps through the front door.

"I'll put the kettle on?" I said, walking towards the kitchen but she took my hand and instead of a trellis arch, I passed, for the last time, through the beaded curtains.

"I loved your drumming," she said sitting on *my* futon and patting the place next to her.

I gulped. "Tania - "

"LSD didn't agree with you, did it?"

I smiled with embarrassment. "Nah... not all that at drinking, either."

Her eyes were the colour of grass after it has rained and her curls that golden matter jettisoned from the sun. She removed her coat and then, to my amazement, her shirt followed. "I don't like injustice Harry," she said, offering her back and pointing to her bra strap. "Undo this. Thanks. Sometimes I march, sometimes I boycott. I believe in acting directly, righting wrongs any way I can..."

"That's okay," I was panting, drifting and humming to the highest of frequencies. "You don't have to - "

She turned around and trained those emeralds on me. "But I *want* to."

I fell into her, cluelessly.

Her lashes batted like the blackest batwings. Bangles jingled, pear drops danced and, once again, I was flying down the wing, leaving defenders spread-eagled and muddied in my wake.

As we dressed, she told me John owned this house and a good few others in the area. His was stinking rich and everyone sucked up to him because it helped keep the rents down.

111

All the musicians, including Gel, were tenants and, for the money it saved, they didn't mind playing his crappy songs once a month.

She put her coat on as I tied my laces. "You really dropped Abdul in it, telling him you were paying a fiver for the bed," she said.

"So, it's cos you felt sorry for me?"

"A bit, but I really fancied you when you played the drums."

"*Really?*"

"Really. There's a look on your face, sort of ferocious…"

I laughed and picked up my jacket.

We stood a respectful distance apart at the bus stop. "Gel thinks you've got the talent; you won't give up will you?"

"Never, Tania."

This was goodbye. Our eyes met in mutual dishonesty. "You're welcome to come over," she said. "But... leave it a while, and discretion at all times..."

"Course."

She hugged her coat to her side. "It's got chilly. Bye, petal."

"See ya," I said, and as she rounded the corner at the end of the road, her hair shimmered magically beneath the streetlight. Then she was gone.

13

The Dress Factory

The shirt I'd fled in was so grimy, it looked as if had been designed with dark grey cuffs and collars. The soles of my boots were now as thin as the knees in my tubular school trousers. Susan's pristine pilot's jacket hid the rag and bone man's wardrobe and afforded a dapper disguise.

That morning, the desk I stood before seemed to have everything a person could want on it: food, cash, pens, matches, fags, paper, scissors, cups (with tea in them). I swayed with fatigue. I hadn't a clue how to proceed with the rest of my life.

After leaving Tania on the corner, I'd climbed back into that school and managed a night by the boiler. Although de-activated for half term, it still had lagging and bits of old blanket to kip down in. When morning came, I'd washed my face in the playground drinking-fountain and set my sights on Hackney and my first ever job interview.

Through the glass beyond the desk, a dozen black-clad seamstresses toiled, their chatter interrupted by sporadic bursts from the sewing machines in front of them.

"Banayamou!" Marios said incredulously into the phone. His chair squealed horribly beneath him when he swivelled on it. He had just returned from a trip back home. I'd watched him field queries regarding orders, deliveries, stock and designs for fifteen minutes, and not once did he come close to losing it. He was tanned, lean, and blessed with an un-flappable Cypriot disposition.

He finally replaced the phone, rubbed his face awake and peered at me. For a moment he seemed baffled by my presence, but only pleasantly so. "Sorry my friend, you go away for five minutes and the business crumbles."

Sipping from a china mug, he leaned back in that creaking chair and toed the door shut. The sound of bazukis and furious needles faded instantly. "So, you're Gel's friend?" he said, appraising me much as he would a jacket held up to the light. I watched him scan for poor stitching and uneven sleeves. "He's a nice boy, Gel... but fidgety."

I nodded.

"He said, you were a good boy?"

"Er..." I was rescued by the ringing phone.

"Marios... endaxi..."

As he spoke, I studied the shop floor. In the centre of the room, a scowling, hirsute man in a vest snaked around a thick pile of fabric with comically huge scissors. I watched his shears carve a sweeping bend in the multi-coloured swatch, it looked like he was cutting through a planet's crust. He paused, spoke to a seamstress, then gesticulated angrily across the room. I followed his gaze to the presser who, through bursts of grey steam, ironed a shirt in half a minute. The presser didn't stop singing, smiling and adding a Hellenic shuffle into the bargain.

The women laughed. The cutter scowled. The presser danced.

"Hey, boy?"

I shook my head. "Sorry, I - "

"You a hard worker like Gel, I said."

"Yeah, yeah."

"But not fidgety?"

"Nah..."

He rocked forwards and stood. "Come on then, I'll show you what's what."

He opened the door and mechanical mayhem engulfed us.

"You see this?" he said, raising his voice just enough and kicking at the scraps of material at his feet. "Cabbage. You

114

sweep it up and bag it up. You do the buttons up for Demos, you put the cellophane on the garments, you put the garments on the rails, you wheel the garments to the van, you put the rails in the van… you sweep up, you do the buttons up, you…"

I nodded.

"You get it?"

"Yeah."

"You not very talkative."

"I, I can talk. Just got nothing to say."

He patted my shoulder, smiled and I went to work.

Marios found me a room at Mrs Hajinickolas', she was his wife's, aunt's, sister's cousin...? Related, anyway. Her sewing machine was in the kitchen and, like the women in the factory, she was also black-clad. I shared the upstairs toilet and bathroom with Louis, Helen, and their three-year-old daughter. They had the big room the other side of the stairs while I had the box room. Louis drove the delivery van for Marios and I'm pretty sure he was related as well. When their little girl awoke she howled the house down so after nine everyone had to walk on eggshells, which was no problem for me, I was a master of the art of late-night landing padding. My old man would go mental if he heard me after sunset.

My room was as small as the one I had back home. The lino had cracked over the bumpy floorboards and the low, bowed ceiling was cobweb-encrusted. One wall was papered in a fading children's design, the other two were bare, pockmarked plaster. It looked like a machine gun had gone off in there. The late Mr Haji or someone had given up re-decorating long ago, because behind the door I found a vat of ancient paste and, embedded in it, a brush as stiff as the cutter's 'tache. The sash window that looked onto the overgrown garden was fractured and hairy with grime. And the door didn't shut (you had to lift it to move it). Against one wall was a hilariously tilting cupboard that only the most trusting of lodgers would put anything in. The mattress had a faint, flowery aroma and that was it.

In my dreams I'd imagined posters: Ferry, Bolan and maybe some kind of statue, figurine? Something out of an advert; a plush leather chair by a working fireplace. A flash stereo *definitely*. Shelves of albums and a classic suede-head's wardrobe like Pat's; two-tone suits stretching into infinity, brogues and tasselled loafers like pretty maids all in a row.

But I wasn't disappointed with my little bolt-hole in Wood Green. In a week, I'd stripped the walls and filled holes and cracks. I bought a tin of whitewash and coated the room. Twice. On Saturday, after a bit of advice from Marios (he'd come by to pick up Mrs Haji's homework), I'd bought putty and glass and replaced the windowpane. The day after, I reset the door (well, put longer screws in the hinges) and scrubbed everything with eye-watering dis-infectant. Standing on the threshold with *Songs of Praise* wafting joyously from the front room below, I felt a novel emotion: pride.

In the doorway, Mrs Haji adopted that hunched, too-much-sewing posture all the women at the factory had. "Thank you, Harry," she said.

I nodded as she peered wistfully into the tiny space. "I wanted to do, my husband, he died... no time, no time..."

"Nah, easy," I said. "Anything else you want done, ask." I sent the screwdriver spinning, let it slap into my palm and tapped a little dotted thing on my thigh.

I never let a plate or cup stay in there after I'd finished with it. There was not a scrap, a speck of lint on that lino either. I surprised myself by how much satisfaction I derived from simply tidying it, making the bed and laying back, hands behind head, feeling the past's scabby lump slowly fade.

Pulling on the sewing-machine wheel, Marios worked the foot pedal and lined up the shirt. I watched the needle slowly nod over its target. "Right, you see, it's marked there, Harry?"

He indicated the edge of the shirtfront and the little chalk scar. "You put it in the machine, line up the mark, then you put the button in there and…" The needle blurred, dotting the button twenty times in a second. He showed me the shirt with the button sewed on. "Got it?"

"Yeah," I said. I had to get it. This was the only move I could make. A combination of shifts on the sewing-machine and my cabbage duties would inch me nearer a deposit for some drums.

"Show you again."

He positioned the shirt under the machine and placed the button in the slot. "Don't press the pedal until you've pulled your finger out. Understand?"

"OK," I said, scanning the room for a moment.

I don't know exactly what Marios had told them, but whenever I looked up from my place, there was a moist-eyed seamstress tilting her kindly head in my direction. Sometimes, when I came back after the break, I'd find a rich, gooey pastry or a plate of stuffed, savoury vine leaves on my desk. One morning, I found a carrier bag with brand new pants, socks and T-shirts in it. When I looked up they were all looking away.

As my colleagues' never unpopular 'Bazuki Hits' was squeezed through the room's tinny speakers, Mrs Constanou winked at me and flicked the switch to *Radio One*. I nodded my thanks even as the cutter shook his 'tache in disdain. It

117

wouldn't be long before tunes from the old country went back on.

As Free's *All Right Now* battled its way through the chattering machines, I pinched a tiny mother of pearl button between my fingers and nodded happily. Great tune *and* I'd learned the beat!

Right. Button in the slot - shirt lined up on the plate - press the pedal - move it. Repeat. I traced the bass drum work as I placed the shirt's chalk-mark beneath the needle and, just as Simon Kirke's juicy bar kicked in, my left hand tapped where the snare drum should go and my foot came down on the pedal in perfect time. Well, I say perfect, but what I mean is, the perfect time in the song, the right place in the bar, but at the wrong time on the sewing-machine pedal. With utter shock, I felt the needle's myriad pricks in my finger nail; I can feel them now, a sort of merciless, reasonless dotting because, once you put your foot down on a sewing-machine pedal, things are out of your hands.

A deep and terrible ache began to grow in the centre of my bicep and work its icy path into my shoulder. I gazed in fascination at the criss-cross cotton mound on my finger pad and the button's glinting rainbow colours in the centre of my nail. "Er…George?" I said to the presser as I held up my hand.

He stopped halfway through a sleeve. "*Banayamou!*" he exclaimed.

In seconds I was engulfed by fussing women.

They led me to the kitchen sink and ran my finger under the cold tap. I could hear them muttering fretfully and fanning themselves while I unpicked another length of pink cotton and pulled it through my finger with tweezers. Paradoxically I felt calm, detached. After a few minutes the button fell into the sink and I turned, smiled, and let them dry and bandage my perforated digit.

I was within touching distance of my table when it hit me, first my legs went and then I did.

With my absurdly bound little finger sticking out like a pennant, I wheeled the empty rail out of the shop and into the van. I took the L plates from the cabin and stuck them to the front and rear. Marios' cousin Nick had been giving me lessons and Marios let me drive on deliveries.

Waiting behind the wheel, I scanned the signs and sale stickers on the shop windows until Marios climbed in minutes later. He smelled of coffee, fags and something else, good will, mates, conviviality? "Everything okay, Harry?" he asked.

"Yeah," I replied, turning the engine over. "She said she'd call you for next month's orders on Friday."

"Good."

I lowered the handbrake and crawled by Finsbury Park Tube.

"What you thinking, Harry?" he asked, as we dawdled at the lights.

"Nothing… just how things turn out."

"You phone your mother?"

"Yeah, all the time." In truth, I hadn't spoken to her since we met and she'd given me my novel twenty quid.

I felt his eyes on me. "You've had some bad luck Harry, but you're okay now?"

"Yeah," I replied, gazing at the multitudes swarming the lights in the Seven Sisters Road.

"Change down Harry, you burn out the clutch."

"Sorry."

"You like it at Mrs Haji's?"

"Yeah, she's really nice."

"It's a bit small though?"

"I can't complain."

119

"You painted the room and tidied her garden," he laughed. "It was a forest."

"It was nuffin."

"Handbrake. You're a good boy."

I turned away and maybe blushed... what a strange thing to have said to you... "If you say so."

"You don't complain."

"Nothing's wrong."

"You see your friends from school?"

"Yeah, all the time… Sundays."

I kangaroo'd the van and stalled it.

"Clutch in. In the café, there's a boy I went to school with in Cyprus, Christos. Amazing… to come here and find old friends. We were trouble at school, Banayamou! We were trouble…" he chuckled, opening his twenty Rothmans.

I restarted the van and we crawled along.

We were idling in the traffic on Kingsland Road when he turned to me. "Harry?"

"Yeah?"

"Louis and Helen are moving out," he said.

"What, at Mrs Haji's?"

"Yes, you can have the big room."

"Will it be more money?"

"Same rent. The baby kept her awake; she says you're very quiet."

My pulse raced above the van's idle. I couldn't keep the urgency from my voice. "Marios?" I said.

"What, Harry?"

"I'm gonna ask you something," I could barely contain myself. "…I'll understand…"

"Get on with it…"

I took a breath, glimpsed into my dreams and saw the thing that dominated my waking and sleeping hours. It was looking at me through the bars that imprisoned it. I was its

120

liberator and when I set it free, it would do the same for me.

"Could you lend me, Marios, er, sub me..?" I asked.

He reared. "For what?"

"I want to get something."

"That's obvious, what is it?"

"Something I need an... *advance* for."

"A car?"

"A drum kit."

"That's not good, Harry."

"Why?"

"Very noisy and, think about it, you'll have nothing to eat..."

"I'll manage. I gotta have some drums Marios. You don't understand."

"You're right."

What was the point of explaining to a grafter like him the aching need to hear what you dream?

"Harry, listen, I understand. When I was a kid I wanted to play football... I just practice, in the dark even, practice, practice. You're at that age when you find your love... it's just that, the drums? You gonna be a rock star, or you gonna starve? Listen, I'll lend you money for a little car. Bannayamou, you stall it again!"

I restarted and, perhaps, over-revved for a second. "You said you understood. I play Marios, all the time, in my head, beats beat up there but that's where they stay. I can work weekends. I don't do nuffin anyway..."

Wearing the same sanguine smile when orders were late or he was refereeing the presser and cutter, he said, "You really want to bang those things?"

"More than anything."

"You mad. Third gear."

We drove on and parked somewhere in Dalston. Another purpose-built maze of box factories for a drop-off or pick-up. At the side of the van, before he slid the door open, he went into his back pocket and counted out the notes.

"Thanks a lot, Marios."

"You can thank me when you're famous."

I smiled. "You never know."

A waiter with slicked back hair slalomed past. I watched him, tray held high, disappear into a restaurant with real, flaming torches outside.

Although it was sunny and noon, I could feel the dregs, the heat of the previous night as I walked past the cleaners scouring the strip joint and night club entrances with their grey, soapy mops. Soho thrilled me; I could have walked its streets for hours peering into the darkened shop fronts, market stalls, cafes and alleys but that day, I was on a mission.

Pausing at the Marquee Club in Wardour Street, I squinted along the corridor imagining the fabulous universe beyond. I'd seen adverts for the place in *Melody Maker*, dozens of bands played there and when there was a review of a gig, you could see the 'Marquee' legend on the wall behind the drum kit in the photo.

"Mind out, mate!" I stepped aside for a couple of blokes with guitar cases. One held the door open for me, inviting me to walk the long dim carpet with them. Mute, I shook my head and backed away.

I headed south and crossed Shaftesbury Avenue. I was so occupied by the theatres and grand buildings, I almost fell into a couple of women in delicate high heels tottering on the kerb.

"Sorry," I mumbled.

Their eyes glistened like cats at pleasure. They smiled and purred their laughter. Both wore dark fur and their perfume made me tipsy for a moment, so I walked a few steps behind, drinking it. "Are you following us little boy?" one asked.

122

Her cheekbones were high and white, the fur at her slender neck, brownish.

I shrugged and smiled.

"He's a baby spy," laughed the other, with pale pink lipstick. Linking arms, they posed and pouted but I let them walk on because I was standing outside the Whiskey-a-Go-Go.

So, this was where it all started, *this* was where I started. They used to argue about that fateful day routinely, so the name of the place was embedded in the shrieks, muffled thuds and footfalls beneath my bed. They called it the Latin Quarter and, in the late fifties and early sixties, women from the East End danced the samba and mambo with men fresh off the boat. Within the passing cabs and buses, I sensed those clave-dotted rhythms dragging me back. I saw myself dawdling outside the front-room in my school uniform as timbales and horns, yelps and shakers, danced around my old house, joyfully at odds with the shitty mood that pervaded.

Recrossing Shaftesbury Avenue, I did a quick left off Wardour Street and walked through a cobbled courtyard to the foot of a wrought-iron staircase. Passing a couple of girls chatting between flats, I heard the familiar sounds of a factory (machines and hammering), emanating from the floor above. I followed the noise and pushed open a door and was trapped in a sawdust mist. My hair collected wooden particles like bees do pollen and I gagged on the dust. A drill stopped and a bloke in an apron removed his protective goggles and asked if he could help.

"I want to buy a drum kit."

"You want the show room."

He led me through a set of doors as if they were stage curtains and waved his hand. "In your own time," he said.

I gasped. There was a score of gleaming sets assembled on the plush red carpet. In a daze, I inspected the myriad sizes, shapes and configurations of them. I'd never seen so

123

many drums in one place. Some had four or even five tom-toms appointed and reminded me of oil rigs or space ships. Some were small and jazzy, they'd fit into a box room, the back seat of a car. There were sixteen-inch bass drums for a warm, thuddy sound and huge twenty-sixers that must have gone off like cannons. Colours were limitless: black, white and red, blue, yellow, gold and chrome. You could have your pick of finishes: matt, gloss, amusingly spangled or playfully striped. For the tasteful, a natural wood look was provided; varnished or unvarnished sombre shells, deep and forest dark. Cymbal trees displayed a gleaming, bumper harvest of gongs, chimes and chinese style as well as regular crashes, rides and splashes. Boxes of sticks in neat cubicles were segregated according to size, weight and balance, while skins of every diameter and type were there for that elusive, perfect response. Entranced, I ambled along lanes of hardware, stands, and pedals. By the time I arrived at the range of towering cases, I was bewildered, bewitched and breathless.

"See anything you fancy?" he asked.

Gazing at autographed posters of the famous and infamous behind imposing kits in fabulous locations, reality chimed in. The cost of even the cheapest set was way out of the league of a potless, temporarily side-lined, male seamstress.

"Fought you made 'em?" I replied.

"That we do." Smiling, he held open the door and we returned to the misty factory.

I had read that they made them here and thought I could cut some kind of deal. But the custom kits they built were as dear as the ones in the showroom. I felt sick. I'd been buttoning up, wrapping in cellophane and wheeling out, like a machine. For the last few months nobody had struck me or called me anything but Harry. I was a more confident and settled person; I was ready, but incomplete. Not having a kit was like missing a limb.

124

"So mate," he said again. "See anything you like?"

"Well, to be honest, I thought they'd be cheaper."

"How much cheaper?" he inquired, using his shirt to clean dust from his goggles.

I told him. He shook his head and leaned against the workbench. "Ever own a kit before?"

"Nah."

"Ever play one?"

"Yeah, course."

He put the goggles down and wiped his palms on his apron. "Why don't you learn the guitar, or the sax? It's a right sodding game, the drums. You're the only one in the band who's not allowed to ease up, rest, miss a couple of bars for a sly half a pint or a fag. The others can pick and choose, click their fingers while you're bangin' away and, just when you think it's all over, they'll delay their *grand* entrance so they can look good for their girlfriend up the back. Once he starts, the drummer has to finish. If he stops, it all does. And the looks you'll get if you drop a smidgen of a beat!... It's a thankless task, son."

I felt dismal, worse than outside Beaky's office or on Bob's mum's couch with the holes in my knees. I wasn't going to get it.

Smiling, he pushed himself off the bench and walked around the room tightening clamps and vices, wiping wood glue off newly turned shells with his finger. "Get something portable. Look what you have to cart about." He pointed to a tower of black cases and boxes. "You're more like a deliveryman than a musician. Watch the rest of the band run for cover when you've got some stairs to go up. You can't have a drink, not a proper one and you have to have a degree in biomechanics to set one up nowadays. Get something light, son, a harmonica."

I shrugged, waiting for the inevitable flea in the ear. Then

125

he winked, beckoned me to the far end of the room and pulled out a stepladder. From a lofty cupboard, bit-by-bit, he handed down a dusty old collection of drums, a sad-looking set of four - taped up, clawed and tired. For a few minutes, he brushed, blew, and wiped it until it resembled something beatable. After tuning and tightening, he stepped back with satisfaction. "You'll need hardware and cymbals," he said.

It was as if I'd asked for diamonds as well as gold.

He pulled out a creaky set of stands and some buckled old cymbals from a storage area. "Yours for a oner," he said.

"I ain't got it all on me."

"Well, how much have you got, money bags?"

I held out the five tenners Marios had advanced me the week before.

"Fifty quid! Tell you something, boy, you got a drummer's chutzpah!"

"Aw, fanks mate," I said, with a soaring heart.

Looking back, he knew I was a devotee, a lover, because he was one himself. I reckon he would have given them to me for nothing if I'd asked nicely, *and* driven them to Mrs Haji's afterwards.

"Hold on, what's your name?"

"Harry Ferdinand," I said, shaking his hand.

"Colin." He nodded, the grin splitting his ruddy cheeks. "Colin Gellor. How you gonna pick - "

"Gotta a van. Be here tomorra at eight?"

"Ten."

I turned for the iron stairs and floated down to the sound of him whistling happily behind me. The girls stopped chatting and looked at each other as I passed. They must have thought there was some serious competition on the next floor up.

14

The Cellophane Warehouse

Marios wagged a cautionary finger. The smile stayed just behind his jowls. "Don't go too fast. The roads have iced up."

"Yeah."

"And Harry," he made sure I met his eye as I turned for the factory door, "don't forget to lock up."

As I dangled the keys for him to see, his voice followed me out. "And make sure they sign!"

"Right."

I slid the van doors shut on the rails of gaudy, cellophane-wrapped dresses we'd been making for the last few weeks; in February's frosty sunshine they looked incongruously lightweight.

After backing into a van-sized space amidst the double-parked anarchy in Fonthill Road, I dragged the snaking garment rail towards Natalie's Trendy outlet at the end of a breeze-block corridor. Music leaked from the room I was delivering to. Before turning the handle, I paused to listen – it wasn't like anything on *Radio One.*

A blistering, unrelenting racket battered the walls as I pulled my rail into a large, grey space crammed with row upon row of dresses, shirts and strides. Natalie burst through the double doors at the far end of the room. Waving and dabbing her face, she turned and glared along a line of clothes. "*Turn that off!*" she yelled.

But nothing turned off. In fact, the level increased, causing her to fan her bosom furiously. She drew breath. "Banayamou! *Christian, switch it off!*"

The din stopped with a click.

"Thank God for that." She turned to me, smiling with

relief. "Ah, summer dresses from Marios. *Christian?*" she called over her shoulder.

As if a monster was hulking up the aisle towards us, the walls of cellophane rippled in ominous waves. The final wodge of garments were flung aside and Christian emerged with a glower.

He was about my age but where I was set, he was wiry; where my hair sprouted wildly, he'd formed his into a copse of defensive spikes. In the home of the six-pleat Oxford bags, rhinestone studs and embroidered denim shirt, his tatty biker jacket, tight black jeans and holey plimsolls appeared deliberately at odds.

He casually wiped his nose with the back of his hand. "Easy Nat," he said. "I'll handle it."

Natalie's stern head-shake couldn't conceal the smile. Smiles always leaked through for Christian. "You drive me mad with this… music!"

Christian winked and surprised me with a small pot of Vaseline produced from a zipped pocket. He dabbed some on his clever lips, the rest he rubbed into his hair. "I know you love it," he said, snapping the lid back.

"Delivery." She exhaled tiredly. "Stack these in three… with the twin-sets. Count them and give the man a receipt."

"Job done," he said, with a nicotine-yellow thumbs-up.

As Natalie left I turned to face Christian but he was already making his way back down the aisle. In seconds the racket again filled the room. His hand fanned across the dresses with absurd speed. "Fifty-two," he said in twenty-six seconds.

I had to shout. "Who's that?"

"The Damned."

I nodded. "Good."

"Yeah, saw them down the Roxy last week. Brilliant."

"Where's that?"

"Covent Garden."

"*Neat, neat, neat,*" he sang, violently miming the guitar.

"Can you play?"

"Yeah," he said, hands by his side, jumping on the spot as if he was going up for a header at a corner.

I was nodding too. "I'm a drummer," I blurted, even though I wasn't really. "Good beat."

"Fuckin brilliant, Rat," he said, scowling. But, even as he menaced, posed and snarled, I detected a vulnerable shade in him. He wanted me to think he was mad or hard or bad, but he wanted me to like him as well. I knew that razor-blade balancing act, I'd been performing it all my school days. I felt reassured I wasn't the only kid that straddled the line between nasty and needy.

Landing with a snarl, he produced a second surprise; a dazzling, all-encompassing smile that looked like the sun coming up. His teeth were pearly and even, like an old film star's. His eyes were wide, secretively grey. His pale skin was literally spotless. He was elfin, a forest creature like a deer, quick to startle.

"We should jam," he said triumphantly.

"Alright… *Rat,*" I nodded with excitement.

He could have said, 'cut your head off and whistle through the hole' and I would. I was drawn to him like a magnet.

Slender fingers beckoned. "Come 'ere."

Hypnotised, I followed him through the maze of cellophane until, with a flourish, he parted a rack of fake fur coats to reveal his red, sticker-caked guitar and amp. My stomach fluttered excitedly. In the few seconds I'd been in his company I knew he wouldn't take the piss if he heard me play.

"Here you are, mate," he said, writing his number on the back of a fag packet and handing it to me.

Sitting on my bed, in my room at Mrs Haji's, I examined

the fag packet Christian had given me at Natalie's outlet. Why had he encircled the 'a' in Christian and why had he written that particular letter in capitals? That 'A' sign was on his guitar as well. All those safety pins fastened to his jacket, what were they about? And holes in everything? He wore a thick leather belt, like Abdul's, but he definitely wasn't a hippie... he wasn't a skin either but not completely dissimilar, especially the way he spoke and sneered. The Damned, what sort of name was that and why the devilish label?

I blew a speck of dust from a cymbal. I'd had my kit a couple of months. It was the last thing I saw at night and the first thing I saw in the morning. It was practically an antique. Colin from the shop had told me it had been the touring kit of some old jazzer in the fifties; in and out of cars and vans, set up and broken down a thousand times and, 'they didn't have cases like they have now back then, son!'

The shells - once silver - were mottled grey, and the rims were dotted with stubborn, rusty spots that just wouldn't come off. With bits borrowed from the dress factory, I'd buttressed the old stands, legs and arms, oiled moving parts and replaced screws, lugs and nuts that had sheared or became loose when I played. It might have looked puny compared to the pro kits in the shop windows but believe me, in a terrace bedroom in Wood Green, it was a monster. My monster.

Mrs Haji, my landlady, was aghast when I heaved it up the stairs into the room above her TV, but I assured her that she'd never hear me hit it. She visited her sister two roads away most weekday evenings. In that hour I'd muffle the whole thing in 'cabbage' from the factory and practise like a demon. Beats, rudiments, patterns and constant repetition. I'd try something new every time I sat behind my beloved, chromium snare drum. I did not go out. I bought no beer or chocolate. My dedication bordered on the holy.

***

Revving the engine, I scraped an icy film from the windscreen and flicked on the lights. Once again, I was on my way to Natalie's Trendy Fashion Emporium in Finsbury Park but this time, instead of floral dresses swaying in the back of the van, I had my drums.

Parking with ease by the outlet, I slid the door back to see Christian standing there, leather collar up, freezing breath rising from his mouth. Wordlessly, he gripped the traps case and hauled it out. I put my hands on bass drum and floor tom case, respectively.

The air about us crackled and hummed as he swore and menaced his temperamental amplifier.

Sitting behind the kit, I felt like a muscleman, too pumped to move, charged and veiny, close to detonation. "What about the noise?" I asked, the sticks trembling in my fingers.

He stepped away from his amp and pulled the rails in closer and closer. The designs were a blur. "Wouldn't hear the IRA in here."

He met my eye and played a fat, teeth-clenching chord. "See?"

We had a battling first rehearsal. I thrashed, he flailed. He changed tempo and so did I but not necessarily at the same time. I was conscious that we were shit, but we were shit together.

When we'd finally run out of puff, he opened a can for me. I swigged mightily; it went straight to my head. "Fuck!" I said, coughing snot and beer all over the kit. "That was brilliant."

"Got a germ of an idea there, Harry."

I tried to look like I knew what he was talking about. "Yeah."

"I reckon I could get at least three numbers out of that."

"You reckon?" I was genuinely intrigued. Was this how it was done? The alchemy of song-writing revealed in a cellophane warehouse.

"Oh yeah. Gonna do me own album." He lit me a fag with an unequivocal nod. "Once I'm sure I'm in the scene."

"The scene?"

"Punk."

"Punk?"

"What, are you a parrot?"

While I broke my kit down, he opened another can and spoke. "Yeah mate, gonna get a cracking band together. Practice like mad... and not in here, proper rehearsal room, with a PA and mics. Gig everywhere."

He was speaking another language but I understood the odd word. Punks, they were all over the papers, hated by the journalists in the *Melody Maker* and the red tops. Christian said they were hated by most people in society because they were pioneers and challenged the status quo. At least I knew who they were.

As I slid the last case into the van he said I had 'something'. "And I don't mean syph. If you ain't doin' anyfin' else, we should keep goin'."

(What was 'anything else'?)

"Alright."

We rehearsed all day on Sundays for a couple of months. I learned fast amongst Natalie's plastic-packed dresses and blouses. The area, just big enough for the kit, amp, and two medium-size teenagers was so compact that there was no hiding place for fumbles and stumbles. Looking back, you couldn't have found a better environment for the exacting, new musician.

In the breaks, Christian fed me scraps about the scene, the

132

bands and girls, drugs and nutters. I have to admit, over pints of Guinness and endless Marlboros, his enticing titbits made me envious of the next stage... the stage.

Now, when the road outside my room was quiet and the yellow street light sliced the anaglypta in two, I didn't look back in shame and regret, I looked forward to a musical fantasy glimpsed between Christian's burps and slurps.

Across the road, through the saloon bar window, The Rainbow Theatre's foyer looked as murky as a dungeon. We had had a particularly heart-busting session; pushing and pulling each other, relentlessly building and crashing as we tried to attain some kind of musical cohesion. These spring sundays were my greatest highlight. I lived for them all week. Up early to peek through the window at the factory van nestling in the frost, breaking down the kit and those ninja-quiet pads past Mrs Haji's room with the gear. A speedy ten-minute drive (because it was Sunday) from Wood Green to Finsbury Park and his face, reluctantly excited, grudgingly angelic, as I slid the van doors across.

He finished his pint and exhaled with satisfaction. "Yeah, definitely an album's worth there."

I wanted to ask, 'where?'

He leaned in. "Gonna see Lucas."

"Who?"

"Only a vehicle..."

"What, like a car?"

"Nah, he's a singer. What I'm sayin' is, I'll get in the scene with him. Get a foothold."

"He got a drummer?"

'Yeah, with a Premier pro plus. Electric blue, 'bout eight fuckin' cymbals on it. Toms everywhere..."

"Yeah?" I said, my percussive manhood shrivelling beneath the scarred old tabletop.

"And he's got three feather earrings… in each ear… fink he's a proper Gypsy!"

Fingering my sad, cod-diamond stud, I said nothing. He rocked back and directed a bluey jet at the ceiling. "Hear about the Russians, them underground explosions? Carter and Callaghan better sort 'em out… be like *Clockwork Orange* the way it's goin'…"

I nodded sagely, rubbery, but inside all was confusion. Let the sodding bombs fall. I was more concerned about this unknown vehicle that would ferry my punk priest away.

"Anuvver?" he asked.

"Yeah."

He leaned on the bar and offered his notes. Hunched up in my pilot's jacket I eyed him warily as did the derelicts, drinkers and local lads in that pub. Who the fuck was this Lucas and what effect was he going to have on future sabbaths?

He returned. After a moment I produced my opening gambit. "So right, they all say this punk rock thing won't last, and - " Guffaws from the builders on the next table broke my flow. They were sneering at Christian's habitual dab of Vaseline to lip and barnet. I could hear 'rotten… anarchy' and 'wankers' through derisive spurts and smirks.

The skinny bastard just turned on them. "What? You wanna photo?" he asked wide-eyed, the deer caught sipping at the lake.

I found myself glaring in their direction too, fearlessly picking out bits of stubble, meeting dull eyes, inspecting spittle lips while my own thinned and stiffened with menace. To my surprise they turned and mumbled into their mild and bitters.

"Let me tell you something, H," said Christian, his voice easily overpowering the country classic on the jukebox. "To be a punk is the greatest honour a British youth can have.

It is obvious that this shit, complacent country needs tearing down and renewing. It's his rebellious heritage and duty to change it, now!" As he tapped his finger on the table, I felt belonging warm me. His eyes drilled into mine. "This is for us," he said loud enough for all to hear. "Not *them.* It's for misfits, the expelled, the unwanted. People that play too fast, can't keep time or play in tune. Our thing, H."

Outside, beneath the darkening sky, Christian placed his hand on my shoulder. "Good today."

"Yeah."

"And the way you stood up for yourself in there."

"I always do," I lied uninhibitedly.

"I've jacked it in at Natalie's."

I was rocked by the connotations. "Have ya? Where we gonna play?"

He wore a consoling grin when he raised my face to his. "Don't worry. I won't forget you."

I was speechless. You can't be the greatest thing an English youth could be on your own.

"I'll call you in the week," he said, hefting his guitar across his shoulders.

As he strode past The Rainbow's forsaken exterior towards Highbury, I had the horrible feeling that he wouldn't. And I was right.

15

Lucas

With the dresses flying around like sailors in a gale, I took my frustration out on the streets. Tearing through reds and ambers, around corners on two wheels, I revved the engine so hard the head gasket nearly blew off.

Even the positive pink blossom along the avenues and park railings couldn't scratch a smile in my rubbery lips. And as for the dawn chorus... what was the point without a verse? I felt as if I'd been tipped off the world. Recently, there'd been murmurings about the noise in our sleepy terrace. Since the cellophane sessions, I'd been playing with such ferocity, I'd had to muffle my drums in ever-thicker layers of factory cabbage. But the fury still broke through.

At around four that Sunday, (and I loathed that day now), I decided to return to my bed. I'd yawned all the way through *Jack Hargreaves* and the *Big Match* and Mrs. Haji was concerned. She tried refuelling me with copious tea pourings from her mismatched army of cups and saucers. (When you opened her kitchen cupboard, there was not one item of crockery from the same family). I'd promised I'd rip out the last of the brambles, nettles and bindweed in her garden. There was just a tiny patch to go but I felt so lethargic, I'd never get it done. Not this rest day.

Night times had become grim, restless torments. Unrequited friendship, lost love and pointless beats had me staring at the ceiling. At four in the morning, I fancied my old man's slapping belt whistling towards me as I searched for oblivion. I pulled the covers up tight.

"*Harry?*" Mrs Haji called from the bottom of the stairs.

"Yeah?" I croaked.

"Phone call."

"Be right down." Bemused, I pulled my trousers on. The only people that knew I was here were Marios and my mum. Marios never called on Sunday and my mum hadn't called in weeks.

I fell into the armchair by the faux-victorian table and plucked the receiver from the pink doily on it.

"It's me."

"Christian?" I said, blinking at a blue willow-pattern cup on a flowery Victorian saucer.

"Can you play for us tonight?"

"*What?*" I'd never been asked that question before.

"Yes or no?"

"Yeah."

"Right." I could hear him speaking through his fingers. "We'll be round in an hour."

"Who's it for?"

"Lucas."

"What, the punk band?"

"Be by the door with your kit. One hour."

"Where we goin'?"

"Chelmsford."

After carefully replacing the receiver and raising an apologetic hand to my landlady, I steamed up the stairs. "It's gonna be all right…" I muttered as the bedroom door shut behind me.

In the centre of the room, my drums squatted mutely. I felt for them as you would a pet whose life you were about to disrupt irreparably. They had never bothered anyone and yet, within a few hours… For a moment I hesitated, heard foreboding whispers and sniffs, 'Can you handle it, *chocolate drop?*'

What was going to happen? I'd never been on a stage. I didn't know how the songs went and these people were nutters, violent gobbers and knifers, reckless swearers on telly, bent on society's destruction. It was proven they didn't think much of The Queen. In *The Mirror*, they were calling them the scum of the earth!

The beat passed.

I ripped the padding from the skins and placed a drum into a case far newer than itself.

Outside the terrace, an engine roared then rattled off. I peeked through the window. A grey Transit had driven into the space Marios' white one usually occupied. A knee-buckling dread-belt squeezed the breath out of me as I took the stairs in two giant bounds.

I opened the door before the chimes rang.

Before me, in black leather, with blacker curls, a white face and a smile, a smile so winning that I gawped, was a man. Wasp-waisted and broad shouldered, wearing a huge bullet belt and calf-length biker boots, he stared unwaveringly at a spot just past my shoulder.

He was like the star of a film. The universal conqueror.

"Lucas," he said, holding out a leather-gloved hand (only one hand had a glove on. Did he take that off when he was putting?).

"Har - "

He released, brushed past, gripped a couple of cases and whisked them to the van. Replacing him was my saviour. Christian barely nodded as he picked up a couple more.

I only had one to carry.

There was a driver, Steve. Steve was also the bass player. He sucked disdainfully on a white filter, raised his brow in my direction and turned the engine over. Steve was tall, lean, enigmatic and his hair was coal-black and pasted on his skull with gel. He also wore a biker jacket done right up and he had pink leather trousers on. I had never seen a bloke in pink before and I didn't know anyone that had. Lucas was motion-less beside him. Everyone held their breath. "Go," he said.

Christian was subdued. Usually in an enclosed space, he'd chew my ear off but he wouldn't meet my eye in the back of that particular van. Up front, Lucas and Steve muttered directions to each other. There were no smiles or banter on the way out of North London. And then, just as fields began to replace houses, Lucas turned to me and smiled for a second time.

Let me be clear, when Lucas smiled at you, you were admitted into a circle for the very fortunate. I studied his face as if it were a painting in a gallery, sure that any moment I'd be moved on and never see it again. White, even teeth, cupid lips and wide fathomless eyes (one of which had mascara on). I took in the details unabashed. It seemed ridiculous that this bloke was sitting in a Transit poring over a map. He should've been, I dunno, on telly.

Leaning over the seat, his face blotted out everything. "Harry?" he said, rolling my name in his mouth as if it were a novel flavour of ice cream.

"Yeah?"

He turned away and slammed his fist into his palm. Everybody jumped. "The *cunt!*" he cried out. Christian sighed and looked out of the window. Steve kept his eyes on the road. "Fucking blow me out, the mealy-mouthed, inbred mug!" He was shaking his head like a wild horse in a field. "Tell *me* he can't do it. Fucking *ten o'clock in the morning!* If I see that Dan again, he's a goner. I'll slit his throat. I know geezers'll chop him up, boy, pour acid down his neck. This is my fucking *career* we're on about!" Lucas smashed his leather-gloved fist into the dashboard over and over.

When he stopped only the indicator ticked.

Who was Dan and what had he done?

Steve put the van into fourth and coasted. "Alright," he said.

"I mean it Steve," said Lucas, his ire ebbing threat by threat. "Call him. Tell him, if I see his pockmarked mug in Chelsea I'll have him. Tell him not to come out of that cave in Brighton." His voice was almost reasonable now. "I'll definitely do time for that bastard," he added matter-of-factly. "Definitely..."

And that was that until we breeched the A406 and Steve said he needed to stop for fags.

"I'll go with you," said Lucas, opening his door.

"Get us some wine gums..." Christian called as the doors slammed.

I watched Lucas and Steve cross the road and walk past a bus stop. The queue was a study in astonishment. Wife nudged hubby, schoolgirl alerted schoolboy, and soon the whole street had come to a standstill. They sniggered and giggled, hugely disoriented by these two leather-clad aliens availing themselves of the sweet shop. By the greeting card display, I could see Lucas waving his arms about and Steve handing his money over with the composure of a judge. A pram-pushing mum giggled as she exited the shop. She parked up and waited for them to exit and when they did, she knelt next to her gurgling sprog and pointed. The punks had landed!

I turned to Christian. "Who's Dan? What'd he do?"

"He's the drummer, or *ex*-drummer. His girlfriend had a car crash and he couldn't do the gig. He's finished. Dead man."

"Blimey!"

"Don't worry. Lucas'll only maim you if you fuck up."

But I wasn't scared or even nervous. If anything, I found Lucas' theatrics compelling. Even that Steve, who virtually blanked me, had an antipathy I felt at ease with.

"Christian, you bastard," I said smiling. "You never called…"

"I did."

"What'll happen? I don't know the numbers or anything. I've never done a gig before, I - "

Christian didn't reply. He snarled, threw back the doors and confronted Lucas by the belisha beacon. "Ya get my wine gums?"

Although there was no context back then, I realise now that they were vying for attention, actually *performing* by some nondescript row of shops in Loughton. They just couldn't stop themselves.

On one side of the zebra, Lucas was bold and smouldering, a man's man, head held high, way above shopping lists. On his side of the crossing Christian was righteously indignant, a tainted elf, wild-armed and impudent, cruelly deprived of wine gums by his eternal rival.

Almost apologetically, cars hooted as the two faced off on the black and white.

Lucas shrugged and strode across.

Fingers rammed as he searched for pennies, Christian stormed into the shop.

Lucas climbed into the van smiling. "Come on, let's leave him," he said, as Christian approached, chewing sulkily.

Steve grinned and turned the engine on.

"No, don't," I said, from my seat.

Leaning against one wall of the tiny dressing room, Steve yawned, flicked ash and folded his arms over his bass. Next to him, Christian, nose running, hair gleaming like an oil slick, frenetically played shapes on his guitar.

I rocked gently in a corner, absorbing it all with my wonky grin, convinced I'd never pass through here again.

The man that rang my doorbell not four hours ago had his

back to us. He was bent over his holdall, compact mirror open - secret stuff going on.

When the compact snapped and he drew the valise's zip, he stood, turned and took my shoulders in both his hands. He'd added white to the mascara and his eyes were Egyptian and vast. My heart thudded as I looked at my boots.

I wasn't much of a punk: corkscrew curls that I tried but failed to flatten, a pilot's jacket and a pair of baggy suit trousers liberated from a wardrobe at Mrs Haji's. But nothing had been said. Tramp boy had left the building (as had nigger, wog, Gunga and all other aliases), and 'drummer in the band', even for just the one night, had skidded into his place.

"Harry," Lucas whispered. I raised my head. "Keep up."

Chaos. Three hundred screaming, spitting fanatics howled as I sat behind the drums. We were the first of six and had twenty minutes to survive. Lucas shrieked the count in, "*One, two, free, forwa!*"

And I played.

Forget technique, paradiddles, rolls, pushes and counting bars, this was a battle between my will to keep up and the gob, beer, and ear-splitting electricity that enveloped us. I did as I was bid. I watched his fist for tempo, (although all the songs were breakneck), and when he brought it down, I stopped. The lyrics, instrumentation and chords were an unintelligible broth of feedback and buzzing speakers. The atmosphere one of shrieks, flying glass, flailing sticks and phasing cymbals. Lucas pounded the air and I did not drop a beat. My shoulders and forearms ached and, however hard I gulped, my lungs never seemed to get enough air in them. But those discomforts ran a poor second to the fear. Not the fear of playing badly and Lucas slitting my throat on the way back to London, anyone could do that. No, what frightened me was failing the hostile hordes of Chelmsford, diluting the

142

event, decelerating their heart rate and leaving *them* indifferent and *me* a nonentity.

Without drawing breath Lucas ended each two-minute thrash with the in-count of the next. The mob heaved and fought, spat and sprayed, and I hammered my little set like a deranged blacksmith. And then, in the middle of it all, I became detached for a couple of seconds. These seconds seemed to last minutes. I imagined myself walking through the school playground in my raggedy parka and all the kids stepping aside. My bushy head entered then exited the school by the gym. Instead of goal-posts and cricket nets in the playing fields there was a stage. Leaping behind a huge drum kit I attained galactic perspective, saw Chelmsford, then the British Isles and finally the blue, blue earth. In the heart of a rainy forest, I located a crimson pulse. It was my heart, and it was happy. Right then, during song three, bar whatever, change of chords, verse or chorus, the past's grey was obliterated by an eye-shielding flash of solar brilliance.

In a blink, the tap of a hat, I was back. The sticks reverberated up my arms and heads bobbed and gobbed a few feet away.

To my left Steve had his bass slung low. Tilting his head back he'd occasionally spit into the air and catch it. He concentrated on that trick more than his playing. The only clue that he was part of this mayhem (not withstanding the throbbing bass-line coating the crowd) was his right hand, which rapidly flicked a pick across the strings the thickness of my finger.

Christian, on bended knees, had his head up the arse of his recalcitrant amp. It sounded particularly horrible, like a banger about to give up the ghost miles from home. As Lucas howled down the microphone, he shot him and it the first of ten thousand, quizzical, irritated looks. With a curse, Christian administered an almighty boot to the AC30's ribs.

The amplifier stuttered with pain. The sound returned and Christian wheeled on the crowd with the cockiest of grins, the surest of swaggers.

In the space before the final number, Lucas breathlessly addressed the mob, "This is the last one... *We... are... Lucas*," he said.

Roaring, they saluted him with two fingers, spit and abuse. Infuriated, he ripped his T-shirt off to reveal his scarred torso. With a vile oath he hurled the shreds at them and in return received a cigarette pinged at his chest.

I could smell the burning when he turned to me, his sweat-drenched face ran mascara like rain down a windscreen.

Sticks raised, I waited for the final count but he wouldn't move.

Christian glowered but Lucas was inert, staring at the back wall, panting like a racehorse.

"*Lucas?*" I bellowed over the demented buzz and pounding fists. He blinked, looked straight at me and gave me that debonair, English smile. He could have been in Surrey, amongst the azaleas, passing a china teapot across a gingham tablecloth to his venerable old aunt. But he wasn't. He was in this furnace with me. My heart glowed hotter and I remember thinking, I'll do anything for this bloke; he's saved my fucking life.

He strode towards the crowd like a homicidal ballet dancer and bellowed, "*Cat, dog, rat, snake...*"

He dived straight in.

I gulped the hall's noxious vapours with astonishment.

He proceeded to roll in all the crap, glass and spittle as if he had a straitjacket on. And the weird thing was, I *should* have been shocked, concerned, at least disorientated, but instead I thought, I'm not going to let it fall to bits. I'll keep time whatever. It's what chocolate drops do... *that's* when I knew that I could handle it...

When he finally climbed to the mic, he shook himself like a wet dog and screamed the song's unfathomable mantra into the metal mesh. I focussed on his right hand as if it were a meteorite spinning at my head; faster, harder, harder, faster.

Then he brought it down and we stopped, *dead.*

The roar was like a last minute goal.

Staggering from the stage, I fell into the corner of the tiny dressing room. Christian ripped the ring off a can and offered it. Glugging, I coughed my elation everywhere. Steve had returned to the spot he'd occupied not twenty-five minutes ago. I watched him blow his refined stream of chemicals into the ceiling, oblivious of me or anyone within a mile of him. In the opposing corner Christian paced and muttered. With his Strat still singing across his shoulders, he drained his tin and opened another as the next band started up.

All of us watched our singer. Pressing his hands into the wall, Lucas sucked in huge mouthfuls of air. His back was filthy with bloody nicks and squashed dog-ends. He retched, spat, and perspiration cascaded into his leathers, turning the black even blacker.

"I need soldiers," he said. It was a statement made to a wall.

I took a swallow and stared at my boots.

He was standing over me when I looked up. With a trace of the smile, I heard him speak. "You're good, Harry. You want the job - you got it."

16

The Vortex

Christian was having difficulties with his sound again. While he tweaked every knob on his sticker-clad amp, Lucas smouldered over a notebook. He played a chord. It blistered in and out, fading with a crackle into the hessian-lined, rehearsal room walls.

"It ain't the gear, H," Lucas said to his book.

It had been a summer spent in over-heated vans and stages and hotels. While people moaned about not being 'out in the sun', I luxuriated in dingy, muggy holes with megatons of electric current and teenage energy.

We were now in the middle of autumn and the shows were still coming. Everyone wanted us. And, after we played, they wanted more. The previous night, we'd played Leeds. It was the thirtieth gig since my first at Chelmsford (I used to keep a diary back then). We'd played Manchester and Plymouth before then but the big one was tomorrow, here, in London at The Vortex. Rumour had it that the suits were heavily into us, their company cars chock-full of squids for potless punks and Lucas was in a frenzy of rehearsal exactitude. Christian wasn't. Well, he liked Lucas to think he wasn't but everyone was keyed up, really.

We were evolving. Lucas demanded accuracy in the execution of his songs, now. He insisted, on pain of theatrical raging hump, that whatever the tempo, individual sections must remain at least distinct from the previous one. With each stringent run-through and chaotic show, the set was infinitesimally less frenzied, a little more composed.

Christian played another chord. The sound was passable.

With a sigh, Lucas approached the mic and I went around

146

my drums. As we collectively inhaled, another head-splitting belt of feedback prevented Lucas from counting in. We all sagged as Christian, unperturbed by the racket he was making, posed in the wall-length mirror; chewing, snarling, profile, front-on, downswing, upswing, tongue out, gob.

Finally, he clamped his fist around the guitar's neck and yelled, "Let's go!"

As if reading from a page in his notebook, Lucas said, "It doesn't sound like a guitar."

Christian sighed. "And *you* don't look like you do on the posters."

Lucas's eyes closed as he shut his book. "Fuck this," he whispered, as if it were the last time he would ever speak, smile or sing.

Swinging his guitar round his back, Christian dabbed Vaseline on lips and hair with venom. "The gear's shit!" he said.

"You bought it!" Lucas spat back, reopening his little book and fanning the pages across.

I took my feet off the pedals and placed the sticks on the bass drum shell. Christian twiddled a spike-end between thumb and forefinger before elongating it into a glistening pylon on his head. After a pause, he addressed his reflection, matter-of-factly. "I ain't got the money for anuvver one, have you?"

I had never met anyone as obsessed with their appearance as Christian. He'd bathe twice a day sometimes, and if his mouth wasn't smoking, ingesting or swearing it'd have a toothbrush in it, the paste leaking down the sides as he scrubbed and scrubbed. But I wouldn't say he was vain. I liked to think I knew about vanity. His attention to self was occupational. Like learning a song (inserting a lick here, a chop there), he made sure his collar was ripped just enough for the job and no more.

Lucas never condescended to a mirror. At least not in front of anyone. He needed nothing and no one to endorse his magnificence. Gazing up from his book with incredulity, he asked, "Money for *your* amp?"

"Well, yeah," replied Christian with exaggerated affront.

"Get a job," Lucas said, returning to his notes.

"A job! It's nineteen seventy-fuckin'-seven. X million unemployed."

"What about your mates?"

"My mates?"

"Yes…"

"Nah. They're all skint."

"Fucking joke."

"Least I got some."

"What?"

"Mates."

"Don't push it, Christian. You're one step from obscurity."

Christian glared around the damp room. "Fuckin' see that."

Lucas nodded. "There's the door."

Their eyes met and the rancour, fed by the stifling hum of PA and amps produced an unbearable tension that only playing would release.

Furiously, Christian dabbed mouth, bonce, mouth, bonce then pulled his guitar to the front. "*Fuckin' count it in!*"

"*Fuck this!*" Lucas stormed out of the room.

With Christian silently *ha ha-ing* and giving me the wankers, I followed Lucas through the door.

On the Caledonian Road the sun had turned puddles to black ink. I caught my reflection in a shop window and paused. Although there wasn't much hair about in those days, no one mentioned my barnet. From the untrimmed hedge of old, I'd encouraged a plateau-like quiff. You could put a hi-hat cymbal on it and it wouldn't have fallen off. In our band, apart from Christian, no one was into distressed clobber.

148

Lucas liked us smart and mainly in black; leather was good so my pilot's jacket passed the test. I never once saw Lucas in jeans, only leathers or tonics. He favoured proper shirts instead of T-shirts (unless they were rubber), and shoes or biker boots to DMs. He was no slave to the spiky-haired vogue. He detested high-street punks and weekenders as much as he did hippies and Tories and Christians.

Back then, Lucas paid me in clothes and records. A regulation, hearty breakfast was supplied any time of the working day because an army marches on its stomach. Post-show, burger and chips was consumed either in the sweaty dressing room, at the stage door (wrapper shielded from a dripping gutter), or in a service station, the bacteria on the patty thriving after a day in its warm, stainless steel bed. Rattling past black fields, dormant chimneys and sleeping hamlets, I enjoyed a rapid and enlightening education with him. What he said, or sang, you never forgot because there was no one around that could back it up like he did. As dawn lit the fields on one side of us, he revealed worlds and scenes I hadn't known existed and all his lessons, like his lyrics and impressions, were laced with a spiteful, arid humour.

For last week's gigs, he gave me the pair of nearly new, calf-length biker boots he wore the first day I met him. He took them from a cupboard in his spartan one room in Earls Court, gave them a blow and brush and handed them across. "Always good to my soldiers, H," he said, buttering the toast that accompanied our tea.

"Ta, Lucas."

Fractionally increasing the volume on the miniest of cassette players he asked, "You like Telex?"

"Really good," I replied with my mouth full.

Back to the wall (there were no chairs only a single mattress in his room), I pored over his Allen Jones, Betty Page and Hans Bellmer books, with lust and horror in equal measures. I read his newspaper when he finished with it and his T-shirts when his jacket fell open. I never managed to read his mind.

The night before the Leeds show he took me to see *Jubilee* at The Screen on the Green. In a whisper, he told me I was sitting amongst the cognoscenti, the ones 'in the know'. He said people will look on this era and be grateful because we were pioneers, brave frontiersmen that would take the beatings, humiliation and travails so that generations to come wouldn't have to. I wanted to tell him that's exactly what Christian thought, but even a hint that our skinny guitarist was in any way (apart from the odd backing vocal) in harmony with him, would have caused him anguish and me a caustic earful.

We'd become close but not matey, not like Christian and me. Lucas wasn't the sort of bloke you'd get pissed and fall about with, he was more instructional, a guide and good influence. True to his word, he didn't smoke or drink. Not a flake of Cadbury's passed his lips and as for drugs, you could put them in the Tory/hippie envelope. He was entirely focussed on his career. He'd do a hundred press-ups, sing his bollocks off then walk into the bear pit and slaughter the mob. He could have been, I dunno, in education.

His reflection joined mine in the shop front. He was looking towards the turrets of Kings Cross and St Pancras beyond. Squinting myopically in his NHS specs and crumpled raincoat, people walked past him without a second glance.

With an imperceptible nod we walked back to work.

Lucas stepped up to the mic. "Ready?" he asked. "*One, two, free, forwa!*"

Lucas wailed while Christian flailed and I remember thinking, at that moment, we've moved up another notch.

We had never sounded as powerful and triumphant. The timing was perfect.

There was a satisfying crackle when we finished. Then, as the music in the cubicles around us seeped in, Steve spoke. "What's that smell?"

We turned in Christian's direction. Smoke tapered from the back of his amp. I leaped across and ripped the plug from the wall.

Christian stalked his smouldering gear. "Have to get a fucking job now," he said, feeling for his Vaseline and embarking on the ritual.

Lucas shook his head and winced. "You know what, try the bogs down Highbury Corner, you look like a fucking rent boy doin' that."

Amyl, speed and lager raced through veins and arteries, fuelling the giant, pogoing organism inside The Vortex. It was the place to play if you wore mohair and bondage trousers. To inflame an atmosphere of quaking volatility, the promoters crammed as many bands onto the bill as possible. The right side of the stage was a bottleneck of agitated punks spiking up their hair and puffing manically as they waited to go on. From set-up to break-down, with a performance in between, the whole operation *had* to take half an hour or they'd pull the plug.

We were on a flick-knife's edge. Lucas had made it clear that if we delivered 'perfection', the word 'deal' might be included in our vocabulary. 'Deal' meant signing-off, an end to nicking food from corner shops, bunking Tubes and poncing fags, it meant also a record would be released. A musical time-capsule of what we were, would be lodged in the public's ear for eternity.

Ten minutes before we went on, he was hooked away by a couple of suits. Their mouths moved but no one heard what they said.

Beside me, Christian strained for the gift of lip-reading. "Oowerday?"

I looked at the two louche, thirty-somethings ingratiating themselves with our singer and shrugged. "Ziff I know."

Lucas returned with only minutes to go.

With the band ahead making a climactic, fearful row, Christian erupted. "Who're dem wankers?"

Ignoring him, Lucas carved out a few square feet for his pre-gig press-ups.

Christian's silver-sprayed Marten edged into his eye-line. "*Oi!*" he bellowed, "Them tossy blokes?"

Lucas paused mid-rep and looked up. "Them 'tossy blokes' are gonna buy you a new amp if we're any good so fuck off and tune up." He returned to his warm-up.

The static crackled as Christian lit a fag with his fag. "Cunts. Straights. Go 'n' chin em," he muttered.

Lucas collapsed. "Keep that rent boy away from me, Harry."

We were hemmed in. The band before us was finishing fast, the ones after pressing. The pent-up energy, barging and heat was distracting me. I needed a moment to get a bit of focus but there was no chance that night.

"Fuckin' secrets are *bollocks*," Christian said, stalking our little patch.

Waiting on the blocks to dart on and set my gear up, I sensed the band behind edge a few feet closer in anticipation. We were pressed against the side of the stage. Lucas and Christian had no choice but to stand side by side. Lucas was in one ear. "I mean it, H. That poser comes *near* me!"

I checked sticks, tuning key and towel. Christian poked me in the back. "Just tell him to tell me who them blokes are?"

The band on stage were giving it everything. I was trying

to estimate where my drums and stands would go as their drummer got his set off. "*Oi!*" Christian yelled in the other ear. "It's only fair we know what set of sell-out bank clerks are gonna sign us."

"Shut that oik up, H," Lucas seethed.

I turned to Steve. He was looking into infinity over his filterless wonder, not the least bit interested in the row that was about to scupper everything. "Steve?" I pleaded, hoping he'd come between them so I could concentrate on getting my drums on. He shrugged. "You're in charge, H," he said, tapping ash unconcernedly.

"Great help you are." I leaned towards Lucas. "Erm, he just wants to know, erm…what label?"

"Tell him it's none of his business."

A belt of fag wafted through my hair. "What am I, the fuckin' driver?" Christian yelled. "Course it's my business. It's all our business - we're a band, ain't we?"

"Ask him what we're called?" Lucas said.

Christian elbowed me. "Ask him how good he'd sound without us?"

At that moment the music on stage ended. My heart galloped as I hoisted the bass drum on and plonked it in the space the other one had been. Adjusting legs and rack-tom arm, I saw Christian getting into Lucas at the side of the stage. I scampered back for toms and cymbal stands. "*Christian!*" I bellowed through the roaring PA. "Get your fuckin' amp on!"

When Christian plugged in, his amp squealed horribly. "*Fuckinfuckinfuckinfing!*" he ranted, punching it in the ear.

Lucas ambled across. "You wanna new one, or what?" he asked with a small smile.

Christian snarled, tapping and tilting the noisy box.

'Where's your rebellion gone?" Lucas continued as Christian knob-twiddled furiously. Finally, mercifully, he played a chord that wiped the howling out.

Lucas laughed. "Welcome to the Vortex, *Christian*."

Christian turned and smirked, cocksure again. "What you doin' dahn here wiv us rebels, then?" he asked, tuning up. "You don't even drink. You don't even eat chocolate!"

Lucas, his back to the crowd, held the mic at his side. The place was quiet for a moment. It was waiting for us. I tightened and shifted tripods as Lucas replied. "You just don't get the movement do you? Cardboard punk prat. It's about your *own* rebellion, not some party for dossers getting cunted on speed and beer. There ain't no script."

Christian shook his head and smiled with pity. "*That* is where you're so wrong, there's a bible mate, it - "

"*One-two-free-forwa!*" Lucas yelled and we were in.

Hefting the cases into the van, a welcome, cold gust cooled the baking skin on my back. I shivered with pleasure. "You ain't hangin' about, Steve?" I asked, re-energised by Soho's chilly air.

"Nah, off somewhere else."

"We were gonna - "

He cut me off. "See you at rehearsals," he said, flicking his fag away and starting the van up.

Lucas was hailing a cab on the other side of the road. On his arm was the tall, leather-clad whipper that had been on the covers of all the fanzines that month. She'd slid all over him beneath the parachute they used as a dressing room. Her pouting, leggy performance rivalled the stage for attention. Opening the cab door, he gave me a nod. Job done perhaps? I'd given everything to him that night.

I winced as I put my hand into my pocket, the blisters on my fingers had opened on the first song and my snare skin was blood-spattered by the end of it. Sucking my digits and waggling them in the cold air, I turned for the doors and the intoxicating rumble, heat and stink emanating below. I headed for the bar, happy that singer and bassist were motoring away. It meant that me and Christian were, at last, off the leash.

At midnight, The Slides came on. They were the all-girl headline at my first gig in Chelmsford. I really liked them. They were originals. Their show seemed predicated on whether they could finish the set with their line-up intact. Without any respect for their instruments and little desire to learn, they managed to concoct these trashy anthems that stayed in your head for hours afterwards. They never started on time or ended in the same place and they'd often stop in the middle so they could have a row or chuck hairbrushes at each other. Sometimes they'd swap jackets or shoes and then change back. At least once during their twenty minutes, the drummer would get off the kit and screech into the mic while the singer picked up the sticks and sulkily tapped along. They were a real punk-rock house of cards. On the brink of collapse at the slightest gust.

They'd inexplicably stopped mid-song when Christian's face loomed in front of mine. Blinking and licking his lips, he bellowed, "Harry, come to the bogs. There's a geezer's got some speed…"

The flickering neon strip exaggerated the vivid oranges, greens and reds at the urinals. "Like water skiing through traffic lights," I laughed, trailing him through puddles of piss and water, but the smile froze on my lips when he pushed open a cubicle door.

Like hairless apes, two leery skinheads were wrapped around the plumbing. The big one looked as if he were holding a bag of chips. He sniffed and gobbed. That was enough for me. I turned and walked.

Christian caught me by the sinks. "Back me up, Harry."

155

"I can't," I croaked.

"What?" I'd never heard him so surprised. "You're my mate, my *best* mate…we're in a band!"

I looked away, unable to meet his eye. The sight of the duo in the toilets shot me right back to my final, catastrophic afternoon in Enfield. Once again, I was the terrified miscreant in line for a beating.

A Slides shambolic arrangement bounced off the clammy white tiles as he yanked me around. "Look at me, Harry."

Slowly, I raised my head.

Although he appeared unafraid I saw, behind the safety pins, spikes and snarl, the fragility that first drew me to him in the storeroom in Finsbury Park. Christian's vulnerability triggered a latent instinct in me. It was strange that an individual with so much bluster and mouth would engender such an instinct but, all I could think was, those blokes could smash his delicate face and he wouldn't be able to stop them. I might let it happen to me but I couldn't let it happen to him.

We returned to the cubicle.

Belch, sniff. "Money?"

Christian, with his hardish smile, fished into his trousers and pressed his gig cash into an open palm. An oxblood Marten rammed the door shut and a balled-up page of *The Mirror* was produced. As it uncurled, I read, 'National Party Win South African Elections' but most of the text was blotted out by the clump of gritty powder in its centre. The big one rolled a fiver and hoovered some up. Christian followed, snorting and gagging. Almost immediately, the skin vomited straight down the khazi, three neat, beery heaves. Christian cleared his nose and was about to move his face over the paper again when it was withdrawn.

"Oi," he squeaked, his face crumpling beneath the amphetamine. "I paid for that."

The seller's eyes bulged. "Nah," he said, shaking his head and rubbing his nose. "Not if *he's* your mate."

"Fucking give us anuvver line!" Christian demanded.

"Fuck off! And you, *paki*." His mate pushed us out.

Christian turned to me. "Don't worry Harry, I ain't gonna let them say that to you."

"I've heard it all before."

"I fuckin ain't."

He pushed the door open. "What you say to my mate, you bald cunt?"

"You what? Bender."

They pushed and pulled the door like a couple of kids arguing over a toy. "Come on, Christian. What's it matter?"

"Nah, fuckin' principle." Christian was sweating, his righteous face, the one he wore when he went into battle with Lucas, stuck on with sulphate. "Slag off my mate and rip me off..."

The door was being pulled when the handle came off. As the two inside swore and cursed, my stomach bubbled with dread. Thoughts of blades and blood made me want to sprint. I backed away and looked for trees to climb and hide in. Was that final afternoon about to be re-enacted here two years later?

The door flew open. Christian swung wildly at the first man out, the biggest of the two, but his blows were as effective as ping-pong balls as they bounced off the pallid cranium and chop-sized forearms. With smirking, porcine eyes, the bloke grabbed Christian by his jacket collar and drew his fist back. I could see the glinting metal on his knuckles and was horrified at what would result when driven into an angelic face.

"You can't," I said to myself. I moved in and half-punched an ear. A head wobbled confusedly.

Christian continued to windmill and squirm but his

assailant held on easily. As my fist retracted, the second man was at my face and neck. I think I bit his hand or bent his finger back; anyway, he yelped and fell away. In the same moment, Christian's opponent had righted himself, planted his feet, aimed and redrawn his arm. I hit him again, harder. Much harder. As hard as I had hit anything in my life.

A shockwave rippled sensuously from my fist to my brain.

In the second it took to throw the punch, I realised that The Slides had ended their set and the DJ was playing these thick cuts of lover's rock everyone was into back then. I think *Curly Locks* was on when the bloke I'd punched skidded gracefully towards the towel roll.

I felt unnaturally calm. "You alright?" I asked Christian.

He didn't reply because reality was rushing in around us. People were zipping up and fleeing. *They* were going to kill us.

We backed towards the sinks with Christian spitting menaces about who he knew and what they'd do if a Vaselined spike on his head was affected. The bloke I'd hit didn't give a fuck about his hair and, in his haste to close the deal, lunged, aquaplaned and grabbed for the nearest thing he could for balance. Unfortunately for him, it happened to be the chain attached to the nose and ear of a huge, honey-monster-sized punk.

An agonised roar cut through the toilet.

All eyes zeroed in on a nose dripping blood and the bejewelled end of a swinging chain. While the other skin returned to the safety of the cubicle, the bleeding punk laid into his comrade, banging him around the piss-sodden chamber like a pinball.

Amid entreaties, thuds, ticking hats and phasing piano, I hauled Christian towards the exit but he pulled away, kicked open a cubicle door and demanded his goods from the quaking man inside. A page of crumpled newspaper was offered.

Christian, in a frenzy, ripped it from him, sending the crystals flying into the strip light. I watched the powder fall through the mayhem and land like yellow snowflakes in the slush.

"Oh bollocks," he sobbed, heartbroken.

Outside the cubicle, dub had replaced lovers rock and the area was crammed with skinheads, punks and monkey-suited doormen. With subsonic bass notes shaking the air around us, we fled.

In the street, sober, relieved and elated, I laughed. "What did you go back for?"

"Fucking ripping me off."

"But - "

"No buts. Nobody rips me off, *nobody… understand?*" he yelled, spinning into the beeping, hooting traffic on Soho Square. He was flailing, lashing out at invisible dealers and kicking the crap out of thieving rubbish bags.

Late revellers turned their overcoat collars up and fearfully crossed the road. The terrible new phenomenon they'd all read about was at the gates of London's trendy West End.

I caught him as he was about to career into a roaring cab. His blows whistled past my chin and ear and then he fell against me, panting. "Saved you though, didn't I, Harry? They would'a killed ya if it weren't for me!"

I hugged him. "Yeah, Christian. Thanks mate, thanks..."

17

Recording

Lucas and the engineer scrutinised my work in covert whispers. As they soloed my beat, I felt my wonky, erratic soul laid open for all to see. Cringing behind a fag I feared the worst, but people were tapping along and I realised it was only me that could hear all the fumbling, amateurish hesitancy.

A couple of tortuous playbacks later, Lucas spun around and gave me a huge smiling thumbs up. I nodded as if I'd known it was ok all along.

"Do us a favour, H," he said, as I was leaving. "Get Steve in here."

I was playing pool with Christian when Steve exited the studio wordlessly. Chalking my cue, I heard, "*Harry, get in here!*" On entering the control room, Lucas was raving. "It's shit, it's shit, it's *shit!*" he yelled, flinging his fist.

I glanced at the terrified engineer. He'd pressed himself into his chair like a fighter pilot halfway through the sound barrier. "What is?" I asked.

Lucas slumped. "We're fucked," he said in a deathly whisper. "It's over."

"Why?"

"The bass... is shit."

Dark clouds loomed. "Is it?"

"Stumbling, bumbling, inept shit. I thought it was bad, but this! It's a miracle we didn't get bottled off *every* night."

"Blimey, Lucas."

"Have you heard it?"

"Probably nervous, give him a bit of time."

"Look, we ain't got no *time*, Harry, this is our one shot. If we don't walk out of here with a mix, a stellar mix, they'll give our deal to the next set of funny trousers. He sounds terrible, horrible. He's murdering my songs, all this time, murdering. It's over…"

"Easy, Lucas…"

The suits at The Vortex had been true to their word. We were here to record our first release, *if* it was good enough.

'A mere formality', Christian had said. We were within inches of crossing the line between pro and amateur and he was displaying an unbearable confidence. Lucas was aghast at Christian's attitude. This session was 'death or glory', we were playing for our 'careers' but Christian had laughed, 'what could possibly go wrong? If they were going to sign us on the strength of those crap gigs, they'll offer their first-born when they hear us in the studio.'

A fair point well-made, I thought. Lucas didn't. He threatened to sack everyone for their lax, flakey, cowboy, shit attitude.

Since The Vortex, Lucas had ascended to new levels of impatience and autocracy. His expectations had been rightly heightened by the offer of a recording contract, but his new disposition bordered on the irrational. But, it wasn't only the deal that had caused this change, it was the needless 'one-off' we did a few days later in Middlesborough. It did what I thought was impossible, it altered Lucas's outlook, and the repercussions echoed through the years.

And, we didn't *have* to do it either. When it was mooted, I can remember thinking that it seemed pointless. We really should be rehearsing for the session. But a gig was a gig back then, so we all piled into the van and off we motored.

We weren't two numbers into our set when a hostile gang burst through the doors at the back of the hall. Yawning gaps opened as the various tribes marshalled and battled. Swinging fists, bottles, and tins flew. The security men were completely outnumbered and couldn't prevent the mob from inevitably invading the stage.

Over the rim of a drum, some leering kid tried to nick a cymbal stand. I stopped and pushed him away. Seconds later, I levered some lump off of my bass drum. He in turn was trampled by two blokes hammering away at each other. It was like playing in the wild west. I pounded away until the stage was overrun and we were hauled into the hot, clammy dressing room and ordered to lock ourselves in. In seconds we realised that Lucas wasn't with us.

For an agonising fifteen minutes we listened to sirens, smashing glass, and howling lads through the small, wire mesh window at the top of the room.

We returned to a stage stained with blood and beer. Someone had kindly swept all the glass, cans and dog-ends into a pile by the PA stack but the tang of violence and mayhem remained. Police in riot gear watched from the wings as the crew righted amps and plugged things back in. I was busy resetting my kit when Christian approached me. "Harry," he said, with a concerned nod towards the front of the stage. Together, we watched Lucas emerge like an amphibian from the pit.

He'd been hacked and battered, properly punched about. Drenched in beer and gob, he looked utterly beaten.

I wanted to go to him, haul him up and put a cloak around him, but he simply wasn't the sort of bloke you went to. As he limped around the stage, he met no-one's eye. A roadie handed him the mic and backed into the shadows. In the eerie, post-ruck silence, he sucked in a huge breath. "*One, two, free, forwa...*" he bellowed, and on we went, determinedly to the end.

Scenes of discontent and anger were on the news most nights. Unemployment and race riots as common as football match brawls. Every high street we drove through felt custom-made for public disorder so it was no surprise there was violent unrest at many of the gigs. It was part of the sound back then. But that night was extreme. There were stabbings and young bones broken. People were hospitalised simply because they favoured a different band or haircut.

Crawling past ambulances and smashed-in shop fronts, Lucas twitched, sighed and muttered in the passenger seat. Nobody had the nerve to ask him what had happened when we were locked up safe in the dressing room. The streets, as well as our van, remained horribly quiet.

As we circumvented a gutted car, Christian attempted to regain some kind of normality from the evening by offering a mild but telling observation about the performance. The sound on stage was becoming distorted, he said, we could do with thinking about the volume levels on there. He suggested we trust the house engineers at bigger gigs because they knew their gear better than anyone. It was amateurish, he reflected, to mix your own sound from the stage, after all, we weren't playing for the benefit of ourselves. It was a fair point soberly made. While we mulled over amp settings and where speakers should point, Lucas slammed his fist into his palm.

We'd been waiting for an outburst. Hoping for one, really. He would get it off his chest, and later - as was customary - we could dredge it up with hoots and requisite Hitleresque impressions when he was tucked up in bed. But that evening's events affected Lucas unusually. As we flattened ourselves against the sides of the van, expecting an episode of apoplectic rage, he stopped short. "Never again," he said, quietly. "Never again."

I'd been watching him from the drums for over two years and I'd come to the conclusion that he only did it for himself. He went through the whole thing, make-up, vocals, moves, for his own analytical critique.

163

While Christian smirked and nodded, threw shapes for his mates and everyone else, Lucas remained self-contained. When he flew into the crowd before the last number, it was as if he'd had enough of introspection and wanted to share himself. But, however rough it got in the pit, the love he received far outweighed the discomfort.

That summer night in 'Boro, he was betrayed by the people he thought loved him, I think. From then on he became a performer, a professional one. No longer locked in his own world of self-analysis, he played to the crowd and did it brilliantly (after all, he'd been auditioning himself for years). But even as the eyes that followed his every move multiplied and became mild and forgiving, I hankered after the old days when he'd smile at me through the chaos, turn and leap into that broth of leaping nutters and grind them into the dust.

From that gig on, nutters and dust were prohibited. A new intensity pervaded every facet of the job. Everyone had the potential for treachery, most were out to steal what was rightfully his. From huge over-reactions to being five minutes late or not having a whiter than white towel supplied when he came off, to the more serious matter of the bass lines on record company sponsored recording sessions not going quite to plan, he was intolerant and merciless.

"That fuckin' bass?" Lucas was shaking his head as if unable to centre his brain. "There *will* be murder. I'll... I'll, electrocute him... in here!"

The engineer stood and edged his way out of the control room.

"They'll drop us like a shitty stick. Gave 'em my word as a man, H," he said, looking through his fingers at me. "Those A&R men are callous bastards."

My pacifying hand was in position A. "His confidence

ain't all that at the moment, Lucas," I blustered. "Let him have another go. I'm sure he'll get it right."

I was met by silence. I called the engineer back in.

My brain whirred and ticked, Lucas smouldered and the traumatised boffin subtly lowered the faders on another of Steve's below-par takes.

I took a positive breath. "I reckon, if we take the verse, well the first half on the first verse... on the second take, right?" I nodded encouragingly at Lucas and continued. "Match that up with the second half on the take before that. Was that the third one? We'll have a listen. The third chorus was nearly there, apart from it coming in a little late. Yeah, if we cut that up and plonk it on all of them... except the last cos we change key... erm, Christian could play that. Anyway, the bridges ain't bad, except for the one when we stop. He plays through that... funny never heard him do that, so... we take - "

"*Shut up!*" Lucas roared.

I winked reassuringly at the engineer.

"I can't go on like this… it's over," he said, moaning into the leatherette headrest.

I felt for Steve but I was angry with him too. The stakes had been getting higher and higher. The pressure to be at our best was plainly there. We sold everywhere out. We'd had all these reviews saying that we *must* be recorded before we implode, that we were the last vestiges of 'fag-end punk'.

Although Christian gave Lucas enough gyp for two careers, he was a feverish rehearser. He'd even put his fabled 'solo album' on hold so he could nail his parts faultlessly. Building up to this session, I was so concerned with perfecting my side of the deal I stayed overnight on the rehearsal room sofa. For company, I had the *NME* and John Peel on the radio. When I awoke, I'd get my ketchup-sodden bacon roll from the chip van and go through the songs repetitively before the lads turned up at twelve.

But Steve had done the minimum. When I mentioned coming in early, running through things, just me and him, he'd sneer and tell me to stop being an old woman. When I suggested different ways we could take the bass and drums he belittled me, laughed at my point of view and ideas and I felt a frisson of old shaming wounds. Finally, I thought fuck him, and got on with my end, regardless.

But I shouldn't have. I should have begged and brought him gifts. Carried him to work on my back, wiped his mouth and lit his fags because now, I was doomed.

Mrs H's sewing machine marked erratic time downstairs while I traced a hairline crack in the ceiling. When the needle stopped I was sucked back into awful real time. The unimaginable had happened. Lucas had split the band up and I'd become a non-musician.

This is how quickly it happens. One minute you're playing pool, the next you're drowning in one.

I'd become his confidant and sounding board. He'd call me day or night and, without preamble, plunge me into his deepest workings, but for the last seven days I'd suffered tortuous, radio silence.

I rolled over and silently cursed him for being super-sensitive and double-dogmatic. I cursed Christian for constantly poking him with sticks and Steve for not trying. Mostly, I cursed my inability to read minds and predict the future.

Turning the other way, I attempted to unravel the beat that had wound itself, like a ball of string, around my memory. I'd heard it as I passed a window on one of my long, anxiety-reducing walks around the neighbourhood. It was one of those complex jazz-rock signatures that has a trace of Latin enmeshed in it. The hi-hat hand was doing a tricky, sixteens shuffle while the left hand, the snare drum hand, chopped the bar in half with an off-beat skip. The bass drum dotted the pattern randomly, punching unexpected holes that moved and shoved you along with it. But of course, none of it was random. It was brilliantly calculated and played by a talent I couldn't hope to emulate (especially as I had to sign on and sell everything). The tempo never faltered and the beat rolled on regardless of whatever instrumentation came in or out. I imagined congas and marimbas chiming in, a shrieking Cuban chorus and cascading trumpets. Of course, it was all going apricot. Even as I picked the pattern apart, I heard my old man, droning my name in that tired, frustrated way as I tried to sneak in after school.

I'd not heard Mrs Haji until she poked her head around the door. There was a little colour in her cheeks. "*Harry!* There's a man for you."

"Oh, I'll come down."

I pulled on my combats, stepped onto the landing and padded downstairs.

Lucas stood in the hallway just as he had on that spring day all those months ago. "Alright?" I said, resisting the urge to run into his arms and bury my tearful head in his chest.

Looking from the clay kittens to the spindly table by the door and finally, at the ill-conceived equine watercolour at eye-level, he said. "We need to talk."

Not many.

That day, beneath a long black leather coat, he wore a muted gold suit. He said it was the one David Bowie wore on the cover of *Pin Ups*. His shirt was starched and white and his hair hung in clean black curls. He smiled a brief, dazzling smile at Mrs H, who wilted and returned to her backs and arms in a blush. "Let's go," he said.

I stuffed my feet into my boots knowing all bets were now back on. When I'd looked up, he'd gone.

167

Jogging up to his shoulder, we walked the thin, snowy streets of Wood Green in silence. "What about the deal, Lucas?" I asked.

"I'll take care of that, H," he said.

In the café on the High Street I scoured my mouth with a hot, sweet brew and prepared myself. Whatever he asked of me, I would do.

From his chair in the corner he gave me nothing. Nine-thirty ticked slowly by and apart from a fat bloke eating liver and onions, we had the place to ourselves. He studied the road outside. I followed his gaze. A bus pulled up with a hiss of brakes and sprayed the pavement with grey slush. Looking away with a shiver, I picked up the newspaper a diner had left: 'SHUTDOWN' was the headline. The country was in the grip of crippling strikes and the shittiest weather in living memory. The ambulance men had stopped going to calls. People were breaking raw bones on the ice and snow. It was the winter of discontent.

"He's gone."

"*Who?*" My tea stayed disobediently at the back of my mouth.

"Steve. Out."

I swallowed hard. "Coza one mistake?"

Lucas blew then sipped from his cup. "Don't be naive, Harry," he said. "We've got to move on. I can't have a meat and potatoes rhythm section."

"We ain't," I protested.

He sipped a little more tea while I fretted. "Lucas, there's no way you can give him a second chance?"

"None. He's obsolete," he said, holding my eye for a rare, split second. "You need musicians on your level, people that'll bring the best out in you. You can't keep dragging him uphill and I won't. End of."

The radio crackled, fried slices sizzled and traffic laboured in the slush outside. He tapped his mug for attention. "I've got someone else."

"Who?"

"First things first, Harry. He's got to go. Today."

"You ain't told him?"

"Your department."

"Fucking hell!"

"He was a good soldier but it's over. Go round there and tell him. And be at rehearsals for two… and bring laughing boy with you."

It was no surprise that I'd have to do the deed. Along with being 'teacher's bird', as Christian liked to call me, I was about to become 'his lordship's assassin'.

Through the window's condensation, milky sunshine enlightened the bus station. Bacon spat and the radio scratched out another top ten.

"Nice suit," I said.

"Ta."

"Lucas…" I said, beginning my final submission.

But his eyes would not meet mine. They were set on sights way beyond our table. He was gazing past the counter and the cook (his spatula nudging onions), beyond the bin yard at the back of the café, and thence, to a horizon further. His gaze traversed port and ocean, desert and forest to finally rest on a mountain, its snow-capped peak, glinting like the gold paper on the inside of a packet of B&H.

And I was looking at him.

"What?" he said absently.

"Nuffin."

In the street outside a mother and her kid skidded on the icy pavement. I returned to the newspaper. They were saying that this number of strikes would cause two million people to be out of work within a week. Poor old Steve would make it two million and one.

18

Kyle

"Who's that?"

I gulped. "Harry."

He buzzed me in and I climbed the stairs to his airy, first-floor flat.

"Cup of tea?" he asked.

My ears were ringing. "Just had one."

I flicked through his vast and excellent record collection while he made one for himself. It was a rare moment between us away from the band and I realised how different from me and Christian, Steve was. For a start, he had this flat in Camden Town (living room, separate bedroom, kitchen and bathroom). He had a girlfriend and a job. She had a job too. His employers let him dip in and out when we had gigs away from home. He went out to eat and took holidays. He'd told Lucas more than twice he couldn't make this or that because he had 'prior commitments'. I couldn't imagine anything more important than the band.

To all extents, he was a pretty successful bloke. He never embarrassed himself. He never ponced chips or fags. He had his own. When his amp went on the blink, there a new one was in its place the day after. He never walked, he always had money for the Tube and at least three times I'd seen him getting out of a black cab at rehearsals, but he lacked the element I, Christian and Lucas were suffused with: ambition.

"What's up, Harry?" he asked reclining on a suitably distressed Chesterfield with a matching cup and saucer.

"You spoke to Lucas?"

"Nah." He lit one of his fags and smiled. I squirmed in the

sunshine pouring through the window. The gutters dripped thawing ice.

"He came round this morning," I said. "To my place."

"You're honoured. Used to come here a lot... in the old days."

I felt unnerved. Exhaling, I looked straight at him. "He wants you out the band Steve," I said, almost laughing at the absurdity of it all.

His face darkened. He flicked ash into a plant pot.

"He said, it ain't working," I stated quietly.

"Oh yeah?"

"Yeah. He said we need to find someone with a different style... sort of."

"And he sent you to tell me."

"Yes."

He got up and put the Velvets on.

"You like the Velvets, H?"

"Yeah. Brilliant."

"How long you been into them?"

"Dunno, Christian got me into them."

"Not long then?"

"A few months... but I do rate them."

"They've been going years. Years before you joined. What were you into, like, blue beat and that?"

I looked down at my boots. "I like all different fings..."

He peered into the mirror and flattened his jet-black hair against his temple. He laughed. "You weren't even in a band before Lucas."

"You know I weren't."

We listened to Nico for a minute or two. Opening a fresh pack of twenty he said, "But you reckon you're a proper 'punk rocker' now?"

"Not... not really... just a drummer."

"Yeah, the drummer that's come to give me the elbow."

171

The track ended.

"Funny how he never does it himself," he said. "Sack people. I had to do it to Mick."

"Has he always been like that?"

"I don't know."

"You've known him longer than anyone."

"But not as well as you. Kindred spirits you and 'im. A right couple of dreamers," he said, shaking his head. It was as if he was conceding the last piece of hard-fought land, except he'd never bothered to fight for it.

"I didn't want this to happen, Steve."

"What about Christian?"

"He doesn't know yet."

"You're a good soldier," he said, enjoying my discomfort. "I was going to leave in the studio. It's all gone to his head."

I nodded. He smiled. He knew I was agreeing for the sake of it. "People think they're in The Beatles. They should just enjoy it for what it is."

"That's what I do, Steve."

"Do ya? Sometimes I think you see it like he does. Like a job."

I shrugged. He turned the track up a little. "It ain't though. Just something kids go through and grow out of. What'll happen when it all ends?"

"Dunno."

"Why don't you do a course or something? Get an apprenticeship, bricky, plumber, you'll never be skint."

"I'll have a look," I muttered.

As we listened to the new track melting in, I felt as if I was again hovering over uncertainty. Playing the drums for Lucas elevated me. I beat the skins like a bird flaps its wings. Playing kept the cold, hard earth a good distance below.

He broke the spell. "Nah, you're alright Harry. It had to be done, I suppose. I wonder who'll do it to you?"

172

It was his parting shot and I hoped I didn't blink. "It wasn't my decision, Steve."

"Oh, I know that. It's his game. We are merely prawns in his salad."

We laughed and said we shouldn't be strangers. I skipped down the stairs and looked up at his window for a last wave, but he wasn't there.

"What's up now, sad sack?"

When I told him he went mental, calling Lucas all the cunts and bastards under the sun. "Pointless... criminal. All that in the van about *the family* and when we sign we'll all share it." His voice ricocheted off the Tube station walls. "How long's Steve been with him? From the start. *Unbelievable!*"

"Lucas said we've got to step out of the new wave soup or we'll drown in it."

His finger jabbed at my face. "*Lucas said*," he mimicked effeminately. "*You* are a parrot with not *one* original thought."

"He's got a point, Christian."

"You're a treacherous cunt."

"Don't call me that."

"Treach - "

The lunchtime commuters began a nonchalant stroll towards the other end of the platform as I rammed him into Finsbury Park's cold, westbound wall. After Steve had put me through that old-time shaming ritual, I wasn't in the mood to take any added vilification from him. "He practically told me I shouldn't be in this band," I said to Christian's snarling face. "He's never rated me, he thinks I don't belong."

"So you went and kicked him out for your lover boy, Lucas."

Christian gripped my arm and squirmed but I held him steady.

"Alright then. You think Steve's good enough, do ya?" His grip weakened fractionally. I released him but didn't allow him to get away. "Well, do you Christian? You think he's worked as hard as you, put as much in as we both have... *well?*" He attempted to sidestep but I covered his move. "What about the studio? We were gonna get a deal for fuck's sake! We'd be signed if he played half as well as you or me."

"Criminal," he muttered.

"Where was he when we stayed late to go through the changes? We asked him and he laughed and called us robots. He took the piss. Always off somewhere else, remember?"

He put his anguished face an inch from mine. "*When's my time then, when are you coming for me?*"

The fight left me immediately. Even as he scowled and sneered I detected flecks of dismay in his grey eyes. He was as insecure as I was, but where I gazed dismally down, he sneered straight into the lens. Gently, I put my hand on his shoulder. "It'll never happen," I said.

His lip trembled. "I bet you said that to Steve."

"Steve and me... we were never mates," I said quietly. "We're like brothers, you and me."

With a giant poster of the Tower of London his backdrop, he unzipped his leather jacket. I exhaled, waiting for him to do his Vaseline thing but alarmingly, he opened his penknife.

His eyes never left mine as he sliced across his palm.

"You're mental," I said, retreating as blood grew from his hand.

Pointing the knife at my face, he said, "Blood brothers."

"This is mental..." I was backed against the platform edge with his blade at my throat. The twenty or so people there were now firmly pressed against the far tunnel wall.

"Bollocks." I took the knife, inhaled and sliced across my palm. He clasped my hand. "Blood brothers," he whispered fiercely as our sticky palms bonded.

We were the silent, lone occupiers of a newsprint-strewn carriage.

Outside Caledonian Road, I trailed behind as he muttered and cursed, booted cans and smoked furiously. He was back to his belligerent ways. There wasn't a hint of the trembling lip and frightened eyes of half an hour ago.

He'd worked himself into such a state that as we approached the rehearsal room, I feared a really big scrap between him and Lucas and it all going tits up again. At our studio door, I put my hand on his shoulder. "Wait, Christian. It's just being professional, that's all."

He shrugged me off. "This movement ain't about *professional*. I hate that muso crap."

"But we're getting paid for this now." Which was true. Lucas had put us on a minimal wage. It covered my food and the very reasonable rent at Mrs H's.

The bass rumble from within curtailed the whiplash oath on his snarling lips. We looked at each other then Christian kicked the door open. I wished he'd use the handle like everyone else.

Lucas was sitting on a chair and writing in one of his many, colour co-ordinated, notebooks. He didn't even look up when we entered. Then, from behind the bass cabinet we heard, for a few seconds, the bass line to one of our songs. I remember thinking how weird it was not hearing Steve's pick action, the sound of his amp and his timing. He'd given the bottom end a cold feel whereas what we'd just heard was warm, accurate, and played with real finesse.

For a second I thought it was the milkman we used to have in Enfield. Johnny, Benny, Eric? We never paid him on time and in the end he'd refused to deliver. I had to go round the shops for something white, wet and cold to put on my cornflakes. I recalled the early morning soundtrack though; the float's laboured, electric drone, clanking crates and the crappy pop tune of the day whistled like a genius, note perfect, as the handbrake went down. Johnny, Benny, Eric was - like his whistle - quite willowy, but this bloke, the bloke on the bass, was stocky but with the same mousy hair, styled in a sort of milk-mannish way.

"This is Kyle. He's your new bass player," said Lucas, looking up from a page and giving Kyle the special smile. Enviously, I wondered if a little piece of him melted like it did in me.

Kyle wore a bomber jacket, high street blue jeans and nondescript trainers. I was surprised. After all that Kings Road, stylised superiority, Lucas had chosen the most ordinary-looking bloke you could imagine.

"Alright," I said. "Harry." I offered my hand and he took it. He looked school-boyish but his grip was strong. There was a confidence about the way he regarded us that wasn't dissimilar to the way we regarded him.

Christian scowled and turned his back. He whacked up his amp and played a spiteful, feedback-laden lick on his guitar. Kyle eyed him carefully as I picked up my sticks. Just as I was about to strike, I heard it. It was ridiculous. Kyle, in answer to Christian's warm-up run, produced one of his own; a faultless sprint up and down the neck of his bass. What he played resembled a section of classical music, something you might hear from a cellist. Every string was touched sympathetically, brilliantly and at lightning speed. I sat open-mouthed, my stick up like a lolly.

Casually, Lucas placed his homework beside the mic stand and gave Christian and me a devilish look. The look said, 'Now we've got a *proper* player in here. Now we really take a step up in class. Weep my complacent, punky pals for we have a virtuoso in our midst and none of us will ever be the same again.'

***

A few hours later we stopped for a break and Christian and me went out for a fag. As the lorries and vans roared up and down Brewery Road, I shook my head in disbelief.

"That bloke's fucking brilliant."

Christian glared at me. "You obtuse cunt," he said, spitting into the street.

On our return to the rehearsal room, Lucas revealed all.

That week, while I'd stewed fearfully in my room, he and Kyle had been in the studio re-recording the bass. The tracks had been mixed and sent to the record company. In twenty-four hours (a twenty-four hours I mulled over that fabled brickie apprenticeship), the suits had said yes, it was all they'd hoped for and were putting it out.

As for Kyle, after three run-throughs he was tight as a drum. The way he played made new songs out of old. He forced my concentration to its limits and my technique to breaking point and when it snapped I re-learned, quickly. In the following months, he asked brilliant questions of me and I relished the inquisition. He tutored economy of movement and exacting synchronicity, advised where to push and pull, when to hang back and even drop out. It was delicious musical food and I wolfed the lot down.

Our journey back was not in an empty, newsprint-strewn carriage. It was with London's knackered, pallid workforce pressed lovelessly against each other. I discerned a malign energy across the aisle as Christian offered his two-penn'orth on Kyle's first rehearsal. "He's a fucking jazzer."

The newspapers held by the bean-counters I was wedged between began to rise.

On the journey in, I was a guilt-ridden, half-baked drum banger with the dimmest of prospects. Now, I had it all. The orders I'd just received from my leader had me twitching with excitement and expectancy. The deal had delivered. As well as being able to up our weekly wage, Lucas had told me to go out and purchase a kit. 'The best one, for the best band, H,' he'd said, with a debonair, film star smile. With my rent still at dress factory levels, I'd have more cash than I knew what to do with. I'd save it. But for what? What more could you want?

Fingering the cassette Lucas had given me (the priceless master with the songs for release on it), I replied, "Great player though."

From his seat across the aisle, his eyes became hot and hostile. "I'm not messing about, you crawling, cow-towing knob."

I sensed the whole carriage stiffen. He just wouldn't have it that we were replete; money, record out, our futures - at least in the short term - assured. It was time to spell things out. "How can you have the chad?" I asked. "We're getting new gear, more dough, a record out for - "

"It's bollocks."

"Easy, Christian."

Sprawling between a pair of tense, dual-fibre suits of his own, he sneered. "That Kyle, he's from the other side. He'll turn us into a jazz/funk band."

"Rubbish. What about the deal? Ain't you excited?"

"Sellin' out."

"Ha ha! You moan all the time about your gear and no money."

"*You* should be worried about ol' Stanley Clarke back there. Jazz, I'm tellin' ya."

"That is such bollocks..." I said, sniggering.

Glancing at a red-faced, pregnant woman hanging off the rail at the end of the aisle, he said, "See f I ain't right."

"See if you're a mental ingrate."

He was up, leaning all over me, fixing me with his death stare; a nihilistic speedy-punk special. I backed into my seat,

178

laughing. "We'll see, you wretched, rhythmic bum-boy. We. Shall. See." As I laughed he became angrier. "He don't belong! We'll split up! You won't be laughing then. Imbecile."

As he glared, a quicksilver, toothbrush-rep lowered his arse over the vacant seat. Christian's boot shot out. "Aint for you!" he snarled, leathers, safety pins, swastika T-shirt. The *Evening Standard's* headline could have read, 'Vaseline-headed-nutter puts silver, sixteen-hole Marten on Tube seat, shock!' The commuter withdrew as Christian theatrically brushed the vacant seat with the back of his hand. With an elfin smile, he offered it to the pregnant woman.

When the train stopped, he flew through the closing doors. "*You're all sheep!*" he yelled into the carriage. I watched him flipping V's until the angle became impossible and the window turned black.

Mrs H's sewing-machine was hammering away as I raced up the stairs to my room. I headed straight for the stereo, pressed 'play' then stepped back half-expecting catastrophe. I flinched as Christian's opening chords chimed in. I honestly thought I'd get found out for being a blagger and a fraud, drum-wise. But, the bloke that picked up the beat, while not being all that technical, played with fire... and he didn't simply mark time either. He added something too.

Christian, like Steve, had his problems. His style was scrappy. Sometimes, you weren't sure whether he'd got in and out on time but he played with such panache it didn't matter if he scraped in. His contribution was integral. Always just rough enough.

I wished he were here in the room with me. OK, he wouldn't stand for formal congratulations and smug backslapping. Momentary eye contact through a wisp of smoke, or a sneer at my lightweight reading matter (he was all Blake and Burroughs; me, du Maurier and Dickens) would have been enough while the track pulsed along. But he rarely visited now. I wasn't much for going out *really* late and he had loads of mates that did. Anyway, we saw each other plenty, no big deal.

Of course, Lucas was right. Kyle *had* been the missing link all along. With his technical imprint on it, our sound had the class and body we'd envied in other bands.

Lucas's strange blend of vocal whimsy and conviction was the highlight. All the darkness, sex and humour I'd imagined when we played live became crystal-clear on the recordings. A prideful lump rose in my throat as his slabs of melodious, twisted prose were laid onto our earnest backing tracks.

Was this really me? A signed recording artist playing on a record? Who'd have thought it? I put my hands behind my head and immersed myself in the sound of *my* band. Then I felt it, that cranial leathery line between two fingers, that inch-long reminder of the past, a past that was being battered into insignificance by my debut single's glorious crescendo. I felt the new fresh legion too. The crusty, scabby line I'd drawn in my palm with Christian's knife on the Tube platform earlier that day. I traced the bloody ridge with my finger. Was he doing the same in Camden with his drinking buddies? Like a film, I saw him for a second on my ceiling. He'd put his pint down to stare directly at me. He didn't recognise me.

Mrs H. served me a celebratory dish of lamb and rice, tomatoes and olive oil. While the TV flickered, blinked and bubbled in the corner, she spoke about her cousins and daughters, their kids, their quirks, faults and gifts.

"They tire me out Harry," she said, hands on hips, bemused.

"I know exactly what you mean," I replied with my mouth full.

Well, of course I didn't. But I was a big fan of other people's families. When someone recounted an episode at Christmas or a cousin's birthday, I chipped in with a touching fabrication that had everybody nodding sympathetically. When it came to other people's nearest and dearest, the most inconsequential stories drew me in like a thriller. Domestic banalities filled the family-sized void in me.

At school, the boys would be agog when I told them of a latest beating or episode of familial abuse. I would be equally rapt when they related episodes of parental harmony; going out together, watching a film, telly. I learned that my way was wrong, perverse. Most dads didn't want to destroy what they created.

"How's your mother?" asked Mrs H, pouring tea.

"I went around there last week. She's very well, promoted again!"

"She told me."

I glanced up warily. She'd not been here again, had she? Hadn't I left home for goodness sake! She'd been here twice in two months. On one occasion, I'd managed to duck down the alley at the top of the road when I saw her little car; the other, I hid in the box room, sitting on the flowery bed and not answering to my name.

She was dogged though, my mum. Up every monday with that office trellis on after a weekend of hiding under beds and ducking out of cupboards. A few weeks ago, we'd been playing The Lyceum and she'd wandered in after sound check! I jumped down doubting the evidence of my own eyes. It was like seeing a dog driving a car. She said she had a book for me. She handed it over and left. I told Christian - he didn't believe me.

Placing my cup on the little tray table Mrs H set out for me (the cup base didn't match the saucer, it sort of balanced - I felt it would tip off), I asked, "She been 'ere today?"

"She's a special person, Harry."

"I know, ta."

The TV mumbled beneath the sound of metal on china.

"Would you like more? I'll throw it out if you don't eat it, Harry."

"You know what?" I said smiling, almost sated. "I think I will."

Minutes later, she toed the door open carrying a salver of Cypriot delights: golden, rich and sweet. She knew I could have a fearful appetite after rehearsals but there was three times as many pastries as usual! My eyes narrowed; she'd brought them in on the pukka silver dish she kept for special, too.

I sipped more strong tea and, just as the treacle oozed from the pastry and ran down my chin, the doorbell rang. Sweet turned to ashes in my mouth as those great, black pupils peered around the door, it was as if a nervous cat had wandered into the room.

Usually and pleasantly, I was trapped behind a kit, steel and wood imprisoned me. Now, I was held captive by red flock wallpaper, the doilies on the back of the sofa, and my little table with all the knives, forks and spoons on it. My mum was office-smart, impressing Mrs Hadji with her status at work, sympathising at how hard it must be to be 'on your own'. I sniggered inside, deep inside, 'if only, eh mum?'

"I'll make a fresh pot," said Mrs H, picking up plates and cutlery and looking down with envy at what must have seemed a touching cameo of a family reunited.

As the door shut I spoke. "How's dad?"

"He's on these new painkillers for his back."

"Can't work out if that lowers or raises his handicap?"

"Why do you have to be like that?"

"Like what?"

"Can't we just have a normal conversation?"

Dabbing at pastry flakes on my jeans, I replied, "*Normal* conversations tend to be about normal people, mum."

She spoke in a whisper, the doe eyes flitting at the door. "You talk as if it was our fault. Look how you behaved, the destruction, in trouble with the police. Being summoned to the school... with *my* job!"

Never heard her voice soft to me. Even as I pressed pastry flakes on my tongue, my pulse quickened. I was back there with all the cowbell confusion and apricot fear. "Your father said - "

"Yeah," I cut in. "What did the great man say, *mum...*"

The rage rocketed upwards, but I was practised at keeping cool and steady now - stages, studios, the pressure to perform in chaos. I exhaled. "Nah, you're right mum, let's forget it. Years ago anyway."

Mrs Hadji reappeared with a salver of disparate cups and saucers. Placing a selection of pastries between us, she said, "They're very sweet..."

While my mother lectured about job opportunities for the mature woman, I watched an idiotic game show evolve like mould on a slice of bread.

My mum spoke. "What are you watching Harry?"

"How can anyone believe that bloke?"

Mrs H piped up. "He gave away a thousand pounds last week. I think he's kind, I think he helps them with the answers."

"It's all bogus."

"Harry's so cynical about entertainment, now he's a 'professional'."

They both smiled and I tried my best to perk up. As the credits rolled the announcer said there was a film on next.

"They've got some good old films on, Mrs Ferdinand."

"Yes they have, Mrs Hajinikolas," said my mum.

At the front door I shivered in a T-shirt.

"Harry?"

"Yes mum?"

"Did you like that book?"

"Really good. Steinbeck. Really good."

"You'll enjoy that one then," she said, nodding in the direction behind me. "I've had a few problems with my salary." She gripped the clasp on her black patent handbag. The lamppost made a halo of her bouffant. "I had to change my account. You know the manager at Barclays?"

"Well no, I don't, but what's up?"

"I'll never ask this again, but, now that you're working, I wonder if you could lend me, and I mean lend, because I'll have the new account set up next month, the holiday's slow, every - "

"How much?"

"Could you spare a hundred?"

"Yeah." I hared upstairs, dipped into my leather and brought down the cash.

"Thank you, we're all proud of you."

"Even dad?"

The smile she gave me was the one she gave everyone that enquired about her enigmatic husband, a polite, blank, leave-alone.

I hugged my arms around me as she hesitated at the car door. "Oh Harry, good luck with the record."

"Probably come to nuffin," I said, backing up and slowly shutting the north wind out.

"That was nice wasn't it, Harry?"

"A lovely surprise, Mrs H," I said picking up the copy of *Saturday Night And Sunday Morning* my mum had brought for me.

184

19

Thursday Night

Christmas one year later.

"Whajewhave?" I asked.
"Jag."
"Jag."
"Daimler."
The dressing room they gave us wasn't at all salubrious, more like an old hospital waiting-room than a pop star's boudoir but, they all had to do it from here.

We were enjoying the NHS-style recliners, opening drawers and admiring the lights that framed the mirrors, when Jenny, one of the many helpful employees from our record company, popped her head around the door. "Union rules, gents," she said, pleasantly.

From TV Centre we took a cab to a budget studio a mile or two away. Once there, we took part in a bizarre charade involving a sloppy re-recording of our single so that the Musicians' Union rep that accompanied us knew that we played on it. When his back was turned, Jenny replaced the substandard tape we'd just recorded with the produced master we'd mime to on *Top of the Pops* and we drove back for breakfast.

The café at White City was strewn with Christmas bunting and hummed with freshly squeezed employees. Pressing our noses against the window, we peered into the *Blue Peter* garden as if it were a portal on the universe. "Look," said Lucas reverentially. "There's Shep's monument."

We were all humbled at the sight. It was like finding out that Santa was actually real. "Can't believe we're here,

185

Christian," I said, squirming with excitement, but Christian gave me nothing. "Christian, I said..."

"Yeah, I heard you."

He smiled but it wasn't the old smile. It was the new one. That's not to say the new one was markedly different from the old. But I knew. The new one was jaundiced and stubborn. Initially, I assumed it was because the drummer's observations and amusing asides now bored the shit out of him, but it wasn't that. He'd been wearing that phoney look, on and off, all the while our single had crept inexorably up the charts. Since it had finally broken into the top twenty, it was more prevalent than the real one.

Kyle nodded. "Remember when they dug that pond?"

A year on, Kyle wore black leather and the mousey mane had been shaved to a severe crew-cut. As Christian's smile waned, Kyle's had broadened.

"Yeah, the pond," I said, marvelling.

Each of us had watched dogs and tortoises age, seen abseiling presenters hand out badges and tuned in weekly as the bulbs lit incrementally on one of those charity pyramids. As we swilled tea and wolfed eggs on toast, we recounted favourite episodes and it was funny, because we all had the same ones.

I lived for these moments when there was just the four of us. It was rare that there weren't any crew or record company bods tugging us towards a stage or car now. Our fledgling brotherhood, when we lumped our own gear and travelled on the Tube together, appeared quaint, an amateurish early chapter, now. It seemed absurd to think that we were once paid in clothes and kebabs and had to make our way home from The Electric Ballroom or Marquee on the night bus with the people that had seen us. These contracted days, we were a well-oiled unit, fed and watered by corporate minions. They laughed at our asides, lit our fags and told us 'Better not'

186

every now and again. We knew our place and expected everyone involved to know theirs too. We'd become pros.

At that moment, I glanced behind me at the end of an era. I recalled the toilets in The Vortex where skinheads sold speed to punks and how it didn't matter if you couldn't play as long as you turned up and looked fierce. There was Christian and me, sprinting past the bemused gentry on the Kings Road with a dozen, middle-aged Teds at our heels dying to give us a kicking because punks slagged off the Jubilee. In my mind's eye, through gales of gob and lager, I played my heart out at the Roxy and 100 Club and everyone was in a band or designing T-shirts or going on a march. But my memories had a dog-eared, sepia feel and I knew, even as I sat eating Weetabix in the heart of state broadcasting, that those delicate, ephemeral years had already been erased by momentum's flat palm.

My greatest regret was that the wind-downs at Christian's flat were no more. Those after work evenings, almost three years of them, drinking beers and listening to him strum his 'album' on an acoustic had become precious to me. Only when I heard his surprisingly mellow vocals could I allow my mind to aimlessly drift. I'd glimpsed serenity while he'd put verse to chorus and changed key. It was around the time we signed on the dotted line that he'd withdrawn my 'sofa' privileges. Now, I only saw him at work but that was no big deal, we worked seven days a week.

So, I wasn't maudlin. I had a record in the charts. I mean, who'd have ever thought that? Mopping up the remains of everyone's breakfast I was imbued with positivity. I wiped my mouth and considered my comrades with satisfaction.

Christian shook his head at me. "Look at him... grinnin' simpleton."

I smiled even more goofily. "Just happy."

"Let him enjoy it, Christian," said Lucas.

"It's the minister of fun…" Christian pronounced, caustically. Lucas raised his eyebrows and looked away.

Although no one wanted any aggro, especially this early, I was marginally relieved that even if Christian didn't feel like smiling, at least he felt something.

Jenny appeared. "Run-through time, boys. Follow me."

I stood and stretched. This was it, pop-pickers.

Passing beneath huge portraits of Bruce Forsyth and Cliff Richard, I wondered what my old man would make of me, his own flesh and blood, among his idols? I'd called my mother and told her that I was going to be on. I couldn't see her face, but by the tone of her voice, I was convinced that the scaffolding had come down and that something very rare had replaced it: a smile. We shuffled along labyrinthine corridors, past make-up rooms and production offices, until Jenny ushered us through thick double-doors and into that famous sound-stage. And there we were, on top of the known world.

Facing our stage were two others with equipment set up in front of sparkling backdrops and walls of lights. I craned my neck at a galaxy of bulbs and TV monitors. My face filled a dozen screens. I waved; it was definitely me.

The operation was very streamlined. We were regarded as little more than musical props, cogs in the wheel of the monolith that was *Top Of The Pops*. While I waited for our cue, I recalled Steve Harley's soulful contortions, Rod Stewart playing football and Stevie Wonder's tank top. I wondered if those gods had performed on this very stage? Kyle wandered in front of the kit. Like me, he was buzzing. "Remember the Stones... The Beatles!"

"I know, mental... *All you need is love...*" I sang.

As was his way, he looked for the correct notes before joining in.

"*Oi!*" Lucas called over his shoulder as they cranked up our intro. Smirking, I watched Kyle scramble confusedly across his fretboard but I stopped soon enough. Suddenly, there was a camera a foot from my face so I looked mean and slapped the pieces of white lino that covered the skins like a RADA-schooled thespian.

Kyle and me tripped and giggled along the corridor on the way back to the dressing rooms. Even Lucas cracked his face but Christian was as preoccupied as ever.

"It's a pop dream come true," I said, gently barging him. I wanted him to sparkle because it was our moment to shine.

He strummed his guitar ferociously and snarled into Valerie Singleton's huge, smiling mouth. "Be fuckin' good if we didn't have to mime," he said.

Lucas walked backwards facing us. "This three-minute slot does more for our exposure than a fifty-date tour. So be a fuckin' pro. Everyone else has to do it."

"Exposure?" he repeated, biliously. "Why do we have to do what everyone else does?"

"Cos we have to compete.'"

"Never compete!" He turned away.

Lucas looked at me and put a forefinger beneath one mascara'd eye. "Have a word with him," he mouthed, nodding at Christian.

The last door we passed before taking the stairs to our dressing room was Dreamstate's and they were *still* number one. During our run through they'd taken their place on the stage opposite ours. They were well used to the *TOTP* routine having been in the charts three or four times before.

I detected very little of the mongrel about them as they flounced around with their expensive gear and record company arsewipes. All were six-footers - styled, manicured and noble. As they posed for some stills, they looked like the

German football team lining up for the anthem.

They acknowledged us as we came off. After all, we were all in the charts now, all 'entertainers'. Raif Le Heart, their drummer (probably the best out there), was dark and built like a middleweight. He shared a joke with the bass player before running around his kit with blurring technique. He was a flash bastard. I tried to memorise the fill he'd played but the sequence was so complex, thinking about it made me walk crooked.

With an hour to go before our big moment I felt my eyes slowly shut. When I awoke there was only me and Kyle in the dressing room. "Where's Christian?"

"Went out half an hour ago."

I sat up. "Where the fuck would he go round here?"

"Said he was meeting someone outside."

I couldn't believe Kyle had let him walk out of the place. "Kyle, what if he don't come back in time?"

"Why would he do that?" As he returned to his magazine, Jenny poked her head around the door. "Ready, boys?" she asked excitedly.

My palm went up. "Fine." The door shut. "Oh Christ, Kyle."

Kyle slammed his magazine down. "He said he'd be back in time, *prat.*" He picked up his bass and I followed him outside.

As was now the way, Lucas had his own dressing-room and we met him by the stairs. He had changed into a mustard-coloured rubber T-shirt. He looked like a tank in it. "Where is he?" he asked, widening a freshly blackened eye.

"Went to get a... sarnie…"

"A *sarnie!* Harry?" he said, widening both eyes with disbelief.

We stood stock still for a terrible thirty seconds until we

saw him weaving through another band and their acolytes at the end of the corridor. "There he is." I almost jumped and clapped.

As he passed me I asked, "Whajewhave, choonah?"

"What *are* you on about?" he said, scowling and opening the dressing-room door. He looked shattered and - what was most unnerving - completely pissed off.

This was, looking back, the first time I admitted to myself that Christian's new brown friend was more attractive than his old one. I'd been kidding myself that this was a phase, some kind of fashion, but his indifference to all that we'd worked so hard for, convinced me I now came a long way second... along with the band.

With Lucas muttering through his press-ups and Kyle executing blistering scales up and down his guitar, I caught my breath. This was it. I began to drum on my knees until I couldn't bear the stinging. It was stupid really, it wasn't as if we were about to play for real.

A moment later, Christian, guitar on, stepped out of the dressing-room. His spikes glinted as he slumped at the foot of the stairs. I wandered over. "This is it, mate…" I held out my hand. I could see the faint purple line he'd made on the Tube platform a lifetime ago. I wanted him to say those words, 'blood brothers' because we'd come a long way from eating scraps and bunking the Tube. He glanced at my hand, looked away and offered the limpest of wrists.

I felt my hackles rise. "Oi!..."

Jenny appeared at the top of the stairs. "Right boys, let's go."

As we walked towards the stage she whispered in my ear. "Can I get him some water?"

"Nah, he'll be alright," I said.

"Post-tour fatigue, Jenny," said Kyle.

"It's quite common," I assured her.

From my kit, I gazed across the floor at a dance act playing a tune I'd heard countless times on the radio. As the girly backing singers beamed into the cameras I tapped along, feeling like a viewer myself. A round of cheering signalled the end of their performance and the intro to ours. As one, the audience turned and surged towards us. Dozens of eyes dissected us from a few feet away.

It really wasn't a gig. The front rows consisted of a mob of cheesy weekenders and little kids. Everyone *had* to look like they were having the time of their lives even though they were being brutally shepherded from one place to another by the show's callous, in-house goons.

The DJ gave it his gushing best and my heart raced as he announced our name and chart position. The track bleeped in and for three minutes we mimed our arses off. It was mad up there with the audience clapping and hooting like we were a covers band at a Christmas party.

Our broadcasting debut ended in a flash and the crowd migrated to stage three leaving us dangling, mute, but ecstatically in the moment. I suppose, like going to Wembley or meeting royalty, it was something to tell your grand-children when you're old and stupid.

Kyle shook his head as we walked along the noiseless corridor to the dressing rooms. "I never ever thought I'd do that, *never*," he said.

Lucas laughed aloud. For a moment, *TOTP* had reduced him to mortality. "We've done it now. Christian?"

His face hardened as he spoke. Christian was miles behind leaning wearily against a poster of *The Two Ronnies*.

Lucas nodded in his direction. "State," he muttered.

With beer in hand I found a phone and triumphantly rammed the coppers into the slot.

"Hello... hello..."

Silence yawned down the line. "Hello?" I repeated.

"Hello, Harry?"

"Did dad see me, mum?"

"How are you?" The scaffold was well and truly tightened. The person speaking was not the one I saw on a monthly basis. There wasn't an inkling of the affable conversationalist, the person that asked, on a superficial level admittedly, about what I did and how I did it. How could she turn to stone so easily? I couldn't work it out. Not seven days ago we had met over a cuppa in Palmers Green to chat and exchange another of her old Penguins for a hundred quid? '*Why so cold, mum?*'

"Just been on *Top Of The Pops*, mum! I told you the other day, in the cafe. You said you'd watch!"

I realised, as I gawped at the emergency numbers in the booth that where she stood, you were not allowed to answer freely.

"We… we watched the other side…"

"I wanted dad to see me… I done it for him, mum," I said quietly.

The stairs creaked behind her. Pressure on steps three, four and five. The receiver rustled for a second.

"Dad?"

His voice was like thunder rolling across the fields at the back of the garden. "We do not watch *shit* in this house."

The line went dead.

Replacing the phone with care, I gazed into Terry Wogan's vast, pixilated eyes. They gave me nothing. When a group of *BBC* sweaters swept past emitting pleasant, ecclesiastical smiles, I returned what must have looked like a death-head skull.

Christian was in our dressing room. I wanted to fall into his arms and weep my hurt and confusion all over him. "Thought you'd be caning that bar," I said, summoning up a trace of the old funky chicken resolve. "Free for us. Record company said - "

"Nah, I'm off."

"*What?* You can't go. There's a huge after-show. It's fuckin' Christmas."

"Something's come up."

"Come up? Bollocks. Let's get down that bar."

He put his leather on and patted his pockets. "They're all wankers," he said.

"You'll be in your element," I replied.

He too, gave me nothing. I blocked his way. "Why you being like this?"

For a second I was aware of a sweet, sickly odour. I'd smelled it before on him. "What you doing to yourself?"

His eye would not meet mine. "Out the way," he said, opening the door and stepping into the passage.

I followed him out, spun him around and thrust my hand an inch from his face. "What about this? Blood brothers. What was all that about?"

Three more chunky sweaters were walking towards us. Each of them wore a Santa beard. One had a scarf of tinsel. I held Christian's arm tight.

"Take your fuckin' hands off me!" he shouted hoarsely, squirming to break free. In regimental order, the three wise men turned around and walked the other way. Still I held him. "Me or it, Christian. You make your fuckin' choice, cos you walk out of here, I'll know it was all bollocks."

He sneered and brushed past me.

All the bands, technicians, liggers and execs were in the bar when I arrived. Feeling numb on the outside but super-sensitive on the inner, I edged my way through the crowd and ordered a round for myself.

Kyle came out of nowhere and gave me a quizzical look.

194

"What's up with you?"

"Nuffin," I knocked back one vodka after another. "Lucas about?"

"Packed off in his car with that Jenny."

"Good. I won't have to look at his miserable boat."

Kyle shrugged. "Christian?"

I shrugged.

"Then I won't have to look at his."

"Its been left to us to uphold our band's good name."

"It has."

Our glasses touched and we drained them.

Kyle, as was his way, had latched on to the backing singers from the soul band on before us. Lorraine was already merry, swept away with it all like me. She said she'd called her mum and dad, her brother and a couple of her mates the minute she'd come off. She couldn't believe she'd been on the show and wanted to make the day count, because you never knew if you'd get on it again.

I chatted with Duffy, the drummer from another band that had been on. We toasted our momentous day. His girlfriend said that their flat was packed with mates witnessing his TV unveiling. He said he'd never hear the end of it when he got home. "Brilliant," I said, downing another.

Dreamstate and their substantial entourage monopolised one end of the bar. "They're *really* doing the business," said Duffy.

"Yeah, number one album as well."

"He's brilliant that Raif."

"Even his miming's great." We both laughed.

I couldn't see the great man. "Where is he?"

"He was there a second ago."

Just then, Dreamstate's entourage opened like petals on a flower. I watched them peel away until only two people remained. With matching frilly shirt and blouse, they looked like the embossed portrait on a wedding invitation. The man was tall, dark and handsome, and in his muscular embrace, a fair woman with short, blonde hair, gazed into his eyes.

In a soft-focus, milk and Smarties moment, my world stopped spinning because, I swear, a few feet from where I stood, Susan was in the arms of my *cha-cha-ing* old man.

Duffy patted my shoulder. "You alright, Harry?"

I turned left and right but the merry throng hemmed me in.

"Oi! Harry mate," said Duffy. "You look like you've seen a ghost."

"Oh no," I mumbled, pressing myself against the bar as Raif and his companion appeared to glide along a luminous path towards me.

I reached out, blubbing. "Not her…"

"Fucking sort yourself out." Kyle was at my side whispering harshly. "Your honour. The band."

"What?"

He took hold of my arm. "Come on Harry."

Startled shouts and spilled drinks accompanied our chaotic bunting-snagged withdrawal but Kyle was unstoppable. "Keep on movin'."

After passing through the reception area with my eyes streaming, I found myself in a stupidly flash limo with Kyle. In there with us were the two girl backing singers and a couple of geezers from their record company. I took a huge wipe at a bottle of vodka as Kyle whacked the music up. The barrier rose at the gate, the old soldier saluted and Kyle began to move his head like a bull on a mission. I moved mine in time with him.

"Ooh, look at the rhythm section," said one of the girls as Kyle and me did our neck dance.

In Legends the new romantics fluttered prettily, their

costumes garish and gaudy. Chatting and pouting, they preened each other's ruffs like camp gibbons. I caught our reflection in the mirror behind the optics. We looked a little basic in our biker jackets, like peasants in the burgeoning age of pomp.

"Changed, innit?" said Kyle.

"Not much," I said, wondering where all the grizzled warriors had gone. These places used to be rammed with the raw-boned combatants that fought Thatcher and ran with the miners. Through my whiskey and coke, I speculated on the fate awaiting those safety-pinned veterans, the frontiersmen that had kicked down the barriers so everyone, me included, could have a chance. Was their destiny to be that of the Beefeaters at the Tower? Frozen in Polaroid, wedged between Japanese grandmas waiting for the flash to go off? They'd won the war but lost the peace.

I swilled the ice in my glass. "Won d' war but lost d' peace…"

"Wha…?"

"Nuffin," I mumbled, directing the glass at my lips.

Like a true rhythm section, synchronised to the milli-second, we decided we'd had enough at the same time. "*We're on Top Of The Pops*," we sang to the synthesised hymn they played. The band singing it had been on the programme with us earlier. I think we were higher up than them? '*Did he listen to them? Tap his feet to that beat and not mine?*' I put my hands under my ears for a moment, I wanted to demonstrate neatness and care in hairdressing to the new ones.

Kyle gave me a beery nudge as we joined in with the chorus again. "*We're on Top Of The Pops,*" we sang, drowning out vocalist's lisping, new wave attitude. "*We're on Top Of The Pops,*" the soul girls chimed (in better style, admittedly).

I was mystified that the clubbers didn't join in. Why they steered clear and chose not to commune with us on this great day? I staggered along the bar and put my arm around a frilly-shirted stranger. "Oi, never mind that," I said, referring to the song that was playing, "Lucas mate, top band..."

"Seen better days," said the courtier.

"What?" I mumbled, pawing thin air.

When our backing vocalists slid onto the dance floor, Kyle and me reeled away to join them. We jumped up and down, knees up muvver style, singing, "*We're on Top Of The Pops*," to everything the DJ played, regardless. My vision blurred and hopped with the beat. I had never felt so drunk.

Lorraine laughed and pushed me away when I attempted to snog her. Losing balance, I skidded backwards, missing Kyle's outstretched arm and pirouetting towards a table of trendies minding their own foppish business. Cocktails orbited my head like a baby's mobile. Through the panic and oaths, I slumped to the floor, a vacant infant, cross-legged at prayers.

Lager was poured over my hair. It cascaded down my neck and back making me shiver and fizz. I caught my breath and touched my face. It was pins and needles, numb. All was slow from down here; people walked like dinosaurs, their legs trunk-thick while their forearms, short and stunted, paddled the space ahead. Sounds became elasticated, ideas clipped and unfinished. Amongst the chair legs and broken glass, I blinked up at a concerned monster and smiled with relief when I saw it was Kyle. Laughing and pointing, he bent to haul me up but was wrenched from my eye-line by a couple of furious dandies. Gasps and shrieks punctuated a synth-coated new wave anthem. Suddenly, nobody was doing that cocky, hip-swaying, finger-clicking dance to it. When I managed to stand, a sobbing girl in a lacy blouse smacked me in the eye. Like a calamitous maitre d', I windmilled into yet another table. On this occasion, the beautiful ones had abandoned it like last week's trousers, quickly. Standing amongst the debris, I flung my arms wide and yelled, "*We're Lucas, you funny-looking fuckers, and we made it!*" All retreated, repulsed by the beer-sodden-leather-clad man with the wonky grin.

It was all too much for a meaty fellow with a beauty spot on his blue chin and a hairstyle like an ice-cream cornet. He rolled up his pleats and headed menacingly towards me. Coolly, I measured his approach. The balls, definitely. A kick in the balls then get the head down and flail away. I raised my foot an inch but he was on me.

My arms flapped uselessly as bangs and flashes went off behind my tightly shut eyes. Holding my collar with one hand and shouting something about his girlfriend, his fist went through my flimsy, booze-soaked guard like a piston.

Kyle pulled him off and waded in. For a split second, the bloke looked like a ninety-nine. The needle scratched across a disc and the room collectively inhaled the silence. Next to me, Lorraine was flinching and crying with her mate. I turned apologetically. "Sorry… good night though," I mumbled, before singing a snatch of the *Top Of The Pops* theme to cheer her up. To my sorrow, she remained cowed.

"Come on." Kyle hauled me up the stairs, past the girl with the guest list and into Regent Street. As we staggered past Hamleys, I stopped and puked my guts up in the doorway.

Kyle watched with drunken detachment. When I looked up from my boots he was studying the Christmas display in the window. "Fancy another?" he said turning from Santa to Soho.

20

Christmas

Oz, one of the blokes in the limo from White City, was at Gaz's Rockin' Blues. "Fucking hell, Harry. You been in a fight?" he said, rearing at the sight of me.

"Minor fashion disagreement," I yelled, over the band wailing away on stage.

He grimaced. "D'you wanna lude?"

"*What?*"

Leaning into my ear, he said, "Quaalude, calm you down…"

"Yeah, definitely. "

He passed the pill under the table. I knocked it back with whatever was handy.

"Here, have some for later," he said, pressing a number into my hand.

"Ta," I said, thinking that Christian was right; you didn't have to pay for anything when you were in the charts.

No one would meet my eye in the toilets. In the mirror, my brow looked Neanderthal with bruising and my split bottom lip had puffed up to twice its normal size.

In a moment of sobriety, I questioned what I'd done. A few hours ago I was on national TV, sparkling, now I looked like a butcher's apron. "It's all gone wrong again," I said and thought about how I always seem to end up in the bogs, leaning on a sink in a sad old way.

I splashed water on my face; it was beginning to sting. It needed anaesthetising.

"You alright, mate?" a stranger put his hand on my shoulder. I shrugged him off. "Course I fucking ain't."

Back at our table, Kyle was talking to Oz about the merits

of Brit soul or funk or punk-funk. I wanted to say something insightful, but instead I slid down the table taking my drink with me. I was blunted. I could have been a chair leg or the corner of a wall.

At five in the morning we fell into The Regency, a secret but well-used drinking dungeon. In that ill-lit, clammy hole we plotted the future with people that didn't have one. I may have taken more pills, may have got slung out?

I'd left my jacket somewhere, so digging deep into my combats, I shivered and headed for the sunlit beacons of St Pancras. Yesterday, a warm, record company-sponsored Daimler (or Jag?) could have whisked me home and I wouldn't have known about, let alone endured, the biting wind on the Euston Road.

Cringing into the carriage window, I peeped out of one purple socket at my reflection. I was undecided as to what hemisphere the blood-stained, ochre continent on my T-shirt resembled most. "Australia," I whispered hoarsely, flicking my scaly tongue across a loose tooth. "South America." As the train hissed to a halt and the doors slid back, I caressed an old friend, a lump on the back of my head, a head that was honour-bound to reap hideous revenge for the previous night's frolics.

Underfoot, puddles splintered into spiderweb shards and I rubbed the pimples on the back of my icy arms. When the old boy who sold *The Standard* outside Wood Green tube gave me an inquiring look, I smiled and shrugged. Although sickly and feeble, I managed to slide to my left and initiate the first faltering steps of the old funky chicken.

At school once, on one of the coldest mornings of the year, I'd turned up without coat or jumper. The kids gawped as I

201

strode towards the sports hall, hands, on this occasion, rammed into grey, trouser pockets.

They looked like crows behind the gym wall, warm ones.

Bob handed me his fag. "Where's your coat, wally?"

"My dad burned it." I shivered and coughed the hot chemicals out of me.

If a space ship had landed on the cricket square, they couldn't have looked more amazed. "Burned it?" they said simultaneously, rocking on their heels, eyes screwed up in bewilderment. They were trying to look into a world where your mother didn't check that every hair was in place before you left for school in the morning.

"Your fucking arms..." Pat was staring, pulling up the short sleeve of my shirt.

I lifted it past my chest and, as they gasped, I slid to the right.

'*You put your left arm up - and your right arm too - I'm gonna tell you - what you gotta do - flap your wings - feet start kicking ...*'

The old boy laughed out loud and offered me a folded *Standard*. "You can have a paper for nuffin, dancin' in this weather, son," he said. I folded it up, tapped a little thing on my thigh and set off in the direction of Mrs Haji's.

I slipped into the house like a burglar. "Mrs H?" My voice tailed off in the cold, empty passage. She'd gone away and wouldn't be back until the New Year. I had the house to myself. A bit of peace and quiet at last.

The curtains were drawn in the bedroom. In the silence, I fancied a woman's even breathing beneath the covers. Dumping my clobber, I got in, looking forward to a warm, sleepy shape to hug up to. I put my head on the pillow, reached out but touched nothing.

***

202

When a sliver of pure, bright light sliced through the curtains, I rose, pushed one leg into my trousers, staggered and fell, taking the table, the phone and all that was on it with me.

On my back, I groaned as the pain seeped into my skull, darkening grey and white matter in spiteful, pulsing swirls. Sweat-beaded, clamminess and nausea were my state. "Don't move," I muttered, feeling ancient welts on hip and rib, amazed they were still there. Drawing a resolute breath, I repeated "Don't move."

Peering across my room from carpet level, I listed all the things I would do over the Christmas period. Obviously, I would not drink any more. I'd get a load of fruit in, tidy and hoover and get my washing done. I'd promised Mrs Haji I'd paint her kitchen. I had a tub of pale blue emulsion, brushes and masking tape ready in my old box room. It'd be a nice surprise.

The carpet's yellow, green and orange fibres stretched towards the dusty skirting board. From down here, there seemed no pattern but I knew there was. "All about patterns..." I whispered, deciding I'd master that fill, that pattern of drum complexity good ol' Raif did at the *TOTP* sound-check. What was it? Two beats left hand on the first rack, one right, repeat on next tom but, in reverse and quick as fuck... *ba ba ding, ba ba dong?* A hot, sticky wave sent my stick-work cartwheeling, disintegrating over jagged rocks and crashing into the sea below. The tide was scummy, greenish, grey. I refocussed on the skirting board and was sure I could see a peachy tinge beneath the grubby white coating.

I shut my eyes. I really should improve my technique. 'You never stop learning little man'. Blessed Gel - if he could see me now. He probably did see me. All of them in Abdul's room would have sat around that telly and looked at the little scamp that had kipped on the futon. Not like you, dad?

I boaked. Clichés fitted nicely into Raifs dazzling run around his drums. 'Like you I was, like me you'll become', *ba ba ding, rest two, three.* 'Always good to my troops, H', *ba ba dong, rest two, three,* 'Your kind can't get up, it's proven'. *Ba ba ding ba ba dong ba ba ding...*

Kyle was playing some absurd classical run. 'Technique gives your imagination wings,' he said, his fingers dancing, the pads kissing the strings.

'Technique's for musos and wankers,' shot Christian, pulling both collars up, all fret buzz, thumbing the neck, making it bleed and blister across the stage.

Again, my fill exploded, fragmenting into icy strikes in my hot head.

Always rows and differences, and yet we're still here and in the charts. It was time for my kind to stand up. The pulsing, banging beat of blood through brain and heart squeezed the breath out of me. I got to my knees. I felt like I'd sprinted up a hill. If I could make it to the bed and sleep a little more, he was bound to tire. But he caught me as I raised my head. I tried to pull away but his strength was legend and I'd never beaten him in a race. After three years, scores of gigs, extensive European travel and a top ten, he'd scragged my collar down the phone in *BBC* central. A deluge; a torrent of cuffs, kicks, chokings and slaps had me ducking, weaving and tripping my way around the room. I begged aloud, "*I did it! I'm on Top of The Pops! I made it, dad. You made me and I made... it?*" But he didn't applaud or light a Stuyvesant in my honour. He looked down that equine bugle and both of us knew that wherever I appeared, I'd be an ugly embarrassment to his lineage, line and gametes.

Beneath the covers I feigned death, positive he was at the foot of the bed, standing over me like Ali did Liston. I heard him; 'Like you I was, like me you'll become.'

What *did* that mean? Was it good to be like him, was he admitting his failings? Was it a fatherly warning not to do as he had done? Maybe he loved me in his hate and was showing me the right road by altering my appearance? I buried my head in my pillow. I smelled grease, frying onions, after-shave and sweat. "Fuckin' stupid poem..." I whispered.

I swallowed another pill. It wasn't for headaches.

Snow had fallen, the world outside was muffled and white. Tossing magazines, ashtrays and towels over my shoulder I found, nestling in the bottom of an unpacked holdall, a jumbo bottle of vodka from the tour. I popped another quaalude. My stomach gurgled.

I was shivering in the kitchen, hunting food again. Opening a cupboard, I caught my breath at the mismatched array of sugar bowls, cups, saucers, plates, tea-pots and milk jugs. This is where she kept them all. I picked out translucent blue and gold lips, rose pink, rose red, tweety birds, venerable Chinamen pouring but couldn't find a double for any of them. My brain spun as I shut the doors.

Nibbling three mould-free slices of Mothers Pride, I remembered I was supposed to be working on my technique. I announced to the icy window, "I'm a drummer." I said it so that anyone near would know for sure who and what I was. Peering at the garden I'd cleared all that time ago, I squinted then reared. Although the view was white and opaque, I was sure I could see a decrepit apple tree and a pile of ashes smouldering next to it. I took a tentative half-step on the cold lino and rubbed a small circle in the condensation. The harder I peered the less was clear. A warm apricot flush enveloped me. I stepped back quickly.

Sitting on the edge of the bed, I tried to decipher the swirls and curls in the carpet between my feet. Flame-orange balls with flecks of yellow intersected black and navy ovals. I recalled I had positioned a battered leather recliner in front of me and turned it around so that its tan, leaning headrest was shoulder level, it was my rack tom. Between my knees, I'd placed a wooden stool with a meaty copy of the Haringey *Yellow Pages* on it - my snare. To my left shoulder was a baby-food encrusted highchair draped in a blanket, a hi-hat as chunky as Bonham's. Lastly, on the floor to the right of the stool, was the cherry on my cake, an old sewing-machine pedal. I'd liberated it from the factory (I had to do without a hi-hat pedal for my left foot).

Reaching for the vodka bottle, I announced, "My first kit." But, even as I winced into the recent past, attempting to recall what it sounded like, an ancient and enduring soundtrack, the saturday morning racing commentary, boomed from below. It overpowered everything with its soaring hysteria. I'll drown it out, I thought, picking up a pair of sticks. They felt like two wet asparagus spears.

Inches from the screen, I examined the paper-thin space between grass and hoof. "Which one's yours, dad?" I asked. "Nah, you never let on, do ya?"

There was a layer of grime all over me. I spat on my arm and rubbed. I *must* have a bath. I stood and reeled into the wall.

Somebody was definitely shovelling snow in the street. Scrape, tip, tap, scrape, tip, tap. I pulled the pillow over my head but voices outside filtered through. The words were indecipherable murmurs, the consonants missing in a powdery world. It *must* be the bin-men. If they'd gone back to work, then Christmas was over? Perhaps it hadn't started?

I drank vodka, popped pills and danced around like a wounded bear to old favourites, Lee Perry, King Tubby and Marvin Gaye, on the new stereo I'd bought to celebrate the baby Jesus.

***

A shout filled the vacuum. "Christian? Christian!" I muttered, bolting upright. That was him, surely? No. Then, it must be the bin-men... but, twice in a couple of days?

I ate spaghetti hoops cold from the tin, then hammered all the Sugar Puffs left in the box. For afters, I copped a 'lude. An advert appeared for this Thursday's *Top Of The Pops*. It was a very peachy, stair creaky, moment. Involuntarily, I threw the empty bottle at the set. The millisecond I let it go, I regretted it. Two milliseconds later the screen imploded. Whomp!

Although I'd smothered myself with everything: covers, jackets, trousers and all the dirty laundry from the tour, a penetrating whine oscillated around me. Damning layer upon condemnatory layer buzzed through the pillow held against my ears. '*Like you I wassss... Bottler, grassss. Zzzyou boy, Ferdinand, my office now, zzz!*' Pathetically, I retaliated. "*Go placidly, go placidly,*" I sang, out of breath. I was waiting for the talons to slice my defence like razors shredding paper. "Don't, dad!" I whimpered, balling up tight. He took his time. Peeling blanket by jacket by blanket. Tiny showers, cracks of cruelty splattered against my skull. The showers sounded like pebbles thrown at a window. Fractionally releasing the pillow, I opened one eye. It *was* someone throwing pebbles at a window, my window.

Easing myself across the bed, I pulled the curtains aside and saw, in the street, the band, Lucas, Kyle and Christian. They were gazing at my window. Lit by the lamppost's yellow glow, they looked like a Christmas album cover. Sinful carollers in the snow. I waved pathetically and opened the window. "Alright?" I croaked. The fresh, icy air was a welcome breath on my face.

Christian laughed. It was like hearing Mozart. "Chuck the keys down you dopey sod."

207

They thudded up the stairs. Click. I hid my eyes from the light. "Harry?"

Squinting through my fingers, I saw Lucas standing by the table holding the ripped out end of the phone cable.

"Oh," I said.

"Fucking hell!" Christian gazed around the room. We all did.

The TV looked particularly spectacular with the arse of the vodka bottle sticking out of it. The table, where the end of the phone cable was, was upside-down. A chipboard cow, dead on its back. Finally, in an almost seasonal tribute, a fine Sugar Puff dusting covered everything.

Lucas's mouth remained open. "Your face!"

"Cup a tea, boys?" I said, flicking my wobbly tooth.

Lucas turned, shaking his head. "I'll see you downstairs," he said. Kyle followed.

Grinning, Christian leaned against the door while I hunted for socks. I looked at him quizzically as I pulled them on. Did he have amnesia? Did he not recall our last acrimonious goodbye?

"You wanna photo?" he asked, fit and clean-shaven.

"You alright now?"

His smile was angelic. "Blood brothers," he said, winking.

Tears welled up as I gripped his hand. "You're finished with all that shit?"

"Yeah, knocked it on the head."

I pulled my trousers on as he plugged the phone into the wall socket. "Go downstairs, H," he said. "Gotta make a quick call."

On the landing I heard him. I couldn't make out anything he said but a wave of defeat washed over me at the secretive tone employed.

Lucas' mouth had shut by the time I stepped into the

passage. He nodded towards the stairs. "What was it, drugs?"

"A failed seasonal experiment, Lucas," I said, pushing my feet into my boots.

"Disappointing, Harry," he said. "Sort it out."

Christian was laughing as he jogged down the stairs. "Leave the bloke alone, Lucas. It is Christmas."

"I think you'll find it's over."

"Not officially. Fink *you'll* find it goes on to January the sixth."

"How perverse that the most irreligious person I know, keeps that date handy," said Lucas, turning and walking out.

Christian grinned, pressed his hands together and looked saintly. *"Tis the season to be...."* he sang shrilly. Then he slumped, pulled a miserable face and finished flatly, *"Gloomy!"*

He walked out of the house, confident that he'd amused with his latest dig at our leader, but I was impassive as I locked the door behind me.

Lucas sat in the front of the car, Kyle, me and Christian in the back.

"Really thought you were in a ditch somewhere," said Kyle, smiling ruefully at the memory of our not-so-legendary last night out. He sported a livid graze across his forehead and plasters on the knuckles of one hand. Although faded, my black eyes were still apparent. He peered at my face. "You look like a panda," he said.

As the cab turned left at the corner shop, I spoke to the back of Lucas's head. "Had that winter flu as well... *and* post tour fatigue."

"Got over it?"

"Completely recovered. It's a miracle, a biblical miracle," I said, rubbing my hands together. "So boys, what's occurring?" Looking left and right I sensed the tension we

209

generated moments before we went on stage. No one would speak or look at me. "Well?" I asked.

"He don't know," said Kyle, genuinely surprised.

"Know what?"

As we drove on in silence an old anxiety bubbled inside me. Again, Lucas spoke without turning around. "You really don't know, do you Harry?"

"Know what?"

He finally turned to face me. He smiled. A pleasant enough experience, but unnerving, apropos of calling for his drug-addled drummer a bit after Christmas. He wasn't performing, or near a particularly stunning girl or interested business man.

"What?" I said, flinching from a smile far too big for a cab.

"I've got something to say Harry. It's very important."

Head bowed, tired and not a little peckish, I waited for whatever fate was going to serve up next. Then Lucas laughed and did something very un-Lucas like, he rapped gently on my forehead with his knuckles. Slowly, I raised my guilty head. His eyes were, for once, trained on me alone. "We've done it Harry," he said. "We're number one."

"What, us?"

A huge cheer went up and they were all patting my dopey head.

As the cab wound its way through North London I could see the driver beaming in his rear-view and who could blame him. I mean, how many times in his life is he going to pick up a band with a number one?

"Jenny reckoned six was as high as it could get!" I said, trying to find some kind of rational, logical reason for this momentous thing and my place in it. "I had no idea."

"If you had a telly that worked…" Lucas said, from the front seat.

"It did... when did you find out the chart?"

"If you had a phone that worked."

"I did..."

"I called you loads. The line was dead. Sent Christian round."

"No one home," Christian chipped in. "So we've been auditioning drummers for a couple of days. You're lucky we couldn't find anyone ugly or crap enough. You're irreplaceable, Harry."

Gentle laughter pervaded the cabin and I felt a warmth and security the rest of the world had never afforded me. Resting my head on Christian's shoulder, I shook Kyle's hand while Lucas ruffled my bonce. For a moment, the tarmac length between lampposts, we remained blissfully flummoxed.

We were only doing what we loved, toiling at something that came naturally, and yet we'd attained this hallowed state. I eased myself into the leatherette and let the satisfaction percolate through me.

Then I sat up. "But tomorrow isn't Thursday, is it?"

"We're pre-recording in a couple of days," said Kyle. "There's so much on. We're in...?"

"Manchester tomorrow," said Lucas, gravely. "Bus leaves the Cally at two, no oversleeping."

I nodded as seriously as I could but, my wonky grin refused to budge.

"Then it goes mad. *Top Of The Pops* again; Birmingham," said Kyle. "Newcastle? They're gigs, then Berlin which is a TV, Saturday, er...."

"Nah, Milan before," said Lucas.

"So gigs, Madrid, Hamburg, Paris then TV Berlin on..."

"Next Wednesday."

"Yeah, Madrid, a TV there as well... on Thursday. It's top ten there."

"Blimey!" I said, overwhelmed.

211

"Mime is money."

We all laughed. The driver loudest of all.

"Pull up here, mate."

Lucas turned around as the engine idled. "Be pros, boys," he said, before striding into the night.

"How many places did it go up?" I said as we pulled away.

"Twelve," Kyle said.

"Unbelievable. 'Ere, Christian?"

Christian was staring through the window. I couldn't think of anything better than to go to his for one of those monster fry-ups. He knew just how I liked it; a little charred, oily and plenty on the side. We'd put something on... probably Al Green or Aretha and he'd strum along and we'd talk about his album and our brilliant future. It'd be just like it was, before... before we'd got up the charts.

"Them stones on the window," I said, shaking my head. "Thought I'd heard something. So, it was you, Chris - ?"

"Stop here, mate," he said, patting the driver on the shoulder.

"But I thought we - "

His face was blank while he located his new smile. "Got this bird, Harry."

"Have ya?" I said, disappointed but not surprised by how easily I entered into this fresh bout of insincerity.

"You don't know her." He stared past me, enthused now that we'd communed on this bogus wavelength. "Met her down The Railway before the tour... Got a bit involved. She had someone else..."

"She come to The Empire?"

"You won't believe this, but she doesn't like us. So no. Sorry mate. You of all people should understand," he said, raising his brow and widening the smile that wasn't really a smile but a collection of muscles doing what they were told.

I nodded quickly, "Course, course..." I said.

He, like Lucas, strode away without a backward glance.

Kyle's eye met mine. I think, at that moment, as we watched Christian disappear into Camden Town's throbbing numbers, we accepted Obfuscation and Denial, our profession's fatal twins, into our band. They slide so seamlessly in when you're right up the charts. I mean, what kind of idiot would imperil the delicate machinery that got you to number one with truth and confrontation?

Kyle nudged me. "You can come to mine, Harry. We do have food and hot water in Hackney..."

21

Manchester

After telling the driver I wouldn't be a minute, I turned and made my way past the low numbers. I sensed the change immediately. My heels overlapped flagstone cracks they'd previously slotted into, while my shoulders brushed privets that once skimmed my hair. Halfway up the road, my fingers traced the mortar contours of a front-garden wall they'd traced a thousand times before.

I would have liked him to come out of that flakey door squinting into the midday sun. He'd be darkest bronze, counting golf tees as if they were doubloons he'd dug up in the garden. Did that curtain twitch just as I did? Was that me, the ravenous truant, peeking out as in one liquid movement, he *cha-cha'd* around the gate stuffing those tees back into hugging, black slacks? From my window relief, I'd observe the ubiquitous quad-stretch at the driver's door, the snap of neck left, right, left before the backward slide into the V8 spaceship, clubs a-rattling in the boot.

"He's gone," I'd whisper to the silent house. Then I'd head for the kitchen, my spirit soaring.

My finger left the wall. I missed him, now. But why? Well, for a start, he did look cool and there is other stuff, there really is. If he came through that door now, my heart would surely soften at the baleful sight of him.

'*Dad, it don't matter. Top of the Pops, fuck all of it,*' I'd say, expunging the years of misery with that simple, banal sentence. Just the sight of him doing what he did best, getting the correct thumb position at the zenith of his backswing (minus club), would have me laughing, leave me comfortable with that attention to a seemingly useless detail - because I do the same thing. Of course he'd scowl at me and say something like, '*You can never be serious like a man.*'

I'd take the keys from him. He'd be addled, posh addled and I'd say, '*Nah, dad, I'll drive you. I owe you that. You always drove me. All them football matches you stood on the touchline. Thanks for your support.*'

He'd still be mute as I turned the engine over. I'd put the clutch in (before putting it into gear) and I'd ask casually (as I mirrored, signalled, manoeuvred away), '*Out of interest dad, why the err, excessive punishment? Did I really grow so monstrous that that was the only solution? Look,*' I'd say, lifting my T-shirt, '*still got 'em....*'

I turned away, passed the squatting yellow blur and unclipped another front-garden gate.

Again I paused. Alan had painted the gate black. I liked it red. Almost everyone had a black gate in the road. They'd also replaced the chequered mosaic that led to the front door with plain, sandstone squares. The door was still red, a bit grubby close up though. With relief, I noticed that the locks were still there, soundly fitted and secure. So much had happened since I'd bolted through that door, with everyone in Enfield - bar her - baying for blood. But I was older, wiser, and a bit taller too. *Surely,* bygones would be bygones? If her dad had a go, I'd fend him off, reason with him. I just had to connect with her if only to hear her say 'Thanks, but no thanks, I'm engaged… to that rugger bloke... keep the jacket.'

I knocked but should have pressed the new bell. I hadn't noticed it there.

Terry wasn't barking. Of course! She'd be running him over the fields. *The fields*. I should have gone there first. As I turned, Alan's shadow loomed, darkening the frosted glass menacingly. I gulped as the door opened. But it wasn't Susan's Alan; it was another one, thinning sandy hair, a little stubble, but a few years younger and broader. He had a blue golf sweater on.

"Susan here? Susan Fernley?" I asked.

He studied my fading black eyes and busted lip warily. The door began to close. "No mate, they moved a couple of years ago."

"Oh... any idea where they went?"

"None." The door shut.

With eyes downcast, I saw, beneath the bushes and shrubs that led to the newly painted gate, a small black rectangle in the earth. It was a one-inch tile from Susan's old path. Picking it up, I spat, brushed the mud away and held it up to the sun.

Sensing the curtains shift behind me, I closed the gate and walked towards my waiting cab.

"Back to Hackney?" he asked.

"Nah, Caledonian Road, ta," I said, placing the little package I'd bought for Susan on the far end of the seat. I'd bought a tour T-shirt for her. It had a picture of me on it. There was a couple of singles and some press stuff.

The driver said his daughter liked the band.

"Er... Like I was saying, Harry, I used to play the drums. Yeah, had this band at school, but it never..."

Although every night was different - stage, PA and room - the rituals remained the same. About half an hour before we went on Lucas, hugging his mac to his sides, would sigh resignedly (as if it was his turn at the dentists) unzip his holdall and remove eyeliner, glove and that night's shirt. At this juncture, he'd be relatively amiable, able to chat about the drive or the hotel and be, as much as he could, one of the boys. But, as he scrutinised his Mary Quant (flicking through the tubes and brushes with a purple talon) his mood would alter. If, after an indiscernible point in his make-up application, you remarked on the weather, or the width of breakfast toast, he'd look at you as if you were mental, some kind of

216

trivial interloper, and you'd shut the fuck up.

After mascara had been applied to one staring eye, he'd begin to pace, mutter dark things and take short, sharp breaths. As the technicians counted and hissed into the mics, I'd tap my legs searching for fluency and feel. Beside me, Kyle and Christian would soundlessly strum, pluck and tune, readying themselves for the job ahead. With seconds remaining, Lucas's mood would intensify alarmingly. He'd perform press-ups, hyperventilate, curse and punch the walls. He'd slag the crowd off. He'd call them sheep. Create a gulf of enmity between himself and them so that by the time he went on, he was a furious, fantastic sight.

When we began, at The Vortex, Roxy and Marquee, we had maybe a dozen or so aficionados, the same faces down the front at every gig. We were on chatting terms with them. We'd occasionally donate beers and fags. Sometimes we'd give them a lift when they'd missed their train or it was pissing down. As time had gone on we'd garnered scores of this hardcore lot. Some had 'Lucas' tattoos and showed them to him while he was on stage. Others had 'Lucas' emblazoned on the backs of their leathers. All had etched his name on their hearts.

Now we were in the charts our fans were legion. The majority wore make-up identical to Lucas, a good few were hardened Christian imitators and, unbelievably, there was an occasional confused youth with a big, black bushy hairdo!

We were bursting to get on at the Manchester show, me especially. The culmination of *TOTP*, the Quaalude Christmas and Susan's inevitable withdrawal from my life had me desperate to batter skins and smash cymbals. I peeked through the dressing room door into the yellow/green wash enveloping the stage with longing.

"Give 'em hell, tell 'em nuffin," Lucas ordered. We were on.

However chaotic things were before I picked up my sticks, up there, where it mattered most, I was in control. I dictated time.

We had developed a set that started with Christian, Kyle and me going on before Lucas and cranking up the intro to our opening number. We stayed heavy, menacing and brooding as we got the feel for the stage and the sound on it. Held by a thread, the crowd searched the darkened areas behind the amps, lights and drums for their idol, but Lucas would leave them dangling a little while yet. As I thumped the tom toms, I picked out the latecomers at the back craning their necks for a better look and the sly voyeurs at the edges come to see what it was all about. Gradually, my focus shifted to the massed ranks in the centre before resting on the zealots up the front, the ones who'd call my name, mouth every word and strike every pose. Finally, after a couple of minutes of slow torture, Lucas would materialise from a blood-red wash, thumping his chest, gesticulating and hurling abuse. He'd stride from one side of the stage to the other brimming with fury. At his pumping fist, I'd pick up speed and the whole place would bounce with me.

From the kit, I watched male and female reach out to him, mascara running like tears, crimson lips smudged, gauntleted wrists and leather gloves clapping. They all paid homage and as we travelled deeper into our set, it felt like we were on an asteroid millions of miles from earth.

By the time Christian played the opening chords of the final number the room was as one. Indivisible. Regardless of player or listener, we had all gathered in the same place for the same event.

Singing the very marrow from his bones, Lucas directed the swaying mass and, propelled by both, I accelerated through the gears to the last, breakneck chorus and, at his signal, stopped and exited, to the sound of love.

***

Backstage in Manchester, my ears rang pleasantly and my wonky grin was unwipeable. The band had not let me down. Memories of panthers and childhood sweethearts were obliterated as one sweat-drenched encore after another pulverised the details. It was happening, we were 'making it' and, like underground tremors, there was nothing to do but hold on. As we towelled down and opened foaming tins, there was an atmosphere of invincibility in our dressing room. The world had started to open up, but it wasn't going to swallow us, it was going to spew our every wish. I took cabs everywhere now. Ate out nearly every night, and not bus-shelter takeaway or shop-awning chips, *inside,* my chair pulled back for me and a menu presented to my left hand. There were people employed to check if I was rested, hydrated and ready. I only needed to ask and my kit was re-skinned. Cymbals marginally smashed out of tune were binned and replaced by new, better, shimmering discs and the sticks I held were always smooth, virgin wood straight from the wrapper. Responsible persons held my passport and took care of my bags, and if my room wasn't to my liking, I'd tap a couple of digits and be offered the quieter side of the passage.

Without realising it, I'd become some kind of man-sized child, incapable of trust, independent thought, or direction. It was brilliant.

Bill Stewart, our wizened, ever-ready tour manager, was a master of surprise. That night in Manchester, instead of the anonymous four-star by the M62, we were booked in at one of the trendiest hotels in the city; a place where all the footballers, top bands (of which we now numbered) thesps and VIPs stayed. The nightclub in there was renowned, it was laid out like the interior of an aeroplane with cabin windows, reclining seats and tray tables.

219

Ambling into the hotel cloaked in my post gig high, I recognised people from the show filtering into the club next to the lobby. We'd been that night's big event and everyone knew we were staying here because *here* was where you stayed. I returned nods and clenched fists. We were all buzzing on the same rare frequency and I felt electrifying portents for the night ahead. I hugged Christian to my side. "This is it, mate. Gonna change this shirt. Comin' up?"

I let him shrug me off. He still had that toothache. "Fuck off," he mumbled, flopping onto a deep, leather sofa and glowering around the hotel's stylish lobby.

I sat beside him.

"What now?" he said.

"Nice hotel," I said, thinking of the not so distant past when we'd drive back the two-twenty miles right after the show or stay, all four of us, in an unpleasantly moist, one-room B&B.

"Fucking full a' poseurs and tossers," he said, grimacing. "Fucking selling out, we are. There's kids there tonight hitched all the way from London. Where are they now? Selfish knob."

"Good point," I said, tilting my head.

"What?"

"I've got this theory," I said.

He turned away, wincing in pain. "Oh no..." he muttered.

"Nah, hear me out."

He smouldered with intolerance. "Well, go on, Einstein."

"As you know, my erm, childhood, wasn't the happiest and - "

"'Ere we go," he said, standing up.

I pulled him back down gently. "Five fuckin' minutes, Christian."

Exhaling, he fumbled for fags.

"Right," I said. "So, I've been thinking about it. I'm looking for erm, *consistency*."

"What?"

"I'm looking for *serenity*."

"Noisiest, whiniest cunt I know."

"I'm looking for the complete reverse of my past. You see, I want calm, logical, cause and effect. I want a yes to be a yes, and a no a no. I don't want *danger* or irrational whacks and slaps simply because ... erm... well, for no logical reason."

"And your point is?"

"Well, I've met your mum and dad. They are lovely people. Dream parents, some might say. Calm, kind, intelligent and they love and are very proud of you. So, what *you* want is, cos you were deprived of it, is dan - "

"*Fuck off!*" he roared, standing over me. The reception area was still. Kyle wandered across. Where my pacifier was the raised palm, his was the sunny, boy next door smile.

"You don't know me," Christian said, jabbing his finger inches from my eyes. "You don't know what I've been through."

"A countryside ramble? Wasn't the picnic up to scratch?"

He dived on me. The punches thudded as I covered up.

Through our mutual heavy breathing, I heard footfalls and gasps as people made their way towards the restaurant at the end of the reception desk or ducked into the club, earlier than they normally would. Kyle wrenched him away and pinned his arms.

"*You bastard, Harry!*" Christian roared, held back, hurt.

Kyle looked into his face. "Oi! Calm down!"

Christian pulled away, snarling. He was flushed with indignation, but inside he quivered with vulnerability. My heart broke as I tuned into that pitiful note. I wanted to tell him everything was all right, he could say and do what he wanted, I'd always forgive him.

"Okay, there's no trouble," said Kyle, beaming at one and

221

all. "That tour fatigue… you know, the stress of it all?"

Meeting Christian's eye I mouthed, "Sorry." He ignored me.

As he sloped off, the atmosphere in the lobby altered once more. An air of excitement and not a little awe permeated through guests and staff. I looked up to see Lucas swathed in white towels, mascara running, entering the scene through the automatic doors. He was flanked by record company flunkies and simpering, tripping dollies. All eyes stayed on him as he strode towards the lift.

Kyle looked at me quizzically and nodded towards Christian. "What you say to him?"

I stood and shrugged. "Truth hurts, Kyle."

"What truth?"

"Goin' up," I said.

Walking towards the lifts, I noticed Christian settling into the economy seats with his mates. He despised me. Why couldn't I keep my trap shut and just let him get on with his life?

Lucas wiped his face as the lift doors shut on his entourage.

"Knackered," I said. "Great show though," I added.

"Not bad, Harry. You keepin' an eye on laughing boy?"

"Course. He looks better than he has for ages, I think."

He tapped his head. "It's what's going on up there."

The doors opened. He stepped out and turned left, I turned right. I paused after a few steps. "Comin' down for a drink? Looks brilliant in there."

"Nah, got a friend up from London."

We were both walking backwards.

"Have ya?" I said. "My girlfriend's left me a message sayin' she couldn't come."

"Not met her, have I?"

"Went to school with her…"

222

"Dija? That's nice."

"Not really. Anyway she's just blown me out. She's got engaged."

"Well, you're away a lot."

"Shame though..."

"You won't be lonely, Harry."

"I know that... I was just sayin'... coincidence that you've got a girl coming up from London and so had I..."

"It happens."

We paused to let Obfuscation and Denial catch their breath. "Bring her down Lucas, have a... cocktail?"

"She doesn't drink."

We turned away from each other and began walking. Then I stopped. "Great show."

"What?"

"I said, great - "

"Getting there, H," he said, turning his key.

I removed my shirt and threw it into the corner. As the door swung shut a great wave of loneliness engulfed me. I was baffled. Everything I'd wanted and loads besides had been granted, and yet there was a sense that I was being duped, that in reality, the rest of the world was having it away and I was simply marking time.

I'd seen my mum last week. We'd agreed the usual pub car-park meet, but seeing her there, cold and furtive, I thought, we can't carry on like this so we went into the pub. Imagine that, me and my mum in a pub? I had a Guinness; she, a coke. "So, mum, *Top Of The Pops?*"

She looked around the bar for a moment. "You know what he's like," she said.

That was a pretty good answer.

I told her I understood without saying I did and it dawned on me that the twins, Obfuscation and Denial, didn't hang out exclusively in bands.

But she did want to congratulate me. She'd seen my picture in the local paper and people were stopping her and saying how proud she must be of me. She didn't actually tell me she was, though. She mentioned that dad had had a row with another doctor over his back. This one said he should go for tests but the old man insisted all he had to do, was keep his left arm straight at the top of his back-swing. I asked about Susan. She said they moved ages ago, didn't I know? Fled the street, apparently.

"I went round there."

That information curtailed her vacant perusal of the lunchtime pub trade. "You went to her house?" She was shocked.

I laughed aloud. People glanced across. Mum shrank, lowered her eyes. I laughed again. "Yeah. Dad's car was there. He didn't come out."

"But... but, what if he did?"

I took a drink and wiped my mouth. "I'd a' give him a big kiss. Silly old bastard."

She blinked. "I thought you were upset about *Top Of The Pops?*"

I felt impervious and didn't regret anything. Look where I was. I'd been a world champion vandal and olympic disappointment to ma and pa, and so what? I took cabs and planes everywhere. The blokes I went to school with, the teachers, I didn't see any of them waiting for their chart position. I doubted they'd be gigging any time soon either. "Well mum," I said. "I was a bit down about it at the time. All them *Top Of The Pops* we'd watched together. I thought, at last! But I know and he knows, I ain't *ever* gonna please him, and neither are you."

"That's impertinent," she said, adopting her haughty, officey tone. Wrong paper clips, junior.

"Ha ha, I'm in a punk band, mum. That's what we do."

224

Her cheeks were red and her eyes moist. Leaning across the table, I sensed the steel bars tightening. I think it was the closest I'd been to her for as long as I could remember. "Why don't you divorce him? It's brilliant on the outside. He's ruining your life."

She pulled her handbag towards her, all buttressed and proud. "I have a life. I have a life," she said.

"Well so do I, but I don't have to live there. It isn't right in that house. Get away."

The scaffolding came down completely. "You really think you've escaped?" she said.

After a moment, she started to talk about someone at work whose kids thought we were brilliant and it'd be nice if I popped into the office to meet them. Give them something. I said I'd try to make it home for Christmas… or Easter or the summer holidays but we were really busy and - apart from the obligatory, cash for old Penguin exchange - that was that.

I flicked the TV on. A kestrel or kite was circling a field golden with corn. As it hovered on the thermals, wings feathering perfectly, I watched its beady eyes scan the meadow below. I was awed by its gravity-defying patience and couldn't take my eyes from the screen. The commentator spoke. I shook my head and turned it off.

Downstairs, Kyle and me stood shoulder to shoulder at the bar. Lining up vodka and lager, I felt brazen, number one in all departments, sparking with energy and intent. Bill informed us on the drive up that all the shows had sold out and there was bad blood between the agent and the record company for our time. We laughed. The suits were actually going to war over us! Eyes tracked us to our table. The room was full of women. Every time I looked up one would be looking at me.

Bill slid into his seat. His face wrinkled with fun. "My boys, enjoying this fine Mancunian night?"

"Yeah, Bill. Brilliant hotel."

"All part of the service. And where is the inestimable Christian?"

"Over there."

Bill gave Christian's table, replete with slouching companions, a cursory glance. "A fine guitarist but a poor judge of character." After ordering from a stewardess, he mopped his brow with his palm. "Good show?" he asked.

"Best yet," said Kyle.

"Excellent work," said Bill, rapping the table top. He looked across the bar. "I like her."

"What? In the fishnets?" I asked, glancing at a laughing girl. She was standing by the rear emergency chute with her mates.

Adjusting his headrest Bill said, "Exactly. It's her eyes. The fluttering." He waved his fingers next to his face.

"I saw her," said Kyle. "She was over my side. Knew every word."

Hovering over the room, I picked out the detail; the long bar and whirling staff, the smoky outcrops, thudding dance floor and airplane seats. I watched a figure place a bottle on his table, stand and wander past the cabin doors to the chute.

The girl was a petite, feisty bottle-blonde in fishnet stockings and oxblood DM's. Her face was purposely pale. Her lips and nails fire-engine red. She did indeed have ridiculously long lashes.

I stood to one side and spoke. "Alright?"

"You got a fag, Harry?"

"Yeah." I lit one for her and our irises made those trillion decisions in the match's yellow flare.

She wriggled to the music as if her clothes were lined with

226

itching powder. "Yeah, it were great tonight. Is Lucas coming down?"

"Nah, he doesn't go out."

"Where is he, then?"

"We keep him in a frozen capsule on the bus."

"Wha?"

"Cryogenics."

In turn, her face registered thought, disappointment and lucidity. I amused myself by momentarily waiting for the schoolboy, high-pitch whine of embarrassment to ring in my ears but it never did nowadays.

"What's your name?"

"Melanie."

"I really fancy you, Melanie. You gotta a lovely face. Good dancer 'n' all." I stepped a little closer but did not touch her. "I'd like to see you on your own, away from here." My arm circumscribed the area at my side in slow motion.

She squirmed tenaciously as the beat picked up. "Why? It's brill in here."

I took a drag. "Too noisy."

When she closed her eyes, all I could see was an indecipherable glistening. She glanced at her mates who looked on impassively.

"Come on," I said.

Without looking behind me, I walked towards the lobby and stepped into the lift. When I turned, she was behind me. I kissed her and pressed the button.

"Did *you* think it were good?" she said, drawing breath.

"Yeah, always good up here." We snogged all the way to my room.

On my bed, I was amazed at the sequence of events. From the minute I approached her to the second she unzipped her tartan skirt and let it fall in the trench between Christian's bed and mine, it was all so automatic.

***

Although we'd connected, both of us understood that this event was rapid and fleeting. A wonderful coincidence to be remembered in the weeks and years ahead with a nostalgic smile. Melanie told me she was an art student at the university. She saw all the 'decent' bands that came to Manchester and she thought we were great. I walked her back to the bar, gave her pale cheek a peck and watched her sync up with her mates on the dance floor.

The club was throbbing and on our table, my half bottle of beer was still cold enough to drink. Kyle was nowhere to be seen.

On the other side of the aisle, Christian slumped and stared, head lolling between his shoulders. I felt guilty for the things I'd said in the lobby earlier. I decided he needed cheering up and I was just the man to do it.

"Alright?" I said, squatting beside him and beaming at his companions.

Over time, Christian's mates had become mine too. I'd look forward to their quirky one-liners and enjoyed being appraised of their latest punch-ups and motorway abandonments. After a tedious drive, it was good to see them at sound-checks and hotel lobbies with their rucksacks and tallish stories. They were the remnants from the hardcore element that had followed us through the snow and ice in the years when we were the ubiquitous 'shitty support band'. I felt a kinship with them. We were all going through the same rites of passage but from different sides of the stage. But, even as I smiled, I knew I was kidding myself because this wasn't the pissed and speedy boys I'd come to know as friends, this lot were strangers. They wore mannish, sort of scruffy clothes. They'd made no effort, and everyone made an effort back then. I was instantly peeved. "Number one, eh?" I said, meeting each weary eye.

228

The uniform insincerity of their returning smiles rocked me. This was obviously where Christian had learned his. As fags were passed round, I examined them further and concluded that it wasn't their mangy aspect, the indelible grime around mouth and eyes, the unwashed antipathy, that repelled me, (or at least had me, even in my post coitus euphoria, wary), it was their simpering, quasi-religious confidence. Their bad-smell smiles gave the impression that our chart position could never feel as good as they did.

Bristling, I tried to reclaim him. "Christian, seriously, thought that was the best yet, tonight," I said, attempting to illustrate that what we did was far more important and vital than their devilish, trifling dalliances. But, in a pause in the beat, I knew that the people at this table didn't give a fuck about me, my faiths and friendships, let alone the band and how well we played. A shiver ran through me as I wondered if Christian didn't either.

One of them deigned to address me. "Yeah, good, Harry. Number one... how's it feel?"

"Whajewfink?" I shot back.

Christian slumped my way and whispered. "I think, *you*, are a wanker. Go. Away."

I reared. "What?"

I felt his lips on my ear. "Piss off..." the sibilance hissed with the dance-floor hats. Although none had landed, I wiped my face of gob.

When I stood, they were all nodding their bogus bon-homie in my direction. I could read their fuzzy minds; 'Harry you're a mug. You're in a band and you don't know how to be. You don't *really* belong. You're a fraud. You're passing yourself off. Face it, you're an inadequate that can only experience life's narrowest, mundane frequencies, whereas we have...'

***

229

Bill fished the bottle from the bucket. "Champers?" he asked.

"Ta."

"What's up?"

"Nuffin."

He attempted to fill my glass but the bottle was empty. Waving at a stewardess, he ordered another and gave me a crow's-feet-crinkling smile. "What a smashing night," he said.

Flushing Christian and his crew from my mind, I watched the stewardess pop a fresh bottle. Andy, our back-line man, slid breathlessly next to me. "All locked up, Bill," he said, handing the van keys across.

"Good lad," said Bill, dropping the keys in his aluminium briefcase and filling our glasses. "Cheers!" he proposed.

"Cheers!"

"One, two, three, four, five, senses working overtime…" I sang along with everyone, including a woman at a nearby table. I was transfixed at how her slender fingers wove through the smokey beat around us. She had dark hair and lipstick, but really subtle. She wasn't wearing anything punky, anything a 'fan' would wear and I wondered if she'd seen us tonight? With a laugh and the toss of her head, she stood and finished her drink. The way she stubbed her cigarette out had an assurance that excited me. It was the act of someone used to saying, 'time's up'.

As she passed, I nailed her with a boozy, chart-topping grin. *A Whole Lotta Love* played in my head as I detected a glimmer of acknowledgement in return. Andy offered the bottle. "Top up, H?"

Watching her stride boldly through the partying groups on her way to passport control, I placed my hand over my glass. "Left something in the room," I said, getting up and patting my pockets.

The toilets were situated between the lifts and the dining room. I loitered by the reception desk examining the logo on the biros, and the bowl of crusty, boiled sweets. As the door to the ladies opened, I turned away. When I felt her presence, I spun around.

Her hair was actually brown in the light and un-trendily long. She wore no make-up but that little dark gloss on her lips. Fine, sceptical lines tested eyes and mouth as she took me in.

"Alright?"

She reared with a touch of addled theatrics. "*Sorry?*"

"You at the Mayflower tonight?"

"What if I was?"

This time, the high-pitched whine sounded like a siren. And, it didn't fade either. What was I doing? This was an adult, probably here with her boyfriend, her husband!

"That your boyfriend?" I nodded at the bar.

"No."

I pushed myself off the desk but she didn't back away. I said the first thing that came into my head. "Fancy coming to my room?"

She stepped back aghast. "You cheeky sod. You don't even know my name!"

Without a witty line or game plan, I took her slim, cold fingers in mine. "It's preordained," I said.

As the lift doors shut, she folded her arms and pressed herself into the purple, carpeted wall. Her hips and thighs were framed in a slinky, figure-hugging dress. I felt my pulse accelerating like the gears and winches pulling us upward.

"What are you smiling at you cheeky bastard?" she said, patently astonished she was where she was.

Stepping across, I kissed her and replied, "The world and all the wankers in it."

"What an incredible ego!"

"Gettin' it seen to…"

Placing my hands on her waist, I felt those elegant, expressive fingers take my shoulders. Her body was instantly against me. I traced her spine downwards, lifted her dress and put my hand on one cold, round globe.

We fell into my room entwined, the door banging open. I back-heeled it as she unloaded in a rush. She was an art lecturer at Manchester University. She'd fancied me when she saw me on telly the other night. When she was young, her brother's mate had some drums in his dad's garage and she used to snog him in there. Her name was Sandra.

"I *knew* you wuz a teacher."

"How so?"

Beneath her long black skirt her legs were slim, firm and very white. She ran half-marathons and loved to dance. She clambered over me and pressed me down.

"How so?" she repeated, patently used to her questions being answered.

"You got that look, don't get me wrong."

While I held my breath, she lifted her dress over her head. She wasn't wearing a bra and had a scar where her appendix had been removed.

"Got nuffin against them," I said, breathing out.

"I have *never* done *anything* like this in my life. You're *such* a little bastard," she said, throwing her head back.

"Neither have I. I swear."

Her face rocketed forward. Her eyes were massive above me. Warm brown pools of mischief. "You fucking liar," she moaned, grinding me into the mattress.

"I aint, miss…"

I was not to tell a soul, especially the people she was with. She said the next time I was in town I should look her up. Art Faculty - UMIST. She shut the door very softly.

***

232

After a long, hot shower I searched for those kestrels or knaves or kites but there was nothing on so I returned to the club.

The party was over. There were a few hard cases propping up the bar but even Christian's lot had called it a day. I wasn't going to bed though. Even if I had to walk the streets on my own, I wasn't.

I returned to the lobby in time to see Kyle waving at a cab's receding window.

"Alright?" I asked as he walked through the doors.

"Yeah."

For a moment we were lost in lustful memory.

Loitering by the boiled sweets with Kyle I felt unhinged, definitely not sated, bursting with expectation still. "It's only three," I said, turning for the lift. "Let's see if Bill and Andy are up. See if they wanna go out."

"Yeah, some bloke told me there's a late club, cabbie'd know where it is," said Kyle.

"I'm up for that. Let's get Bill."

Walking along the corridor we sensed music before we heard it. Kyle knocked and Bill opened the door.

Inside the room, Andy was puffing on a joint as reedy as himself. In the background an old film rattled on the telly, and seated by the window were a couple of blokes that had something to do with the PA or the bar. There were cans and bottles on every surface and the customary spew of clothes from suitcases. I had a drag and passed it to Kyle but it didn't take any edges off of me because, resting against the headboard of one of the beds were two, strawberry blonde girls in 'Lucas on tour' T-shirts.

"Thanks Andy," said one of them earnestly. They were *ever* so grateful. By way of reply, Andy magnanimously waved an elongated hand. He told us later that he'd promised the girls they'd meet Lucas or at least the band and lo, he'd delivered on his word.

It didn't take ten minutes for Kyle and me to wheedle the two women out of the door. Kyle took his to his room. I was less fortunate. A volley of Christian abuse greeted me at mine. I had hoped that he'd still be out painting the town and the room would be vacant for a little longer. But, not to be put off, Andy's friend and me made do with the fire escape.

After this leg of the tour, we were booked in to record our debut album. I was now on a wage commensurate with any professional. I bought little clothing, as designers asked us to wear their fabrications as a favour. I paid for the occasional meal, but most were on one firm or another. If I wasn't sleeping, I was drumming, and if I wasn't doing either of those, I was moving forward at unnatural speeds. My friends were the boys in the band, the crew, and the odd industry bod. As for a girlfriend, it was impossible to consider dates ahead (meets in bars, parks or outside cinemas), we were booked and marked down for months. But I wasn't ever lonely. I only had to ask a name, or politely enquire where I might buy some fags or a paper, to inculcate myself with a person of the opposite sex. I could stroll through a record company corridor, smile wonkily at a publicity girl and be in her flat in Vauxhall once she'd finished her calls. I was able to nod at the studio receptionist knowing, without doubt, it'd be just me and her in her Oxford-bound car, once the overdubs were tidied. When I'd grin at best friends linking arms in a cold Scottish queue, it was written that I'd pass through the stage door with them and the flight-cased gear hours later.

And when the curtains were flung back, the phone rudely rang, or Bill pounded on the door, the warm brown or ice-blue eyes picked out by the back lights over Christian's Stratocaster, would have their cab fare home and I would have the night.

22

Born To Run

One year later.

Fighting for breath, a fat, heavy hand muffled my airway. My neck strained against the force while my eyes bulged with alarm. My arms were pinned at my sides and my knees couldn't stand. My chest heaved its last. It was the end, my end.

Kyle nudged me from a choking sleep.

My panic-stricken blink into daylight was accompanied by the shimmering, cabassa-laden intro to *The Girl From Ipanema* (piped through the airplane speakers). Breathlessly, I tore my eyes from the apricot-coloured seat-back inches from my face. As was now common, instead of one of his damning lines of prose, I heard her confident enquiry uttered in a pub in North London over a year ago, '*You really think you've escaped?*'

The bass player and I glanced at our dozing guitarist and then down at the glorious sight thousands of feet below. The statue beckoned as the sweat dried on my back.

"Bit of a nightmare, H?"

"Post-tour fatigue again... even though we're still on it."

Kyle swirled the ice in his plastic cup. "Fancy going down the Village?"

"We got press."

"Oh yeah. After, though... stave off the lag."

"We've only come from Texas."

"You know what I mean."

"Oh, yeah." We had entered the time of code.

Tuning into the icy rattle in his cup, I conjured up a nightclub's dusty light, washes of white and blue against a throbbing floor. I discerned bass notes and seductively incomprehensible chatter in the frozen cubes. A girl asked a question. It was an irrelevance. The answer was all that mattered.

"Remember that waitress at the Red Parrot?" he asked.

"Yeah." I didn't.

"She works in some flash store, Chelsea… get a cab after the press… she knows loads of parties." Probably doesn't.

"After we check in…"

"Oh, yeah…"

"But after, definitely, Kyle… *Whoa!* The great man rises from his pit."

We tucked our knees in as Christian squeezed past and staggered towards the toilets. He had slept the whole way.

"Bloke stinks," said Kyle.

Our eyes didn't meet. I stood, picked up my little medicine bag and made my way up the aisle.

An hour later we were in a checker flashing past the graffiti-caked walls of Queens.

"Ain't it great to be back east, Christian?" I asked.

Jammed together in the back seat, I felt his recoil at the sound of my voice. "Yeah, brilliant," he mumbled. "Bill," he croaked to the front, "can we go straight to the hotel?"

"You've got some phone interviews at the record company."

"Can't his lordship do them?"

"He's doing a TV."

"I'm fucked. Ain't we got a show tonight?"

"We have, big 'un at the Ritz."

"I need to get my head down. Talking shit to clueless yanks…"

"Come on Christian," I said. "They only want you to talk about yourself. You normally excel in that regard."

"Fuck off!"

236

Beside me, Kyle bristled, glowered and bit his lip. I feared it was all going to kick off before we'd even checked in. But I was saved, because just then Manhattan, dotted by infinite twinkling rectangles, came into view across the East River. Motoring towards it, glass and steel seemed to meld into some new, refractive material whilst buildings bonded for life only to separate, unceremoniously, seconds later. Endless avenues vanished into strips of sun-dazzled grey revealing soaring, red and blue towers that punctured the leaden sky above. Again I caught my breath, but this time it was as we plunged into the Midtown Tunnel's blackened, sooty mouth.

Yawning, Kyle replaced the receiver and sipped his coffee-flavoured drink. "I mean how many times can you say you *love* it out here?" he wondered.

We were all ready for bed, and notions of a pre-sound-check charm offensive to Greenwich Village were suitably left a couple of miles in the sky. I rubbed my ear; I'd finally completed the last of six, adenoidal rock-based inquisitions. I blew out my cheeks exhaustedly and caught Christian's eye.

"Still thinking of a little loft space out here?" I asked.

From his desk across the room he barely shrugged.

Kyle was watching us. "I bet you were a font of in-formation," he said.

He put his finger to his lips theatrically, "*Christian?*" he lisped in camp, mid-Atlantic. "*You're an experienced rock and roll tourist, could you give our listeners an insight into the comparative difference between American and European audiences, response-wise? Sorry Chris, what was that? Shrug? Can't really hear 'shrug', ol' buddy. What was that, 'bored sigh'?*"

He placed his cup on the table and peered into Christian's face. "Don't you think you should knock your dirty little hobby on the head?"

Christian snarled. "Look, you fucking muso wanker, you don't know me - "

"No-one does. If *he* sees you like this again… you're putting this whole album in jeopardy."

I felt queasy at the mention of our second album and couldn't help thinking it should have the legend, 'ill-fated' before the title. Lucas, a man usually accomplished at detachment, had begun to fret. He couldn't ignore Christian's physical state, tardiness and dire live work any longer. A fretting Lucas would be catastrophic combined with a useless Christian. Compounding the issue were the knowing looks from the hoary New York record execs, the signatories of these massive cheques that paid for us to make our music and financed our careless lifestyles. They'd seen it all before, and although their smiles and gestures were as wide and lavish as Fifth Avenue, you knew they'd drop you like a shitty stick the minute Christian dipped below the industry's degenerate plumb-line.

"Tosser," muttered Kyle.

Christian stood, scattering ashtray and coffee. "Fuck off out of my face, Kyle. I *mean* it…"

He was shaking, fists clenched, enraged, and Kyle and me exchanged an encouraging glance. He was up. He had a bit of fight. We might make this sodding record after all. My pacifying palm was up as I toed the door shut on a couple of passing secretaries.

The New York Ritz was a theatre from the same lineage as the Shepherd's Bush Empire or The Lyceum; you felt that if you stepped outside you'd be in The Strand with hackney carriages scattering guttersnipes, snowflakes on toppers. It was a bit of an away home-from-home for us, a comfortable old pair of slippers. As the front-of-house tech babbled through the fold-back, I sighed. My sound-check application

238

had dwindled to a few sultry taps and a half-arsed verse and chorus. As well as my bed, I dreamed of a day when, like the *really* big bands, your roadies checked the sound for you and you could sleep right up to stage time.

As Andy replaced a crackly lead, I spotted Christian, guitar on, at the back of the vast stage. Lost and forlorn, he looked like a sad old Artful Dodger, but not so artful anymore. He pinched and raked the festering scab on his forearm and I winced in shame for him. In the toilets on the plane, I had cleaned and bandaged it, but he'd peeled the bandage off at the record company. I cleaned that wound every day but it was pointless, a few hours later, he'd be in there with his grimy, yellow digits, picking, picking, picking. He sported a week's bum-fluff but it could have been a month's. I remembered when his cheeks were alabaster and his mohawk was as manicured as the bowling green over Grovehills. "The devil's in the detail," he used to say, running a razor across his skull, tapping the sink and smiling into the mirror with those unfeasibly white Hampsteads. We all knew where the fucking devil was now.

Kyle stepped onto the drum riser. "He should live in a flight case, travel with the gear…"

Laughing humourlessly, I played a little shuffle on my hats. "Yeah, open the lid in time for soundcheck, then put him back in and close it…"

"Wait, leave it on stage by his mic, then when we go on, Andy can open it and he can sort of, 'rise miraculously' up… with his guitar on…"

"Red, velvet-lined flight case, coffin-shaped, with 'Property of Lucas' on it…"

"Okay, ready," said a voice through the speakers.

To my right, Christian looked like a dog chasing his tail as he tried to plug the lead into his guitar. Andy did it for him. He did everything but play his parts these days.

239

"He'll be alright on the night," I said with a grin that Kyle didn't return.

"*Play!*" yelled Lucas.

We jumped and Kyle returned to his amp.

Lucas stood at the microphone, motionless. "For *pity's* sake, play," he begged, quietly.

"You ready?" I called to Christian. He nodded and sniffed. "Right, *one, two, three, four.*"

A few hours later, striding on for the second encore, I looked for Christian. The guitar started this song but Christian wasn't there. Lucas shot me a fearful glare. Taking the initiative, I thumped a pattern that got the crowd's hands clapping and killed time. A whole minute later, Christian ambled on and plugged in.

"*Alright, New York?*" yelled Lucas. A huge roar washed over his beaming face as he stared into the blackness beyond the front rows. Thankfully, he was unaware of Christian's backwards stagger into the kit and subsequent levelling of half the mic and cymbal stands around it.

We flopped backstage.

"Where is he?" asked Lucas, scowling around the room.

Bill winced. "He went off with some… people."

"Well, fuckin' get him!" he whispered, barely in control.

Bill could only shrug and scratch his head. "It'll be murder trying to find him out there, Lucas. Hundreds of punters - "

Lucas rounded on me. "What did I fuckin' say, Harry?"

"He's been - "

"I fuckin' said to keep an eye on him. They will not have it, mate."

The 'they' Lucas spoke of were the scary, hoary ones. The grizzled cheque-signers and dinner-buyers we'd promised our firstborn to in the contract.

"They don't mess about over here," he continued. "They got blokes... they take you into the woods, garrotte cunts like him..."

I glanced at the dressing-room door. Any second, I expected 'them' to wander in with their spouses and kids, albums and posters for the signing of, photos and pleasantries. *"Harry, what cymbal stands do you use...?"*

"Lucas, he's tire - "

"He's gonna blow it, Harry." He was ramming towels, shirts and fruit juice into his holdall manically. "The album..."

I didn't look up. "He's really tired. It's been hard. I'll have a serious word with him."

"Remember Steve?" he warned.

"Easy Lucas, for fuck's sake - "

"Don't fucking 'easy Lucas' me. You know who was out there tonight?"

"They loved it - "

He peered at me. "Are you sure, Harry?"

"I didn't imagine two encores, Lucas."

"Standards, mate."

"We played alright."

"He was shit!"

In the ringing silence we ruminated on the blatancy of Lucas's observation.

"He's got that flu - "

Lucas glowered. "Next week, in Florida, with Kenny. If the tracks don't cut it, I'll have to make decisions. Understand?"

"Not really, Lucas," I said.

"Okay, I'll spell it out. If those songs are not ready - and by ready, I mean *stellar* - for my vocals by the time I walk into that vocal booth in Florida, I'll get the yanks in to do it for me."

"*What?!*" we chimed, as a rhythm section.

"You deaf as well? If there's one element, and you both know what that element is likely to be, that isn't up to standard, I'll get someone else in."

We were aghast. Bill opened the dressing-room door as Lucas hoisted his holdall. He paused in the doorway. He wasn't finished with us yet.

"You ain't so cocky now, are ya?" he said, peering one-eyed around the room the way he did on stage. "Amateur hour, this ain't. I've had enough. Nearly two bleedin' years to sort this soddin' problem out. The lies and bollocks. The stink. The grubby fuckin' blokes hanging round!" He threw his holdall through the door and filled the frame with smouldering discontent. "You promised me, Harry." His voice boomed and his finger pointed. "A fahsand dozen times you said you'd have a word." A stage smile passed his lips as he calmly re-entered the dressing-room. Gently, Bill toed the door shut behind him. "He'll be alright, you keep sayin'. Look at the geezer. Where is he now?" He stopped by the beer bins and jabbed his finger into his palm. "He should be in here. We should be talking about the tracks." Humming tunelessly, he began pacing from deli tray to coffee-maker and back again. "That key change still ain't right and there's got to be an intro on that number. Sounds like a load of hippies strolling in 'n' jammin'!"

He shook his head in the silence then collapsed in a corner.

After a minute he whispered, "All these years we've been at it." He looked up and slowly shook his head, wordlessly begging our understanding. "Can't you see? If we get this right we're sorted!"

"Blimey, Lucas!"

He rose agonisingly and took a huge breath, like he was counting in the last tune we'd ever play. "*Where. Is. He?*"

242

he roared. Bill opened the door and he flew through it.

Quickly, Kyle filled two beakers with vodka but took his time getting the orange quota just right. We sipped.

"Those girls, the really tall ones from The Red Parrot turn up?" I asked.

We scoured a suite at the Iroquois Hotel with the aid of a couple of upstate go-go girls but he wasn't there. Then, in the gilded lift, with the girls bumping and grinding so hard the old cage shook, I recalled he said he'd be at Danceteria. We hailed cabs and scoured every floor, but of our guitarist there was no sign. Later, Kyle managed to round up a posse and out we went a searchin'. The girls from The Red Parrot suggested a party downtown, then a bar on the borders of Harlem hours later. From their great height, for they were indeed lofty, they said anyone who was anyone was going. We must have missed him by inches.

Shielding our eyes from the sunlight glinting off the sky-scraper tips, we ambled up to the bouncers outside the Mudd Club, unbowed. We were here to double-check, and squander our last few dollars with our trusty, early morning drinking pals, Obfuscation and Denial.

By the time we fell through the Gramercy Park lobby doors on the way to our beds, the Manhattanites were looking forward to their lunch break.

23

Pacific Coast Highway

I'd left Christian baking in his oatmeal and returned to my room to shower, change and pack. Lucas and Kyle had left the hotel to mop up the farthest flung interviews hours ago. We were to pick them up on our way north. The record company publicist had booked a paltry three local chats for Christian and me, but they wouldn't happen; Christian could just about answer his name these days.

Stewing in the lobby of the Sunnyside Hotel, I ruminated on the previous night's encounter. Jim had called the shots and I had played my part. "Yes, indeedy," I muttered, I had played my part. How could I hit those skins without him and her coming to mind now? I shook my head and smiled humourlessly. Events barely touched the sides. It was as if I were paid in sexual encounters. My worth as a musician was now totted up in how many and how weird.

The door from the pool opened to reveal last night's karaoke preppies wheeling a long rail with cream, cellophane-wrapped suits and dresses through the lobby towards the exit. The rail paused in front of me. From my armchair by the fronds, I could see nothing but the swinging, empty uniforms in their see-through casings. A moment from the past, out of focus but as tangible as my breath, threatened to play.

The rail passed, to reveal Bill settling up at the reception desk. He wore sensible road-wear; loads of useful pockets in his knobbly safari shorts and a 'Lucas World tour' T-shirt, just so you knew. Snapping his case shut he turned and offered an avuncular smile. "And then there was one," he said, through his peppery stubble.

I stood tiredly. "Where's Chris - "

"In his bunk."

He paused, squinting into his memory banks. "Oh, there was a couple looking for you last night. I think it was the drum rep fellow and his wife?"

"They found me."

"Good." Fixing his shades, he strode towards the exit while speaking over his shoulder. "Picking up vocals and bass in Santa Barbara and then, San Francisco here we come. Last one before Florida." He pushed the door to the street half open, paused and gazed back dolefully. "Come on, H, not as bad as all that, is it?"

"Course not, Bill."

I followed him into the dazzling, white light.

A little way down the hill, the preppies were loading their cellophane rail into the back of a mini bus. I stood transfixed as a scene played, just the other side of my memory's curtain.

"Harry?" Bill called from the entrance of our rather more elaborate ride. Shaking myself, I climbed in and the doors shut with a hiss. I flopped onto the nearest bench and we made our ponderous Hollywood escape.

We had a Silver Eagle luxury tour bus. It had two toilets, a downstairs kitchen and lounge, a rear lounge, a front lounge and enough sleeping space for a band three times our size. I remembered the thrill of stepping into one of these for the first time with the boys. We were all grins; pulling back curtains, opening useful storage hatches and claiming bunks. Back then, Lucas was happy to occupy the front of the bus on his own; there was no smoking allowed up there and no booze either. There, he could repose and reflect, or bury himself in a wartime biography, and when he'd finished reading, he could get on with his favourite travel pastime: staring steely-eyed past the driver's shoulder at his freeway of destiny.

The back of the bus was ours, a haven to booze, fags, porn and music blasted through the Eagle's arse as we tore up and down the heat-hazed interstates.

But that was then.

Weaving along the aisle towards the back lounge and Bill, briefcase open, poring over contracts, I stopped and pulled a bunk's curtain aside.

He was asleep. Beneath his pillow, I noticed a jewel sparkling. It was caught in the light streaming in from the front lounge. Without waking him, I raised the pillow with the back of my hand. But it was a trick of the light, nothing precious at all, just a ball of stained brown, silver foil.

I held on as the bus rocked around a corner. Like washing on a line, all the curtains billowed and for the third time that morning, a recollection flickered on my conscience, tantalising my memory.

I returned to the front lounge and slept.

Pulling a stupidly large carton of chilled juice from the cool box, I sat on the step next to Big Bob, our humongous bus driver.

He growled into his CB and smiled down. "Way to go yet!"

"Blimey," I replied, shaking the sleep away.

"What's that?" he said quickly, his eyes straying for a second as he leaned towards me.

"Blimey? Sort of like, wow!"

He chuckled. A huge paw scratched the mammoth ab-domen beneath his 'Nugent on Tour' T.

We were balanced on the Pacific Coast Highway, a strip of tarmac like a felt-tip line separating sea from land. Bob's feet danced on pedals and his ham-sized forearms wrenched levers, releasing clutches and gears that hissed and thudded.

"Man, I *love* the Allmans," he whispered reverentially, turning the radio up.

"They were good, Bob," I said.

Although we were proceeding in the opposite direction, my thoughts were now firmly on Florida and recording our second album. Once there, I would really go to work on Christian. Get him into shape. I was prepared to stick my tongue right out and lick the crusty bottom of my well of optimism to get this done. It would be the most important week of my life. Failure was not an option.

"What's that, son?"

"Failure is not an option, Bob."

"I hear that, Harry boy, I hee-er theyat!"

To a blast from the horn of a passing chromium truck, we inhaled and ascended a mountain pass. The hills on our right rose green and monumental, their peaks in wispy cloud. To our left, the land fell away and the angry ocean burst on the jagged rocks below.

Bob glanced down and winked. "Yep, awesome ain't it? Stay in this business and you'll be up and down the PCH, sure enough." His eyes glistened with pride at the nature around us. "*Damn!*" he whispered almost tearfully.

He was the blacksmith in a one-horse town. I was the bloke that minded the donkey. "See those mountains, Harry? A few miles inland you can't move when the roads ice up, and… Hey, Christian, good goddamn *mornin'* to ya!"

I blinked at the shadow over me. Christian was swigging from the carton of juice I'd opened minutes ago. I stood, left the step and fell onto a bench opposite him. I smiled.

"What? Dopey sod. Another childhood trauma recalled?" He winced and coughed; pallid, knackered, teeth of yellow, eyes of fog.

"Thinking about when we met, the dress factory. Fucking icy roads. I used to skid all over the shop in that Transit,"

247

I laughed. "...Rat. Happy days?"

"Happiness is just an illusion..." he said.

"Filled with sadness and confusion," I sang.

He almost smiled but the bus had come to a halt. The doors hissed open. With the Santa Barbara sunshine at his back, Lucas was framed in the aisle. He gave his guitarist a withering glare.

I stood, peacemaker-palm the right way up. "Alright Lucas? What was it, radio?" I was pathetically bright and rightly ignored.

Lucas and Christian, in time-honoured tradition, sneered at each other in mutual loathing.

Kyle wandered past, obliviously. "Alright, H? Shattered," he said, making his way to his bunk.

The bus doors hissed shut. Lucas blinked, reared fractionally and nodded at me. "Three radio, two magazine and a telly," he said, as if ordering without looking at the menu.

In silence, we watched Christian, draped in his oversized oatmeal tracksuit, make his way along the aisle to his dreadful pit above the wheels.

24

Florida

In the far recess of a live room the size of a penalty area, Christian was bent over his amp. His last five minutes of mumbling, pick-dropping, and level-adjusting had been witnessed in embarrassed silence. He looked like a baffled old man. When he finally played a chord on the one, he'd distorted his sound so much, it obliterated any of the notes he may have got right. "Run it," he said, hoarsely.

I heard my sticks count time but he was in late again.

Kenny Jett's Brooklynese cracked the awful silence. "Hey, *hey*, Christian baby, why don't you come back in?"

A few days ago, we had shivered as our long, black 'gator of a limo crawled out of Miami International. So flat and blue, Florida. So blisteringly hot. Kyle rubbed the back of his arms. "Do us a favour mate," he said to the driver. "Set the AC to stun."

Across the chromium and leather interior Christian dozed, his feet on the decanters. From the passenger seat the record company rep spoke without turning around. "We'll take you guys to the restaurant now. Kenny's already there."

Kyle pushed Christian's boots. They fell to the floor with a thud. "Wake up. We're meeting Kenny in a minute."

"Fuck off!" he snarled. And, even though the driver *had* let a little heat seep in, I shivered.

Our producer, Kenny Jett, rose to greet us as we walked in. He was six foot four, broad and balding, and wore cut down denim shorts. He had a jagged rectangular scar across one knee. A souvenir of the Vietnam War, he said. Overlooking a lagoon hemmed in by swaying reeds and bulrushes, we ordered shrimp, crab and chilled beers.

We'd met Kenny in New York months ago. He'd been to see us on the road three or four times and genuinely loved our sound. Most importantly, he had an ethnic sincerity that upped even our jaded pulses. "Men," he beamed. "In my humble opinion, we can make the best rock'n'roll - hey sorry, new wave. New wave, right? - album, *ever.*" Nodding confidently, he scooped a portion of guacamole with a shovel-sized chip.

A distant motorboat startled a colony of flamingos. I watched them glide across the setting sun with a feeling that yeah, we could make some sort of stand here. We had the marines on our side, after all. The food was freshly caught and plentiful. Knowing that I wasn't eating, checking, gigging and partying after, caused me to relax and take my time. Minus the tour routine, I was able to savour the fish and sauces, the crisp, cold beer and salty fries. I relished the wind down amidst the scenic views and ideal temperature.

Kenny crunched a crab's smoking limb. "Hey Chris, you look a little fazed. We can do this real quick and you can hire a boat for a few days. Feel the wind on your face, bracing - "

"Feel a bit tom and dick, actually," he replied, standing and heading for the toilets.

"You can get a bad prawn," Kenny said, wiping his hands on his bib and mercilessly breaking another carapace.

Kyle scowled. "Story of my life, Kenny," he said, watching Christian's feeble exit.

I stood. "I'll see if he's okay."

He was retching in a cubicle. When he emerged he looked like a ghost, pallid and blueish. "You look dog rough. Whajew'ave? D'lobstah?"

In the old days that would have elicited a smile at least.

He grimaced and clutched his guts. "Tell that fucking muso not to talk to me - "

"Yeah, okay. So that'll be Lucas not talking to you, Kyle not talking to you, and Andy's had enough of your shitty moods, and Bill - "

He coughed violently into the sink. I held my right hand up for a change.

We made our way back through the restaurant. The diners were golden brown. I was virtually black. Christian was as white as chalk.

Kenny asked him if he was okay.

"A bit tired. The flight and the rest of it."

"Post-tour fatigue…"

Bill stood. "I'm going to the house. Make some calls. Any takers?"

Christian stood. "Yeah."

Kyle, Kenny and me watched them leave through a wicker arch garlanded with blossom.

"He okay?" Kenny looked a touch addled. "We really gotta hustle. The record company are breaking my balls on this and you know I've got a thing in Detroit straight after."

"He'll be fine. You know, *guitarists*," I said.

Kenny broke another claw in his massive mitts. "All I know is that they've been telling me how slick you guys are, how *professional*."

"Don't worry Kenny," said Kyle confidently. "We're British, hard. We'll handle it."

"*Briddish!*" beamed Kenny, leaning so far back on his chair I feared its collapse. "We saved your ass when you were running round Egypt in your short pants!"

Christian put the guitar down and sloped across the glinting parquet towards us. He landed like a sack of spuds in a deep, red sofa. He couldn't stop yawning.

Kenny swung around; it was as if the jagged scar on his knee frowned on the company. "Listen, guys. You know I love you, of that there can be *no question!* But I can't work like this." He peered at Christian who was fumbling for cigarettes. "Christian, these guys got bass and drums down in four fucking days here, and you can't deal with it?" There was a humourless crease about his avuncular eyes. "I'm gonna call it a day. Let's come back in the morning and go again."

After chasing the giant setting sun for a few miles, our cab gave up and deposited us outside a gorgeous, stucco mansion on the edge of the sleepiest lagoon. The place the record company had rented was sprawling, ultramodern and spotless. It had six bedrooms, three living-rooms and innumerable bathrooms. A Londoner could lose himself behind its rendered walls and bake on its myriad patios.

The cab's engine gave way to the sound of water gently lapping and we padded through the front door in hushed reverence at the Eden we'd so fortuitously tipped up at.

A cooling zephyr shifted a frond by my face.

"Look at this, Harry."

I opened my eyes on Kyle. He was sitting on the low wall by the pool enticing a lizard with some crisps. A light went on somewhere in the house. He darkened. "Fucking bloke..."

"Look," I said. "Go easy… I'll talk to him. It'll be alright."

And so dense was that moment of obfuscation, so weighty and pregnant of bullshit was it, that it tore through the fabric of reality and deposited us both on some freezing, pissing down with rain, rubbish-strewn high road back home. Through the icy squall our eyes met in sadness at all we may have lost.

A squawking bird of paradise brought us back.

"Your optimism is your strength, Harry boy," he said, nudging the crisp along.

Agreeing he had a point, I put my hand theatrically on my heart. "Strength in optimism," I announced stoically.

He smiled and raised his arm in Nazi salute, "Strength in optimism." We laughed and then he stood up. "My lizard's gone. Fancy another?"

"Ta," I said.

The following day, waiting around the back for our driver, sunlight bathed the lagoon as it had done for the last billion years. Standing bronzed beneath a shady palm, his eyes blue and eager for work, Kyle laughed. With his dark glasses clipped onto the neck of his cap-sleeved T-shirt, he looked like a poster boy for the Miami Tourist Board. "Good idea… 'ere Christian, what d'you reckon? If we get Lucas on the lake we can push him in, like in *The Godfather*."

Christian was curled on a lounger. He coughed then croaked. "Yeah, I heard."

It was eleven, already baking and he had on one of his outsize tracksuits. He looked like a tramp beneath a grubby old blanket.

"Up for it?" I asked him.

"Yeah, bit cold, that's all," he said uncurling slowly.

"What, out here?" Kyle snarled, waving his arm at the outrageous backdrop.

"Yeah, out here. *Is that all right?*"

Stepping across, I put my arm on Christian's shoulder. "Calm down, we're only - "

He shrugged me off. "Fucking old woman."

"Easy - "

"Shut up and leave me alone."

All three of us shuddered in the heat.

We didn't get any guitars down that day either and re-convened in the afternoon heat by the pool. Well, Kyle and

253

me did. While he hunted for his lizard, I gazed across the lagoon. In the distance, an inkling of music emanated from the property mirroring ours. I wondered if someone was looking at our place the way I was looking at theirs. " 'Ere Kyle," I said. "what if someone's looking at our place, like the same time I..."

At that moment Christian walked out and picked up his fags. As he turned for the house Kyle leaped across and spun him around. Christian staggered. He didn't even raise his hands so addled was he. My heart broke as he blinked at me like a little boy.

Tearing across the poolside, I pulled Kyle away. "Leave him, he's... not well..."

Kyle shrugged me off and steamed towards the jetty as Christian collapsed on a lounger. When I walked up behind him, he looked as if he were about to dive in. "Kyle?" I said.

He didn't turn around. The wind changed subtly, pleasantly, and I heard a woolly bass thud wafting across the still water from the house on the other side of the lagoon. When Kyle turned around, he looked perplexed and sanguine at the same time. "You've known him miles longer than me," he said. "How long 'as he been doin' it? The hard stuff."

"A while."

He nodded. "I reckon it was around the first time we came here. There was that nervous girl, she had a boyfriend with the limp, in Rhode Island. The promoter said they were junkies, well known. What?"

I shook my head.

"Before?" he asked.

"Before *Top Of The Pops*, the first one."

"Nah."

I nodded. "He'd been dabbling, getting in and out, he finally succumbed around then. Never been his old self since."

Kyle smiled sadly. "I just thought he hated me, cosa... me?"

"Me as well. Been kiddin' myself we're best buddies. All that finished ages ago."

"Oh."

I looked into the clear blue sky. "Funny, you'd say, 'best years of your life' these. The countries, the laughs and girls and... success. He's gone through all that in the grip of some shitty chemical. He's never really experienced it like, free. Not actually held it in his hands... life, I mean. He's had this big heroin glove on. Laboratory conditions. Desensitised. Which is a shame, really."

"Was there nothing you could do?"

"It's hard to say to another man, specially one like him, 'No you can't.' However much you care about them they got their own free will. You kinda kid yourself and say, 'Well, he's a really bright bloke, he can't possibly fall for this bollocks, gotta be a phase?' Anyway, he just got deeper and deeper into it and I just got further and further away... what with working in the band... hard enough, aint it?"

He walked past me. I followed. "So," I said (to myself as much as him), "that leaves us where we are now."

"I just don't get it," Kyle said quietly.

We were standing beside Christian's lounger. I put two hands to my face and rubbed. My eyes were dry. Christian was rooting around for his Marlboros. His were too.

When I looked at Kyle, a tear ran down his cheek.

"My mum cleaned houses for rich people," he said, sniffing and wiping his face. "They found out at school. Whenever I thought I was doing alright, someone would always remind me that mum was a cleaner. She's got arthritis now. Don't do it anymore." He smiled and sighed. "She's got one whole wall covered with pictures of me... and you, Christian. She thinks the world of all of us." I slumped exhaustedly onto the white, low wall while he continued.

"My old man lost his job at the print a bit after I joined. Started there when he left school. His whole life in Wapping. They got nuffin now. There's only me. I'm all they got."

Christian coughed and curled up on his lounger. His spine looked prehensile through his tracksuit.

"They see me on telly. I got that nice car and I drive them about when I'm home. After this album, when they give us our advance..." he tailed before rallying. "I *was* gonna buy 'em a bungalow... in the country, well, Broxbourne, and move 'em out there. Lived Beffnall Green all their lives." He took a breath and bit back his tears. "My mum.... She used to walk past the school gates with her shopping, and a couple of the kids'd laugh, call her a charlady. She didn't care though, H. She gave me the dough for my first guitar and amp. Think about that. Back then, what it meant."

As I thought about what it meant, the music wafting across the lagoon became more distinct, easier for the head to dilute.

Kyle spoke to Christian's motionless back. "And you, with your shit, selfish habit are ruining it for all of us."

Kyle wasn't easily confused, or deterred, so it was most unsettling when he pushed his hand through his hair in utter bewilderment. "Is it that much better, drugs, heroin?" he asked. "Is it better than being in a brilliant band with me and Harry... and an album, the girls, money in our pockets... You never pay for anything. You travel the world. People go out of their way just to..." He scratched his head and blinked cluelessly. "Is it *really better?* You got any, cos I'll take it now. Just to see how brilliantly better it is than..." his arm now circumscribed the pool, the fronds, the palms and the sun-dappled expanse of blue lagoon, "this? *You selfish bastard!* Can't you see you're ruining it for everyone."

By way of reply, Christian snored evenly.

Kyle turned to me. "Harry, you explain?"

***

A car crunched the gravel at the front of the house. I opened my eyes to twilight and Kyle. "Going to the Grove," he said.

I hadn't moved from the pool while he'd gone to his room, showered and shaved.

I stood up. "Hang on, I'll get my jacket."

Kyle shook his head. "Nah, don't H. I need a break from all this."

"Okay."

I must have drifted off again because the sound of a car door slamming had me blinking awake. My heart soared. Kyle had come back for me. What a mate, what a bloke! Another thing is (and Kyle well knew this), on the road, a laugh isn't really a laugh when it's just you having it. Padding through the house, I expected to hear southern, female laughter and Kyle impressing with talk of his five-string or colour-coded effects pedals but the house remained quiet. Perhaps they were outside the front door, dancing on the crusty fronds, carousing with cicadas, loitering with lizards? Beaming, I opened the front door on Kyle and his freckled, sun-bleached babe but there was nothing but fireflies and the blackest of outlooks.

Just then, a set of brake lights flared then disappeared at the end of the road.

Christian's door shut on the landing. "Billy…" I whispered.

In the beginning there were the clubs and pubs. I used go down there with him for a few pints from those smelly, plastic pots. I can bring to mind a collage of dabblers, pavement pukers and Tube train narcoleptics that sniffed and popped to the bands, with a smile. Back then it was a young thing. As rebellious as not tidying your room.

***

The first time I really took any notice of Billy was... maybe Chicago... Cleveland, Columbus was it? Billy definitely wasn't the limping partner with the girl from Rhode Island.

I recall there were cold beers and huge steaks, chips and onion rings on that particular table. We were all sitting around it and I was happy, so very happy. Back then there was no equivocation; it was glorious touring the U.S. Here, we were respected as professionals. Back home they thought you were on the dole, poncing, if you were in a band.

The motels on the highway, the inns on the freeway, or the big hotels in town were invariably a pleasure to frequent. Always had somewhere to eat a hearty American breakfast and they always had someone insisting you had a nice day... so I always did. Most had a pool as well; ideal for chucking plastic furniture into when you got back late, or even immersing a knackered carcass on a rare afternoon off. I can see the three of us now, floating, our heads just above water, fags clamped between teeth, tequilas on the poolside. But was that Christian beside me and Kyle in the water, or Andy?

Our initiation began in small, quirkily named towns, Poughkeepsie, and Schenectady, then, we graduated to the cities: Buffalo, Boston, Pittsburg, Cincinnati and Chicago, Philly. We circled the industrial north-east like a spirograph and spread, like a great musical stain, out and down. From eerie Minneapolis and bustling Cleveland, through the devastated Washington suburbs and hollowed-out Detroit, we gave it everything. And the locals reciprocated. Always. Rumbling through the Carolinas (North & South), we entertained ultra-polite Tennessee, Alabama, Mississippi and Atlanta, fell blinking into white, bright Miami, before steaming through Tampa, Tulsa, Texas and Oklahoma and then, then... Apparently the west coast was hot for us so we had to get out there as well.

258

We even played on a riverboat on the banks of the Mississippi. Fuelled on Wild Turkey and fizzy beers, we reeled along Bourbon Street dancing to the blues. I thought of all those cheesy musicals my parents ogled on telly and wondered if I'd ever bother to tell them I'd actually been to those cinematic locations. It would so disappoint them that streets didn't erupt into high-kicking dance routines the minute someone saw a tram.

But even as I looked back at the Technicolor flash of those dates and places, I saw Christian, frequently distracted or sleeping or simply not there. He'd returned to the hotel because he was knackered and had that flu.

"Wha?" I said, with my mouth full.

Kyle was speaking as he carved his Ohio steak.

"I was asking Christian."

I swallowed. "Askin' him what?"

"Where he met him," said Kyle, chewing.

"Who?" I said, not chewing now.

"Who?" said Christian, not chewing.

"That bloke you were talking to at the bar last night."

"Billy? New York," Christian replied.

"I saw him at Providence. Green Bay the night after," I said.

"So?" said Christian.

"Is he going tonight?" asked Kyle.

"Fucking questions," he said, pushing his food away and standing up.

"Christian, hang about - "

"What, for your mother's meeting? No thanks."

After the show that night, Billy poked his head around the dressing-room door. His clothes were new and trendy but something grubby remained. Something soap could never shift. "Great show, great show, guys. Chris you coming? Got the car outside."

259

"Give us a minute, Bill," said Christian, rummaging for his jacket.

"Can't hang around, buddy." He turned and left.

I looked at Christian. He was panic-stricken, throwing clobber over his shoulder and cursing. He found his jacket and hared through the door. Me and Kyle just stared at each other. It was definitely Columbus... Columbus, Ohio.

Closing the front door on the car, I returned to the dream kitchen, a marble-floored and granite-surfaced space, bigger than my flat. Christian was nibbling crisps at the table. I pulled two chilled beers from the fridge and opened them.

"Kyle gone out?" he croaked, wiping his nose.

"Yeah, Coconut Grove."

"Nice."

His toothache was perpetual. Face-ache. "Christian, think I should call a doctor."

"It's nuffin."

"You're fuckin' ill. We gotta do something. I told Lucas we'd have 'em down by now. Kyle's losing it."

"What *are* you on about?"

"Whajewfink? The tracks!"

"We got ages."

"You haven't recorded one minute of guitar!"

Beer untouched, he rose and left me.

I took a breath and followed. As I climbed the stairs I felt like the priest in *The Exorcist*.

"Fuck me, it stinks in here," I said, pushing the window open.

"Don't, it's freezing."

"Freezing, you cunt! It's thirty degrees."

"Let me sleep." He covered himself up. There were blankets, coats, T-shirts, he'd emptied his entire case on the bed and crawled beneath. His eyes were two gaunt, glass depressions. Like a doll's on a skip.

260

"You gotta stop *now*. Look what it's doing to you!" I ripped his pathetic defence away.

He cowered, fully clothed. That whiff I'd noticed, that odious sweetness, emanated from his bed. I reared as he coughed. "What?" he said. "The smell?" A twisted grin appeared. "Chicken soup, Harry," he whispered avidly, "*Chicken soup*. This is what it's like when you come off."

The scary unknown had me glancing left and right, anticipating hoards of long-backed, razor-toothed vermin, swarming the bed from under the door. Fearfully, I asked, "Come off? Who was that in the car?"

"Methadone... I'd run out."

I squinted in dismay. "So, what you like when you're doing it?"

His ghoulish, yellow toothed smile defied me. "I manage," he said.

As I turned, he groaned horribly. "Ahh," he doubled up. "*Ahhhhhhhg!*"

"Fuck me, Christian." I knelt by him. "I'll get help..."

"Bin..."

As he wretched dry into an ethnic wicker basket, I picked up the phone. Before I could dial, he'd leaned out of the bed and ripped it from my hand. He lay on the slabs in foetal prayer. "It's retribution, Harry... payback for the life." His teeth chattered.

"What have you done?"

He shivered. "I'm cold," he said.

I tucked him in and leaned against the wall. From his mountainous bedding he watched me out of one frightened eye.

His room was far smaller than the one I had on the next floor up. His was about the size of the box room at Mrs H's. The one with the precarious, tilting bookshelf. The rooms Kyle and me had had TVs, fridges and sofas. You could easy

261

live in one. In the old days *he'd* insist on having the biggest and best. He didn't give a shit now.

The breeze kissed my face. Echoes of laughter and rhythm rippled from the house across the water. "I bet you regret ever starting."

He blinked. "State the fucking obvious."

"It was in Bristol... the first time."

He pulled the blankets down and looked at me in amazement. "Owja know that?"

"Stuck in my mind. About a month before the single got in the charts. We did a gig there, went to party in some flats after. There was a grey table in the kitchen, wooden, like a garden table, and there was spoons and foil on it and some right charmers sitting around it... you were never the same after that. The gig was ok-ish."

"Oh, H," he whispered and I was swept back years to the party in those flats a little right of Wales.

"Yep, I was with this girl, fuck, what was her name... *Joan,*" I said triumphantly. "Really nice, she was. Lived on the outskirts near a pylon. She was worried about radiation or something evil from the electricity. Her dad had run-ins with the council..." and on I went, recalling the music they played and the weather, the bare boards in the rooms. "She'd never heard of Lucas, which was weird, because we were consumed with it back then. Like school kids we were, drawing the logo on bits of paper, bog walls, remember? The single had just got in the charts. We were so proud, Christian. Our record. Us," I said in wonder. "Remember how we used to go into the shops, like, 'disguised', and look at it in the racks? Brilliant those days..."

He struggled and sat up. "Always thought the production was a bit lightweight on that, that first album too..."

"Funny you should say that. I was round that drum rep bloke's the other night, I told you, in LA. They were playing it. Hadn't heard it for yonks... Could've been heavier, and then I thought, nah, it was a record of the time, a sensitive thing... it'll stand the test..."

"Yeah, but still...." He winced and an imperceptible nod to his left had me lighting fags for both of us. "I reckon Kenny'll really heavy this one up..."

"I shoulda just got hold of ya, pulled you out of that fuckin' kitchen. We'd a got away and - "

"I woulda got it somewhere else, H."

The wind shifted. The music emanating from the house across the water became so clear, it was as if the band had set up by the pool downstairs. A rumba shimmered into Christian's room; halftime shakers and random congas, timbales on the change of chords rebounded. A Spanish guitar picked and punched, while a Cuban wailed at a wall of laughing trumpets.

But I was dismal. Even as I tapped my thighs, sideways, with devil's horns my old man danced in from the chipped apricot skirting. I shut my eyes but there he remained, miming the words while lighting his lover's cigarette. I wiped the image away and tracked a few bars. There must have been four or five people hitting things on the track. Every strike, shake and flick fell in delightful repetition, like a section of early raindrops on the pavement in front of you. The softest of mallets struck the core of me and a question was asked; if he loved the drums like I did, and he *really* did, why did he never speak of them to me? Merciless irony was piled on when Christian croaked from his stinking pile, "Cheer up, H. Ain't the end of the world."

"I'm alright mate," I said, gazing at Florida, still so flat and blue.

Amidst chinking glasses the party over there bumped and floated but the whole thing was remote, like music from a rapidly passing car. It was as if I'd never go to a brilliant party

263

like that again. I attempted one more flashing chance, a shot from forty yards. "That's why…" I said, as a tear plopped onto the back of my hand, "you gotta get that guitar down. You'll shine on this album, Christian. Come on, mate?" Wiping my eyes, I implored him. "We've got all those songs. All those parts. The work we've put into it. It's the *most* important thing in our lives… the next album, Christian. Always the next one…"

"…Don't you think I know that!" he said, glaring at me. That once venomous look now resembled one an irate old lady blocking a shop doorway would give. He groaned and fell sideways. His eyes fluttered and his face contorted as he wretched dry over and over again.

After a moment of silence he grinned with triumph. "This thing Harry, it's like God, you can't defy it."

"You sure?"

"Positive."

At that moment, my shot sailed way over the bar.

He dozed then went into spasm again. I held his hand while he thrashed about. Covering him up, I talked complete crap, told all the lies you tell to your junkie brother.

Darting from him to the house across the lagoon, I felt I was hovering in that unfathomable space between hope and resignation. His eyelids fluttered and he blinked in pain. I just couldn't put it back together again. There was no palm-up rational, bridge-building, sucking-up or funky chicken moves that could save me now. I'd burned all the libraries, pulled down all the goal posts and exhausted all my happy-ever-after fantasies with the girl next door. I was on my own.

As I sat, hugging my knees, listening to Christian's fitful inhalation, my old man's derisive mantra, '*Like you I was, like me you'll become,*' came dancing across the blue in true Latino style.

264

25

Where's Kyle?

As I rolled up my blinds, another beautiful Florida day was magically revealed. I showered and made my way downstairs for breakfast but the little Mexican lady that did for us wasn't there. Selecting a couple of slices of un-mouldy white from the bread bin, I trudged back up. I knocked for Kyle. He didn't reply. When I pushed open his door, I saw that the bed was stripped of its bedding and there wasn't a trace of his stuff. Had he eloped? I toed an inch of Christian's door open. That sweet smell leaked out. I let it close silently. Outside, the pool's whitewashed borders gleamed beneath irrepressible sunshine. I stared at the bulrushes, mute with fear.

A beeping car horn brought me to my senses and I made my way to the front door across those cool, marble slabs. At the end of the drive, Bill was standing by a cherry-red hire car. He smiled and waved when he saw me. "*Yoo hoo!*" he called.

"What's happening, Bill?"

"Is he up?"

"Nah."

"Tell you what, H, pack your gear and put it in the car."

My heart hammered in my chest. "Why?"

"Not my department, son. Do it and wait by the pool."

He strode past and took the stairs two at a time.

Christian's window flew open and the sound of Bill's cajoling banter hovered over the pool. As he passed the window with a handful of shirts on hangers, my skin prickled. I knew somewhere, not far away, Kenny was enjoying a hearty American breakfast before an internal flight to Detroit and, not a million miles from him, Andy was wheeling our flight cases (including the moribund ones with guitars and amps in them), from studio to truck.

The house across the lagoon was quiet, a shimmering white cube in jungle green. "Where's Kyle?" I whispered.

On the first floor, as Bill gently chivvied him into packing his belongings, Christian's protestations were a dental whine, a sound like a mower trimming Bermuda grass borders.

In the back of the cherry-red hire car, Christian sweated like a wax model. I sat up front with Bill and let the AC do its work. Too fast. The lagoons and lakes, the motorboats and storks went by obscenely quick. The radio murmured about gigs happening all over the state: Tampa, Jacksonville, Fort Lauderdale. I'd have given anything to be on my merry way to a sound check at one or any of them. And what was strange was, if I were, I'd have happily whiled away the miles talking crap with Bill, but because of the situation, neither of us said anything.

He pulled up at the airport, opened his aluminium briefcase and glanced at me over the lid. For a moment I was reminded of my mum and her scaffold countenance. Bill's whistle-while-you-work bonhomie had vanished, and instead his eyes portrayed a spaniel sadness at the turn of events. He took a breath. "Tickets, boys," he said.

A wash of panic caused me to wipe my brow. "Ta."

Staring into Christian's face, he tucked passport and documents into his jacket. "You'll need these at JFK. Don't lose 'em."

"I won't," Christian whispered.

"Look after him, H…" he said, as he turned for the car.

"Bill?"

"Harry?"

"What's gonna happen?"

"Take this flight to New York and get the connection to Heathrow."

Christian leaned in. We both reared from the fumes. "Ere Bill, could you sub us?"

I couldn't bear it and looked away.

'Could you lend me, Marios, er, sub me…'
'For what?'
'I want to get something.'
'That's obvious, what is it?'
'Something I need an… advance for.'
'A car?'
A drum kit.'

That advance wasn't really an advance. Marios continued to pay me the same and never asked for it back.

I had a kit in every port now. After that first set, I hadn't paid for a single right-handed drumstick. I was plied with stands, pedals, skins, *and* the spouses of the people that made them. I had clothes aplenty too: T-shirts, sweatshirts, gratuities from colleges, gigs and radio stations across the US. In my wardrobes at home were perverse, sail-shaped trousers, exploding jackets and half-open headgear, gifts from outré European designers.

I'd moved out of Mrs H's and into a flat in Highgate. My views were not of a thin urban terrace but of St Paul's, and The Heath. I hadn't been back to Wood Green for years. Recently, I'd imagined returning. I'd been planning, itemising every job I'd do in Mrs. Hajinikolas's garden when I did. Firstly, I'd cut back all the trees and bushes, (they'd have gone wild in the seasons I'd not tended them). I'd trim the lawn, re-seed it too. I'd have a great big bonfire up the back, eat gooey pastries, drink strong tea and after, I'd watch

Match Of The Day from my armchair amongst the doilies. I peered up at the little box room. Behind that new window pane was the set of drums I'd bought in Archer Street. It was stacked in a corner, and over the top of the fourteen-inch tom-tom was Susan's pilot's jacket, and in the pocket of that jacket was the black, one-inch tile from her drive.

'That's not good, Harry,'
'Why Marios?'
'Very noisy and think about it, you'll have nothing to eat...'

Bill peeled off a few notes and handed them to Christian. He stuffed them into his jeans. I knew those notes wouldn't be on the firm because we were no longer on it. Bill would have given them to him from his own pocket.

I took a deep breath and turned to him. "Where's Kyle?"

"With Lucas."

"What's happenin', Bill?"

"Not my department," he said, inadvertently mocking our oft-amusing 'road' aside. "Harry, believe me, I don't know. Everything is on hold. You're to go home with Christian and await orders."

"Bout the recording?"

He shrugged.

The skycaps were loading our bags up. "But Bill - "

He shut his door and wound the window down. "Be a pro, son," he said, starting the car up.

"Right."

I pulled Christian out of the sunshine and into the terminal. "You ain't got anyfin' on ya?"

He flinched as the tannoy went off over our heads. "Nah."

"You sure?" I had to shout over the announcements.

He shook his head, yawned and gazed uncertainly at the bustling terminal. "Search me."

268

I bellowed, "You know…" my voice softened as the speakers relented, "what's going on?" Panic and confusion flitted across his eyes. I took his hand.

"We're going back to London," I said.

"Where's Kyle?"

"He drove up to Lucas last night."

"Where's Lucas?"

"New York."

"Why?"

"Dunno… seeing the record company."

"Why, H?"

I eased him out of the way as a family - black bloke, white woman, three brown nippers - shuffled past. As we joined the snaking line behind them I answered his question. "I really don't know."

"Gonna get some fags…" he said almost inaudibly before leaving my side.

Bewildered by the terminal's wraithlike figures to-ing and fro-ing, I experienced that erstwhile high-pitched ringing in my ears. My fists wouldn't clench and there was an embarrassing flimsiness about my knee area. Taking my time to inhale and exhale, I attempted to read, with phonetic patience, the information on the huge display at the end of the line. I was mumbling, "At-lan-ta," when I was knocked off balance by one of the kids in the queue in front of me.

"James, apologise to the may-ern!"

"Nah," I said, looking into the frightened brown face that peered into mine, "that's alright."

"Apologise now, soldier!" said dad.

The little mouth moved but the words reached my ears milliseconds later. "I'm sorry, sir."

"Don't matter, honest… it's cool…"

Smiling, I looked away but felt the kid's repentant eyes on me.

On the other side of my memory's curtain was a nippy spring morning where sunshine blinded my still-sleepy eyes but a dash of optimism pervaded, nonetheless. I was drawn to the light. The prospects of a new day (even at school), energised me. Closing the front door, feeling the chill on my face, I heard my name called. "Harry."

"Goina' school, dad."

"Today…" big theatrical pause, "you are not."

"Dad, it's football…" I said, shutting the door and settling on the chipped apricot skirting.

With head raised heroically, he gazed at the suburban pampas then lowered his dog-dead eyes on me. His instructions were grave. I winced as his aftershave wormed through my sinuses. "*You*. You do not speak. *You*. You do not come near. You stand away and only when I call, near you come."

Off he strode in his neat all-black, his shoulders wide, his samba hips sliding past the award-winning rhododendrons over Grovehills. A couple of times, to test, he glanced casually behind. Obediently, I affected apathy, kicking at nothing, scratching at mid-air.

Emerging from the woods (with me back that respectable distance), he surveyed the targets dotting the knolls and pathways around the café. From up here it appeared that the area was strewn with slowly moving, pink and pale blue bunting.

He sniffed high and began his sultry, Latin incantation. "*Pa di di di pa. Da de de da da de de da...*"

Below us, a mid-morning herd of young mums had recently dropped their toddlers off at the nursery at the west end of the park. On tuesdays and thursdays, a good number liked to pop into the café for a cup of milky coffee and a natter. Careful not to startle, he circumnavigated the lake and wound himself alluringly between the black, wrought-iron east gates. There, he was practically invisible. Only yards

270

away, with buggies in gear, their banter blending pleasantly with the distant, quacking mallards on the lake, they approached the exit oblivious of the waiting jowls that would take their hinds and flanks. From the bus stop across the road I watched as, in irresistible all-black, he padded amongst them: panther.

They were intrigued, genuinely so (well, what female wouldn't notice this statuesque, muscular androgyne), but unwilling. Politely reticent.

To siphon one away he had to get serious. First up, he utilised the quad-stretching-dancer/hurdler stratagem but, although she liked Tito Puente and sports, she wasn't a fan. He modified to the wincing-back face but 'this one' wasn't a healer or physio and had pain of her own. Digging deep into his predatory tool-kit, he retrieved one of his basest weapons: the cringe-worthy baby doter. Squatting by pale blue booties he tragically proclaimed that, '*this is the most beautiful child in creation!*' But alas, she was aware of that anyway and was in love with the child's father. None succumbed to his ways and blinding cologne on that safari.

For a moment he was like me, a forlorn male unit, staring at the retreating rumps of the buggy pushers as they progressed the ones yet too young for nursery back up the hill.

We ended up in the yellow Rover. Even with the sunroof down his aftershave was stifling. Overriding that was the stench of righteous indignation at being blown out so quickly by so many.

At eleven o'clock the old V8 crunched the gravel of a pub car park in Barnet. I daren't open my mouth. Rejection had him addled. The puppy's tilting head and double posh mumbling had replaced the commander's steel and clear instruction. Stock-still, I stared through my window at a grubby privet until an irrational quiver had me ducking below the dashboard for my life. But he hadn't struck. He'd opened and

271

shut his door so quickly, I wondered if he had actually left the vehicle. He loafed on the warm bonnet until, through the saloon doors, a young, apron-wearing woman emerged with a bin. Her brown hair was sensibly tied back while her mouth was screwed up disdainfully at her menial duties. I felt the chassis rumble as he said something in bass. She turned, smiled into the sun, and sparkled bashfully at his approach. Looking left and right, she reddened but was unable to stop herself falling into his arms. They kissed, and then appeared to argue. She pulled herself away.

My stomach buckled as she tore into the pub with her bin, her hair loose from its tie.

Robotic, angry eyes steamed towards the car. He glared at me and I glared at the privet (ugly, stunted, dirty little bush) knowing that if a fibre twitched, I'd feel something heavy and hard across my temple. He wound the roof up at lightning speed. Gravel flew as he tore out of the car park.

For more than an hour my teenage vitality stewed to a bubbling nothing in that car. Shop fronts, bus stops, and turnings flew past. I dozed, strapped in and stifling.

I awoke with a start. He was no longer muttering.

"*Cow, putan, bitch!*" he roared, twitching with volatility, the sinews in his forearm undulating iron as he squeezed the breath from the wheel. With the wipers going mental, he sped through boroughs, hooting, turning without indicating, punching the dashboard and slamming the anchors on needlessly. At one point, his hands left the steering wheel as he accelerated through pedestrians at a red light, the engine screaming in the wrong gear.

It was a merciful relief to both car and passenger when he finally ratcheted up the handbrake and turned the fucking thing off. With his heart thumping behind stone-slab pecs, he nodded at my door. Before getting out, I dared to glance.

His eyes were wet and red, incredulous with hurt.

I stood with my father in a high street as bleak as the weather. Grey, low, wet cloud had chased the morning's optimism away. "Wait," he warned, before walking towards an attractive, smoky glass facade a few shops from the confectioners we'd parked outside. The sign above the purple-tinted glass read, 'Camden Massage' which was good for me because it meant that I wouldn't have to rub his back later. Sometimes, I felt like I needed a chisel to get between the furiously inflamed sinews in his traps and cervical spine. Perhaps the muscular relief he'd receive would improve his mood and he might buy me some chips… or a Mars bar. It was nearly end of school and I'd have eaten anything, to be honest.

Between the massage place and confectioners was a bookies with a picture of Georgie Best in the window. Next to that was an electrical repairs shop that looked quite interesting. It had a varied display of radios and a really cool little telly up the back. For a couple of minutes, I amused myself by waiting for all the clocks to strike the half hour at once. I recall there was a sports shop across the road which looked good as well, but the traffic was busy and I was knackered and cold. The rain persisted so I parked myself under the sweetshop awning until the man inside gave me the customary look and waved me away with his thumb. I walked to the massage place, slid down the glass frontage and, hugging my blazer, closed my eyes.

"Weak, weak, *weak child!*"
I awoke and scuttled instinctively. From inches away his lashes batted like Dusty Springfield's.
"What dad? What?"
He was aghast, blowing and pointing at the purple glass behind me. "Against this you sleep! You are not a man?"

"Sorry dad, sorry..."

"Men stand. Their spines are strong. They are upright. But look at you! You slouch in public, *here?*"

A snapshot of passers-by had stopped; some early school kids, a bloke in a kaftan with a fag and a middle-aged lady with a flowery shopping bag. Fleetingly, I looked to all for succour.

His weight subtly favoured the left side as he drew his hand back. I went left to roll with it. But he'd done me again! The right slap was short and well aimed at the temple area, it sent me spinning across the puddles. Through the pattering rain and that familiar, shitty ringing sound I heard childish giggles but they weren't gleeful because it isn't...

And then a fat man in a leather waistcoat and medallion opened the door of the massage place. Unshaven, oily scalp and scabby-lipped, he eyed our domestic like he'd trodden in turd. "Not here," he said.

Pulled by the hair towards the family car, I watched the grebo spit in our direction. "Fucking wogs," he muttered, closing the door.

"You shame me. On purpose, you shame me..."

His grip on my hair tightened, pulling so it hurt my ears. As one hand burrowed into his golf slacks for keys, the lady with the cheerful bag approached us tentatively. "Leave t'choild," she said in soft Irish, hugging her bag agitatedly.

He glared and responded in supersonic, wounded posh. "How dare *you!* I am with son. We have been," - preparing himself for the final section of indignation, his eyes bulged - "to the hospital!"

"Sir, please."

"*Fuck off, whore!*" he raised his arm. She backed away, stunned and powerless before the nutter.

Head hit frame (always too big for that car) and foot connected with arse. My ears exploded as he slammed the door.

"You hate me so?"

"What, dad?"

I was the cat he kicked, the door he slammed, the Spalding he drove (occasionally), so sweetly.

"You okay, buddy?"

I blinked up at the concerned black face. "Nuffin..."

Father and sons were staring; wide, warm inquisitive brown pools peering into a past I'd die before retelling. Raising one saintly hand, I realised I was on my back with our bags scattered about me. I smiled. "Sorry," I mumbled.

"You sure you're okay?" said dad, pressing a miscreant son lovingly to his side.

I nodded, and as I did Christian's white face, a cue ball amongst the colours, appeared. "How long to go, H?" he mouthed beneath the bellowing airport tannoy.

26

This Is Valley Farm

Four months later

Sleep was fitful. Fingers tugged at my bedding. Exposed
skin became cold in seconds. There were monsters in those
cupboards, and at about eight, I heard one scratching around.
The front door slammed, shaking the rattly sashes. I looked
through the window to see Christian ghosting into a minicab.
There was a firm across the road and they were always lined
up. Dressing quickly, I flew downstairs. His cab was speed-
ing towards Manor House. Climbing into the one behind, I
told the driver to follow the bloke in front.

Outside the Electric Ballroom, the scene of many an early
triumph for us, I feigned interest in African beads, fertility
icons and reggae compilations. Rubbing my hands for warmth,
I glanced at one of the flats above the shops opposite; he'd
been in there half an hour but I knew he'd emerge sooner
rather than later. At nine he blinked into the damp Camden
traffic and made his way towards the Lock. Some places were
already open, an electrical shop and a bookies, but the second-
hand record shop he loitered outside was, as yet, not.

Cupping his face in his hands, he peeked through the
window for a moment. Then, after an excited half-skip, he
knelt and called through the letterbox. A moment later he was
admitted. Following a pace behind and with eyes downcast,
I quietly flicked through the soundtracks.

His palms bore down on the counter. On tiptoes, he willed
the bald man with a red goatee to dole the tenners out faster.
I left *The Sound of Music* and joined them. He hadn't a clue

I was there. "These ain't his to sell, mate," I said, picking up my gold discs: three of them, two singles and an album. Both were speechless. The owner and his goatee reacted first. He snatched his money, slammed the till and stepped away.

"Thieving, treacherous cunt," I said over my shoulder as I left the shop.

Black drizzle pooled and slid into the storm drain. I hugged my industry awards and ruefully shook my head. He actually drop-kicked me. I almost met the Chalk Farm bound bus going the other way. Arching and wincing, I rubbed the small of my back. As ever, sanguine Londoners gave us ample room.

He was outraged, pointing at my face. "No trust, you *fucking* Judas!" His voice clambered to a panic-stricken change of key. "I said I'd pay you back but you never believe me. Anyone else, yeah. But you never listen to me... *never.*" Tears pricked his eyes as, pouting and scowling, he dance-stepped from side to side in his desperate little quadrant.

I did not move. His indignity dissolved. Holding out a trembling hand, he said, "*Please,* Harry."

I remained still.

Cowering, stooping sideways and shuffling towards me, he flinched and pleaded, "Give 'em back, mate."

I shook my head.

He offered his palm. It was pale and thin, the scar was red and livid. "Bonded in blood, H," he stated, his eyes brightening hopefully.

With revulsion, I watched his attempt to dredge up the prose that would persuade me to give him *my* discs to sell for poxy drugs. His lips moved in feverish wavelets across his teeth.

I'd long since dispensed with a pacifying palm. "You've lost it, pal," I said. "I know you nicked that jacket and the cash, that watch from Hong Kong... what the fuck happened to you?"

"*Me,* you look at!" He threw a few wild, mid-air hooks and accidental back-fists. He'd become an indignant Norman Wisdom with his old leather hanging off one scrawny shoulder. "With your *pathetic* mementos of that fucking *average* band. Wait till you hear *my* fing... I got tunes, mate and I'll get a fuckin' drummer with *bollocks.*" He roared the final word until he coughed and choked.

"Gotta go to work," I said.

A new, cruel squall blew unpleasantly through the stalls, causing the T-shirts and combats to twist and billow on their hangers. Raindrops followed, rapidly dotting the pavement, and Christian got his hands on the discs and pulled. I pulled back. We danced and snarled until those gold-sprayed vestiges of the dream world we'd once inhabited went skidding into the street in time for a council gritter to run them over.

Through the dirty, wet shards I read, '*Harry Ferdinand... five hundred thousand...*' I picked up the corner of a frame. The thing disintegrated in my hand.

On our return to London, I'd rented a first floor flat on the Seven Sisters Road from a cousin of Marios. Like most of everything since I'd got back, the visit to the old factory had been a humbling event. The needles stopped in mid-air when I walked in. Even the presser's iron stopped hissing. A lump rose in my throat as a round of applause, accompanied by Cypriot felicitations, grew to a crescendo. They'd hung a huge poster of me on the wall over the cutter's table. I stared down from a fiery drum kit, ferociously. Inwardly, I cringed at my cocksure visage. I really thought I'd be up there forever.

After visiting the four corners of the earth, I stood on the cabbage-strewn factory floor, chastened and quiet. I'd never said, 'thank you' for the job and room; I'd mumbled, chewed my wonky lip and looked at my boots. These people had fed me, entrusted me with their purses and jackets and the keys to their vehicles, but most importantly, they'd given me self-respect.

"We watch you on telly so many times, Harry," said Marios, His eyes looked like they did when unfolding a new, exciting pattern on his desk. "We are so proud. I tell my niece that you work here and I give you the money for your first drum." His smile broadened. "She don't believe me. Kids," he said, shrugging.

I had half-prepared a classic, self-exonerating speech where I'd mention, 'random acts of kindness shown by strangers to the youth and the right road indicated' etc, but it all evaporated when I looked into his harassed, kindly eyes. "Blimey, Marios. If it weren't for you... I'd be nowhere..."

He was nodding encouragingly when he replied, "So, Harry, where are you now?"

Hunching my shoulders against the freezing rain, I crossed at the lights at Finsbury Park. Out of the corner of my eye, the street people huddled around a brazier by the iron gates. I felt its vaporous warmth through the icy needles on my cheek. Ahead of me, the brick ranks on the north side of the Seven Sisters Road marshalled into ramshackle order. An impenetrable metal sheet had settled above the roofs. There was no longer a sky to reach for. Water cascaded from gutters, dripped from bus-stop shelters and jetted nastily, laterally, from passing tyres. Damp and disoriented, I began to half-jog to my block. Minutes later I trod the spicy, tatty stair carpet and re-entered the flat.

But while I'd walked, Christian had bussed. The clobber-strewn, forest track in his room had changed since I sped after my gold discs. He'd returned, and left our flat quickly. Scanning the area, my heart smacked a couple of times in my chest because the door to one of the myriad cupboards in our rented rooms was ajar. He knew what nestled in the bottom of it and when I opened the door, it nestled no more.

He'd nicked my snare drum: Ludwig Black Beauty. A spare from a tour over here. A great instrument. Sharp, great crack on it. No rings or overtones but sensitive to a sparrow's breath, and loud as fuck, too. Industry standard backbeat. Three hundred quid's worth, never beaten. Oh, what delights for him on my drum.

Weather-wise, the outlook was magically transformed as we drove out of London. The roads were dry and sunshine dappled the fields we motored past.

"This is it, Valley Farm," said Rod.

We'd pulled off the A-road and bumped down a gravel track. On one side of our Transit was a wall of perfectly clipped ferns, on the other, horses stood like statues behind a white picket fence. Our wheels crunched the shingle of an open courtyard. With a cheeky wink, Rod parked it between a Porsche and a Range Rover.

On the way here, Mick had informed us that this was some TV celebrity's new home. Apparently, they'd spent squillions doing it up. We were here to make good and keep our heads down. I became aware of the lad's awed murmurings when I opened the van's back doors. Turning and shielding my eyes, I took in a glorious Georgian mansion set against a vast blue backdrop of sky. Rod pocketed the keys with a whistle. "What a gaff..."

Intersected by running red creepers, its countless windows reflected the valley and tree line we'd just driven by. Through curtains billowing on a balcony, female laughter floated towards us.

I was walking towards the front door's grand pillars and gleaming brass knocker when Mick called my name. "Oi, Harry, you're not in the bands now." He had paused at the corner of the house. "Tradesmen's for us, mate."

Turning on my heels, I held the old palm up and followed.

From an area at the back of the house, I ripped out bell-bind, dandelion, and spiny bramble. I raked, swept, and filled my barrow much as I'd done for Mrs Hajinickolas many years before. The patio slabs were, I'm sure, cool and smooth, but I wouldn't have felt them beneath my steel toecaps.

My dustpan overflowed as a set of bright, grey female eyes appeared around a curved, freshly rendered wall. She was tall and willowy and wore a blue and purple sarong. Beneath a nose that flared with equine sensitivity, she held a cup of steaming coffee. She blinked at me but didn't speak. Her gaze was on the manicured lawns and trimmed hedgerows of the grounds behind me.

Momentarily, my memory's gauze curtain shifted in the breeze. I *knew* her. She and Christian had really hit it off. It was some TV.... *Channel 4* or *BBC Two*. We were on at six but we had to get a flight straight after. She wore jeans and a T-shirt with 'Pimp Floyd' across it. He wore a blue drape and creepers. He had a quiff then. It looked brilliant. I remember she'd induced a modicum of civility in him and I thought, as they chatted at the make-up room door, she'd be really good for him, give him something to live up to, because he'd been seen out with some ripe undesirables around then. I couldn't recall the outcome, because next thing we were in the car with Bill... can't even remember what record it was for.

Leaning on my broom, I smiled straight at her. 'Mime is money' we used to say. She blinked and reared with more than a fleck of disdain at this particular builder's mate. I wanted to tell her that we'd met before, on a '*professional level*' but she'd turned her back. "Try not to bring the dirt in," she said, floating around the curve.

281

The jobs were menial and minor: sanding down, wiping off, clearing away. We were there to tie a pink ribbon around the dream home of some buzzer-ringing, wheel-spinning, TV host and that was that.

By four we were done.

Unseen, in a corner of the acreage, smoke smouldered from a pile of dampish leaves and we kicked a ball about waiting for the boss to tell us we could finally chip off.

Mick squared it to Rod, and Rod squared it to me.

"So, how d'ya like your new career, Harry?"

I flicked it up and half-volleyed it to Mick. "S'all right."

"They'll call ya, mate. From what you said, you're just on leave." Mick chested it, let it drop and side-footed it to Rod.

"Gardening leave, ha ha." Rod did a couple of knees and nudged it to me with the outside of his foot.

"You miss it, Harry?" Mick asked.

Flicking it to Rod, I allowed the gauze curtain to brush my face. I would have wept if I'd pulled it across. "It's like I'm someone else now," I replied.

The men looked at each other, amused by another of my obscure, but nonetheless diverting references.

"Pass," I said. Rod pushed it to me. I trapped it. Sole on the ball, arms folded. Old style 'team photo' shot. "Fing is," I continued. "I would have paid to be in that band. I'd have done this all day for nothing just to get on stage with them at night... I'd have worked down a mine, lived in a tent. I'd have done double shifts in the take-away under my flat after, *just* for the honour of drumming in that band with those blokes."

I passed the ball back but they didn't see it. They were staring at me. "Was it that good, Harry?"

"Better," I said, jogging past them to retrieve it from a hedge.

Mick stroked his chin. "What you gonna do?"

Ushering the ball, instep to instep, I said, "Last I heard,

they were gonna call me and tell me what's what. That was three months ago." I flicked it to Mick who dragged back and dragged back then put his own foot on it. "So, no money?" he rolled the sole of his boot across the ball contemplatively. "But, ain't they s'posed to pay you for recordings? Like royalties. I mean you done well out of it?" He chipped it over to me.

I trapped it. "Yeah, there's money there for me but they ain't gonna let me have it. Legal reasons. We didn't finish the album we were contracted to do. My mate got ill and couldn't do the guitars. Then, they stopped all the royalties. People got very irked. Serious business. Serious geezers running it."

Mick looked at me. "So, how much is there?"

I shrugged. "Thousands, mate," I said, flicking it up and gently volleying it across smouldering leaves.

"Fucking guitars! I'll do 'em..." Rod said, nutting it to Mick who nutted it to me.

"Probably sound better than - "

I juggled; one, two, three and was about to pass when the boss entered the field of play. "Lads, one more job. Her ladyship," he nodded towards the house. "Volunteer for the kitchen. Only a quick one."

I flicked the ball to Mick with the outside of my right foot. "I'll do it."

The kitchen was spacious, pristine. A white and chrome expanse of gadgetry and Italian styling. 'Her ladyship' (the girl from the TV show years ago), scuffed a dainty sandal across the floor and looked concernedly at the boss. "It's the tiles, Ralph..."

"Just a bit of cement. Harry, you'll need a toothbrush. Just get that layer off the glaze..."

"Yeah."

"Bit of soap and water..."

The taps, basin, and surfaces were brand new, I daren't touch anything higher than knee level in there. So, I went outside, got detergent from the van and filled a bucket at the standpipe.

When I returned, the lady had a female companion. She was a little curvier with shorter hair. Her pussycat eyes squinted with mirth at my bucket and me. Chatting at the breakfast bar, they sipped freshly-squeezed orange juice while I dutifully knelt.

The tiles were beautiful: one-inch squares, aquamarine, dark blue and jet. My job was to get on down with my soapy brush, scrub each one and wipe it to a shine. When requested, they'd move to let me work and, as I did, I'd watch their feet; red and plum toenails, tendons and veins in sandals and cream heels shuffling from view.

They uncorked champagne. Understandably, the mood was celebratory: but for a few grubby kitchen tiles and the grubby bloke cleaning them, the place was finally done.

At the edge of a unit, I encountered a crumb of grouting that refused to come away with the brush. I got beneath it with my nail and as I scratched it off, my eyes again rested on tanned calves and dimpled knees shifting languorously. They were almost touching. I was eavesdropping on a conversation between pairs of female legs.

Minutes passed and the radio played. I was aware of pins and needles and the stiffening of my lower back but my task had rhythm. I scrubbed, wiped off and moved on. And then, with just the final quadrant to go, her ladyship said, "Remember this?" and she turned the radio up.

It was us.

I stopped, uncurled and listened. I recalled the session, maybe not the exact take, but the session, yeah. Instead of toothbrush, rag and bucket at eye-level, I saw a score of mics.

They were there to pick up every nuance and buzz, exaggerate every weak strike and stumbling fill, to scrutinise my ability to the microscopic limit.

But I was good. We were good.

"What ever became of them?" the cat-eyed one asked while I scrubbed and wiped my way through the first chorus bridge.

"Someone in production said they had a new album coming out. Not entirely sure what happened to it."

"This was great." She hummed the chorus, a little sharp.

"They did the show a few years ago. Typical lads, full of it. You know the sort?"

A smirk, and flutes refilled on the granite top.

"You *didn't?*"

"Chance'd be a fine thing." Slurred, sexy laughter and a change of legs. "Good song..."

They sang along. I hit the final cymbal and stood up. "That's it," I said.

The lady scanned the glimmering floor. "You've missed a bit, there."

"Nah, that tile's damaged - "

"Fine." She turned her back.

27

Double Booked

"What's up with you, Harry?"

"Knackered."

Mick's grime-encrusted brow furrowed. "Piece-a-piss that."

"Post-tour fatigue."

Rod glanced at Mick. "What?"

"Nothing." I smiled, comforted by the addled glance they exchanged.

We'd stopped in the service station car park. "You want something?" he said, nodding towards the entrance.

"Nah."

Just then, the complex's automatic doors slid open and, arm in arm, two incongruously gorgeous girls walked through. Mick looked at me and I looked at Rod and Rod made the 'oooh' face. We laughed and the girls glanced across before tightening their grip and accelerating away.

As the van doors slammed shut, I glanced into the rear-view but the girls had gone. "Peaches and Cream," I whispered.

Scrolling and re-scrolling against the car park backdrop I found, between a rep's Ford and a gas fitter's Bedford, a dark area in the wings on the other side of the world.

'*H, you're on, get on.*'

"Right," I said, readying myself for our finale.

Amidst ardent stamping and clapping, I jogged to my drum riser. Four minutes later, I stepped off to something marginally less intense.

Bill handed out fresh towels. "That's it, boys, terrific show..."

Claps on the backs, whoops and hollers ushered us to our horribly quiet bunker miles below. How remote and impersonal our gigs had become. I remembered when I knew

286

every face in the first three rows. Now, half the time, I couldn't tell you what town I was in.

I massaged my little finger. It itched now and again. Andy shuttled past from stage to dressing-room. "Your button finger, H?" he said.

"Yeah, Andy." I tracked him as he worked around me. "I thought I was fine, got all the cotton out and then, smack. Passed clean out..."

He nodded encouragingly.

"And that's how it started, sort of," I continued happily. "See I had to - "

"Drive the delivery van, H?" he said, displaying a familiar smiling patience.

"Course, you know all my old stories, Andy, don't ya?"

"Serendipity," he said, gathering sticks, strings and guitars.

"Dipenserity... " I repeated.

"H." He had stopped to hold my attention. "Don't forget. The drum rep bloke. The skins. You've been using them for the last half-dozen gigs. He's coming to tonight. He'll be in the back stage bar."

"I won't forget, mate."

He turned away and I joined Kyle at the beer bin.

He made the 'ooh' face.

"I thought it was an alright show," I said, defensively. "What Lucas say?"

"Why don't you ask him?"

"Fink he's gone."

I swigged and shrugged. "Standard three encores."

We didn't look at each other.

"I'm off to the bar," he said.

"Just gonna... erm, sit here for a bit."

"See ya, H."

"See ya, Kyle."

I put the bottle down, shut my eyes and drifted off.

"You got'n headache, son?" Bill was staring down at me.

"What?"

He dipped a single corn chip into a vat of salsa. "You're rubbing the back of your bonce."

I stood up and stretched. "Nah, Bill, just remembering something... long time ago."

"Care to share it with the class?" he said, scanning the empty dressing-room and picking up Christian's jacket.

"It's nothing. You going back to the hotel?"

"I am."

"I'll go with you."

"There's a decent after-show upstairs?"

I shook my head.

As I left the dressing room, I looked behind me at the surplus of food and drink. "Such a waste, Bill."

"Excess, Harry. This games's middle name. Our drive awaits." He gave me a kindly smile and that's when the girls walked past.

"Hi, Harry," they sang.

I took a cab with them to the Sunset Strip. We dropped by The Roxy and Rainbow, but it was noisy and chaotic and I wanted to see them on my own. I felt an attachment to them. They took the piss out of me in a gentle, humorous way. They evoked something from the past that wasn't dark.

So another cab was hailed and, with me in the middle, Peaches and Cream shot benign, verbal bolts at me. I fizzed in their light, sardonic persecution. They were clever, insightful and toxically droll.

By the time we'd got back to my suite on Alta Loma, I was a bit pissed (but on a comfortable level, only) and because they'd been such great value (and it was such a bleak time for the band: Lucas a stranger, C a c, Kyle knackered,

288

the gigs too big and impersonal, distances huge and, of course, the terror of recording the second album ahead), I decided I'd perform for them.

Arranging them on the divan, I turned away then spun around to face them. They hugged each other in mock fear. But it had a bit of real fear in it too because I wasn't quite myself. Like Gielgud I began and they hugged tighter. "You do this me to?" I coughed, lowered the register and corrected myself. "Me to?... *You*, will weep blood at my grave and your hearts will break and crumble like, like... Digestives! Yes they will. Bastard. Family. Of. Mine!"

It was the first time since they'd strolled on stage that I'd seen them speechless. With dead dog eyes, I stretched out one leg and grimaced in time-honoured tradition. "My death will cause," I continued, "rivulets of tears from you, son and wife!" I pointed like he did and one of the girls, Cream, I think it was, flinched and said, "No, Harry - "

"*Harry I'm not!*" I roared. They retracted and squealed with smiles that were, again, not entirely convincing. With fists pounding heaven and hell I railed, "*You* will put me in the earth cold of this fucking island with its white, bony men and creamy-arsed females. Here I will die and... *and! If* either of you wretched cunts dare to shed a tear, my hand will break through my sarcophagus's iron lid and I rise, I *swear!* and flay you both!'' Then I reverted to me and sat down opposite them. "Whajafinkadat?"

They collectively exhaled and one, Peaches it was, asked, "Did you act, Harry? Before the drums?"

"Like a nutter," I said.

The van doors flung open, and Rod and Mick leaped in.

They dropped me off at the chicken takeaway below my flat. Rod leaned across Mick in the passenger seat. "You're welcome to come out with us, mate."

The rain patted the shoulders of my jacket like it was trying to get my attention. "Nah, I'll have an early one," I said. "Really tired."

"It's only half six. You've slept the whole way!"

"Go placidly amidst the noise and haste..."

After another baffled double-take, Mick said, "See ya, H."

I slid the door across.

Nodding at the lads at the deep-fat fryer, I put my key in the lock and flopped exhaustedly onto the unlit stairs. As if a pillow were compressing it, the city fell silent. Momentarily, no hissing, humming and banging could penetrate that quiet.

In the flat above ours, the refugee mother started to sing her desert lullaby to her youngest and the void instantly filled. On the other side of the staircase wall, industrial fryers hissed and spat. Traffic grumbled outside and the step creaked beneath the bones of my arse. As I was about to stand and trudge back up, a burst of drumming, shuffles and shakers, obliterated everything and I recalled a couple of Brazilian blokes had started in the takeaway beneath our flat. They were mad for the sound of the old country. Suddenly, I was intoxicated not by a hundred and one secret herbs and spices, but by the smell of lean meat and sizzling onions borne on the rhythmic tide that flooded my childhood with bogus joy. '*Harry.*' My name from his lips sounded like no other. The vowel was practically nonexistent and the H a growl, but this wasn't a growl, it was a wince.

I looked up. My mum was standing at the foot of the stairs and amusingly (not out of fear of a whack), but out of genuine surprise, I scuttled backwards up steps five and six. "What the bloody hell you doin' here?"

Shaking drops off her brolly, she said "You left the door open."

"Oh," I said. I hadn't seen her for two years.

"Something's happened, Harry."

"Er... come up."

I flicked the switch on the wall. In the rush-hour traffic outside the takeaway, a number seventy-three marked time. The passengers on the top-deck, peering cluelessly into the room. "What's happened, then?"

"Something," she said.

This sounded good. This sounded like what I needed. The last time we'd spoken was before I embarked on the mammoth tour I'd just been slung off. She was in real bother, financially. I remember she followed me to the bank. It was one of the more absurd moments in my life; her at my shoulder, licking her lips nervously while I added two, then three noughts to a cheque for her. It meant nothing to me. I was happy to help. 'Thank you Harry', she had said, 'I'll pay you back, I promise.'

And lo, here she was with my dough. "Mum," I said. "Never had the chance to say, ta, for all the books and that... sometimes, they were all I had."

At those words, the scaffolding vanished and I saw the woman beneath. She was timid, un-starched and incredibly vulnerable. "Mum?" I said, standing, concerned. But, even as I straightened my legs the tubing and bolts reappeared, the lattice of steel between us.

Outside the window, the bus lurched. Beneath the assault from the engine's vibration, the old windows rattled alarmingly. It sounded like a missile had hit the building. You had to get used to it. "*Sit down mum*," I bellowed. "Cuppa tea?" I offered, as the bus passed.

Tightening and re-enforcing, she replied, "No thank you, Harry."

I realised she was not here to repay me but, as she had said, to tell me 'something' and I began to feel nervous.

291

In a room lined with sun-flaked old cupboards, chests of drawers and wardrobes, she perched noncommittally on the edge of a satiny, armchair. She checked the clasp on her hand-bag as I parted the useless, light-enhancing nets. In the wet, tar-shiny street below, red tail-lights glowed as the traffic inched towards Tottenham. Without turning around I asked, "How's his back?" Why were our conversations always so short and stilted? Why did we not speak to each other as we spoke to others?

Raindrop landed on raindrop, smudging and altering the teardrop tracks down the glass. It was all too late. Like him with the drums, my mum and me had much we hadn't shared. Rain cascaded into the storm drains on the Seven Sisters. Cabbies munched chicken wings and tossed the bones through the windows. Around their idling vehicles, pigeons strutted, cannibalising the remains. She'd still not answered my question. I let go of the nets, turned around and awaited a reply.

Click, click. Eyes downcast, she flicked wordlessly at the clasp.

Just then, I detected a whiff of powder or whatever it was she always wore, and was wrenched back to Enfield, apricot skirting and all. Golf balls rolled to the lowest point as canned laughter emanated from the front room. Desperate to stay in the present, I asked, "How's the office?"

To this question, she addressed her fascinating bag. "Fine, fine."

I looked around for something to hold onto, something that would stop me, like those golf balls, from rolling back. Christian's door was ajar. The rags he slept in strewn across the floor he refused to sweep. Perhaps I'd talk about the band? She knew nothing of my travels, the people, the places, the food and weather. I was living her dream, the dream she was promised when her education was complete.

Continents and culture, wine and song: the prize she had reached for but failed to grasp. '*Mum,*' I wanted to say, '*you never guess what, I've been on a barge from Kowloon to Hong Kong and mum, they hang all their washing out... and, and mum, on the banks of the Bosporus, they bring mackerel, just caught, they like, fry it on the boat, yeah? Honest, the taste, with lemon and onions on bread fresh... mum?...*'

For the millionth time, I remembered that, in a few chilly months, my world had shrunk from oyster to winkle and I wasn't going first class anymore. I travelled by van mostly and my horizon was only ever a mile or two away. The work was dusty, hard on the lumbar spine and hands, and the food was for energy only.

The clasp clicked. In the yellow neon wash from the chicken sign outside, I scanned her face. "Mum?"

She wouldn't look up.

The building shook again, but this time not courtesy of a furious, City-bound Routemaster, but from the kitchens below. The old furniture practically hopped to the Latino throbbing upward. It was at that point that I gave up. There is nothing on earth that can distract you from beats like that. Syncing instantly, I tapped my left and right foot as a Cuban chorus accompanied the opening of the gauze curtain on a familiar, household scene.

Instead of my mum's standard, the expressionless visage that meant 'yes, no and who cares?' at the same time, I observed the pupils dilate in her terrified eyes. Blood leaked from her nose and dripped on a starched office blouse creating a new, rusty island. Her clawing fingers missed our front door latch by millimetres.

That miss was as good as a mile because the panther had her.

I considered how peculiar her brand of humiliation must feel at his hands. She too had a funky chicken world but hers was far more consuming than mine. In my grey school shorts, from a chair in the corner of her office by the bus depot, I'd witnessed an authority, a composure *never* displayed at home. Grown men in suits revered her, pretty girls did her typing. There was a smile and a laugh at an office aside, she was happy. But she was a stranger to me. Were those biannual workplace visits her legacy? Was she showing me that there *was* a life beyond the shitty apricot skirting if you forged it for yourself?

Yet, here she was, trapped in my amber memory, stuck in the passage, reduced to slave status, sobbing and bloody, stripped of all dignity in front of her son, an equally hopeless victim of the great suburban tyrant. How those contrasting frequencies must have burned and throbbed in her double life.

The golf balls had rolled to their gravitational end in that narrow, un-hoovered area at the foot of the stairs. The club heads chinked as my grip tightened around his legs.

Perversely, I felt at ease with this random episode. I had, at least, retained that strain of my past even if I'd blown my career. Staring at my mother's pink nails and handbag clasp, I wondered if this was the new way: a life spent washing and drying at the sink of my reminiscences?

Through the curtain, he dealt a couple of downward thumps but they were ineffective because all of his effort was centred on holding onto his terrified Mrs. And I held on tight, tighter. '*No dad don't, don't, don't...*' I sucked in snot, her powder, his cologne, meat rind and grass cuttings from the clubs. With the cabbassa and horns belting out of the over-heated front-room we banged, sighed and strained like some leaden, supine conga.

She wriggled closer to the latch.

In my arms, his body felt like granite. Such a man machine but, on this occasion, his muscles did him no good. I had jammed myself between the doorframe and the foot of the stairs. He'd have to snap half a dozen bones to get rid of me. '*Leave her dad, please don't...*' All apricot and drums, it was.

The 73 passed like an earthquake, obliterating the soundtrack downstairs. With relief, I focussed on one of Christian's oatmeal tracksuit tops. It lay in a sad puddle by the rad. Where was he, who was he with? Had he an inkling of me or what we'd done together in his drum-nicked 'heightened' state?

My mum broke the spell. "Harry, I've got something very important to say." She was looking up at last. The scaffold had given way. I fancied I could hear the blokes throwing the poles into a flatbed truck outside. Her face was not timid and vulnerable, it was serene, approaching angelic. My heart thudded. "He's gone," she said.

"Owjamean?" I replied, glancing into Christian's room then back at her. In that fraction, I imagined his room empty; the ragged carpet ripped out, the floorboards sanded and glossed. The sombre furniture had been removed and was burning somewhere while the walls were smooth and whitewashed. My pulse raced as I looked along a gleaming, knot-free skirting. It appeared to stretch into the white, misty infinite.

My mother tilted her head at a kindly angle. She was dealing with me. I was an inquiry at her office door. "He's dead, Harry," she said.

"Who?"

"Your father is dead."

"Blimey, mum. When?"

"A week last Wednesday."

I stopped squinting. "Howj'you find me?"

"I went to the record company."

"Oh yeah..."

At that moment, a cowbell pattern, so hooky you couldn't

help but shift when you heard it, ticked and clicked through the ancient rug beneath us.

"Noisy," she said, involuntarily clicking the clasp in time.

I glanced into Christian's room. Was he sniffing, scuttling about? He'd not come back, had he? Leaning forward, I peeked further into his den but all I could see was the three of us, mum, dad and me, linked in the passage of time.

Weirdly, I couldn't remember how many balls had rested against the skirting. I couldn't read 'Spalding' or 'Dunlop' on them either. Usually, I'd see which balls were cut because you didn't want to give him one of those when he snapped his fingers on the first. I felt uneasy behind my curtain. These details were usually etched so sharply. Panic flicked at me. I gulped. Something else was missing. I couldn't smell my dad's cologne. That aroma had followed me from San Diego to Tokyo, Hawaii to Berlin. The muffled shriek and roar I heard at a truck stop, hotel lobby or girlfriend's house, had a comedy echo on it. Someone was having a laugh with my private soundtrack.

When I returned to the passage, the front door, open living-room door, and foot of stairs had vanished. I knew where they should be but couldn't see them. No music played or telly droned. I wanted to cry like a child at my loss. "He's gone," I whispered in the silence. Mum, me and dad were hovering in clouds, our torsos ghostly, our limbs powdery and thin. I looked into his eyes, his last remaining human trait. They did not emit disdain or contempt for once, but the warmth that only respect engenders. His final thought was that his son, in his puny infantile way, was protecting his mother. He was being the hero he'd always thought he was.

His last act was to thump the top of my wiry bonce. It felt like a caress.

"I think that's very succinct, Harry," she said, nodding.

Startled, I said, "Did I say something?"

296

"Yes. You said, *'What you sow, you shall reap'*."

I smiled and she looked away, subtly amused. My mum and me liked our clichés and codes.

"How?" I asked.

"We all thought it was his back but it was a tumour," she said, brushing a fleck from her skirt. "Cancer. It's been growing for years. It finally killed him. Last Wednesday, around four o'clock."

In the remotest corner of my mind, filmed on the smallest, highest tile in the mad mosaic from a rich lady's kitchen, my mother finally slipped the latch and was free.

"I'm really sorry, mum," I said, recalling the reverb-coated sound her clacking heels made as she sprinted past the Fernley's towards the safety of Green Lanes. The tears and roars faded but the music remained.

"I'm sorry too, Harry. Now, are you going to answer that?" she said.

"What?"

"The door."

I blinked. The doorbell was ringing. There was no music.

Pulling up the rattly old sash, I peered down. The rain had stopped.

Three of them. Lucas, Kyle, and a hatchet-hard upholder of the law stood by a yakking police car in the rain. They were looking up at me. I glanced from them to my mum and back again. It was as if the past and the future had fused in the present.

Lucas' face was etched with smouldering concern. Turning to my mum I said, "They can't sack you twice, can they?"

28

Funeral

We convened on a beautifully dismal day in north London. Beyond the gates, rows of solemn tulips dipped and bowed as if each were a departing soul offering a final, stoical farewell. The dress-code was black. Those gathered looked like futuristic actors, their elongated silhouettes reflected on the sides of cars parked neatly on the gravel. Amongst the assembly were a few of his old girlfriends. Smoking in a huddle by a redbrick arch, they faltered on the pebbles in incongruous high-heels. On seeing me, fingers fluttered and sad smiles were exchanged. When I waved back, one of them lifted her veil and blew me a kiss. I imagined it floating across the car park and detonating inside me.

Accompanied by the sound of spiralling organ chords, I took my seat next to a girl I knew but hadn't seen for years. When she glanced at me, she began to cry, igniting everyone in there. I listened to the dirge drowning beneath the weeping arpeggio, feeling dry and numb. I'd not cried yet.

The coffin looked like a package delivered by mistake, *'The wrong number on the docket. Couldn't tell if it was a seven or a one, mate.'* I found the whole event bizarre, a practical joke, surely? It defied all logic that *he* would be so still and take it.

The music levelled out and the vicar started telling us of his life.

When he had concluded, family members tentatively rose and said their piece. Finally, it was my turn.

Amongst the sea of heads I picked out Lucas. I glanced at the box. "We ready?" I inhaled. "A one, two, three, four…" I heard a couple of sympathetic chuckles in the gap where the song should have started. "Nah, only joking," I said, raising the old pacifier. "I just want to read something first… from school. I sometimes read it to him." I coughed to clear my throat. "Go placidly amidst the noise and haste…"

There were plenty of lads from way back shuffling about; gnarled punk rockers and toughs, their jutting chins and vicious sneers softened by the terrible occasion. They belonged in a throbbing club with plastic pint pots and a deafening PA. To see them meek and mild amongst the geometric flora gave the day an even more unreal air. Kyle tapped my shoulder as I sipped a Coke in the beer garden of the pub across the road. Apart from a subdued hello at the flat last week, I hadn't spoken to him since he said he was going to Coconut Grove and actually fucked off to New York to plot my downfall with Lucas.

"Great turn out," he said.

I could see his point. Like me, he felt a little spare, irked that we weren't playing to such a good crowd.

As I was about to speak, Andy gangled over and embarked on a monotone irrelevance; something to do with the engine capacity of some parked car and then, just as he was getting onto the cylinders, he began to well up. With his hands at his sides and his teary head bowed, he looked like an abandoned lamppost. Reaching up, I patted him gently on the shoulder. I failed to understand why men couldn't wear veils in these enlightened times.

At a table across the garden, Christian's mum tended her flock. Her face was red raw with agony and yet, she remained dignified and like him, well, sort of stroppy. It took all the courage I had to walk across and to squint into her face.

Words failed me because I felt, they all felt, I'd failed him.

"Are you alright, Harry?"

"Fine, fine…"

"Lucas came," she said.

And went. With flash bulbs going off round him, I'd watched him slide into a waiting cab ten minutes earlier. I didn't recognise the model/actress he was with. Needless to say, she was stunning and taller than most.

"They were very close," I said. "He's very erm… sorry."

"I know, he told me…"

"Mmmm."

"Nice bit of reading there, young Harry."

"Well thank you very much, Bill. Something I penned at the lights on the way over."

"Ha ha."

"Ha ha."

I sipped. "You've done this before?"

"Too many times, son. Too many funerals for the young and gifted. It's a sad thing, very sad, but..." he sniffed and dabbed an eye with his hanky. "A decent enough send off."

I nodded. "Really difficult."

"Impossible."

"Yeah."

"You alright?"

"Yeah…"

We sipped and looked around the bar. He coughed lightly. "Sorry to hear about your old man, Harry."

"It was coming."

"How long, you know, had he had it?"

"Oh years, eating away at him."

He winced. "Sorry son..."

But I was bright. "Nah, he had a good bat, erm, 'round'. He loved his golf. He lived the life he wanted."

"Well, that's something, isn't it?"

I nodded. They'd whacked the jukebox up. Some of the

mourners were dancing. Voices bubbled. Laughter, as ever, leaked through.

"What about your dad, Bill?"

"Lost him to emphysema ten years and, let's see... " He paused and looked into the ceiling. "Three months and a week ago."

"Sorry, Bill."

"Yeah. Devastating. Couldn't get going for months after."

While I nodded gravely, he picked out that spot in the ceiling again.

"He was a great bloke, my dad." That quiet sentence hung between us for a moment. When he continued there was a prideful element in his tone. "Told jokes. He'd get them off cereal packets, or lolly sticks, sweet wrappers... tell them at breakfast. Every school day morning, a crappy joke. I can see him now, Harry, laughing across the milk and teapot as me and my brothers and sisters winced at the corniest cracks you've ever heard. It got to the point where we'd duck under it, the table, I mean." He smiled at something unimaginably beautiful in his heart. "Towards the end, it was like a family tradition, as soon as he started, we'd take our bowls and actually sit under it to eat... the table, I mean..."

I laughed out loud. "So funny, Bill."

His eyes creased with mirth. "Hilarious. Blue chin, grey, kind eyes. Shirt on always ready for work. Council electrician. Never missed a day. Fishing at the weekends. The bloody jokes, H..."

He began to sob. To see him, the unflappable man that had gently ushered us around the planet - equipment knack-ered, passports lost, cases missing, drugs, fall-outs, planes cancelled, miles driven through the dark American nights - to see him broken, even for a moment, was the sorriest sight of the day.

"Bill, mate."

"I'm fifty-three and I *still* miss him. His smile. The decades of graft for his kids and mum..."

I stood in front of him so that people wouldn't gawp.

After a minute, with the aid of his white hanky, he'd got himself together. "Sorry, Harry. Hogging the grief."

"Nah... it's good to erm, let it out."

"Thinking about it, that's what we're here for."

"What, for grief?"

"To be dads. Good dads."

I nodded. "Yes." But it wasn't in me to be one. The thought of having *his* genes and producing a son seemed criminal. There was a monster in me. A monster that couldn't cry for anyone.

"Ah well," he sighed. His familiar smile broke through. "I forgot, one of the lads gave me this. From a girl. Very pretty, he said..." He handed me a piece of paper and winked, "Proud of you, Harry. Ever on the pull, even here."

Smiling cluelessly, I said, "I didn't talk to anyone, Bill."

He smiled, with road-style admiration. "More credit to you."

We - Lucas, Kyle and me - re-convened in one of those empty offices you always find at a record company. There was a poster of the new album in the corridor. Lucas looked heroic on the cover. The boys in the band (me included) were mere shadows in the background.

He was smart and perfunctory. He had an endorsement photo session followed by a meeting with a designer for the tour's stage-set right after the one with me and Kyle. We were effectively, his 'eleven o'clock'. He handed me a cheque as soon as the door shut. The amount was absurd. I folded it with a nod and shook his hand. He, in turn, gazed resolutely past my ear at a shelf of empty files, a hole-punch and a pen-tidy.

So we three sat with cups of tea not knowing what to say. It was the sort of moment *he* would have filled with some caustic observation that would have us wincing and smirking simultaneously. And it was strange because at that moment, Lucas smiled to himself and muttered, "Fucking rent boy…"

Smiling in return, I allowed an initial tear to drip down my nose. I sniffed as, once again, a moment of profound silence seemed to fall. When I looked up, Lucas and Kyle were looking at me concernedly.

Kyle coughed and glanced at Lucas. "So, auditions then?"

"Wait a minute," I said. I felt the need to evoke Christian before we replaced him forever. It was important that his essence be at this assembly. It should be *him* passing over the reins he'd held with such finesse.

Unable to think of a suitable phrase that would do this, I said, "Jewfink, we should have, like, a memorial gig? Erm, somewhere to lay flowers... a plaque?"

Lucas spoke. "The music will be his memorial."

The office sounds - typing, yakking, walking corridors - continued outside, but in our office, a full minute's silence was respected.

The spell was finally broken by the sound of a sobbing man. Grief had finally snagged me amongst the disconnected phones and staplers in an anonymous room in the West End. I was overwhelmed at all I would see and do that he wouldn't. The years stretched ahead for me but for him, there was no more. I moaned, twisted and writhed for my passionate brother, the kid behind the cellophane curtain that had given me all this.

Why had he taken *that* fork in the road? Painted himself into *that* particular corner? As I tried, for the millionth time, to find an answer, a torrent poured from my eyes and through the fingers of my hands. "The thing is, right... *his* album," I said to them both. "He's been playing it to me since I met

303

him. You'd think all the numbers were hard and fast and heavy, but you know what? They're the most soulful, melancholy, delicate things. He wasn't what he seemed." Wiping my eyes, I peeked at both of them. They nodded. I sniffed and exhaled. "So, auditions then…"

Kyle leaned forward. "Yeah, we're thinking rehearsals for the week after next. There's a couple of blokes I know…"

29

The Circle Squared

I'd treated myself to a really nice car but there was still loads of money left over. I was tempted by the requisite toys and clothes all flush musos should have but felt apathetic on matters of style and gadgetry. Perhaps I was destined to be tramp boy however much dough I had? Books were cheap, and a passion, so I got a load of them in. I had music a plenty. I ate okay, but nothing flash. I felt a bit of a berk in the corner of a restaurant ordering for myself.

My youth had come to its natural end. I had been to the four corners and back again. Since I'd left school, life had been all about me. I had settled all my scores and revenge was no longer my motivator, amorous or not. Adulthood, the majority of my song, stretched ahead. I was as clueless how to proceed on this phase as I was on the last.

Sitting in my car, with nowhere to go, I wondered if I should give the lot to charity. I felt the need to contribute to a higher cause than my wardrobe or stomach. The idea that I should have a 'cause' began to dominate like beats did in earlier years.

I had declined Kyle's offers of parties, girls and Mediterranean breaks and, instead, began buying presents. For Mrs H, a proper tea service was bought: all matching, plenty of gold leaf, tongs and milk jugs. I donated a quality stereo and speakers to the factory, (put a little 'bottom e' on those mental bazukis), and for Marios, a top swivel chair with arm rests - a silent one.

I'd bought a suit too, and that morning, had a meticulous shave.

"You look every bit the young executive, Harry."

"You're kidding, Bill?" I said, wincing into the mirror and pulling the shirt collar from my neck.

"You'll tear it off!"

I didn't of course. I'd been staying at Bill's and playing along with the new album in a little practice room around the corner. I wanted to get up to speed before rehearsals with the boys began in earnest. Bill was in pre-tour frenzy: flights, hotels, stages, get-ins, outs, budgets and insurance, so our paths didn't cross, much. I felt a bit like a nagging kid on a long journey, which amused me because in a few weeks I'd be taking up that role professionally. So, I played a bit, sat in my car, walked around the park and looked at the sky for signs of Christian.

Bill said, best not be mawkish and go and live the richest and most fulfilling life in honour of those that no longer can. But if there's no one about and I need a bit of feedback (like I did about the phone number Bill had given me at the funeral), I'll ask the sky. I'd like to think it bequeaths immortality.

I had a couple of pretty monumental tasks that day. The first, though important, was banal and right; the other, a step into the unknown and probably ill-advised.

She'd done her hair different. It wasn't all puffed up like a Coldstream Guard's, teased to scare the enemy. It was modest and tidy. She was waiting at the corner shop with just one medium-sized bag. After all those years, that was all she took.

"Is this your car, Harry?

"Erm, yeah, I erm… made a few quid, mum."

She smiled, "I probably owe you enough for another one."

"Nah, all the books. I'da been a proper imbecile without them. Fink how good I did at school?"

"You did okay."

We both smiled at that.

"Never said ta, for that twenty quid you put in *Night Flight.*"

"It was the least I could do," she said.

For a moment, I became excited, we were saying, 'thanks' and 'that's all right'. Normal stuff.

We drove towards the centre and we were sad and quiet because there were galleries, parks and restaurants I'd never go to with my dear old mum.

"So, France then?"

"Yes, going to stay with my sister Sarah."

"Didn't you do French at school?"

"I did. Lost it all..."

"Lost it all," I echoed.

"Well, mum, there you go."

I put her bag on the pavement.

"Erm... Sorry, about all that, Harry."

"Nah, all's well that ends well... Getting into a bit of Shakespeare in my old age."

She smiled again, turned and walked towards the coaches.

I was glad she was still in London, even if right on the very edge. Driving through her estate, I thought about how we start, how we end up and all the fragility and chance between. There simply is no reason or plan, it seemed to me. Nothing is preordained or deserved. There are no angels on our shoulders, spirit guides or lucky charms. Events happen randomly. If they didn't then, surely, there'd be the cruelest of Gods mixing our sound up there.

A group of leery teenagers on pushbikes approached at speed, their mouths agape at my shiny, German wheels. I parked and switched the engine off. Through an untamed, tilting privet, I double-checked the number daubed in white emulsion on the red brick. For a second, I thought of restarting and turning around. Recalling the ironic, scaffold-free smile my mum had given me after I'd handed her the novel for the ferry to Le Havre, I removed the key from the ignition and stepped out.

Glancing up, I noticed that the sills were rotting. A length of guttering had come away from the eves and some tiles had slid into it. They could fall and smash a head at the slightest gust. Through the gap where a gate once was, I trod the crisp-packet strewn, tarmac path feeling lighter and faster than I'd ever been in my life. What had gone on before, was no longer a preoccupation, no longer the default excuse for my disposition. If I were reminded of those times (as I was now), I felt that those events had happened to someone else, some kid. Passing the flaking door, cracked bay window and raggedy nets at the front of the house, I arrived at the side and the door to the flat upstairs. A rusted pram and car battery stood like sentries either side of the step.

I'd bought flowers (his idea). It was the first time I'd done that for anyone. I took a pleasant, excited breath and rang the bell.

Footsteps tripped lightly down and my heart thumped much as it did before we went on. When the door opened, I couldn't stop grinning. She was struck so delightfully dumb. She too then laughed. It was *really* funny. I'd put an effin' tie on. "Don't look like I'm selling insurance, do I?" I said, tugging self-consciously at my lapel.

"You look like a film star."

"Blimey."

"Are those for me?" she asked.

"If you'll have them."

She clutched the bouquet to her face and inhaled. For a second, a chewed-up tennis ball arced across the blue and I floated weightlessly in her gaze, again.

308

After following her up the narrow stairs and along a corridor, I hesitated, made my fearful face and nodded. A telly was chattering away in the room at the end of the passage. "Who's there?"

"Only us." She opened the door and stood aside.

Two feet from the TV screen, with his back to me, was a little boy. In one hand he held a yellow toy truck; in the other, a crisp. He held the truck with a firm chubby grip, the crisp he held delicately, between thumb and forefinger. The boy was engrossed in a cartoon. There was an explosion on the screen and he mimicked it with his truck.

"Louis. I want you to meet someone. Turn around, love."

He turned quickly and stared. I froze. She walked to the TV and turned it off. "*Mumm,*" he protested.

"Sit with me, Louis."

She picked him up and put him on her lap. "Sit down, Harry," she said carefully, not taking her eyes from mine. I sat a foot away from them on the sofa.

The boy had brown eyes and his hair was quite light, nowhere near as black as mine although, like mine, it grew in a wild uncontrollable bush. His complexion was sallow to brown. Again, not as dark as me, but not as light as his mum. He pursed his lips, examining me from the safety of her lap.

"Louis, this is Harry. We went to school together."

He whizzed the truck past my eyes.

Then, like hers did across the desks years ago, a solemn goodness shone. Carefully, he took my hand, opened it and placed the toy in my palm. "You play," he said, patting me.